A love that makes life drunk

First published 2008 by Pink Cup Cake Publishing, PO Box 4766, Rugby CV21 9FT

ISBN 978-0-9557911-0-9

Cover by Design One and courtesy of The Black Apple

Prepared and printed by:
York Publishing Services Ltd
64 Hallfield Road
Layerthorpe
York YO31 7ZQ
Tel: 01904 431213
Website: www.yps-publishing.co.uk
Printed by Biddles Ltd, King's Lynn, Norfolk

A love that makes life drunk

Karen Roderick

For Carl, Parka and Jackson

Francesca and Paolo

'Jefferson?'

Someone must have left the damned door open again.

'JJ?'

But I have to finish this paragraph.

'I've got someone I want you to meet.' Luke appeared at my office door, someone in tow, 'Jefferson this is my girl,' as she emerged from behind him, I stood up, 'Lily.' She put her hand out, I took it; my head felt light. 'Lily's a writer.' Luke had a stupid yet proud look on his face that I had to admire.

'Not published though.' Lily jumped in.

'What sort of books do you write?' I leaned casually against my desk, feet crossed at the ankle, still in a black suit after my meeting with Henry, my white shirt tails creased and hanging out.

'Dirty stuff.' Luke grinned; I turned back to Lily, she didn't look impressed.

'It's not like that,' her frown faded as she turned back to me, 'I call it contemporary women's fiction, with a lot of, well, you know...'

'Sex?' I stepped in to help since she obviously had a problem with the word.

'Yes.' She said with increased confidence, '*sex*.'

'I knew you two would have loads in common,' Luke was notoriously naïve, 'cus Jefferson writes all that sleazy shit too.'

Lily and I shared a smile only a fellow writer could appreciate.

'I have to ask you not to refer to my work as *sleazy shit*,' I said managing to tear my eyes from Lily's, 'I prefer "sex", or "fucking".'

'I'm not trying to score points when I say this,' Lily's delicate interjection impressed me, 'but I've read all your novels, and when I found out you were Luke's brother, I couldn't wait to meet you,' my chest tightened. 'I've been following your work for years.'

'Years?' I was curious of this demure, but resilient twenty something standing infront of me.

'Yes Mr Howie, I admire your guts.' Lily tucked her hair behind her ears, lovely ears they were too. 'A friend introduced me to your Independent column when I was a student the first time around and...'

'First time around?' I was painfully aware I was repeating everything she was saying.

'Yeah,' Luke chipped in cheerfully, 'Lily's in her first year of a Masters,' he folded his arm around her waist dragging her slim frame into his much larger one; I twitched. 'Brains as well as completely gorgeous hey?'

'I'm studying the History of the Book.' She said ignoring Luke's compliment; she was demanding to be taken seriously. I could smell it. I liked it. 'I originally wanted to do Creative Writing,' she smiled, 'and you don't have to say anything, because I already know what you think about that.'

I laughed gently; she wasn't lying about reading my column.

'You mean my feelings about a writer being "born" rather than "made"?'

'Yes Mr Howie.' The nagging in the pit of my stomach made me feel uneasy. 'But actually, I don't care what you think.'

I raised my eye with a smile,

'Well Lily,' I said uncrossing my ankle, and standing at least 7 inches above her, 'I've got to say, I'm glad to hear it.'

'You are?' Luke said bewildered.

'I like a fighter,' I said combing my fringe from my eyes, then adjusting my specs, 'too many budding writers give up because of my egotistical comments.'

'So why do you say them?' Lily's confusion was adorable.

'Because I can.'

'So you don't believe them anymore than I do?' Was it possible for her to be anymore beautiful, even when she was frowning?

'Like I said, I do it because I can.'

'So you really are pretentious?' She said it with such earnest, I almost smiled.

'Pretentious with a capital P.' Luke grinned kissing her cheek, but she backed away; she hadn't finished with me yet.

'I hoped the students were wrong.' The softness in her voice had disappeared, 'a lot of us read your column, and I defended you, I preferred to think you were...' she pondered, I wanted her more, 'misunderstood, a bit of a maverick.'

'Well thank you for defending me Lily,' I walked around my desk, I was waiting for an e-mail from Henry, 'but now you can see I'm not *misunderstood* or a *maverick*, I'm just plain arrogant.'

If I was trying to impress her, I was going the opposite way about it, and that my friend, was no accident.

I looked up from the PC; Lily was staring at me. She had a wounded but determined gaze in those incredible blue eyes,

'Maybe I should carry on defending you Mr Howie,' she grimaced, 'ruin that image of yours.'

I ignored the e-mail; she'd got me now.

'No need Lily,' I smiled leaning over the desk; her perfume, divine, 'it's already ruined.'

My name is Jefferson James Howie and I'm a very bad man

'Of course, there is a legitimate reason why he isn't married mum,' Jeremy grinned over lunch, 'did you read what he said about Henry Miller's writing in relation to women?'

'I was merely passing a literary comment, I wasn't defending him.' I said.

'Who's Henry Miller?' Luke chipped in; roast potato spewing across the table.

I caught Lily's eye and we smiled; that same appreciative smile we'd exchanged almost 12 months ago.

'I read it,' Lily said picking up her wine, 'I thought it was brilliant.' She didn't look at me, just straight ahead at my folks. 'All Jefferson meant was that Miller is sometimes misunderstood.' She said, 'the way he writes about women doesn't offend me, and when it comes to the degradation of women, you know I'm easily offended,' she shook her head, 'I believe Nin when she said as a lover he was soft and weak, nothing like what he wrote,' a true genius ponders; it made me smile, 'or at least that's what she thought at the time...'

'Who's Nin?' Luke stretched across the table and stuck his fork in the last roast potato; his t-shirt dragging in gravy.

'Anais Nin.' Lily and I chorused.

Luke looked perplexed; how the two of them got together was beyond me, well, OK, my youngest brother is a handsome fucker, so I'm pretty sure that helped.

'Well,' my father said rubbing his belly, 'I'm sorry guys, but you've completely lost me.'

I glanced over at Lily and winked; she nodded appreciatively.

I arrived back in Convent Garden with Lily heavy on my mind. I went straight to my office (or my *"High Place"* as Lily has nicknamed it); I needed to write. I'm so violently inspired at the moment, which is no coincidence, as the woman I've spent all afternoon with (albeit with my family of course), continues to batter my emotions senseless.

'Every writer needs their space,' Lily and I had been talking in my parents kitchen earlier, 'Luke doesn't understand that, he comes in, sits on my desk, rifles through my work and loses it's order and when I get annoyed he just grins and kisses me...' I adore seeing her smile, but I don't love hearing about their intimacy. 'Anyway,' she quickly added, 'your place is cool, it's like Nin's retreat at rue Schoelcher, her *"High Place"*.' (Did I mention she speaks immaculate French? *Non*, well, she does- remarkable woman.)

The menacing red light on the answer machine was annoying my eyes, so I took off my specs and rubbed the sockets, kicked off my shoes beneath the desk and started trawling through my messages.

'Jefferson my friend,' it was James Allen-Tait, 'listen, I'm sorry we had to cancel our dinner arrangement at such short notice, but keep your diary free for two weeks time.'

Beep,

'Hi Jefferson,' it was Joseph, 'look fella, there's a party coming up in Mayfair and Flo's going over to stay with her folks, fancy some free champagne you old shyster...'

Beep,

'Howie,' Madeleine doesn't talk, she purrs, 'dinner; tonight; my place.' And she hung up.

I groaned; when the hell did this pseudo relationship disturbingly become dinner on demand?

See, people assume keeping up the pretence of being a best selling author as well as a "prestigious" journalist must be hard graft (and glamourous of course), but believe me, it's nothing compared to the thornier area of my life, and that my friend, as demonstrated above, is women.

I love women; all kinds of women, and over the years I've enjoyed a fair few of them too: women of friends, female associates, socialites, holiday "romances" or mere fateful opportunities, and then I met Gracie Miller.

Gracie was a twenty three year old writer teetering on the brink of supreme recognition, when her agent invited me to the launch party of her debut novel. She was intelligent, incredibly naïve, and very much on the rebound. I openly fell in love with her, and in return she changed everything for me as far as the opposite sex was concerned.

OK, so I'm going to be arrogant here and confess it's rare I'm turned down by a woman. Even unavailable women I've worn down, real tough cookies too, and with Gracie, the fact her childhood sweetheart had recently dumped her, and shipped himself out to New York to live, was not going to stand in my way, so, I pursued her, got her, and convinced myself I could keep her. Well, that was a lesson learnt, and a harsh one at that.

See, with Gracie, and the reason we've been able to stay friends, is because I know she tried to love me, that she did everything she could to stop thinking of Eliot, but she couldn't, and that, combined with his name lovingly tattooed across her navel, didn't exactly help my growing insecurities.

Well, a year later, and a trip to New York, guess who turns up, and he's so handsome it's painful, (as well as being the most promising contemporary artist on the planet), and unsurprisingly, he wanted her back. Anyway, it's a long and complicated story between them, and Gracie went on to write about it, but I knew they belonged together, so, like a gentleman, I walked away, and for the first time in my life, it took every bit of strength I had, because I honestly believed I'd met the woman I was going to marry.

Anyway, before meeting Lily, Gracie and Eliot (very cool guy- no hard feelings), got married, and last week I saw them at an Art exhibition at the Tate Modern (his exhibition I'll add) and she's pregnant and I'm happy for her, because I have a lot to thank her for, she's a woman who made me love; who opened me up to a world outside of blasé sex, and do you know what, it felt fantastic, only problem is, I'm finding it incredibly difficult to revert back, so it comes as no surprise that I'm having inappropriate thoughts about one woman who is dangerously unavailable, and why am I having these thoughts, well, I'm pretty sure it has something to do with her hair, yeah, I know, but believe me, when the sun glistens on that hair, it would be criminal to describe it as anything other than Heaven on Earth.

So, because you don't know Lily yet, let me enlighten you; she's a *Red.* A bone fida, alarmingly stunning redhead, and before you feel cheated that she isn't a *blonde* or a *brunette,* let me tell you a few things about this woman that might change your mind.

Lily is auburn; make that *smouldering auburn,* a delightful vision that captured my breath the moment I saw her. OK, so I've always found redheads sexy and mischievous, but I've never actually physically engaged with one before, never had the chance, and then I met Lily; the allure in her eyes, the fire in her voice, the passion in her words and I wanted her, every bit of her, from her delicious body to her teeming brain, and after 12 months that hasn't changed, in fact, it's far stronger and much more complex than I anticipated, least of all because she's in love with Luke and not me.

So, I've become infatuated with a redhead.

OK, you're probably asking yourselves, why is this guy so obsessed with her? Well, maybe it's because I spend so much time talking with her, or maybe it's because she's incredibly beautiful and easy to be with, or is it because I hear *reds* are the feistiest lovers? You see, Lily runs free; to her the usual rules don't apply, she makes up her own, and I want to follow those rules too; in truth, I just want to follow her and I'm pretty sure it's because of her hair (crazy I know).

Right, so you know about the hair, but I love Lily for many reasons; her vibrancy, her youth (not essential; I'm not a guy who bottles out on a woman over the age of 30), I love her freshness, her passion, her raw edge, her cute naivety, her strength, her innovation and creativity, her intelligence, her body, her beauty, her open mind, she's trustworthy and kind, generous and forgiving; in a phrase, I want to be like her, and because I never will, I need to be with her, so please, sympathise when I tell you, I will never get close to this woman, I will never have the opportunity to follow her and abide by her boundless rules, and why, because she's in love with someone else, and as one-dimensional as I am, I just don't think I could do it. Not to her. To me. To my little brother, and yet I do nothing to stop it.

Lily Ellen

What I know about Lily comes from twelve months devious orchestration of "placing" myself where I know she'll be, and this largely comes in the shape of a writers circle in North Camden.

The great thing about being an established journalist and author is you get to know a lot of people in the industry, and Jon is one of them; he runs the Camden group, hence how I get away with attending without being a member.

Now, the amount of times I've been tempted to ask Lily to have a drink with me or take her to dinner is phenomenal. See, I'm never quite sure how she feels about me. She has in the past told me I'm a complete cock, but on other times, our eyes meet in a way that perhaps they shouldn't, and it's this silence that encourages me to pursue her.

OK, so I've never got around to asking her for that drink (sounds too obvious, even for someone as squalid as me) but a lift home – sure, because that's acceptable isn't it? Well, of course that depends how long we sit outside her place in the car talking – two hours or more? Still acceptable? I have no idea – worthy of the risk? *Jesus* yes.

On times though, I loathe my deviousness. See, last summer I walked into my parent's garden to see Lily shimmering out of their swimming pool and now I can't forget wet auburn hair and a glistening body slinkily clad in a pink ruffled bikini. (I actually felt myself blush, honest); so now when we sit in the car talking, sometimes this vision drifts into my head, and I have to nudge my conscience to remind myself who she is (this is beginning to happen more frequently).

See, with Lily it's easy to forget she's Luke girlfriend; her conversation is rich and vibrant and her laughter gets me right in the gut; her smile makes me want to keep her and I feel regret when she's gone; I am in love her; it's that simple – but of course it's anything but.

OK, let me introduce you to Lillian Ellen Mills.

Lily is twenty five and was born in Camden. She has a 1st Class Honours in English Literature and in the autumn she'll be going into her final year of a Masters in the History of the Book, with the aim of teaching or lecturing. She's currently studying at the University of London, and hangs about in Holborn to use the library. She's a grafter and takes her work seriously, but that's just a small part of her.

See, during many Howie traditional Sunday lunch gatherings, Lily has told me that after completing her first degree, she undertook a Certificate in Translation at the University of London Institute in Paris, and stayed on to become a translator.

'I needed to get away for a while,' she said to me across the table as the others talked drivel, '...needed to see things.'

And see things I'm sure she did; hints of "hanging out" in bohemian artists' squats on the Left Bank leave me restless.

But this aside, Lily is passionate about Paris, and I adore listening to her, see, I also had a year out in Paris in my mid twenties, so I know a little of how she feels, and whether or not this is a prissy comment to make, she's like me, but with a *graceful brilliance* I lack.

Anyway, after leaving Paris, Lily returned to the UK, caught up with old friends and went off to Cornwall for a holiday, and guess what, Luke was in a surfing tournament, took one look at her, and had to have her (sound familiar?) well, it seemed Lily liked what she saw too, and you know the rest.

So, apart from having a man 12 years her senior leching over her, Lily supplements her University bursary by working at 'Refuel' restaurant on Richmond Mews (yes, I have 'placed' myself here too), and when she's not there, she's with her sister Livvy and husband Tom on their farm in the Cotswolds, or hanging out in a rented house in Chalk Farm with two other students, and since Luke travels quite a lot, I'm grateful someone as exciting and inspiring as Lily doesn't waste her time sitting around waiting for him. Not that he expects her to, because in fairness, I love Luke, he's crazy and unique, which I can't think about too much because of how I feel about his girl.

Anyway, a few weeks ago, Lily invited me to her 25th birthday party. It was arranged by Livvy and was being held on the farm. Now, I didn't think I deserved an invite to Lily's party, after all, I'm just Luke's brother, but I accepted, (and without hesitation I'd like to add). It was the *raison d'être* I'd been waiting for to get close to her, it was also the grounds in which I used to corner her in my parent's kitchen the Sunday before the party.

'How are the arrangements coming along?' I said.

'Yeah, everything's under control.'

'Good.' I hovered in front of her, thinking of a way to keep her with me a little longer; we rarely had this opportunity, despite my efforts.

'So, it's a barbeque then?'

'Yes,' if she gripped her wine glass any harder it would break, 'Did Luke pass on the details about the hotel?'

I took the glass from her,

'Yes,' I said filling it with red wine, 'I've booked myself in already.'

She thanked me for the wine,

'I didn't expect you to come,' she said perching herself on a stool, 'I know you have a lot of important dinners to attend.'

I laughed,

'Pretentious dinners you mean?'

'Don't put words in my mouth Mr Howie.' She grinned sending me into complete raptures.

'Anyway I'm curious about your sister's farm.'

'It's nothing special,' she shrugged looking down at her feet; sexy, lightly tanned slim feet with perfectly cut nails with no polish, sitting elegantly in a pair of the cutest sandals; pink with a butterfly motif. 'But I love their chickens,' I adore that laugh, 'and I love the scrambled egg.'

Right. Cue.

'So, apart from chickens and scrambled egg, what else does Lily like?' See, we usually only discuss books and writing, avoiding the questions I'd much rather ask.

'Lots of things.' She said putting her wine down on the table, 'Music, Art, food, drinking, going to parties...'

'What music, what art, what food?' I said with a grin.

'You're taking the piss aren't you?' She eyed me with mock suspicion.

'Lily, I'm very interested in a woman who reads Henry Miller, because despite his sometimes bigoted attitude, you still manage to talk about him with a passion.'

I think I stunned her.

'Oh right, well...' she said looking up at me, because honest, I do tower over her, which makes her a little more demure and a little more beautiful. '...at the moment I'm listening to a band called The Kooks,' she said, 'and Nerina Pallot – she's very cool.'

'Art, food, parties...?' My mission was a desperate one.

She laughed, leaning forward, her arms folded, her glorious hair falling silkily from her shoulders, the radiance of the auburn penetrating my eyes,

'How long have you got?'

'As long as it takes.'

'Oh, right,' she stopped laughing, 'OK, well...' she looked up at me, smiling, and I wondered whether those eyes were for real, 'I love Lowry, especially the industrial scenes, and a cool American artist I've just discovered, The Black Apple, umm, I love olives and Champagne,' we smiled, 'dinner parties frighten me,' she's kooky; I love it, 'and I wish I was as classy as Audrey Hepburn.'

She is; I'll tell her one day.

'Favourite writer?' I asked; even though I knew the answer.

'Anais Nin.' Said without hesitation

'Ah yes, Nin.' I smiled, 'not the easiest literature to read, but magnificent.'

'I know she's most famous for her diaries, but I love her novels equally, I mean,' she said turning to me, arms unfolding, so she could elaborate, (I'd noticed this a few times), '"*Spy in the House of Love*", I so love that book, the plot could easily be a contemporary fiction storyline, but written with such class and beauty that you just don't see these days...' she stopped talking; looking a little awkward.

'Carry on.' I said softly.

'You're just being polite aren't you,' she looked into my eyes, 'humouring me whilst I gabble on about nothing.' I didn't believe that; I had a feeling most people wanted to worship this woman.

'Are you calling Anais Nin "nothing",' I raised an eyebrow, 'then shame on you.'

She smiled,

'It's just that I get used to Luke blanking me and Livvy losing the plot.'

'Well,' I said clinking her glass, 'you have now officially found someone who can match your passion.'

I hadn't meant that as it sounded, but once it was out, I wondered if it was true in the sense we were both thinking, I had a wicked feeling it was.

The following week I drove to Stow on the Wold, curious to experience country life after so long in the City, and I wasn't disappointed, because pulling up outside the old quaint farmhouse my eyes were fixated on a pair of stunning legs (OK wearing pink floral wellies but I barely noticed these) beneath a short frayed denim skirt. I ran my eyes the whole length of those legs to a pink vest; jersey fabric sculpting delicious breasts and the red halo blowing aimlessly around her face; she has the loveliest, most alluring smile I've seen in a long time.

'Jefferson?' Lily, surrounded by chickens, came over to me as I got out of the car, 'what a day for it hey?'

'It certainly is.'

I wanted to hug her. It felt natural, after all, it was her birthday and I'd travelled from London to spend it with her (OK so had about twenty others), but we'd only hugged once before and that was at my New Year's Eve party last year, but by the time I'd pissed about wondering, she'd already got her dainty arms around my neck, on tip toes, holding me.

I slipped my arms around her delicate waist and held her tight, too tight maybe, and buried my face into her hair; breathing in her skin was the moment I knew I was alive.

'Happy Birthday.' My arms felt empty without her, 'I've got you a little something,' I leaned into my car and took out a small pink gift wrapped box (I chose pink purposely; it is officially Lily's favourite colour).

'Oh bless you,' she said taking it from me, 'that's really kind J, but you didn't have to.'

'I wanted to.'

She ripped into the gift,

'I love the paper,' her eyes twinkled as she looked up at me, 'I'm a bit predictable aren't I?'

'There's nothing predictable about you Lily.'

I didn't mean my voice to sound quite so soft, and yes, Lily did notice because she looked at me a little longer than she should have, but I liked it, and I think she knew I did.

'Oh my God,' she looked up from the diamond necklace; her eyes were watering, and I felt a bit of a shite, like maybe I'd gone over the top, 'Oh Jefferson, this is stunning, honest it's beautiful, thank you so much.'

I looked up and noticed the man who was responsible for, firstly, introducing me to Lily, and secondly, making sure I never have her.

'JJ!' Luke swaggered over like the jock he was, hands in baggy jeans, showing his underwear, 'you made it then?' he said reaching us, immediately slipping his arm around Lily's waist and pulling her in.

'In good time.' And we shook hands.

'Look what Jefferson bought for me.' Lily showed Luke the necklace.

'Whoa man,' he grinned, 'bet that cost a cool...'

'Stop.' I said holding up my palm, 'don't.'

Luke's like this about money; he thinks I'm loaded, and OK, I am pretty well off, but he has this irritating habit of mentioning it whenever we're together.

'Sorry man, don't want to ruin the moment eh?' And he laughed before smothering Lily's neck.

I smiled defeated but Lily caught my eye over his shoulder and winked, and that my friend was my moment of hope.

At the party, Lily's parents didn't waste anytime introducing themselves.

'Hello Jefferson,' a slim, small lady with red glossy hair approached me in the kitchen, 'I'm Laura, Lily's mum.'

I shook her hand,

'And you obviously know who I am?'

'Yes, we know who you are.' And she smiled, sort of mischievously, (see what I mean, *redheads* hey?) 'Lily's told us all about you, she's even made us read your column, not that Jim or I usually read the Independent.'

Cool.

'This is Jim,' Laura said taking hold of the muscular arm of a tall broad man who had been talking behind us, 'Lily's dad.'

Jim was forced away from talking to Tom, who I already knew was Lily's brother in law.

'Jim this is Jefferson, Luke's older brother, wrote the book that Lily lent you.' Oh Jesus, her dad has read one of my books.

Jim shook my hand, eyeing me with caution, and I wasn't surprised, especially if he'd read the line "*...reds, I've heard they have a built in fucking manual, I'd like to give it a go, like to plunge in and out of the red stuff.*" I swallowed nervously.

'Jefferson.' His voice was firm, and if I was being honest, I would not want to mess with this man under any circumstance, even if I am taller than him.

I saw Lily across the room and indulged my senses, visually pursuing her from person to person. Earlier this evening, she'd exceeded my expectations as she strode into the lounge before the party; her hair tumbling effortlessly around her shoulders, her body marching sexily towards me in a navy blue silk ruffle dress. She has amazing legs elegantly emphasised by thought provoking silver heels.

'Hey J,' she completely blinded my vision, 'new suit?'

'Yes it is.' I said looking down at my black jacket, then fingering the lapel.

'It's lovely.' She sat beside me in a delicate vapour trail of perfume and I flinched, 'What do you think?' she said putting her dainty hand to her chest, showing me the necklace.

'Beautiful.' I couldn't catch my breath.

'That's what I thought,' she ran a finger tip over the diamond; 'I love it, thank you again J.'

Dragging myself back to the party, I struggled to tear my eyes from Lily who was currently being molested by my little brother, but when I did, they were met by Laura's; fuck, why do I always do that?

'It was very kind of you to buy Lily the necklace.' She said.

'Not really,' I said leaning back against the dining table, 'I just wanted to buy her a gift.'

That sounded suspicious; but it's the truth. I want to shower Lily with gifts, of everything she likes, (books, music, flowers, clothes, dinners, champagne, shoes, handbags) and things I like (underwear; in particular pink satin, maybe a corset, peek a boo panties – they had definitely been wanking fodder for some time).

'Hey mum,' Lily joined us; it was cute that she slipped her arm around her mum's waist, 'you've met the infamous JJ then?'

Lily makes me sound human. I like it. Most of the time I live in a land of ego's and bullshit, with Lily it's, well, it's free.

'I lent my dad *The Northern Road*,' she said, 'he thought it was, well...' and she smiled at me; he had definitely read the part about "*reds*", '...intriguing.'

I started laughing, I couldn't help it, thankfully Jim had disappeared, but even better, Lily was laughing too,

'We're both open minded,' Laura assured me, 'we have to be with this little lady roaming about.' And she kissed her daughter's head and I looked at Lily, the "little lady" and we smiled, but I couldn't help wonder what Laura meant by her last comment. Lily had just become even more of an enigma.

The opportunity to speak to Luke about Lily is rare. Inbetween surfing, clubbing and I guess getting intimate with his girl, I don't see him much, but after copious amounts of alcohol at Lily's party, he started to open up.

'I've never met a girl like her,' Luke was slumped against the stable door, watching Lily talking with her sister and some friends; I looked at Luke smiling adoringly at her and felt a stab in my gut.

'Why?' I was curious. Luke had never been short of women.

'Oh come on man,' he said, 'you've talked to her, I mean, how cool is she?' Luke finished his drink and I took the glass from his hand, otherwise it would have ended up like the other one; somewhere in the haystack behind us. 'She's good you know,' he caught my eye, 'you know, in the sack.' He looked away thoughtfully; he was watching her; I wanted her more than ever. 'I've never known a woman so openly, you know, in to shagging before.'

We looked at each other,

'Think yourself lucky then.' I turned back to Lily. I think she was looking at me.

'I mean,' Luke continued, 'is a chick supposed to be like that, you know, making all the moves?'

I laughed; Lily Ellen was so wasted on my little brother.

'You've obviously been short changing yourself for years?' Talking about her like this made me feel bad, and yet I craved to know more.

'Maybe I have,' Luke said grinning, 'you know, she's even crazier after booze,' he said nudging me, but my gut wrenched at the thought of it, 'real disinhibited.' His eyes widened.

'Piece of advice,' I said not liking the way he was talking, 'memories are so much better when they're not shared.'

I bided my time all evening and kept well out of her way. I spoke to everyone at the party I could; most of whom I didn't know, in the vain hope I might just get her alone, and as the party was dying down, she found me.

'Mr Howie?'

I was scanning her sister's bookshelf; obviously not an avid lover of books like Lily, but there were some acceptable offerings present.

'Since it's your birthday, you can call me Jefferson.'

She laughed softly, and I didn't like to think of her being disinhibited with Luke, or with anyone for that matter.

'Well thank you "Jefferson".'

'So,' I said looking down at her as she stood beside me, our backs against the books, 'how's your party?'

'I'm having a great time,' she had small pink glossy lips, and when she smiled, she showed her lovely white teeth, 'catching up with people I haven't seen for ages, and some I'd rather not.' I nodded in appreciation. 'I finished reading "*Grey Rain*" last night, for the second time.'

I wrote *Grey Rain* after breaking up with Gracie. It wasn't about her, but the mood was dark and there was a fair bit of filth in there too; things I knew Lily could handle.

'Criticisms?' I asked.

'It's a masterpiece.'

Her announcement shocked me a little. This was a woman who read a lot of books; a lot of classics, a lot of trash and a lot of fucking brilliant pieces and she thought I was a "masterpiece".

'You're too kind.' I said.

'But...' she looked up at me with a raised eye; cute or what? '... you gave it a happy ending.' She smiled leaning her head against the books, her hair sliding from her shoulders, revealing demure ears and glistening diamond studs. She turned her head and looked at me; she is divine, 'life would be boring if everyone had a happy ending don't you think?'

'Personally Lily,' I leaned in a little closer, mentally counting the freckles across the bridge of her nose, savings them for later, 'I love a happy ending, so I have to disagree that life would be boring if we all had one; I hope to God we do.'

She looked thoughtful for a moment; wearing an unfamiliar frown; I wanted to rub it away,

'You're right.' She nodded, 'excuse my cynicism.'

'I've got you down as a lot of things Lily but cynic isn't one of them.'

Silence.

'In Paris,' she's very good at changing the subject, 'there was this really great café close to where I lived,' she pondered, 'I miss sitting there with my espresso and croissant,' I wanted to kiss her, 'that was my breakfast you see, then I'd pick up a pink cup cake from the patisserie on the corner, go to work, come home, shower, go out with friends drinking, maybe dancing, get in way too late, crash out and start again the following morning.' when she laughed, my stomach went ballistic.

I laughed too.

'An espresso, a croissant and a pink cup cake hey?'

'Yes Mr Howie,' she is so beautiful, 'some of my favourite things, along with the ballet, crunching autumn leaves under my feet, snow and Love.'

'Ah,' I raised my brow, 'a side to Lily Ellen that's hidden away; what a regret.'

There. I'd said it. "*Lily Ellen*", my name for her, accept she didn't flinch.

'So,' she said, 'what are your favourite things Jefferson?'

That was easy, although I had to eliminate her from the line up.

'A very mature Glenfiddich, no ice, or a mature red; a book, and a bath, preferably all three at the same time.'

'I wonder about your life,' she leaned her head back against the books, offering me visual access to her smooth slender neck and magnificent jawline. 'I imagined you'd be like this.' Her eyes were heavy on mine.

'Like what?' I dared to ask.

'Amazing company.'

But I failed to return the compliment, because Luke came bounding over,

'Hey babe!' he called out, 'I've been looking for you everywhere.'

Luke was a man who needed to be mothered, and although Lily seemed happy to cuddle him and stroke his hair now, I didn't think she'd want to do it forever, no, because from the little I'd learnt that evening, Lillian Mills was one redhead who demanded to be taken seriously, and I was right on board.

My infatuation with Lily catapulted after her birthday party but I was no closer to her, so when I arrived at my parent's house for Mum's birthday a few days later, I received an unexpected surprise.

'Hello!' I called from the front door, directing it at the lounge where I could hear voices, 'it's JJ!'

I'd had lunch with Henry at The Wolseley. I'd given him three new chapters to keep him quiet.

'Jefferson!' Mum looked pleased to see me; in fairness, she always did, but not as pleased as I was to see Lily sitting in the arm chair beside the window; I winked at her over mum's shoulder and she smiled.

'Happy Birthday mum,' I said handing her a small gift box. 'I hope you like them.'

'Oh Jefferson, you know I will.'

As mum started opening her present (pearl earrings; she's been going on about them since Christmas), I sat down in the chair beside Lily.

'So,' I said, 'how's it going?'

'Pretty good,' she smiled and sitting so close to her, I had an incredible urge to hold her hand, 'study day.'

'Ah yes, study days,' I empathised, 'which actually translates into the day when you have to get everything else done because you've neglected it all week.'

'Exactly.' She has a soft laugh that chokes me; it always does.

'Oh honey,' mum called out over my thoughts, 'these are beautiful, oh really you shouldn't have, oh Lily come and have a look.'

I watched as Lily got to her knees beside mum. Her denim skirt rose slightly, exposing a generous amount of her smooth thighs; I swallowed.

'Jefferson,' Lily said turning back to me, 'you have good taste.'

'It's all those lovely ladies he courts,' mum looked hopeful, 'they're all well bred ladies you know.'

Lily caught my eye and smiled,

'I'm sure they are.' Because she knew damned well they weren't. 'I'll put the kettle on,' she said getting back on her feet, her beautiful heaven like hair spilling around her shoulders, and I couldn't help it, I simply could not take my eyes off her.

'Jefferson,' Mum's harsh tone made me jump, 'stop it!'

'What?' I asked guiltily.

'You know what.'

Lily returned carrying a tray. I immediately got up and took it from her, my fingers briefly touching hers. I looked for a response, but she was completely oblivious, still talking to mum about the earrings.

'I had a friend in Paris who was mad about pearls,' Lily sat back in the arm chair, legs crossed at the knee, she was wearing those sweet pink butterfly sandals again, why I'm so crazy about them I have no idea, after all, I'd had delicious sex with Madeleine last night and her Jimmy Choo's should have been enough to keep me satisfied right? 'Her boyfriend was a struggling artist, but he spent months frantically selling his paintings so he could buy her pearl earrings for her birthday, it was so lovely.'

Romantic as well as sensual. I like it.

'So, do you prefer diamonds or pearls Lily?' I asked innocently. Mum was staring at me again and I had the feeling this wasn't the first time she'd caught me leering at Luke's girlfriend.

Lily smiled and lifted her hair revealing her ear; I knew she was a diamond girl. Pure class in a denim skirt and girly flips flops, and for me, her beauty is unparalleled.

'Do you miss Paris sweetheart?' Mum was taking out her hoops and slipping in the pearls.

'Sometimes.' She said, 'I miss some of the friends I made,' then she looked at me, 'Jefferson and I went to similar places didn't we?'

I liked the way she linked our lives.

'*Deux Magots* is brilliant for people watching,' she grinned, and I couldn't help thinking she was quite naughty when she did, 'I used to go there in the afternoons and watch writers discussing manuscript with their agents wishing it was me.'

Cute.

'Do you still keep in touch with any of your friends?' Mum asked innocently.

'Well, no...' Lily's eyes met mine, 'not anymore.'

I knew it; Lily would have been a struggling artists Heaven.

'Oh what a shame.' Mum added fiddling in her handbag.

Lily gently raised her eyes at me; I nodded to let her know I understand her awkwardness.

'Lovely museums out there I hear.' I was happy Mum liked her earrings; so far, she'd spent most of this conversation (which she initiated) studying them in her compact mirror.

'*La Generale* was my favourite, and *La Barbizon* was pretty cool for watching films,' she said in a wonderful French accent, sending me into complete raptures, 'a lot of my...friends were artists you see, ' And I looked at her, but her eyes were firmly on mum messing about with her jewellery, 'they taught me a lot.'

I know *La Generale*, I went there last year with James Allen-Tait, it's the largest "art-squat" in Paris. We sat in a room with empty Champagne bottles on the floor; I guessed they couldn't be "struggling" that much.

'Ooh, sounds exciting.' Mum said, but I didn't think she'd been listening.

'Does that explain your passion for Art?' I smiled at her, because; well, because she's so damned lovely.

'Yes.' And she smiled back, and I swear, there it was again, Lily's eyes hovering on mine for longer than they needed to. 'Comes second to writing.'

The doorbell went, and I got up to answer, but mum waved me down,

'It'll be Annabel.' (her sister). And as soon as she'd disappeared, I took the opportunity.

'You speak brilliant French,' I said.

'Oh thanks.'

As she leaned over to put her cup on the table, her skirt rose and honestly, believe me when I say this, I did attempt to drag my eyes away, until I caught a glimpse of her underwear; pink satin; *Jesus Christ*!

'You visit Paris quite a bit don't you?' She said crossing her legs.

I nodded sipping my tea; I could smell her perfume again, I think its Calvin Klein.

'Friends of mine have an apartment there,' I said hoping to impress her, 'I stay there when I can.' Thought I'd try my luck and impress her further, 'they're both writers actually,' I said putting my tea cup beside hers, 'James and Helena Allen-Tait?'

'I don't know them.' She said leaning forward; eyes focused, and if body language experts were right, she was interested in what I was saying.

'Well James writes crime fiction and Helena writes Erotica.'

'Erotica?' that got her, 'sounds interesting.'

'Look her up online,' I said fuelling her interest, 'she's been published for about seven years now.'

'I will,' she said writing down the website address in a pink notepad, 'I'm always looking for new inspirations.'

God, I love this woman.

'So, where in Paris do they live?' she said elegantly slipping her notepad back into her satchel.

'Montparnasse.' I said. 'Actually I'm out there in a little while.'

'Oh you're so lucky,' she said sitting back, pulling her skirt down slightly. I hoped she hadn't caught me looking, 'oh I bet their apartment is stunning.'

'It is,' we'd found another shared passion, 'it has authentic shutters and ivy growing around the window; you'd adore it.'

We looked at each other and I swear she was reading my mind, or rather my eyes, because to take Lily to Paris, to have that time with her, well, I'd do anything I could to make it happen.

'I'd love to see it.' If I wasn't mistaken, her voice had turned soft.

Mum arrived back with Annabel and I knew this would kill our conversation. Something always happened to stop us talking, and I wondered if there would come a time when I could get to know her without it looking or feeling suspicious.

'How would Montparnasse compare to your days in St Germain?' I said hoping to cut in before Annabel and mum stole her away (they love Lily; the whole family does).

'I don't think it could.'

I wondered again about her previous lovers. Her apparent insatiable sexual appetite had been haunting me.

'Good.' And I winked with a smile.

'Hello Lily,' Annabel hugged Lily briefly and I'd have done anything to swap places, 'how are you sweetheart?'

'Good thanks.' She said fiddling with the straps on her satchel; she was obviously getting ready to leave.

'And when's that tearaway boyfriend of yours back from far away shores?' Luke was currently out in Australia. He left at the weekend.

'Not until next month.'

'Four weeks!' Annabel cried, 'oh pet.'

'Do you need a lift Lily?' I interjected.

'Well only if you're sure.'

'I'm going to Camden anyway.' This was the truth, despite Mum's eyes flicking between the two of us.

'Actually Jefferson,' she said turning awkwardly from Mum, 'I'm going to Holborn, so I'll make my own way if that's alright, but thanks anyway.'

'Of course; no problem.'

But it was a problem, a huge one, because if I didn't let go of this infatuation, and leave her alone, one day, Luke was going to come home, ask her to marry him and they'd go off and live in the Bahamas; then I really would be fucked.

Good Day

A week later and I'm due to meet Joseph for lunch in Café Pasta. I haven't seen him for ages, well to be honest, I've been avoiding him because he's been after the four of us going out for dinner (by four, I mean with Florence and Madeleine); so there I was, walking down Monmouth Street, when something caught my eye in the window of Coco de Mer. I stopped and went back on myself; swallowed, and walked in.

I browsed for a while because this isn't the first time I've been in, in fact, I've bought a few gifts from here, none that surprisingly gave me the response I'd hoped for (OK, maybe a glass dildo was a bit presumptuous for a second date; very poor decision making, agreed and never to do again.)

I went back to the window display. I could see her in it. That delicate waist, the luscious curve of her hips, tender round breasts spilt over pink satin; delightful against pert nipples, and by candlelight, that auburn hair would be *heaven on earth.*

'Can I take this please?' I turned to the shop assistant and pointed to the pink satin corset with it's delicious pink ribbon, as you've guessed, it's proving much more difficult to let her go than I originally thought.

I was wandering around whilst the assistant sorted the right size corset, when something took my eye,

'And these please.' I said pointing to a pair of panties, well, I call them "panties" loosely because they are no doubt made for all kinds of filthy fucking sessions; white transparent fabric with a pink satin bow at the back (it unfastens too – perfect).

Handing over my card, I noticed a small book on the counter. It was a cute little thing produced by Playboy; a collection of Playmates with varying shades of red hair. *A must have for this boy.*

'I'll take this as well thanks.' I'm fortunate money isn't an obstacle, but where should I draw the line, after all, hadn't I just spent almost eight hundred pounds on gifts I'd never beable to send?

Joseph was already sitting outside the restaurant with a bottle of red wine when I arrived, I hoped he wouldn't notice I'd been shopping.

'Hey fella,' Joe got up and we shook hands, then he nodded to the bag, 'looks interesting.' He grinned.

'Just a gift.' I said sitting down and pouring myself a drink; I still couldn't believe what I'd done.

He leaned over to look into the bag,

'Very boudoir.' He smiled raising an eye.

'It's for Madeleine.' I said before thinking.

'Well let's have a look then?' Fortunately the Café wasn't busy. 'There's no way that's for Mads, this is tiny.' I took the corset back and put it in the bag, hidden amongst torn tissue paper. 'You're not playing away are you Jefferson?'

'Of course not.'

'Then what's that all about?'

There have been many occasions over the last year where I've wanted to confide in Joseph. To confess that steadily over the last 12 months, I've been falling in love, but he'd laugh; hysterically, but he'd end up crying when I told him who I'd fallen in love with.

'Look, Luke asked me to get it for Lily; he's away until next month and he wanted to cheer her up.' That was a very cruel lie.

'Ooh, the lovely Lily hey?' Joseph's eyes twinkled. He'd met her a few times at my place and on every occasion he'd commented on how lovely she is. He continued to stare at me, and I swear it was written across my face, so I picked up the menu,

'Know what you're having?' I said.

'Mussels.' His eyes bored into me.

The thing with Joseph is, he's become well and truly "married". He's conveniently forgotten how many women he's shagged or the couple of times he's fucked about without Florence knowing (OK, not actually fucking, but I'd say a blow job comes pretty close) but now he's all morals and judgement, and that majorly pisses me off.

'Go on,' I said putting the menu down, 'there's obviously something you want to say.'

Because I've known Joe so long, we can have these conversations.

'I just wondered what was happening with you and Mads.'

OK, "Mads" is best friends with Joe's wife, Florence. They went to the same girl's school and somehow I've managed to enter into some sort of "relationship" with her, which was never my intention.

'Not a lot if I'm being honest,' I said pouring more wine; this conversation was making me want to get pissed out of my skull, 'me and Madeleine are just messing around.'

'Mads doesn't "mess around".'

This I already knew.

'Well I made it clear I wasn't looking for a permanent fixture.'

'I saw Gracie and Eliot last night,' he always does this; blames my "lack of commitment" on the fact Gracie left me, 'she's looking amazing, even with her bump.' This was old news. 'Anyway, how you fixed for next Friday?'

Oh fucking hell.

'I need to check my diary,' OK, big lie, 'I'll get back to you.'

Joe raised his brow at me; he knows me too well, but honest, I know this is cruel, but I so do not want to get into anything with Madeleine, well, OK, maybe just one thing, a warm soft thing, just for now though, until I get the one I really want.

I left Joseph in Neal's Yard talking to a friend of his from college and headed towards Piccadilly. I had a couple of books on order at Waterstone's and I'd had a call to say they were in. I was working well on the new novel, but even so, Henry can be a real pain in the *ass* when it comes to deadlines.

I took off my sweater; it was muggy today and I wish I'd worn something a little lighter than moleskin trousers. Brushing the hair from my eyes, I adjusted my specs and ran to the third floor. At least the air conditioning was working today, which didn't stop me craving an ice cold beer when I saw the sign for 5th View.

As the assistant began bagging my books, I saw Lily, almost as though I'd wished her. Well, at least I thought it was her; she had the same beautiful hair, although tied in a sleek low hung ponytail, and the formal attire threw me a little because the Lily I know is usually quite cool and casual. She's turning around, Christ, it is her.

Lily was reading, so I snatched the opportunity to allow my eyes to deliciously linger. She was wearing an olive green flower print scarf teamed with a snug black t-shirt and a black A-line skirt that sat at her knees. I even stared at her feet, yes, perfect; black ballet pumps. She is magnificent.

I clinched my bags between clammy hands, thinking of pink satin and black ballet pumps and I was getting one hell of an erection. I closed my eyes to stop thinking, but I was thinking even more and when I opened them, she was looking right at me.

'Jefferson,' she closed the book and strode over to me, 'how's it going?'

She gripped three books to her chest, that cute brown satchel strapped around her ultra feminine body.

'Lily,' I smiled trying to act as though I'd only just seen her, 'I'm pretty good, you?' The fact I'd shared a bottle of wine with Joseph was helping.

'Well,' she shrugged, 'beginning to wish I'd never started this MA,' she looked pretty pissed off, 'I just never get time for anything else, and

I'm desperately trying to work on my novel but everything together is just crashing in on me.'

'What you doing now?' I said catching my breath.

'Well,' she checked her watch, 'I should be working, but I got side tracked, me and books you see...' And she started laughing.

'I understand,' I smiled, 'come on, how about we have a drink and I'll see if there's anything I can do to help.'

Now, I did try and salvage this situation by suggesting we take the stairs to the cafe, but Lily wouldn't hear of it; it had to be the lift. The doors closed and standing in such close proximity to that hair, I failed to keep my promise not to admire her. I shifted a little closer; her perfume was divine and when I glanced at our reflection in the doors; she was watching me too; we both smiled.

'You look different without a suit,' she said as the doors opened. 'I guess it's because you wear one quite alot.'

'Is that good or bad?' I thought about what I was wearing; brown moleskin trousers, check shirt, sweater in my hand, dark brown Camper shoes, black bag strapped around me and specs.

'No, it's good,' she looked me over; it felt wonderful. 'I like it.'

We were shown to a table beside the window. I could see the Eye, which of course I've seen many times before, but being here with Lily, everything feels fresh.

'I like your scarf.' And I did; but more than that, I was desperate to compliment her, I had been from the moment she walked into my life and because she is extremely sexy, if I hadn't mentioned the scarf, the words "pink satin" and "fuck me" might have got me arrested.

'Oh, thanks,' she sounded pleased, but a little surprised, 'I got it from Covent Garden,' then she shrugged, 'God knows why I just told you that.' And she started laughing.

'Orla Kiely.' I added, 'I pass her shop most days.'

'Yes.' She looked as though she was inspecting me. 'Mr Howie, it's true, you are a genius.'

I laughed, because sometimes she's real kooky, I didn't tend to find that much in the women I dated.

'So, have you been somewhere important?' I said, my eyes loitering over her outfit.

She shook her head without looking up from the drinks menu. I knew what I was having.

'After we talked about Paris last week, I felt inspired.'

'You look good in black.' I took a slow breath, daring to push myself further, 'but pink butterfly sandals are good too.'

She put down her menu and looked at me, and for one moment I really thought she was going to land one on me, instead she started smiling,

'Bit of a contrast hey?' She looked down at herself.

'Parisian chic meets surfer girl.' I smiled.

'Is that what you think of me?' She laughed; she was great to be with.

'A little,' I shrugged, 'and you carry both off with an equal amount of charm.'

She was still laughing when the waitress came over, so I ordered two glasses of Prosecco, then changed it to a bottle with a side order of olives and ciabatta.

'So,' I was admiring her freckles, contemplating telling her, "*redheads are the only women who come with a built in sex manual. Think freckles. Think Connect the Dots.*" (I read it in that Redheads Playboy book. True? I'd give anything to find out.) 'what's troubling you, and can I help?'

'Well...' as she pulled her satchel from beneath the table I noticed her grinning, 'Coco de Mer hey?' whoa, what naughty twinkling eyes, *my name is Jefferson James Howie and I am a very bad man.*

'It's nothing.' I said, which was the most bizarre comment I'd made in some time and since this was Lily and not Madeleine, there was no way I could get away with it.

'It is for Madeleine?' she tilted her head in an attempt to see inside the bag, 'can I have a look?'

I didn't want her to see it. I didn't want to see her holding it. The thought was too much for my already badly straining trousers and as I handed her the bag, I remembered the Playboy book, so I took the corset out and took back the bag.

'Oh Jefferson,' she said running her fingers lovingly over the satin; delicious tingles rushed to my groin, 'how beautiful.' She looked at me, smiling, the sexy pink satin reflecting her active mind, and then, Oh Jesus, she held it up to herself, and started laughing, well, a giggle actually, and seeing it up against her, seeing how perfect she would look in it, I couldn't speak.

'I'm sorry.' She held the corset firmly between her hands as though she didn't want to let it go, 'that was insensitive of me.' And she carefully folded it and handed it back to me.

The Prosecco arrived and our awkwardness soon disappeared.

'Let me read your work?' I poured us another glass, and for a moment, I left my body and stood by the entrance, looking over at our table, watching us together as I often did during Sunday lunch at my folks place, wondering if people thought we were a couple, were we suited, did it look as though we were in to each other as we clinked glasses and laughed as she told me she was nervous about me reading her work.

'I'm not worthy.' She grinned.

I took off my specs and gently rubbed my eyes. Blinking her back into vision, I couldn't believe the way she was looking at me.

'I've always liked your glasses.' She said taking me back a little, 'the thick black frame looks lovely because of your chocolaty brown eyes.'

I started grinning. I couldn't help it. Was it my wishful thinking, or had we now given each other two compliments. This was a good day.

'You're laughing at me,' she smiled fiddling with a cocktail stick in the olives, 'do I sound that bad?'

'No,' I said meeting her gaze, 'you sound that good.'

We searched each others eyes, but she lowered hers and a change of subject was desperately needed.

'So Lily, talk to me about your writing?'

OK, so we've done this many times, but love me or loathe me, I just wanted to keep her with me for as long as I could.

'I'm old fashioned deep inside, but with a contemporary edge,' she said, 'after all, we don't date like the Bronte's or Austen anymore and saying, "some things are better left to the imagination" doesn't always work for me,' she picked up her glass, delicate fingers lightly gripping the flute, leaving marks in the condensation, 'I like people falling in love and I think a lot of other people do too, but the thing is, to get to the point of falling in love, you have to "experience" that person, you know, real nervous intimacy; full on fucking.'

I had an olive stuck in my throat.

'I agree,' I nodded with a cough, 'intense love stories need a certain amount of detail,' I said honestly, 'sex scenes need to be lovingly brutal in order to make the characters passion believable, because isn't that what people do when they're in love; that insatiable and animalistic urge that comes when you're deeply in to someone,' she nodded thoughtfully, 'but I'm not sure you have to have fucked someone to fall in love with them, that simply compliments the feeling.'

'Really?' she smiled, raising an eyebrow.

'Sure,' I grinned, 'so sometimes that "imagination" thing you talked about does work.'

She laughed a little between sipping her drink,

'I think you're right.'

I know I'm right Lily Ellen; you are living proof.

'Anyway,' she finished her drink so I topped her up, 'I shelve so many of my ideas for being unfashionable,' she said pulling at a piece of bread with shy fingers, 'when I think about some of the things I've written, the sex, I can't ever imagine getting published, let alone getting an agent.' *Jesus Christ. I love this woman.*

'I think you're a fucking genius Lily.' And I did.

She looked up at me; her eyes steady on mine and then she started smiling,

'You are such a piss taker Jefferson.' She laughed and clinked my glass, 'but hey, at least you listen.'

'Can't you talk to Luke about it?' I had to ask this question, because their pairing still confused me.

She shook her head.

'It's not really his thing.' She shrugged, 'I think it embarrasses him.'

'Let me help you Lily.' I leaned forward, 'let me read what you're working on, I'll make some comments and then we can meet up and go through them together.'

'You'd do that for me?'

'Sure I would.'

'I haven't got anything on me at the moment though,' She said, 'perhaps I can send some on to you?'

'Sure you can.'

She took out a notepad and a pen and handed it to me. She watched as I wrote down my address, and just for good measure, I put my mobile number on there too.

'I should give you mine too, just in case.' and so I watched as she wrote down her address and *Holy Jesus!* – her mobile number.

'Better idea,' I dared to say, 'are you going back to your place tonight?'

It was only when we left the tube at Chalk Farm that it hit me; I'm going to Lily's place.

'Hey Lily?' I said.

She turned and looked at me. Her hair had fallen out of its ribbon a little, her skin looked flushed and a little tired, she'd removed her scarf hours ago, but she still looked like the most beautiful creature to me.

'Are you hungry?'

'Yeah,' she said with a cute smile, 'You?'

I nodded,

'Takeaway or eat out?'

'Takeaway,' she said pushing her key in the door, 'craving pizza at the moment,' then she stopped and looked back at me, 'is takeaway pizza good enough for the refined Mr Howie?' and she winked.

I smiled and followed her in; she's dangerous.

Entering Lily's house felt as intruding as undressing her, but I still ordered the pizzas and let Lily show me around, thinking this is a place I shouldn't be, and yet following her into the kitchen, I felt like I'd been here before.

'Seriously J, are you sure a takeaway is alright?' she said from inside the fridge, and seeing her emerge with a smile and a bottle of beer made this about the best day in a long time.

'Us pretentious folk do lower ourselves to eat the occasional takeaway Lily Ellen.' And I winked at her.

'Lily Ellen?' she sat herself on the table, her ballet shoes had gone and she was swinging her feet in a lusciously girly manner; I could feel the familiar rush of blood to my groin at the thought of ripping off her panties, opening her legs wide and fucking her right here on the table, it was just too vivid for me to deny, 'How do you know I'm "Lily Ellen"?'

'Luke told me.' This was true.

'Is that what he calls me?'

I smiled, shaking my head,

'It's what I call you; it's supposed to be endearing,' I said walking over to her, imagining opening those thighs and holding them wide around me.

'It is endearing.' She said holding her legs together as though she could read my mind, 'I just never imagined Mr Howie did "endearing".

'Mr Howie does a lot of things that might surprise you.'

'A pink satin corset doesn't surprise me,' she raised a pretty eyebrow, 'I know about bad men like you.'

Is she flirting with me?

'Lillian babe is that you?' a female voice called from somewhere.

'It's Susie,' she said elegantly slipping off the table, her arm brushing mine, but I couldn't tell if it was accidental; maybe I shouldn't let her have anything else to drink. Too disinhibited; too soon; I can't even think about it. 'I'll just say hi, then I'll pop upstairs and get my work for you.'

'Of course.' I watched her leave the room, padding barefoot along the wooden floor, and then she disappeared into the next room.

I checked my watch. I'd been with Lily since two o clock; five whole hours of Lily Mills and then my phone went off. It was Madeleine.

'I'm standing at your door Howie wearing not very much, so I'm disappointed to find that you're not answering.'

Now, don't misunderstand me, Madeleine is stunning; attractive in an obvious way; curves, sculptured cheeks, gorgeous black hair, and her impulsive sexual urges arouse me beyond belief, but the moment she opens her mouth to speak, I want her to leave, and after the last five hours, I don't even want to fuck her anymore.

'We didn't make plans tonight did we?' I said hovering in the hallway; I could see my girl (well, not my girl yet, but after today, I feel a step closer) and another girl, Susie talking on the sofa.

'No darling,' Madeleine purred, 'just thought I'd chance it.'

'I'm with friends,' I said, 'won't be back for a while.'

'Oh damn,' she sighed impatiently, 'well I'm not hanging around for you Jefferson.' And she hung up; typical Madeleine.

'Hey J,' a breath of fresh air danced around me as Lily emerged from the lounge, 'come and meet Susie.'

Susie was older than Lily; she was definitely more worn.

'So you're the refined Jefferson Howie.' Susie was, yes, confident. 'I was beginning to think the lady was dating you.'

'Ignore her,' Lily replied unfazed, 'I do.' But Lily winked at her friend, and I felt kind of nervous.

'Well you guys,' Susie got up from the sofa, she was wearing a silk dressing gown in green and black; eccentric, just like the owner, 'I'll leave you to it.'

'Are you out tonight?' Lily was tidying the coffee table; a pile of magazines, some newspapers (all The Independent – I am seriously flattered by this woman), two white mugs and a plate with half a white bread sandwich left on it.

'Archie's taking me to "Honey's".'

Lily stood up, holding a worn copy of *Tropic of Cancer* to her chest,

'Cool.' She smiled, and I wished I'd opted to dine with her when I had the chance, not knowing if we'd have another opportunity. 'He's finally treating you like a lady then?'

'Oh yes,' Susie gushed, 'chocolates and flowers.' She snorted, 'very cliché.'

'Nothing wrong with chocolates or flowers,' Lily said putting the newspapers into a nearby rack, 'I think it's lovely.'

'Whatever,' then Susie turned to me, 'well Jefferson Howie, nice to meet you; I trust you'll be here in the morning.' She looked at Lily, and so did I, but Lily just frowned and then the doorbell went.

'Oh, that'll be the pizza.' Lily had been rearranging the throw and cushions on the sofa, and in just five minutes, she'd transformed this typical student lounge into a cosy sitting room.

'I'll get them Lily.' As I walked out the room, I could hear the girl's talking, like girl's do; girl's of any age.

'Ooh Lily, sexy older man hey,' Susie's voice was hushed, 'why didn't you say he was that gorgeous; are you playing with fire little lady?' Susie was laughing.

'Fuck off!' Lily whispered, 'Jefferson's a good man.'

'He looks like a very bad man to me.' Susie laughed again, and this time, I heard Lily join in,

'OK, he is a bad man, but he's still refined, handsome and sophisticated and he knows stacks about books and writing...'

'An easy way to you then?'

The doorbell went again, so I quickly opened it, still a little disorientated after listening in on their conversation, wishing I could have found out more, *fuck, when did I turn into such a sleaze? Always Jefferson; always.*

I can't remember the last time I did something like this, sitting down with a couple of beers and a pizza, in such great company, actually, make that, fantastic company.

'This is pretty cool isn't it?' Lily closed her box and folded her bare feet beneath herself as we sat on the sofa.

'I've had a great day Lily.' I closed my empty box and smiled, 'thank you.'

'Even though I've taken up almost your whole day.'

'I'm not complaining.'

She laughed with the kind of softness that got me right in the gut.

'Me neither.'

'So Lily,' I said turning to her, 'apart from parties, is this how you spend your evenings?'

'Sometimes,' she said, 'but only if I'm with Susie or Lauren, a lot of the time I just want to be alone, do you know what I mean?'

'Writing is a lonely profession, but we like it that way right?'

'We do.' She shook her hair from the sleek ponytail and let the auburn richness fall about her shoulders; she is so beautiful.

'So what else does Lily do with her time?' There was music playing softly; I like this mood.

'Study, eat, sleep,' and she smiled, 'write, go out...'

'And where do you go?' She looked a little surprised by my interruption.

'Well, local usually, Honey's, The Tavern, The Earl, Daisy Deli...'

'Daisy's?' I said. 'My friends own that.'

'Really?' she sat up, beaming at me, 'that place is so cool, have you tasted their carrot cake, oh I love it with an espresso.' Then she looked at me, 'you know some cool people don't you Jefferson?' she was looking at me in that way I can't work out, 'but then you are pretty cool aren't you?'

'I'm very flattered you think so,' I was buzzing inside; definitely good for one's ego, 'the nearer I get to forty, the more strokes I need.'

She started laughing,

'I don't believe that,' she was sitting cross legged, a soft pink cushion in her lap, 'I've seen you in the papers and magazines with your "well bred ladies" and then the pink satin corset, I mean, a man with your prestige and reputation does not need strokes from a twenty five year old...'

'You're kidding right?' *Calm down JJ.*

She shrugged awkwardly lowering her eyes,

'Anyway, tell your friends at the Daisy Deli I love their place.'

'Lily?'

She looked at me,

'Yes J?'

'We can do this you know.'

'Can we?' her eyes were alert, and I wondered if we were talking about the same thing.

'Of course we can; I think we can learn a lot from each other, and I'm happy to set aside a part of my day to go through your work and discuss it with you.'

'Oh, right, I see what you mean, yeah, of course, thank you, I'll be grateful for your help.'

I was a bit perplexed by her reply; now I know we'd been talking about different things, but hers excited me.

'Right then,' she said getting up, the pink cushion falling onto my lap, 'I'll get that work for you.' I watched her go to the door, and then she turned back to me, 'do you mind waiting?'

I caught my breath at the thought of what I was about to say,

'Can I come with you?'

It was close to midnight, and I've been with my brother's girlfriend for most of the day, and if anyone close to me knew this, they'd know it smells bad, and yet I still follow Lily upstairs to her room.

She opened her bedroom door and immediately an overwhelming breeze of her perfume wrapped its sweet arms around me, and for a moment I couldn't breathe.

'This is the real *High Place.*' I felt eighteen again.

Her room was kind of sexy. The walls were bright pink, articulately decorated by silver framed prints of Degas' ballerinas and a couple of pencil sketched nudes. Another wall was taken up by books, with an over spill on the floor, and there were CD's lying around, Kings of Leon, The Strokes, John Lennon; another shared interest, which I find difficult to put into words because between us, is what I'd call a substantial age gap.

I didn't know what to do with myself, after all, I wasn't a kid on a first date, and yet that's how I felt; the whole room reminded me I shouldn't be doing this, and yet I couldn't walk away, her presence was too strong, this vibe too powerful, and the feeling of losing control was frightening, but my feet remained firmly on her wooden floor.

'J,' she sat down at her desk and pointed to her double bed, 'sit down a minute.' So I did, noting it was firm, comfortable; no squeaks.

Whilst Lily sorted through a variety of files, I continued taking in her boudoir. Her wardrobe with the elegant black chiffon dress hanging up, making me wonder what she does and where she goes; her double bed covered in a pink and aubergine floral duvet, a white fur throw slain across the bottom; the white iron wrought head board with it's tiny white flickering lights entwined around the curves; I see her holding it, lying on her back, knuckles white because I fuck her deep, I closed my eyes, then opened them and blinked.

There were a few used candles scattered about: bedside table, the floor, the window ledge, the dresser. Yes the dresser, I'm gawping at like I've never been into a woman's bedroom before. I was right; CK Eternity. There were make up brushes, a compact, lipgloss, Body Shop hand and face cream, bath soak, everything that makes her what she is. I turned to the radiator; laundry; panties: white cotton, pink chiffon, black lace. They all look so demure; so innocent, yet so naughty and I don't think I've ever been in this situation before.

'Jefferson?' Lily was holding a pink A4 binder and I wondered how long she'd been watching me. 'I thought I'd give you this to start.'

I took it from her, holding it securely. I know I'm holding her life's work in my hands.

'You'll probably find it a bit amateurish, but I know you'll beable to look beyond that.'

'Of course.'

She sat beside me on the bed and I looked at her. She's so young; I can't believe how badly I want to fuck her, but more than that, I can see those freckles and I'm joining them up, they're sexy and sweet and I want to trace my finger over them.

'What?' she put her hands to her face, laughing, 'what are you looking at?'

I didn't know what to say.

'Can I take a look?' and I nodded to the pink binder.

'Please.' Her thigh was pressed against mine forcing my erection to thump beneath the binder; I started reading at random,

"He was surprised that for such a young pretty girl living alone, she didn't close her blinds at night, and so, as she peeled off her jumper, swiftly followed by her vest, he admired those curves in silhouette against the fairy lights..."

I flicked through again,

"...I'm running my hand up her skirt to her thighs, holding her skin between my fingers. She's motioning beneath me and I want to fuck her but she deserves more than this, she's majorly on the rebound and yet I've got my hand on her ass feeling the crevice through her barely there pants..."

I closed the binder. I couldn't read this stuff with her so close to me.

'You hate it right?' She was gazing at the closed binder.

I laughed to shake off the intimacy; I couldn't.

'Lily Ellen have confidence in yourself.' I had both hands on the binder otherwise I feared one might have crept into hers. 'When can I see you again?' OK, so that came out pretty badly, so I'm glad she laughed.

'Well, that depends on you J; I know you're busy.'

Right; how quickly can I turn this over for her?

'Saturday?'

'Umm,' as she pondered for a moment, I looked over at her chiffon dress, forgetting she was a busy and sought after woman, 'Saturday what time?'

'How about we do it over lunch?'

'OK.' She smiled.

'I'll book us a table at The Wolseley, say 12.30?'

'Great.'

Now it was time for me to go, but as I followed Lily downstairs and to the front door, I desperately wanted to stay.

'Jefferson?' Her voice was soft and tired, and I would have given anything to hug her goodnight. 'Thanks for everything; it's very good of you.'

I climbed back up the steps until we were level,

'I was a struggling writer once Lily,' I said, 'I can't do much to influence your fate, but I'll certainly do my best to help it.'

She gently kissed my cheek, and the touch of her lips melted my skin. I folded my arms around her warm and welcoming body and held her against me. I closed my eyes as her arms slipped around my neck and carelessly my head collapsed against hers. She stroked my hair, the fallen fringe tickled my nose and the comfort I felt from this woman was undeniable, and so I'll forever regret that someone whistled at our "lover's" embrace, because she immediately withdrew.

Crossing the road to my apartment, I could see a ghostly figure hovering outside the door.

'Jefferson!' I couldn't believe she'd been hanging around all night, Christ, it was almost 1 a.m. 'I kept dropping by; hoping; oh I'm desperate darling, please?'

After pushing her inside, I made sure the pink binder was safe before pinning Madeleine down on the stairs, ripping open her Mac and carelessly pulling down her panties, but all I could think about was the white cotton on Lily's radiator, and my flounding dick rose to spectacular proportions.

As soon as the rubber was on, I snapped her legs open and drove straight in. Her cries echoed in the hallway, but I needed it; this filthy release, because if I couldn't have Lily, I'd have to take this instead.

Madeleine was trying to make some kind of loving out of it, but I just needed a fuck; I needed to come, I needed to feel sharp nipples rubbing furiously against my chest, needed to plunge in and out, over and over, and now I'm coming, Oh Jesus, I'm coming...

Hollering, I closed my eyes tight, thinking of her, of Lily, seeing her beneath me, her mulled wine hair, her dot to dot freckles, her smile, oh Lily, and she's watching me, wanting me, loving me.

Completely out of breath, I collapsed, holding Madeleine to my sweat slicked body. I was exhausted, seeing stars, but feeling strangely empty; how quickly euphoria fades. Madeleine pushed me off and stood up, straightening herself out.

'That was quick.' Her voice penetrated me; made me nauseous. 'And who the fuck is "Lily"?'

'Lily?' I was trying to pull up my trousers.

'Yes you fuckwit.' I thought she was going to land one on me.

'I'm sorry.' God that sounded pathetic.

I shuddered as Madeleine slammed the door behind her. I looked to my left and there, safely on the stairs, was the pink binder.

Hummingbird Bakery

I woke up face down, naked on top of the duvet. I felt like shite. Christ knows what time I went to sleep, but it was late. After the Madeleine episode, I dragged my sorry ass to my apartment, undressed, threw myself on the bed and started reading Lily's work.

I guessed dinner on Friday was off, since Madeleine would have me down as the World's biggest prick, which probably wasn't far wrong after what happened last night, but to be brutally honest, I didn't want see her again; however, there was one thing playing on my mind, and I'd only thought of it after she'd slammed the door in my face.

See, I've known enough women in my life to be confident that Madeleine will be talking to Florence today about what I did, or rather, said. She'll tell her I've been cheating on her and that she's wasted all this time on something that's going nowhere; although I told her that three months ago (but not in those words); I'll be the world's biggest *bastard* and between them both they'll never forgive me or speak to me again. Fine. Well, except it isn't, because when word gets around that I accidentally called out Lily's name as I was coming (yes, I know, I can't excuse myself on this one), Joseph will know exactly who "Lily" is, and it was freaking me out big time, so I prepared myself for a call, but instead, I was blessed with this.

'We need to talk.' Joseph snapped through the intercom.

Hanging about in a pair of joggers and a t-shirt, I knew I looked how I felt.

'One word…' he said storming into my apartment.

'Lily.' I wasn't in the mood to fuck about.

'So you're not denying it then?'

'Fuck it Joe, get off my case will you?' My head was pounding even though I hadn't drunk much last night.

'Mads is in a right state.'

'Well "Mads" shouldn't have been hanging around my apartment until all hours.'

'Look, I know she's a royal pain in the arse, but she's not in a good way.'

'It was a mistake.' I said sitting on the window seat; Joe was sat on a stool at the breakfast bar, 'I'd been with Lily, going through some work, it took longer than I thought and I get back and Madeleine's feeling frisky, what am I supposed to do?'

'Be honest?' Joseph raised a judgemental eye and that did it.

'I've been trying to be fucking honest since I met her and if you and Flo could have kept the fuck out of my business...'

'Are you fucking her?' he said. 'Lily?'

I got up and pulled my hands through my hair.

'No.'

For the record, Lily is not a woman you just "fuck". After reading a fair bit of her work last night, she needs and wants so much more.

'Christ Jefferson, you're thirty seven years old, what the fuck are you playing at, she's twelve years younger than you, and she's your brother's girlfriend; what is this, mid life fucking crisis!'

Did he think I hadn't thought of that?

'There is absolutely nothing between Lily and me, I am simply helping with her work.'

'Well, fortunately for you, Flo hasn't clicked,' he said as though he was doing me a favour, 'and I'm obviously not going to say anything.' Then he sighed and threw himself on the sofa, looking more like the Joe I'd known for the best part of fifteen years. 'Look mate, I don't give a fuck what you're up to, but where's your state of mind? You've been fucked up since Gracie and now...'

'Joe,' I said sitting beside to him, 'there's no need to keep bringing Gracie into this; I've moved on, completely, in fact, I see her and Eliot every month at the Arts club, it's over, and this has nothing to do with it.'

'So, you have a thing for Luke's Lily?'

I didn't like to think of her being "Luke's Lily"; I didn't think she belonged to anyone, like Mark Twain said, while the rest of us descend from apes, redheads come from cats.

'She inspires me alright; we have a fair bit in common, and we enjoy talking to each other.' I sat with my head between my legs; I should tell him; it might help, but then again, it probably wouldn't.

I looked up; he was watching me.

'Just be careful; it's not just about you Jefferson.'

'I know.' I was defeated before I'd started; but he was right, for once in my life it wasn't just about me, and yet last night, being alone with Lily in her room, I wanted it to be about me; about me and her.

Joseph left, and I headed to the bathroom. I promised I'd make notes for Lily and I intended to. I checked myself in the mirror to see if I needed a shave, and that's when I started studying my reflection.

God, I was looking tired. I closed my eyes tight and opened them again, the deep brown of my eyes at least gave me some life and I knew once I'd washed my hair, showered and put on some decent clothes, I might feel more like myself.

Standing in the bedroom in just a towel, I dried off my hair and waxed it back into its usual style. I like it better since I've grown it a little longer, that and my side burns. Throwing the towel on the bed, my mobile was flashing. I had a text. I picked it up, hesitating in reading it. There were only a handful of people who text me apart from my brothers, and that was Joe and Thomas, and if it was Joe, I really didn't need another conscience prick.

"Hey J," but there's only one person who calls me that, *"just wanted 2 thank U again 4 yesterday, it was real kind of U 2 take the time out 2 entertain me! B gd, C U Sat. Lily Ellen x"*

I sat on the bed staring at the phone. I did and did not need that. After my verbal battering from Joseph I've been reconsidering my position, but after reading her message, I can't believe the affect it's had on my mood.

"Lily Ellen, pleasure was all mine, enjoyed yr company, look 4ward 2 more enlightening discussions on Sat. Don't work 2 hard, J x"

I caught a glimpse of myself in the mirror. I breathed in; for a man of 6 foot 2, I'd let myself go a little, and in comparison to Luke, why would Lily choose me?

OK, so I wasn't that bad, and I haven't had any complaints so far, besides, I don't have the time to work out anymore, infact, I don't even have the inclination, but I thought of Luke: fit, toned, well defined muscles, tanned, nubile, and I breathed in again, looked at my mobile and pressed "send"; *cest la vie.*

Throwing my phone on the bed, I slipped on black briefs, followed by a pair of grey cords. Fumbling about in my wardrobe for a casual shirt, I heard the mobile go again. After pulling on a tank top I grabbed it.

"J, have a question 2 ask; think U might know the answer? Lily Ellen x"

I smiled; this was cute.

"Go ahead x"

"What year was "For Esme – with Love and Squalor" published in the USA? x"

I lay out on my bed, grinning; this boy is mad about Salinger.
"1953; originally published as "Nine Stories" Anything else I can help with? x"

"Yes; where can I get a decent cup cake in London? xx"

I started laughing; this was real cute, and ironically, I did know a place.
"Hummingbird Bakery; Portobello Road. They even have ones with pink icing. J xx"

"Are you serious!!? This is the best news I've heard in weeks. Do U like cupcakes Mr Howie?"

Is she flirting with me?
"Yes; but I have to draw a line at pink icing xx"

"How do U know if you've never tried? x"

She is flirting.
"U have a point madam; but U could always persuade me xx"
OK, so now I'm flirting.

"Busy?"

"Sorry?"

"R U busy Mr Howie? Maybe I could persuade U 2 give pink a go?"

If only she knew the connotations in that last text, she might not have worded it quite so, but then again...
"U got me."

"Say, an hour; Hummingbird Bakery?"

Is this for real, or is someone fucking me about here?
"An hour it is. J xx"

On the tube, my conscience was nagging away at me. Usually I'm pretty good at ignoring it, in fact, through my twenties, I don't think I had a conscience, but even so, I had every intention of meeting Lily.

I found her standing outside the bakery gazing through the window,

'Seen any pink ones?'

'Christ Jefferson, you frightened me.' she was laughing, holding her hands to her chest.

'Sorry.' I smiled, wishing I could hold one of those hands, 'shall we?' I opened the door and signalled for her to go first.

I know this place from when I had the apartment in Notting Hill, but I never imagined the significance it would have.

'Wow,' she said leaning over the cake stands, and with the light behind her, I could see her shapely legs through the flimsy fabric of her skirt, 'these are amazing.'

They certainly were.

'Like Paris?' I said leaning beside her.

She turned and our eyes locked; I swear she grows more beautiful by the day,

'Not quite,' her voice was soft 'but I'll be forever in your debt Jefferson.'

Whoa, I didn't know how to reply to that.

'Let me treat you Lily.' I said as we stood back up, and again, standing beside her; her femininity aroused me beyond belief.

We made our way outside and I took a cup cake from the box and handed it to her,

'This is a momentous time for me Jefferson,' she said taking the cake from my hand, 'care to join me?'

I looked at the pink cup cake and then at Lily and with a raised eye we both started laughing,

'It's just a cake J,' she was unpeeling hers, 'I promise I won't tell anyone.' And she winked at me.

'I started reading your work last night.' I said as we sat in Suburb on Neal's Yard.

'Gosh,' she said sitting back on the sofa, 'you must have gone to bed late.'

'I started reading it on the tube home; I was in the flow.' There was some nubile guy sitting on the next table making eyes at Lily; she'd noticed too. 'My intention was to make a few notes for you, but I got a call from a girl who wanted me to eat pink cup cakes with her; how could I decline?

Lily started laughing; it got me inside.

'Was she worth it?'

'Every bit.' I let my eyes hover on hers for a while; I want her to know, and because she's looking back at me over the rim of her coffee cup; I know she does.

'Have you given Madeleine her gift?' Lily put down her cup and crossed her legs at the knee, the nubile guy got a generous glimpse of her thighs and I didn't think I liked it.

'No...' I said, 'actually, I might as well come clean; we're not seeing each other anymore.'

'Oh, right, sorry.' She looked quite embarrassed. 'Gosh, can you get your money back on the corset?'

My mouth twitched into a smile,

'Maybe.'

'You're laughing at me aren't you?' She was laughing too.

'You say some sweet things sometimes that's all.'

'Oh God, "sweet", that sounds awful doesn't it?'

'Not at all,' this was true, 'you are sweet, but you're also a lot of other things too.'

We had another coffee and talked more; infact, I know more about Lily after the last two days than I'd learned during the last 12 months, and why it chose to start happening now, I honestly have no idea.

Strolling onto Monmouth Street, I had that urge again, the one where I want to hold her hand; tight.

'Do you see many famous people?' She was referring to my apartment being opposite The Ivy.

'On occasions,' I noticed the missing corset from the window of Coco de Mer, 'but there's always paparazzi hanging about.'

She started laughing,

'No room for discretion then Mr Howie?'

'No,' I grinned, 'none at all.'

'I'm sorry about being nosey yesterday,' she said as we approached my apartment, 'about the corset and asking if it was for Madeleine...'

'In all honesty Lily, we weren't really together.'

'I sort of guessed that.'

We looked at each other standing outside my apartment block; I couldn't remember how we got here or why, but I had to send her home.

'Heard from Luke?' Yes, that was my feeble attempt.

'We've been e-mailing...' She has a lovely smile. 'We could go through some of my writing if you're not busy?'

I swallowed thinking about what Joe had said, "It's not just about you Jefferson." *No it's about Jefferson and Lily.*

'Sure, why not.'

I opened the door and my eyes almost popped out of my head. I tried to close it again, but it was too late, Madeleine had seen us.

'Front door was open.' She glared at the beautiful young woman at my side; it was frightening, 'you must be Lily.'

Mental note to kill whoever it is that keeps leaving the damned door unlocked.

'Yeah that's right, hi.' Lily has an innocence about her, but she's no idiot.

'Lily, this is Madeleine.' My aim was to keep this brief.

'Well, I was going to suggest we talk, but I can see that would be a complete waste of time.' I felt sorry for her; my conscience had been pricked; it was letting all sorts in.

'Lily,' I said turning to her, 'can I just have a minute?'

'Of course,' she said holding her satchel to her chest, 'I'll wait over the road.'

I closed the door,

'Look Madeleine I...'

'I knew she'd be young; Jesus Jefferson take a look at yourself, she's half your age.'

Bit over the top; but I let it go.

'She's just a friend...'

'I don't believe you.'

Now, if I hadn't called out Lily's name during sex, I could have told the truth, but for obvious reasons, I can't.

'Look, I'm sorry but...'

'Fuckwit.' She threw open the door and I watched as she ran down the steps and over the road to where Lily was standing; they exchanged words, but Lily has free rules, I told myself, which has to be why she's walking back over to me,

'Shall we have that drink now J?' and her smile blew away any thought I had of asking her to leave.

She Moves in her own Way

One thing that's become apparent, is that Lily rarely talks about Luke. The only time she mentions him is if I ask and when she replies, it's always a little, well, vague.

'So what does Luke think of your writing?'

We've been talking about her work for over two hours now, and so far, we've covered three chapters; she is a confirmed brilliant writer. I poured us another glass of red and re- joined her on the sofa.

'He doesn't want to read it.' She must have caught the expression on my face, 'you're surprised by that?'

'Well, yes I suppose I am.'

She smiled, curling her naked feet beneath her bottom,

'Why?'

'I just thought, you know, he'd want to.'

'Well he doesn't.' there was firmness in her tone, 'besides, I don't think he'd understand.'

She's staring at me; her glass in her lap resting on the A4 pad we've been using to make notes, and watching her, it feels as though she's been here hundreds of times when it's just a handful, but she looks comfortable and I feel comfortable with her; she fits in with my life, drinking wine, reading books, listening to music, discussing, analysing, laughing...

'Luke says I'm a free spirit and he finds it difficult to deal with sometimes.'

'Which sounds strange coming from a man who spends half his time travelling around the world without you.'

'But he's wrong J,' she put her glass on the table and turned to me, 'I'm not a free spirit, I'm actually quite a homebird.'

'Creativity sometimes frightens people Lily, it makes them wary.' I said softly, 'I understand that well.'

'Susie can't understand why I'm with him.' She shrugged, 'she says physical attraction can't last forever.'

'I'll be honest, it has crossed my mind.' I said cautiously.

'I used to see a lot of things in him.' She looked at me; 'a year is a long time isn't it?' she was being exceptionally vague.

'It can be.'

'Anyway,' another Lily change of subject, 'I see you've stolen my CD collection.'

I watched her get up, her skirt rising. She was wearing white lace panties; I wish I could stop getting such corking erections around her.

She hovered over the CD's, picking out a few, reading the cover, then slotting them back and whilst she was doing this, I took the rare opportunity to admire her; the auburn halo resting iron flat against her back; gorgeous against the yellow of her t-shirt.

'Wow Jefferson Howie,' she was looking at my black and white photographs of Paris; I'd recently had them framed, and since she appeared so interested, I joined her. 'Your hair's a little shorter, but you look just the same; very chic; very sophisticated.'

'A little younger though.' and we smiled.

'But every bit as refined.' I am seriously flattered by this woman. 'Oh, these make me miss Paris so much,' she said moving on to a photo of Café de Flore, 'I'd love to go back.'

'I'd take you out with me, but people might talk.' I laughed gently, to gage her stance on the situation.

'Talk about what?' She replied vacantly.

'It was just a joke Lily Ellen.' I smiled, and to my surprise she winked, and I couldn't help getting the impression she wasn't as naïve as she liked to portray.

'So when are you next out there?' She moved to the next picture. The Eiffel Tower.

'Three weeks.'

'Three weeks?' I swear I heard the cogs rotating in her head, 'Luke will be back by then, otherwise I'd catch a lift over with you.'

I could not let this opportunity pass.

'That's not a definite date though,' I said sitting against the back of the sofa, crossing my feet at the ankle, 'I'm not a man who can commit easily; too busy.'

'Yes,' she grinned, 'so I can guess.'

Her flirting is delicious.

'You've got me worked out all wrong Lily.' I laughed, holding my hands up.

'I haven't got you worked out at all Mr Howie,' she said tilting her head to look at me, 'in fact; we don't really know each other at all do we?'

'But we're making a start.'

'Yes.' She smiled. 'We are.'

I offered to make us food, not imagining for a moment Lily would agree, but she did, so I cooked us up some noodles with stir fried vegetables and opened another bottle of wine.

The lovely thing about having Lily with me, is she moves in her own cute way. She flutters around my kitchen, talking, helping, asking questions, and letting me catch her watching me in that mysterious way she does, and then of course there's the picture on the fridge; the one I'd forgotten about.

'Who's this?' Lily was holding a colour picture of a naked redhead, 'she's gorgeous.'

'Ah, well...' God, I felt like a complete prick, '...just an old picture I found,' I said taking it from her hand.

Now, let me quickly tell you the story behind my "pin up"; she is the spit of Lily. I found her in that *Playboy Redheads* book; I can't believe how much she reminds me of the beautiful young woman smiling at me right now.

'Deanna Baker,' Lily said reading the caption at the bottom of the page, '1972.' Our eyes met, 'do you think she's beautiful J?'

I swallowed,

'She's...impeccable...'

Lily smiled, then she started laughing; *God I love her,*

'Then you have good taste.'

'Yes,' I couldn't take my eyes off hers. 'I think I do too.'

'So J,' Lily was picking at a dish of olives on the lounge table; it was lovely having her this close to me, 'where do you hang out?'

'Places I think you'd find pretentious.'

I adore her laughter; she brings so much fresh air into this apartment without having to open a single window.

'You're not pretentious Jefferson.' The softness in her voice provoked a silence in me, so I gulped my wine in the hope of swallowing the noodle that had become lodged. 'I think I just misunderstood you at the beginning, although it didn't deter me at all.'

I didn't know what to say. I'm not used to be complimented in quite this way.

'Well,' I'd finally got rid of that trapped noodle, 'I go to different places with different people; with Joe and Thomas, it's *The Wolseley, 5th View* or *Carluccio's,*' she hasn't taken her eyes off mine; it's a little unnerving; I want to be in control; I'm not. 'Whereas Henry prefers *Racine,* which is a great place, but very Knightsbridge; very Henry.'

'So what about Jefferson,' she grinned, 'where does he like to go?'

I smiled,

'These days, I have to say somewhat quieter places, like *Arbutus,* on Frith Street; have you been?'

'No.' she put her drink to her lips; I couldn't take my eyes off them.
'It's French,' I said, 'I know it's somewhere you'd appreciate.'
Our eyes met for longer than was deemed necessary.
'Will you take me there J?'
'Of course,' my hands twitched to hold her, 'perhaps we could have dinner there instead of The Wolseley.'
'I'd like that.'
'Then it'll be my pleasure.'
'"*Breathless*",' she said nodding to the large black and white framed movie print I'd bought on eBay, 'I love that film, but I haven't seen it for ages.'
Right. Cue again.
'Here,' I said leaning over to the DVD's, 'do you fancy watching it?'
'Yes please,' she is so beautiful. 'that would be great.'
I put it on aware it was already ten thirty. My logic was to keep her here for as long as I could, but I wasn't going to force it.
The introductory titles came up, and Lily took my plate and hers to the kitchen, I could hear her stacking them, padding about bare foot on my oak floor and when she came back through, she poured me another glass of wine, and I finally caught my breath.

Although I speak quite a bit of French, it's nothing compared to the standard of Lily's, so for my sake we had subtitles, but I struggled like hell to stay focused, choosing to spy on Lily instead. She's stunning when she concentrates; a sexy furrowed brow with poised eyes, I've noticed she gets into her space very quickly.
Unexpectedly she looked at me, as though she'd felt me watching her; the lights were low, a candle in the middle of the table, her one side of the sofa, me the other, then she smiled and I smiled back.
'Lily?' I asked softly, 'did you love in Paris?'
She smiled,
'I had a good time if that's what you mean.' *Oh she makes me ache.* 'Did you?'
'I enjoyed myself.'
Her gentle laughter is contagious,
'There's nothing wrong with having a good time and enjoying yourself.'
'None at all,' I noticed we were sat in the middle of the sofa together, 'I'm actually doing that right now.'
'Yeah,' she nodded thoughtfully, 'me too.' She checked her watch; yes, I know, it is past midnight. 'I should go.' She said shuffling to the edge of the sofa.
'Let me call you a cab.' I said reaching for my phone.
'Its fine J,' she said slipping her folder into her satchel, 'I'll get the tube.'

'No you won't.' I stood up; towering over her, my little lady. 'It's very late.'

'I do it all the time.' She replied nonchalantly; it was quite charming.

'Well you shouldn't; and tonight you're going home in a cab, either that, or I'm coming with you.'

'Honest J, it'll be fine.' She laughed.

'Crash here instead then.' And I meant it.

'Now the neighbours will talk,' she grinned, glancing out of the window, 'any paparazzi hanging about? Up here!' She makes me laugh, 'Mr Jefferson James Howie is about to be a bad man!' Then she turned and shot her gaze right at me; my stomach in raptures at the sight of her, 'I'll keep out your way,' she said softly, clutching her satchel to her chest, 'and I make a great cup of tea in the morning.'

I grabbed a couple of blankets from the bedroom, struggling not to stare at Lily sat on my bed. I'd agreed to sleep on the sofa, but watching her stare at her watch, the one she'd just taken off, I couldn't help but think I wasn't the only one orchestrating this progression.

'Goodnight Lily.' I stood at the door thinking she looked a little lost,

She looked up; she has tired eyes, but beside the heavenly glow of the bedside lamp, I can see how blue they are.

'Night J, sleep tight.'

Why am I hovering? *You know why, you're a bad, bad man.*

I shut the door, leaned against it, and closed my eyes. In less than 24 hours, I'd done more with Lily than I'd done with any previous dates in 24 months, and now I wanted her, a little too much.

I woke with a start. It was dark outside and we were having a storm; violent rain stabbing like spears against the window, ear shattering thunder making me shiver. I sat up and rubbed my eyes, thinking of Lily alone in my room.

I tossed back the blankets and sat on the edge of the sofa, I had one hell of a crick in my neck. I painfully rubbed it, then lay back down to encourage sleep, but every fucking crash of thunder prevented it.

Stumbling to the kitchen, I flinched again as the room illuminated, and after grabbing a glass of water, I turned to see a demure figure standing beside the breakfast bar; I almost leapt out of my fucking skin.

'Sorry,' Lily was wearing my old running t-shirt; way too much for a *boy* like me. 'I didn't mean to make you jump.'

Now, I'm painfully aware I'm standing in just my jocks and she's looking right at me. So I chose to ignore it.

'Can't sleep either?' I said putting the water down.

She shook her head,

'There's something unnerving about a storm, even though I love listening to them.'

Actually, I did too.

'Well let's sit and listen then.'

We went to the sofa and Lily covered her legs with a blanket. I slipped on my jeans and sat beside her as more thunder ripped through the lounge. I looked down as she slipped her hand into mine and held it pretty tightly, so I curled my fingers around hers and swallowed.

'J?'

Despite the darkness, I think we were looking at each other.

'Yes Lily?'

'Would you mind if I stayed on the sofa with you?'

'I wouldn't mind at all.'

Beneath the blankets, Lily has her arms around me, her head on my chest, and I think now is the time to acknowledge this feeling is mutual, but I have no idea what to do next.

Of course, I knew exactly what I wanted to do, which is why I spent most of the night, keeping my groin area firmly away from her; it was the most persistent erection I'd had in some time, but with Lily's lovely legs thrown over mine, I wasn't surprised.

It took a while for me to fall asleep; my head brimming with Lily. Every sigh, every shuffle, every fucking breath she took I was there, living the dream and now I know we're potentially heading towards a full on collision, it's just a case of how hard and when.

'Jefferson?'

I don't want to wake up.

'Jefferson James?'

Lily.

'Morning,' she smiled as I opened my eyes.

Am I still dreaming?

'I made you a cup of tea.'

Thank you God. She really is here.

'I can't stay,' she said kneeling beside me, 'I've got to go to work.'

'Can I see you again?'

She laughed gently, stroking the fallen fringe from my eyes,

'I hoped we'd still meet for lunch tomorrow,' she's playing with my hair; I like it, 'I'm looking forward to eating at Arbutus.'

I dragged myself up, feeling like the two and a half bottles of wine we'd consumed last night. Lily sat beside me.

'Did you sleep well?' I said twirling the ends of her gorgeous hair around my finger.

'Yes thanks.' There was distance between us, which felt strange since we'd spent all night wrapped up like lovers. 'Did you?'

I looked at her; I love her.

'Yes. Thank YOU.' And I pointed to her, and she smiled.

'Right, got to go,' my eyes pursued her as she stood up 'I've tidied up, it's the least I could do to say thanks for entertaining me again.'

'And like before Lillian, the pleasure is all mine.'

'Not quite.' Was that a grin? She grabbed her satchel and strapped it around her lovely feminine body, and now I'd had the good fortune of holding her, smelling her and having her against me, I didn't think I wanted to let her go. 'See you tomorrow then?' She kissed my cheek, 'be good.'

I stood up and followed her,

'Texting is a great way of keeping in touch ...' I leaned against the door as she stood on the stairs; hoping to sound casual.

'E-mail is better,' she said walking back to me, 'more room for longer conversations.' She took out a pen and paper, wrote something down and handed it to me.

lily.mills@virgin.net

lily.mills@virgin.net

I needed to catch up on my work, so after Lily left I managed to type off ten pages. Sitting back in the chair, I rested my eyes on Lily's manuscript. It's fair to say she's one hell of a firecracker when it comes to writing sex scenes, and because she's so passionate about her work, even as we discussed it last night, she remained unfazed about its content.

Actually, I've been tempted on several reads to give it to Henry, to see if he can make room for a little one; maybe I'll ask her tomorrow if she's comfortable with the idea. Anyway, there's this line she wrote that gets me everytime,

"...I can feel his warm sticky semen between my thighs and yet neither of us moves; not even as the music plays, and people sing and shout next door, but in this room, this dark unfamiliar room, something is happening, something strange and I don't think we know how to make it stop."

I flinched as my mobile started ringing. My nerves are in pieces.

'Thomas, how's it going?'

I haven't spoken to Thomas Eliot for about two weeks now, the last time being his birthday bash, where I happened to get extremely pissed and tell him I *liked* someone I shouldn't.

'Good my man, listen, I know its short notice, but what you up to tomorrow evening?'

Right, OK, pause. I'm having dinner with Lily at 12.30, and if our last two "meetings" are anything to go by this could easily sink into the rest of the night.

'What you got planned?' I said leaving my desk and glancing out of the window. It was still raining.

'We're having a dinner party,' he said, 'just the usuals.'

OK, so I know what you're thinking, "dinner party", sounds

pretentious with a capital P, but Thomas and his wife Leigh aren't like that, their dinner parties are actually quite cool, because they're very chilled people, and besides, Leigh doesn't do "dinner parties" in there traditional "sit down around a table" sense, it's very relaxed; the ideal setting for Lily and I, if, by some chance she were to agree to accompany me.

'Sure, sounds good, what time?'

'Seven thirty?'

'Magic.'

We chatted for a while, having a pretty good crack, then asking the usual pleasantries – how's the family, is Luke still away, how does his girlfriend cope, and finally, how's Madeleine?

'You mean you and Madeleine are no more?' He was laughing; the git, 'not that it comes as a surprise Jefferson.'

'Yeah, you and everyone else.'

'So, come on, how did you break it to her?'

'I didn't have to,' I went back to my desk; eyeing Lily's manuscript, 'she got in there first.'

'Oh mate, you must have done something unforgivable,' he was still chuckling, 'you never did the dirty did you?'

'No,' I laughed; irony hey? 'But she thinks I did.'

I could hear a child crying in the background,

'Look JJ, gotta go, Daisy's crying, but we'll continue this tomorrow.'

Throwing my mobile on the sofa, I went to the kitchen, eyeing Lily's e-mail address on the breakfast bar. I picked it up and headed back to my office; since Lily had shared her work with me, I'd quite like to give her something back.

To: lily.mills@virgin.net
From: jjhowie@msn.com
Subject: The Storm

Lily Ellen,

What did you think of the storm last night? Did it inspire you? I've written ten pages about it so far and since we experienced it together I wondered what thoughts it provoked in you. Very interested.

J xx

To: jjhowie@msn.com
From: lily.mills@virgin.net
Subject: The Storm

Hey J, good question.

Right, can I be honest? It made me think of brutal sex.

1. Lovers fucking in the back of a car, rain hammering against the windows and the bonnet, thunder crashing with their cries, the lightening providing privileged access to shimmering skin as they slither against each other.

2. Lovers having an argument, and in the throws of anger, they fuck like mad, the storm playing out their emotions.

3. A softer example would be a couple making love instead of just fucking; full on intense love in a cosy room (for example, your *High Place*); touching, watching, smelling, listening as the rain attempts to penetrate the windows, but they're warm and safe inside because they're together.

Interested in what you wrote.

Lily Ellen xx

To: lily.mills@virgin.net
From: jjhowie@msn.com
Subject: The Storm

Your thoughts fascinate me; they give me an insight into what goes on inside the agile but brilliant mind of Lillian Mills, but listen Lily, I wrote about the same thing; sex, but in its most animal form.
Listen honey, I know you know my work, so I can write this to you, and you'll understand:

"...I'm hurting her because she's tight, honoured to be invited into her unused cunt. I stroke the well trimmed kitty and immerse myself in that fervent purr, and now she's relaxed, I plunge into her as brutally as rain batters the car. She convulses with the thunder and her ass opens, allowing a privileged but well earned glimpse of the tiny bud I'm eager to invade...

This is exclusive material Lily Ellen; wrote it just an hour ago. There is more, and I'd like to share it with you next time you're here.

J xxx

To: jjhowie@msn.com
From: lily.mills@virgin.net
Subject: The Storm

Oh J, that was amazing. I feel privileged; really I do. I have always adored your animalistic love scenes, and the way you use colloquial language with a pinch of literature to boost their passion; it gets me every time.
J, when I read your words, mine feel immature. I've tried writing like you but never quite manage to pull it off, maybe it's because I always add a little too much "love" to the ingredients; what do you think?

L xxx

To: lily.mills@virgin.net
From: jjhowie@msn.com
Subject: "Love" is good.

Lily,

Please don't change your style; its magic, it works, you have to believe me. It gets me thinking; wondering things I shouldn't; things I'll ponder on for hours, but will probably never know the answers. Adding a sprinkle of "love" to your scenes can only ever make the sex more real; more satisfying and have the reader begging for more, like Nin said, we need sex and love together to create Heaven, and believe me, reading your manuscript, it does.

Jefferson xxx

To: jjhowie@msn.com
From: lily.mills@virgin.net
Subject: Genius!

Jefferson Howie! You are amazing! A poet, an artist, a fucking genius! (I'm laughing can you tell!) Today is a good day; I like it, even if I can't get my head around it. Do you have good days J. Describe to me a good day and let me wallow in it...

To: lily.mills@virgin.net
From: jjhowie@msn.com
Subject: Good Day

Lily,

I wish I found it as easy to talk to you as I do to write, but as writers, I think it's a burden we carry; I sense the same in you.
Today is a good day Lily Ellen, but there are additions to my day that can make it a brilliant day. See, I adore great company, someone I can talk and laugh with; share good wine and food, and know it's equally appreciated.
I imagine a moment's silence, but to not feel intimidated. To discuss a manuscript into the early hours and feel inspired. To watch an old movie, to listen to music, to read a book, to write, to look into the eyes of someone beautiful and try and guess what they're thinking.
To anticipate, to kiss, to undress and be undressed; to touch; to smell; to fuck; to make love; to listen to nervous breathing; to hear them coming; to come; to watch them sleep; to fall asleep...

J xxx

To: jjhowie@msn.com
From: lily.mills@virgin.net
Subject: Good Day

You are a man that makes life drunk...You are like me.

Lily's right; e-mailing is superior to texting, and the way I've opened myself up to her today is unparalleled. As a rule, I'm not very good at expressing myself, not just to women, but men as well, (which I struggle to explain since I'm a writer.) As you can imagine, this has got me into endless strife with previous lovers accusing me of secrecy, so my opening up to Lily has made me wonder whether I'm now following a few of her free rules.

But I need to find out more about this woman who is inspiring me; the real Lily; the Lily who has been writing to me today; the Lily who lay asleep in my arms last night, who is making this spark inside me turn into a fire out of control.

Little Lady

I wondered whether I was drinking too much. I've always enjoyed a drink, but it feels recently I've been drinking more than my body can cope with; or maybe I'm getting old; maybe I'm just a drunken fool who needs to face up to a few things.

I was lying faced down in bed. I turned to my left, opened my eyes and smiled.

See, I wasn't going to bother going out last night; I wanted to keep myself fresh to meet Lily for dinner, but Joe wouldn't let up about this damned party, and since Florence was in Portugal, I was his second choice.

I didn't even know whose party it was. Some guy Joe worked with at the bank; some multi-fucking millionaire asshole who gets off on parading money and women. Anyway, it was at his apartment in Mayfair, which to start with I found passé, but hey, free food (for what the food was worth, I loathe fish eggs), but the Champagne was good: Cristal, can't be bad can it?

Anyway, I'm not ashamed to say I captured a fair bit of attention from the ladies; again, good for one's ego, however, I'm not disappointed to confide I didn't fancy one of them; not one single fucking one of them.

'What the fuck's up with you?' For Joe, it seemed to be a case of *whilst the cat's away,* for which he usually blames me ("I just went along to keep Jefferson company.") 'You've not gone soft have you Howie?'

The same blonde approached me no less than three times, and after the third blow out, I honestly thought she'd got the idea, instead she sent her friend over. So, I'm thinking to myself, yeah, this would be easy, I could fuck her, satisfy an urge if nothing else, but then I caught hold of a conversation going on behind me,

'Do you know that in ancient times redheads used to be burned at the stake, even buried alive,' said a female voice, 'and sacrificed to the gods.'

'And?' a male voice interrupted, 'what's your point?'

'The point is Nicholas, it's a miracle redheads survived at all; it means we really should take our hats of to them.'

'I find redheads exceptionally sexy.' Rasped another male voice. 'And naughty; sort of wild.'

'My wife's a red; don't you dare get any ideas over dinner.' And they all laughed in that awful guffaw manner that only the rich can, and with that, I headed straight out the door.

I haven't done this for years, wandered aimlessly around London. I had no idea what the time was, or where I was heading but I wanted to write. I wanted to put my storm piece into my work and then shake it up with a bit of *naughty, sort of wild*; what a wonderful way to describe her.

I ambled through Leicester Square. Lily was also at a party tonight; I got the feeling she went to a lot of parties. I wondered if she followed up any admiring eyes like she did mine. I hoped not.

On instinct, I sauntered towards Covent Garden, but I didn't want to go home; I felt inspired, it's the Twenty-First Century for Christ's sake and I'm in London; I can do anything I want! I wanted to find a late bar; carry on drinking, land back home in the early hours, drunk with no regrets, but most of all I wanted her; I needed Lily.

I took out my mobile and scrolled to "Lily Ellen". It rang off, diverting me to voicemail; so I rang again, and she picked up.

'Jefferson?' It was noisy in the background; voices shouting, cheering and loud music. 'Let me go outside.' The noise stopped; just the odd passing car in the distance. 'Hey J, where are you?'

'Looking for you.' I laughed; I was pissed; should just go home.

Lily was laughing too,

'Are you still in Mayfair?'

'Party was shite; wanna meet up?'

'Sure.' She sounded happy; I needed her happy. 'Where?'

'A late bar.'

She laughed again,

'Meet me at Bar Italia, Frith Street.' And she hung up.

I wasn't far from Frith Street, so dragging my sorry ass back the way I came, I wondered how long it would take Lily to get to me. I didn't even know what time I'd called her, and then I heard this,

'Jefferson Howie is a man who makes my life drunk.'

I hurried over to her, scooped her up and spun her around. She was laughing, holding her arms out grasping the air, I slowed down and she folded her arms around my neck and leaned her forehead against mine, her feet slipping to the ground.

'This man is drunk.' I whispered.

She smiled, drawing away slightly,

'Then let's go and get another Mr Howie.'

I took her hand and followed her inside. We sat at a table at the back and I ordered us a drink.

'Champagne J,' she smiled as I poured, frenzied bubbles spilling provocatively over the top of the flute, 'what are we celebrating?'

'Shite parties.' I lifted my glass and tapped it gently against hers.

'To shite parties.' And she laughed with sparkling eyes; *naughty, sort of wild.*

Lily's party had been in Holborn; after my call, she got a cab straight over.

'Will your friends be looking for you?' I said re-filling her glass.

'They know me,' she winked over the rim of the flute, 'they know what I'm like.'

'And what is Lily like?'

'What is Lily like Jefferson?' What an amazing grin.

I smiled; she's too clever sometimes; but she was most definitely not drunk.

'Lily has free rules.' I shifted my chair closer to her; I couldn't focus, this place gets so busy, 'Lily runs free; Lily is wild. Lily is beautiful.'

'Jefferson is a man like me.' Her confidence sometimes overwhelms me; then she smiled, 'Thank you for calling me tonight,' she said, 'the party was awful.'

'Any admirers?' Slight flirt; but I know she can take it.

'There was this one guy,' she said picking up her glass, 'but I said no.'

Right. OK. Wasn't expecting that to feel quite as bad as it did.

'Do you know him?'

'Oh yes,' she said nonchalantly, 'he's in my class at Uni.'

Right. So she sees him everyday. Not so good.

'He knows I'm not interested.' Ours eyes met, 'but he keeps going at it.'

'He obviously likes you.'

'I don't like him,' she shrugged crossing her leg at the knee, 'he pretends to be this big intellectual man, but he's a phoney.'

'Phoney?'

'Yeah, walking around with books all the time; big names; Dostoevsky and Proust, and yet I doubt he knows the first thing about them.' She sat forward again; sometimes she's like this; can't keep still. 'What about you Jefferson,' we gazed at each other; her perfume is heavenly. 'A party in Mayfair? So many glamorous and beautiful women wanting a piece of my J.'

'My mind was elsewhere.'

'Of course,' her smile faded, and she sat back, 'I'm sorry about all that stuff that went on with Madeleine yesterday; I felt really bad about it.'

'History.' I smiled. 'Now, drink up little lady, let's move on.'

Lily is effortlessly elegant. Her glorious hair lay sleek and glossy around her shoulders and parted neatly in the centre. She is wearing a black shirt with short sleeves, a ribbon tied beneath her breasts, and a pair of dark jeans, and every time she turns to me, the diamond necklace I gave her for her birthday, glistens back at me.

She took my hand at Old Compton Street.

'You don't mind do you?' she said as I looked down at our joined hands, 'say if you do.'

I firmed up my grip and we smiled at each other.

'I know a place,' I said, 'it's tucked away, it's a late bar.'

'Well it's still early,' she said looking at her watch (it was actually after midnight), 'let's go.'

"Chabrol" was supposedly a Paris inspired bar, but to me, it felt more like New York. We sat at the bar and I ordered two single malts.

'Lily,' I said turning to face her, one foot resting on a bar stool, the other on the floor, 'I'd like to invite you to something.'

'That sounds exciting.'

'It's quite a public affair, and some pretty big names in publishing will be attending, and I want to introduce you to them.'

Her eyes widened,

'Public affair?'

'It's The Costa Book Awards at the Grosvenor.'

She gasped; I heard it; even over the Blues.

'My God Jefferson,' witnessing her gratitude gave me a lot more pleasure than I'd anticipated, 'I don't know what to say.'

'Say you'll come with me?'

She smiled; then she laughed, the one that gets me right in the chest,

'Of course I will,' she is the most beautiful woman, 'I'd absolutely love to.' She couldn't stop smiling; it was proving contagious, 'you're very good to me J.'

I remained silent; I didn't think I could take credit for trying to steal my brother's girlfriend.

'So little lady,' I said propping myself up against the bar, 'why Nin and why Miller?'

She smiled; took a gulp of whiskey and put it on the bar,

'Sex.'

I swallowed.

'Elaborate.'

'It was my awakening.' She still hasn't taken her eyes off mine, 'when

I was younger, I was really restrained, even though I wanted so much more, and to feel so much more, to convince myself it wasn't wrong for a woman to feel such intense sexual urges,' she looks so beautiful when she's this passionate, 'so I allowed my femininity to inspire me, and only then was I confident enough to express my sexual self.'

She was making me just a little fervent.

'All because of Nin and Miller?'

'Mostly Nin, but how can you read Nin and not Miller?' she said, 'after delving into her diaries, I read Henry and June, and after that, I started to read Miller too.' She was expressing with her hands again; I love it. 'See, a lot of women go through a Nin stage, wishing you had her balls, that sexual licence that men have with no regrets or judgement...'

'Do you have the balls Lily Ellen?'

She lowered her eyes; then flicked them straight back to mine,

'Do you?'

'Depends how badly I want something.' Risqué. 'Now answer my question?'

'You're very demanding Mr Howie.' She smiled.

'So are you madam.'

We started laughing, but her smile quickly faded.

'I don't know if I do,' and I think it was the first time she'd broken through that air of vagueness that follows her around, 'but I think about it all the time.'

'There will come a time when you have to stop thinking about it Lily.'

'Right now J, I can't see it happening.'

'It will.'

'When?' She was firm.

I smiled.

'Very soon.'

Now, I wasn't quite sure we were talking about the same thing, but I had a good idea we were, and if I was right; this feeling; this weird emotional game we've been playing is verging on exploding.

'*Vous voulez boire un verre*?' and she grinned showing me her empty glass.

'*Oui belle.*'

She ordered two more whiskeys. I don't want to leave this place; it feels like ours; the world outside can go fuck itself, Lily's here with me, and I think it's where she wants to be too.

'This is more like New York don't you think?' Lily has her legs crossed; she's wearing silver shoes with the sexiest point I've ever seen.

'Yes.' I was still looking at her shoes; *wondering.*

'Jefferson?' Her voice is chocolate. I looked at her; empty glass in her hand. '*Chez toi ou chez moi*?'

I finished my drink and took her hand.

'My place.'

I closed my apartment door and watched Lily kick off her shoes. Most of the night my conscience had remained quiet, but now it was alive, and I couldn't; I just couldn't...

'J?' she said opening the fridge, 'will you read to me?'

'Of course,' it feels so like we're lovers, and yet we haven't laid a finger on each other. 'What would you like me to read?'

She took out a bottle of water and handed it to me,

'Salinger.' She opened her water, '*Catcher.*'

I took her hand and we went to the sofa. I read for ages, actually, I felt as though I could read the whole book, firstly because Lily adores it as much as I do, but mostly because she's curled up beside me, watching me read to her; I could honestly do this for the rest of my life.

'You do a pretty good New York accent J.' she said shifting slightly so her head lay against my shoulder, 'sorry,' she winked looking up at me, 'carry on.'

And now I know what people mean when they write the word "forever".

Lily had fallen asleep so I gently carried her to the bedroom. She looked so young, forcing my guilt to re-appear, but only to vanish as she held onto my neck,

'J?' she whispered, 'don't go will you?'

'No *belle*, I'm right here.'

I lay her on the bed, where she curled up like a flower out of sunlight; bare feet beneath her. I took off my specs and cautiously lay behind her, spooning at a distance, but she sank into me, granting me silent permission to cling to her. I rested my head in her neck and swathed my feet around hers. She turned to face me; eyes closed, and slipped her arms around my waist, her fingertips like electric as they unintentionally touched my skin where my shirt had come loose.

I held her head to my chest, stroking the soft satin strands of her hair, and I wanted her so badly it was painful. She sank deeper into me, so deep I thought she might crawl into my skin. She took hold of my shirt; I checked her eyes; still closed; cautious fingers running across my lower back. I closed my eyes; cock straining for freedom, not sure what she's doing, or if she knows she's doing it, either way I didn't care, my conscience had clocked off, my fragile body in tune with her fingers. I moaned softly; couldn't help it, then she withdrew, but it was too late for self control.

Shifting away from her slightly, and on high alert I slipped my hand into my jocks and grabbed my dick, almost coming from the friction, from the intense aching in my balls. I began to rub, gently at first, I didn't want to wake her, for her catch me like this, but I can smell her perfume, her skin, her hair and I'm rubbing a little faster now, the occasional moan threatening to expose this filthy act, but fuck it, I want to come, gotta come, Oh Holy Jesus!

Standing in the bathroom, I was reveling in how much I'd come. When I left Lily sleeping, and went to clean myself up, the fabric of my underwear was awash with sperm.

I stepped in the shower and closed my eyes. I love her, but do I tell her? If I tell her, will she sever this link? I didn't think she would; this interdependence we've created is too powerful and intense, and isn't that what we both live for? Strive for? What we've been writing about for years?

Drying myself down, I thought back to our earlier conversation in Chabrol: *"There will come a time when you have to stop thinking about it Lily"*, but then what? An affair? Slipping on a pair of blue joggers, I headed back. Lily was fully clothed beneath the duvet, so I slipped in beside her, and immediately we held each other, but at least now, after that huge release, I can sleep with her head and her hand on my chest.

Prelude

I rolled from my front to my side and opened my eyes. *Lily.*

'*Salut.*' She's naughty; it makes me smile, 'sleep well?'

She was facing me; real close; what a way to wake up.

'Yes thank you.'

Her delicious mouth twitched into a smile,

'Me too.'

'Did we drink a lot last night?' We were holding hands beneath the duvet.

'Copious amounts.' She laughed softly; she still looked tired. 'How's your head?'

'Like shite.'

She sat up slightly and kissed my forehead, and the urge to possess her got me, so I playfully caught her and sank my face into her neck; she giggled delightfully, and trailing dangerous hands beneath her shirt, her satin skin swathed in goosebumps, she rested her forehead against mine; her magnificent mane concealing our intimacy, and with a tenderness I'd never known before, she rested her hand on my cheek, so I covered it with mine.

'Tu as de beaux yeux, tu sais?'

Having Lily tell me she thinks I have lovely eyes, and for her to do it so lusciously in French, was fucking about with my head on a grand scale.

'Merci beaucoup belle.'

'But it's our secret right?' She whispered.

'Pourquoi?'

'Je ne veux pas d'ennuis.'

'I don't understand.' My French is poor compared to hers.

'I don't want you to get into trouble.' She repeated in English.

I watched Lily get up, hard on throbbing in my joggers; but hang on, I want to get into trouble,

'Lily?'

She turned to me at the bedroom door,

'J?' she said, seemingly ignoring I was going to ask her something, 'can I shower?'

'Of course.' I sank back defeated.

'Then I'll make us a cup of tea.' She winked and left, and I didn't think I liked it much.

It felt good hearing Lily in the shower. Like I've mentioned, after Gracie, I missed the intimacy of being close to someone, so knowing Lily is standing beneath my shower, I feel a great sense of contentment.

I switched on the coffee machine and opened the kitchen window. It was another beautiful day, and I wondered if Lily fancied doing something with me. I didn't know what, just something, after all, we were already having dinner today, and I didn't have to be at Thomas' until later, until then, I just wanted to be with her.

The intercom buzzed, interrupting my devious planning.

'Hello?'

'Jefferson.'

'Jeremy mate,' this was cool; my brother. 'Door's open.'

Getting another cup out, the shower stopped, and I remembered, *shit,* Lily isn't mine, has never been mine, even if it did feel like she was, and Jeremy was going to know; he was absolutely going to know.

Grabbing a t-shirt from the bedroom, I heard the door open, and hurrying back to the kitchen, I combed my hair from my face and adjusted my specs.

'Hey mate, long time eh?' and we hugged; that pat on the back thing.

Jeremy had been out on tour with the RSC.

'When did you get back?'

'Last night,' he said grabbing a stool, and despite my cheery persona, I was becoming anxious about Lily appearing, 'I thought I'd come round and see how things are going with big bro?'

'Yeah, things are...'

I never got to finish, instead I swirled around to see what or rather who Jeremy was gawping at, and my skin prickled with fear.

'Hi Jeremy.' Lily emerged nonchalantly from the bathroom wearing, get this, just my white shirt from last night; fresh faced, hair towel dried and laying about her shoulders; just about the sexiest thing I'd ever seen, honestly. I wanted to get on my knees in front of her.

'Lily...' Jeremy's voice faltered. 'how are you?'

'Very well thanks.' She came over to us; I couldn't take my eyes off her; running them up and down her legs, trying desperately to catch a glimpse of her ass, her sex and catching my eyes on her nipples, oh man, she makes me giddy. 'How was the tour?'

'Umm, yeah, brilliant.' It seemed he couldn't get his breath either.

'I love Richard II.' This was true; she'd told me before. It was her first Shakespeare play; she was seventeen years old and it was in Stratford. She fell in love that night. 'Right then, I'll just get dressed.'

I caught her eye before she moved away from us, and we simultaneously smiled; it gave me a delicious feeling inside.

'Jefferson?' Jeremy was staring at me; blinking, completely confused, no, make that, bewildered. 'What the hell's going on?'

'Lily stayed over last night; nothing untoward, we had a few drinks, we got pissed and she fell asleep.'

'Why were you and Lily out together getting pissed?'

'I'm helping her with her writing.' I set the cups out for coffee; I did not want to be confronted with this, especially by someone so close to me. I didn't want to lie.

'But she's in your shirt.'

I needed to play this down; act casual.

'She wanted to use the shower, that's all.'

'Jefferson?' Jeremy's tone was a little harsher, 'this is inappropriate; you can't just...do this sort of stuff; she's Luke's girlfriend...'

Jesus; she was Luke's girlfriend; I'd conveniently forgotten, and I think she had too.

'I didn't want to put her in a cab in the early hours when she was pissed.'

'I didn't realise you and Lily were this... well, friendly.'

'We've always been friendly.' I said truthfully, 'it's the books.'

I could fool a lot of people, but not Jeremy.

'No,' he shook his head, 'I didn't like the way you looked at each other; what the fuck are you playing at?'

'Oh Jesus,' I scraped my hands through my hair and took a deep breath, 'just leave it will you?'

'My God, are you having an affair with her?'

I looked up; we were having an affair; just not physical.

'We're not lovers.'

Jeremy studied me, and then he nodded,

'OK, but I've been defending you to mum for weeks now.'

'Mum?' I frowned.

'Yeah, she's got it into her head that you've got feelings for Lily.' Jeremy eyed me, 'you have haven't you?'

I closed my eyes briefly and sighed.

'How can anyone not?'

He didn't look surprised.

'Come on Jefferson; you need to put this into perspective, people will get hurt, very hurt.'

'Nothing will happen,' I actually meant this; not on my part though, (I remain a very bad man), 'she's great company, she's intelligent, she's fun, she's fresh, she's creative, she's a free spirit with free rules...'

I can say these things to Jeremy, maybe Thomas, but no one else.

'Jefferson?' Lily's voice was a welcome relief, 'I should go now.'

She was standing in last night's clothes; I want to go with her.

'Is 12.30 still alright?' I said.

Her eyes darted between me and Jeremy; scrutinizing; she'd heard everything.

'Yes.' She smiled; she's like me; so fucking much like me it's frightening, then she looked at Jeremy, 'will I see you tomorrow?' she said, 'Sunday lunch?'

Even when Luke's away, Mum insists she comes for dinner.

'Sure.' Jeremy smiled; a genuine smile, because although I know he absolutely arbores what I'm (thinking of) doing, he's a good man.

I walked Lily downstairs.

'I'm sorry J,' she said as I opened the door, 'I told you I didn't want to get you into trouble, and it's already started.'

'Don't you worry about that,' I touched her face with my finger tips and her eyes closed, then opened and she put her hand over mine and our fingers linked, 'I'm not a good person sometimes,' this was the first time I'd seen her eyes without glitter, 'but I can't help myself.'

'You are the woman who makes my life drunk.' I whispered.

She clung to my neck as I picked her up at the waist and squeezed; *people will get hurt; very hurt*, but we just can't help ourselves; we just can't stop.

After Jeremy left, or should I say, after my hour lecture on morals and values, I had to write. Being with Lily over the last few days has fuelled my desire, and I wanted to get it on paper. I checked my e-mails, I was expecting feed back from Henry, but instead, I got this.

To: jjhowie@msn.com
From: luke.howie@yahoo.com
Subject: My gorgeous babe.

Jefferson man, how the devil? Look, this is a quick one, but I wondered if you'd do me a favour. Lily told me you've been helping her with her work, so since you're seeing a fair bit of her, I wondered if you'd check out the situation for me. She's been acting a bit weird this week, not sure why, don't think I've done anything, anyway, she's been spaced out on the phone, well, that's when I can get hold of her and it takes her ages to answer my e-mails.

OK, look man, I know how I sound, but I wondered whether she'd met someone, there's always loads of guys hanging about her place, asking her out, shit like that, and all those parties and

stuff she's in to. Would you keep an eye on her for me?
Cheers bro.
Luke

That was all I needed.

Her J.

I'd just arrived at Arbutus when I received a text.

"Hey J, wait for me inside, tube problems at Euston. Lily Ellen xxxx"

"Lily Ellen, I'll be waiting xxxx"

"For how long?"
She's flirting again.

"How long what?'
Yes, now I'm flirting.

"How long will you wait for me?"

I smiled; couldn't help it.
"As long as it takes. xxx"

I didn't mind being tested by Lily, in fact, I found it exciting. I hoped it was an indication we were on the same road.

'Sorry J.' Lily sounded breathless as she hung a rather chic cerise pink shoulder bag on the back of a chair, then hugged me. I caught her around the waist, adoring her delicious bottom perched in my groin. She's smells gorgeous. We looked at each other, grinning, it was a pretty wonderful moment, but regrettably she got up and sat opposite me, 'wine looks good.'

'It goes well with oysters.' I said pouring her a glass, despairing at my dick begging for freedom.

'Oysters hey?'

We tapped glasses and sipped, watching each other over the rim; she is truly beautiful, with her divine hair around her shoulders, parted in the centre but delicately pinned to the side with a diamante clip.

'Did you manage to get any work done?' Lily was studying the menu, but I just wanted to study her, this lovely woman in straight dark jeans, a white snug t-shirt and elegant taupe cape.

'A little.' I said, admiring silver heels at the side of the table, 'actually Luke sent me an e-mail.'

She put down the menu,

'Cool.' Her eyes betrayed her.

'He's a bit worried about you.'

She frowned,

'Is he? Why?'

Right. OK, how do I word this?

'He said he's finding it difficult to get hold of you.'

She nodded,

'I'm very difficult to get hold of at the moment,' she leaned back, 'my J needs my time; and I need his.'

I started to smile, and so did she,

'So what should I tell him?'

'That I'm living every waking minute with you.'

'Are you?' I raised an eyebrow.

She looked down at the menu.

'Yes; as you are with me.'

And now I know just what she's saying.

The oysters arrived, and we smiled at each other. They were deliciously presented on a tray of crushed ice with wedges of lemon, and I'm thinking "aphrodisiac", though I doubt either of us needs it. Ah, just as I thought, Lily has done this before, look at the way she elegantly tips her head back, the oyster sliding into that delicate mouth; how she holds it momentarily, and then swallows.

'Lily Ellen?'

'Yes Jefferson?' she reached out for my hand, so I linked my fingers firmly through hers.

'Do you have a party to go to tonight?'

'I do.'

'Would you be willing to change your plans?'

'What's on your mind?' She has gorgeous eyes.

'You.'

She laughed softly,

'Me?'

'Yes you.' I couldn't help grinning. 'Come to a party tonight,' I said lowering my voice, 'with me.'

'What sort of party?'

'It's a dinner party with a difference,' she gazed at our joined hands, smiling; my chest remained tight. 'The hosts are close friends of mine, Thomas and Leigh Eliot, but they'll also be a handful of writers, a couple of artists and the odd poet, I think you'll enjoy it.'

'I'll need to change first.' she said looking down at herself.

'So that's a "yes"?'

Her beautiful lips spread evenly into a smile,

'It's a "yes".'

When we arrived at Lily's, Susie was hanging about in the kitchen.

'Here she is.' Susie sang, 'Lily and "her J".'

These girls have been talking.

'We're going to a party.' Lily slipped past Susie and opened the fridge, 'aren't we J?'

'Yes we are.' I thanked her for the beer;

'I thought you were already going to a party?' Susie also took a beer.

'I changed my mind.'

'Ah yes, the older man has that affect on you doesn't he?'

Lily shrugged; she remained unfazed.

'Jefferson's party sounds much more exciting,' she said sitting on the edge of the table, swinging her legs, 'and J's much better company than Mark and Adam.'

'That figures.' Susie smiled at me as she left the kitchen.

'Mark and Adam?' I had to ask.

'Friends from years back,' she said, 'its OK J,' and she slipped gracefully from the table and walked past me, 'they're gay.'

I couldn't take my eyes off her; her sexual energy penetrating me to the core; she turned and looked at me over her shoulder,

'Coming?'

I took her hand and followed her upstairs to her girly boudoir, the one that's featured heavily in my writing of late, under a different guise.

'What should I wear J?' she opened the wardrobe door as I sat against her desk, watching her, 'skirt, dress, jeans?'

'You look beautiful as you are.'

She laughed,

'That's not what I asked.' My God, she's standing between my legs.

'OK,' I smiled linking my fingers through hers and holding them up at eye level; I love flirting with her; it's completely delicious, 'denim skirt is good,' I smiled as she leaned closer to me and I supported her with my hands, 'silver sandals...and that.' And I nodded to the wardrobe door, where a small black shirt and olive silk scarf were hanging; the one she'd worn the day we met in Waterstones.

'Sure.' She withdrew from me completely, but I reached for her hand, pulling her back into me, she gripped my shoulders, the tips of our noses touching. I swallowed. Now I had her, I knew just what I wanted to do, but the door hurled open, throwing us apart, and a girl with peroxide blonde hair in ponytails, looking like something out of a bad porn film stood staring at us.

'Oh hi,' she smiled unperturbed, 'you must be Jefferson,' she came over and shook my hand, 'pleased to meet you, I'm Lauren.'

I shook her hand completely bewildered. I didn't know what the fuck was going on. Lily was collecting her clothes, throwing them on the bed.

'What do you want Lauren?' She said without looking up.

'Your grey military jacket.' Lauren was rifling through Lily's wardrobe; I sensed unrest.

'No Lauren.' Lily sighed, 'that's my best jacket.'

'I've worn it before.'

Lily looked up at her; her eyes watering.

'Well you shouldn't have.' She snapped.

'Oh go fuck the old man.' And Lauren slammed the door behind her, making Lily jump.

I left the desk and sat beside her on the bed. I prized her chin up and we studied each other. She was crying; just a little, but enough.

'Jefferson?'

'Lily?' I held her cheek with my hand, brushing the tears away with my thumb.

'I hate it here sometimes,' there was a small sob in her voice; it touched me deeply, 'they're cruel you know.'

I pulled her into me and we folded our arms around each other. I could feel her crying. Her warm tears on my neck. I was seeing a side of her tonight I sensed existed, but never thought I'd be privileged to witness; her vulnerability.

She put her hand on my cheek, stroking my skin. I closed my eyes, her touch almost unbearable. I opened my eyes,

'Is it time to stop thinking?' her voice was soft, and I wasn't sure I was hearing her properly.

'Yes Lily, it's time.'

I stole her mouth completely. Sucking her air; breathing her free life into my lungs. We wrapped ours tongues around each others, her sweet saliva dousing my mouth and chin. I swept her hair from her face, leaning her back slightly with the force of my kiss.

The softness of her tongue lashing with mine made me hard. I thought about guiding her hand to it, imagining her girly fingers smoothly rubbing the coil; *oh Lily, my Lily.*

We slowed, but I continued teasing her, tenderly biting her top lip, then her bottom, and hers trying to catch mine; she's delicious, and hearing her gentle laughter through our kiss made my chest tight.

'My name is Jefferson James Howie,' I whispered; grinning; her forehead against mine, her delicate fingers exploring my face, 'and I am a very bad man.'

We started kissing again, Lily holding my face between her hands.

'I should get dressed,' she kissed the end of my nose, 'we don't want to be late.'

'Lily?' I grasped her hands as she stood up, 'How long?'

She smiled; but her eyes were watering,

'Before we'd even met.'

As we walked from Lily's place on Hartland Road to Thomas and Leigh's on Arlington, I couldn't remember feeling this proud. Luke was right, guys love her, and why wouldn't they, she's absolutely beautiful, and if her kisses are anything to go by, fucking this lovely woman was going to be immense.

I seized her hand the moment I could. Tonight she's mine, and OK, I wasn't sure what was happening between us, whether our kiss had been the backlash of her disagreement with Lauren, or if we'd finally collided. I preferred the latter.

The *usuals* were at the party: John, Lawrence and Seb (writers- strictly Literary. Loathe my novels, but love my column), Mel (poet- two volumes published) and Jez and Sian (artists), and as soon as my lady walked in and I introduced her, no kidding, everyone, (even Mel) couldn't take their eyes off her; her modest charisma was, well, blinding.

'So Lily,' Seb was first in, 'what's your genre?'

Followed by John,

'How can you enjoy the dirge that Howie writes; honest, the man has no morals.'

Morals? No, I have absolutely none. That was confirmed the moment I let my mouth stray with Lily's.

Then, Lawrence; kind, gentle, intense Lawrence,

'Is that auburn?' he said admiring her hair, 'it's just, well, breathtaking.'

'Oh, thank you.' Lily seemed genuinely surprised; surely she knew?

After the first round of drinks, I found myself in the kitchen with Thomas.

'So, Lily is the "someone" you like but you really shouldn't?'

I stared into my drink,

'Transparent as well as a cunt.' I smiled.

'Just a transparent cunt then?' Thomas chuckled, 'is it serious?'

I looked up,

'I'd like it to be.' I said honestly, 'but my conscience is working over time.'

'How does Lily feel?'

'I'm not completely sure.'

'She seems pretty smitten.' Thomas leaned against the breakfast bar, 'so are you guys, you know, getting it on?'

I laughed a little,

'No.'

'Not yet you mean.' Thomas was a devious git at times. 'Are you in love with her JJ?'

I nodded.

'Cruel world.' He was right. 'So what are you going to do now?'

I didn't know whether Lily's free rules would let her fall in love; but I had to give it a shot.

'I have no idea.'

Thomas took my glass; I watched a generous amount of whiskey being poured into it,

'Here,' he said sliding it to me, 'loosen up those inhibitions.'

'I'm not sure that's wise.' But I took the drink anyway.

I returned to the lounge to see Lily talking with Leigh. They were sitting on the floor, Lily with her legs elegantly to one side, glass of red wine in front of her, animating with her arms, looking every bit the chic Parisian I've been living with in my head for the past 12 months.

I stood at the door, whiskey in my hand, legs crossed at the ankle, watching her. Finally she looked up, we smiled simultaneously and I winked, and she did it back.

I joined John and Seb in one of their pretentious literary debates, but I wanted to get Lily involved. She's fascinating in these discussions; she speaks from the heart with such passion and conviction that I become just a little more infatuated.

She accepted my invite, and as we talked, I noted how admirably she took their criticisms of her literary preferences; but then how she cleverly played back their arguments, until they were nodding in agreement with her.

'Your girl,' Leigh sat beside me on the sofa and we watched her, 'she's lovely.'

I can't take my eyes off her.

'How many people do you know that could do that?' I said, 'turn an argument 360 degrees?'

Leigh was grinning, yeah, OK, I sounded like a cunt.

'She's an amazing woman Jefferson.' We looked at each other, 'so, what you going to do?'

Yes, what am I going to do?

'Lap of the gods,' I knocked back my whiskey, 'lap of the fucking gods.'

I wandered into the garden. The others were discussing Sylvia Plath, well, I had to draw the line somewhere, and that's where she found me.

'J?'

I held my hand out and she came to me.

'My Lily.'

I steered her amongst the over grown crawlers sagging lazily over the pergola.

'*Restez calme.*' Her voice was soft; concerned.

'I am cool.' I said '*tres.*'

'Tell me what else Luke said in his e-mail?'

'Why?' I said stroking her hair,

'It's freaked you out.'

She leaned against the wall, I moved in, gripping her waist, resting my head against hers,

'He thinks you've met someone.' Our eyes locked, 'have you?'

She laughed a little,

'Yes J.'

'Tell me who?' I can feel every delicious sinew of her body against mine.

'It's you.'

I smiled; I couldn't help it, even when I was trying to suppress it, it just kept growing. We started kissing; I lifted her up and gently perched her on the patio table hidden amongst the wisteria. She wrapped her legs around mine, her skirt rising. My hands wandered to her thighs, pushing her skirt higher, breaking off and looking between her legs; pink chiffon.

She was biting my chin; she sounded different; hot; white hot. I grabbed her mouth greedily, pushing her skirt over her ass and slipped my fingers beneath her panties, the fabric tantalising my skin, the friction making me want to fuck her.

My head was spinning, but I pushed a finger inside her bud. She jolted slightly; my finger in her ass; but she moved with it, her head back, mouth open, sexy hair down her back, breasts full and heaving.

She had a hand between my legs, rubbing my dick.

'I want to fuck you,' I whispered in her ear, 'I can't stop thinking about it.'

I smoothly slid my finger from her ass and glided my other hand inside the pink chiffon; her hair was short, neatly trimmed; I've been dreaming of matching cuffs and collar; oh how magnificent.

I ran a finger the full length of her sex, smearing the creamy juice over her clit; small, delicate, soft and ripe; I can smell her excitement.

She relaxed her legs and sat her feet on the edge of the table; I couldn't stop staring between her thighs,

'J take them off.' she whispered; *wild; naughty; filthy Lily Ellen.*

So I did; in one swift movement, revealing a sexy strawberry blonde. Her gash was red and wet, sweet folds of velvet, wide open. I got to my knees, discarded my specs and thrust my mouth into her cunt, eating her, sucking her, licking her over and over. Her hands were on my head, moving her sex up to meet my mouth; panting, stifling her moans, but thrusting vigorously as I took her harder, sticking my tongue deep inside, plunging a finger in for good measure.

She grabbed my hair; Jesus, she's ferocious.

'J don't stop, oh no, don't, oh holy fuck...' and stretched out, knees up, my head between them, she rocked relentlessly against my tongue, tensing her thighs around my head, snatching every precious bit of that luscious orgasm.

Steadily I retreated, her cool juices, smothered around my mouth. I looked up at her; the moonlight casting shadows across her spectacular body, I can barely believe I'm privy to this after so long.

'J,' she whispered, 'if you fuck me now, I'll be tight.'

I looked at her, pink chiffon panties by her side. I put my hands out and she took them, and bringing her closer to me, she appeared a little confused, but I know she'll understand.

With care, I closed her legs and re-placed her skirt. I folded my arms around her and, sank my nose into her satin skin, suffocating on her perfume, *oh I love you, I love you,* and these fucked up emotions make me want to cry, and standing here, in her arms, I feel safe, me, Jefferson James Howie, 37 years old, in her arms, this 25 year old woman, who doesn't belong to me, but who I'd give almost anything to be mine.

A Letter

Have you ever known a man intentionally put a woman's pleasure before his own? I don't mean the kind where he lets you come first, knowing he'll enjoy the fruits of his labour moments later, I mean the type of selfless pleasuring when he just wants you to come; no ulterior motive required. No? Well neither had I, until tonight.

Holding Lily in the aftermath of her pretty spectacular orgasm, we parted slightly, but not so far that I couldn't feel her warmth.

'You're not a bad man Jefferson,' she whispered, 'please don't feel guilty.'

'Lily,' I held her face between my hands, 'like you, I can't help the way I feel.'

'I've been trying so hard, I promise, I just couldn't stop it...'

'Lily I don't want you to stop.'

'I know,' she was looking right into my eyes; she did that a lot, 'that's why I let go.'

'Can I see you again?'

She was laughing gently, nodding,

'Of course.'

'When?'

We were both laughing,

'Anytime you like.'

'You're a busy lady, I know that.'

'I've already been cancelling things all over the place to be with you J.'

I kissed her,

'You are so beautiful Lily.' I grabbed her face, taking her mouth completely, 'inside and out.'

'Mon bel J, mon bel J.'

*

OK, you may not believe this, but I didn't sleep with Lily, and it was totally my decision. See, she made it clear after she'd come that she'd like me to make love to her, and after the things we'd been saying to each other during the evening, it was inevitably going to happen, but not tonight.

I'm not going to analyse why I didn't fuck her, but I know it has a lot to do with how I'm feeling right now, see, I know when I do lay with her, that'll be it for, I'm all hers, whereas for Lily, I'm not quite sure yet, but one thing I am sure about, is since that first kiss, our inhibitions have been gliding off us like oil.

'You've been watching me Mr Howie,' Lily had whispered as we stood at her front door to say goodnight, 'and your mum has caught you on more than one occasion.'

I grinned,

'She's obviously heard about my reputation.'

'What reputation?' Lily laughed; she's gorgeous. 'I'm not afraid of your ladies Jefferson.' She said slightly more seriously.

'You have no reason to be.' I said squeezing that dainty waist.

'Tomorrow at lunch, will you still sit opposite me, will you still "accidentally" touch my leg with yours, and will you watch me whenever I get up, hoping to see something you shouldn't.'

I honestly had no idea I'd been quite this obvious with her; no wonder Mum was doing her nut.

'Do you want me to?'

'Yes.' I love the way she never hesitates. 'Sundays have never been so exciting.'

I arrived back at my apartment in the early hours. After leaving Lily, (reluctantly I might add), I walked home. Humidity was high and strolling through London, surrounded by life helped me feel less lonely.

'You're wild Lily; you're free.' I'd said as we held each other outside her place.

'Then capture me J.' she'd whispered.

Back at my desk, I wanted to write to Lily. I figured I expressed myself more honestly like that, whereas Lily has the gift of both. I took off my specs and rubbed my eyes; dragging my hands down my face, I held my fingers to my nose. I could smell her. I gulped at it, deep breaths sucking her in, and the pain in the pit of my stomach burned.

I got up, undressed and lay on the bed. I turned to my side, she wasn't there. Then to my other side, she wasn't there either. I grabbed my mobile from the floor with every intention of calling her up, "get a cab", I'd say, "come over now; I need you." And I know she would.

I threw the phone down. My conscience hadn't clocked off yet. I had Luke on the brain, surfing blissfully in Australia, trusting me to protect his girl from predators, when I'm the one he should fear the most. I closed my eyes. I'm tired; I can't sleep; it's humid; I'm perspiring...I sat up; the mobile was bleeping. I had a message.

"J, (Louveciennes, March 1, 1932), "...I am running away from peace and have begun to live like you...And both kinds of lives lead to the same madness." L xxx"

I leapt from the bed and dashed to the living room, almost breaking my neck on the sofa. Limping to the bookshelves, I skimmed the rows, and there it was: "*Letters of Anais Nin and Henry Miller*". I knew what I wanted to write, I just had to find it.

Frantically flicking the pages, I found it on page 16. I slumped to the floor and started to text,

"Lily, (March 4, 1932), Three minutes after you have gone. No, I can't restrain it. I tell you what you already know – I love you...I can't say much now – I am in a fever...Without realising it, I have been living with you constantly...I thought it would terrify you. Today I had planned to bring you to my room...But it seemed so sordid, leading you to my miserable hotel. No, I can't do that. You will lead me somewhere – to your shack, as you call it. Lead me there so that I may put my arms around you." J xxx"

I lay out on the floor. My head in bits; my stomach in raptures. I love her; I love her so much; I had to tell her; forgive me.

I didn't know how long I'd been lying there, on the freezing floor, maybe I'd been asleep, but it was the bleep of the phone that brought me back.

"J, (Louveciennes June 11, 1932), "Things I forgot to tell you...That I love you, and that when I awake in the morning I use my intelligence to discover more ways of appreciating you...That I love you.

That I love you.

That I love you."

Collision. Full on; at last.

I went to dinner at my folks place impatient to see my girl. Like a fool, I chose my outfit with great consideration, and with eager anticipation I drove to Hampstead, and instead of my mulled wine lady, I was faced with this.

'Lily's not coming today,' Mum was stirring the gravy; she was wearing some sort of weird red and white kaftan, 'her sister made a surprise visit.'

Holy shit; my stomach hit the floor and catapulted back up my gullet.

'You look nice JJ,' Mum finally looked at me, 'all this for Sunday lunch?'

'Jefferson,' Jeremy appeared behind me, 'got a meeting later?' he said looking me over, Jesus; I was only wearing jeans and a red sweater, 'cashmere?' Jeremy nodded to the jumper, 'very nice.'

'No meeting.' I replied firmly, 'just lunch.'

I left the kitchen. I wondered if Lily had regrets about last night, or perhaps Luke had been in touch again. Not a lot I could do about it now; it was done.

Through lunch, Jeremy and Mum watched me in turn and it was beginning to piss me off. Anyway, since when had they joined forces, usually Jeremy couldn't be bothered with Mum when she had a bit between her teeth.

'How's the new book JJ?' Dad said as he poured himself another glass of red wine.

'Good,' I said helping myself to more roast potatoes; in fairness to Mum, she knew how to roast.

'Are we allowed to know what it's about?' Mum put down her knife and fork.

'You know I never disclose anything until it's finished.' This was true; some stupid superstition I'd started years ago.

'Luke rang yesterday,' she added, 'he said you've been helping Lily with her writing.'

'I have,' I said continuing to eat; I know she wants a reaction. What she'd do if I came out with it I have no idea, 'she's brilliant.'

'She is that,' Dad chipped in, peas flying out of his mouth; god bless him, 'our Lily, shame she couldn't come today.'

Yes, shame indeed.

'So, any other news from our little bro?' I said looking at Mum.

'He's in the next round.'

'Not a surprise,' Jeremy said, 'he is superb and...'

'Anyway, he's missing Lily.' Mum's interruption annoyed me.

'I'm sure he is.' I said.

'Well, he'll be back soon,' Dad smiled oblivious, 'and they'll be reunited.'

I swallowed. But the potato was well lodged in my throat.

I was loading the dishwasher as Jeremy poured himself a drink.

'Look Jefferson, I want to apologise for what happened yesterday, with Lily.'

I stood up,

'It's forgotten.'

'It just looked a bit weird that's all.'

'I appreciate that.'

He was hovering; he had something else to say; I could feel it.

'So, you have feelings for Lily then?'

'I thought we'd forgotten about it.'

'I just wondered, because, it must be difficult for you that's all.' He shrugged, 'because of Luke.'

I smiled,

'I'll live.' But I wasn't quite sure I believed that.

'Listen Jefferson, I know it probably won't help, and you know I hate this sort of thing, but I do sometimes think she chose the wrong brother.'

I shrugged, then smiled; *what did it matter now?*

'*Cest la vie.*' and I left the room.

Driving back to my apartment, I wondered what the hell to do with myself. I thought about going to Chalk Farm to beg Lily to come and live with me (OK, bit drastic), or I could get totally smashed, if I could be bothered to drink.

On the way in, I picked up a letter from my mail box. The front had been handwritten with the initial "J". I had a gut feeling this could be a "*Dear John*". Kicking off my shoes, I went to my office and started to read:

"Jefferson,

Livvy arrived this morning, and although I was happy to see her, I was totally gutted I wouldn't see you for lunch.

I didn't sleep much last night. I couldn't stop thinking about you; about us. Are you always this intense? Do you make all your ladies feel this good inside, this alive; this wild!

Oh J, what we did in the garden last night has fucked my head up, but please accept my apology for asking you to make love to me, I realise now we need time to explore, to get to know each other, and there's so much I want to do with you, my head is crammed full of the stuff, from gentle love making, to violent fucking, I just can't stop, I'm carrying it with me everyday.

Listen, I must tell you, no other lover has travelled around my sex like you did last night. You are a thorough man. I have to say I rarely come like that, but you J, you were amazing; breath taking. I wanted to cry because my orgasm was so intense; I think it was the way it all happened, especially the way you looked at my underwear after you'd taken them off. I imagined you putting them to your nose, or slipping them in your pocket to masturbate over later, either way Jefferson, you arouse me so badly, and to fuck you now is the right thing to do and I know you feel the same. I've known for ages.

Do you know, that first time I met you, you were so beautiful, so completely gorgeous, with your dark trousers, your shirt tails hanging out, your shiny square toed shoes, your sexy hair tousled carelessly in your eyes; brown velvet eyes, hiding behind your glasses. Jefferson, seeing you leaning nonchalantly against your desk, I knew then it would lead to this; you did too; eyes are windows; this is true, but in our case, they are also mirrors.

Tell me J, tell me honestly, am I burning out of control here? Will I implode? God, listen to me, I sound like an idiot, like I'm losing my head or something (I'm laughing at this madness!), like Nin said, Love does crazy things to an intelligent woman.

Listen J, I'm at a party tonight, it's Susie's birthday and she's having a load of assholes around, but I said I'd go, but I'm thinking of you; always thinking of you. I love you.

Vraiment,
Lily Ellen xxx"

Right, so if I can't see her; I'll write to her.

To: lily.lills@virgin.net
From: jjhowie@msn.com
Subject: I love you completely, madly...

Lily, my darling Lily,

You are a *"genuine spark of the divine fire"* and I love you madly. How do you write like that, the things you say astound me and now I crave you more than ever. How I kept this thing under control before you let go and opened up to me I have no idea.

Oh Lily Ellen you say I fuck you up, that's nothing compared to what you do to me, with your mulled wine hair and your dot to dot freckles, Oh Jesus Lily to fuck you would be to go to Heaven, but last night, I just wanted to make you come, to see your pleasure; you taste of seashells, of fresh life. I still had you on my hands last night, I breathed you in, then curled my fingers around my dick and fucked myself, your juices soaked into my skin, and when I came I imagined shooting my sperm deep into your womb, and you opening your legs wide so I can witness my burning seed oozing out of you.

Oh Lily, I have thought such bad, filthy things about you, I want you, here, now, with me, I want us to fuck all night and day, to talk all day and night, to love for a very long time, I don't want to let you out of my sight, shall we Lily? Shall we do it?
I have never met a woman like you; I'm ashamed at 37 I have only just found you.

I don't think I can keep a woman like you Lily; you're too fresh; too brave; too free; too young. Oh Lily, let me follow your free rules; let me run beside you. I love you.
Yours,
Jefferson xxx

Ps. "Never like this" x

PPs. That day in Waterstones, that was my Good Day.

OK, so I gave in, I had a whiskey, actually, I had two, then one for good luck; my head's gone; I'm fucked. I'm good for nothing. My phone's bleeping, I pick up the message.

"J. I hate this party. Come join up my dots and drink my mulled wine hair x"

The Pink Room

I hate this fucking place sometimes. It's impersonal; busy; ignorant; blind, but as I stagger towards Chalk Farm, I'm cutting through it, and I'm going to her. No one knows what's happening; no one knows how bad, yet how good this feels, or how fucked up my head is, except her.

I slipped down some steps on the Underground; graze my face; there's blood; I don't care.

'I'm looking for Lily.' There's a guy staring at me on her doorstep; he's looking at my cheek; the blood, so I wipe it with the back of my hand.

'Lily!' he yelled over the thrashing music; it echoed real bad in my head. 'Some fucking geezer at the door for you.'

Then she emerged; a red glow around her.

'Jefferson!' she ran to me, pulling me into her arms, 'what happened?'

'I slipped.' I couldn't take my eyes off her, I kept touching her hair, 'it's nothing.'

'It's not nothing.' she fingered my blood. 'Come with me.'

I took her hand and we arrived at the pink room. She closed the door behind us, numbing the music, but the beating through the floor was like the thumping in my chest.

'Sit down.' She said bringing a towel over and tenderly wiping my cheek.

She stood between my legs; I gazed up at her and pulled her in close.

'You came?' she said softly, brushing my hair from my eyes, 'it's all better now.'

I stopped smiling; so did she; my hands on her waist, hers on my face,

'Do you love him?'

'No.' She whispered, 'I love you.'

I ran my hands from her waist and beneath her dress, effortlessly gliding her panties from her thighs. She elegantly lifted her feet in black ballet pumps and I held the black lace between my fingers. Our eyes met. I put them to my nose, closed my eyes and breathed in, then slipped them in my pocket.

We started kissing; wild, luscious deep kisses. She delicately removed my specs, then led my hand beneath her black chiffon dress and I cupped her kitty in my hand. She was wet. I slid my forefinger back and forward, her eyes closed and she groaned so I pierced her with two fingers,

'Oh J!' she cried, 'Oh, be bad!'

I withdrew my fingers, drenched with her juices and dragged her into me. I unzipped her dress, dazzled as it shimmered to her feet. She raised my arms and pulled off my sweater. Freeing myself from my jeans, I pushed them to my thighs and she seized my jocks and my dick unfurled. I looked at her; she was taking me in. I liked it.

I kicked the remaining clothes from my feet and pulled Lily onto me, then lay her back on the bed and her legs opened.

'Do you want me wide open, or tightly closed?'

'Both.'

I lay over her, holding her legs apart, my head was spinning. I sucked on a nipple and our eyes met, and beneath this lust, this dirty desire, I love her.

She took my dick in her hand and smoothly rolled back the foreskin until I could smell myself; everything was heightened, even the usual awkwardness of grabbing a rubber felt erotic.

The heavenly sight of her neatly trimmed cunt deliciously sucking in my cock, choked me. She ruthlessly met my every stroke, devouring my dick. She threw her arms back, tossing her head from side to side, her hair a sea of red.

She opened her legs wide, and lifted them up, forcing me in deeper. I felt her shudder, her feet on my ass, pumping me hard, tightening the grip around my cock with her well toned kitty, luscious hips thrusting in perfect rhythm as we fucked. She brought her legs down and laid them flat beneath mine, rocking frantically under me, oh Jeez, her hunger makes me crazy.

She squeezed the wrought iron head board, her smouldering hair like nectar against the pillow. She studied me with a sweet frown, her breasts bouncing. I went back to her eyes, they kept opening and closing, she's close to coming.

She howled over the hum of music below us, clenching her thighs around mine, digging her heels in my ass until it hurt; her back arched, her breasts heaving into my face, her knuckles white as she crushed the bed frame, her glorious skin like velvet beneath my fingers.

Oh please, no, I'm not ready to let go yet, I want to make her come again, and I'm trying to hold it, oh honest I am, but I can't, Oh Holy Christ, I'm shooting, choking, my mouth's dry, I'm suffocating; is that me I can hear?

Gasping, but succulently spent, I prized my heavy head from the snugness of her neck but remained inside her, because despite our heat slicked bodies, clammy in the aftermath of our spectacular collision, I wasn't ready to leave. My hair had flopped carelessly into my eyes; hers ruffled from where my hands had been, but we couldn't tear our eyes from each other; I wallowed in the obsessive silence.

I lay my hand on her cheek and she shielded it with hers and we kissed. I rested my forehead against hers and we kissed again, and now I'm having an out of body experience, watching myself lying between the open legs of my girl, who's stroking my hair as I stare at her in disbelief, but I'm smiling; content; safe and loved, here in her arms.

'Do you know,' I smiled, 'we've been staring at each other for the last...' I lifted my head from the pillow to glance at Lily's clock, '...hour and ten?'

She grinned,

'Is that how long it takes to join up my dots?'

I started laughing,

'Oh it takes a lot less than that madam.'

I wrestled her onto her back, pinning her arms above her head; my beautiful girl, and I was just about to wickedly prize her open, when the bedroom door knocked, and I remembered where we were.

'What?' Lily shouted with a slight frown, but it softened once she looked back at me and smiled. I still had her pinned beneath me.

'Lily are you coming out?' Called a female voice.

'Susie.' Lily whispered to me.

'Everyone's asking after you; what the fuck's going on?' Susie called back, 'is this cus of what I said about Jefferson?'

I looked at Lily; she shrugged,

'Tell you later.' She looked back at the door, 'I'll find you,' she called, 'just need some space OK?'

'Cool.' And she was gone.

'Listen,' Lily said to me, 'Apart from Livvy, Susie and Lauren are the only ones who know how I feel about you; Susie said you were a dog I'd never beable to keep on the porch.'

I started laughing;

'A dog on a porch?' I pondered aloud, 'I'm not sure that's altogether flattering Lily Ellen.'

'They weren't my words,' she smiled, tilting her head to study me; I liked it, 'anyway, she's wrong.'

'She's very wrong.' I said, and although sometimes she can be incredibly difficult to read, I could see she was surprised by the force of my reply. 'I'm the one who should be insecure Lily.'

'I love you,' she laid over me, her thighs parting over mine, 'there's nothing more I can say to reassure you.'

I cupped her cheek,

'I'm crazy about you,' I felt choked by her presence, 'to hell with fucking about Lily, I want you.'

She laughed, that soft gasp that gets me right in the stomach,

'Oh J, you make me drunk,' she gathered up her hair and let it descend about her shoulders, Jesus, I want her, then she stared right at me, 'to hell with fucking about,' she whispered, her sharp nipples penetrating my chest, 'I want you too.'

Oh, *Holy Christ*, Lily on top; and just look at that beautiful body, *oh Lily, my Lily*, and I know she's displaying it for me, because she likes me watching her, I know she does.

Grinding her hips, she devours my dick, drenching me with succulent juices, because did I mention, she's already come once, and she's going for a second.

I trickle my hands over luscious jiggling breasts, tweaking the nipples and listening to her moan; oh, she is erotica herself. My hand strays to her belly, that soft, smooth, slightly curved belly, it slips between her legs, I brush my thumb over her clit; she's fucking me faster, head back, tits out, Jesus I'm going to come pretty soon, and then I look at her, ah yes, the best part, her raw and honest reaction to orgasm.

I sit up, shove her back, haul her legs apart and drive straight in, elevating her from the bed.

'Do you fuck ass?' she panted over my growling.

'I'll fuck your ass.' Oh *Jesus,* too late, I'm filling her up.

I quickly pulled out and gazed between our legs; my dick was gleaming, slicked with her come. I went down on her, nibbling her clit, parting her lips with my fingers, screwing my tongue into her hole. She thrust her cunt in my face, holding my head to her, panting brutally and ramming my nose into her sex, rubbing it against her clit, until exploding into number three, oh God this woman; this most wonderful woman...

I woke with a start; I could hear shouting outside the bedroom door. I sat up alone. I dragged my hands through my hair and checked the clock. It was mid morning. I threw myself back down, re-covering myself with Lily's duvet; yes, *Lily's duvet*, because that's where I am, where I spent the night, in her room, with her.

I lay with my hands behind my head; grinning. Honest, her insatiability gives me palpitations; it's just the small things she says, like this,

'J,' she whispered earlier, laying over me, rubbing herself against my thigh, 'let me see under your arms.'

I held the headboard.

'Oh it turns me on,' she said bringing herself off, 'thick and black against your skin; it's so masculine, I want to fuck it.'

I watched her speed up; she was so wet she was gliding over my thigh. It gave me one hell of a boner, and after she'd come, I pushed her to her hands and knees and fucked her from the rear, my hands on her ass, stretching it apart, drooling over her bud and sliding in and out of her squelching cunt.

Thinking about it again has given me a huge hard on. No kidding, I've had a permanent erection since entering the pink room last night. Even after we've fucked, blood quickens to my groin again, I can't help it; it's all a bit crazy, even for me.

The bedroom door opened and there stood my Honey. She was wearing nothing but my red cashmere sweater and holding two mugs. Her hair against the jumper fuelled me; she is Fire.

'Hey J,' she said softly; *oh how I love her.* 'I hope the shouting didn't wake you,' she handed me a mug and sat cross legged in front of me; giving me an amazing shot of her beautifully ripe cunt, 'Lauren's having a spat as usual.'

'Does anyone know I'm here?'

'I'm afraid they do,' How did she do that? Sound so innocent? 'I'm sorry.'

'Hey you,' I said taking her hand, 'I'm just thinking about you, that's all.'

'You're very kind,' she said looking at our joined hands, 'but you don't have to.'

'I can't help it,' I said, 'besides, I want to take you away from this place; I hate seeing you with these people; you don't belong here.'

She tilted her head,

'So where do I belong Jefferson? A first floor apartment in Covent Garden?'

I started laughing and took the mug from her, putting it on the floor with mine,

'I forgot,' I said pulling her onto my lap, the jumper rising, revealing my hands on her bare ass; I wanted it. 'Lily's a free spirit.'

'J, will you run with me?'

'Ah yes,' I said dragging the jumper from her glorious body, 'as fast as we can.'

I don't know how many times I've fucked Lily in the last eighteen hours, (excluding the head splitting blow job in the shower, and me fingering her against the desk; girly pink panties hitched down) but it's been one hell of a wild time, and I guess my age must be showing, because I'm totally, well, fucked out.

I was sat on Lily's bed tying my shoes when she slinked back into the room wearing a black lace bra and matching panties. It unnerves me that she walks around like this, in this house, knowing there are still a few guys hanging about from Susie's party.

'What?' she must have read my mind.

'You.' I smiled.

'What about me?' She sat over to me; oh Jesus, not again, I can't...

'Just worry about you.' I rested my hands delicately on her waist, unable to stop the urge to stroke her belly, the lace of her bra tantalising my finger tips as I reached her breasts.

'I know you do.' She took off my specs and leaned forward, her eyes level with mine. 'J, you have the most beautiful eyes; I want to look at you forever.'

I couldn't catch my breath.

Lying out on her bed, hands behind my head, I watched her getting dressed. She sprayed herself lightly with perfume, and then pulled on her jeans, the ones that rest on her hips, revealing a little of that satin skin. She slipped a black vest over her head and after adjusting it, reached for the Orla Kiely scarf and tied it without looking in a mirror.

'J?'

I'm overwhelmed as she brushes her red velvet hair; resisting the urge to do it for her.

'Lily?' I smiled.

'How did Madeleine know who I was?'

'Because I called out your name.' I'd come more times in this woman in the last few hours than I had in years; now wasn't the time to avoid intimacy.

She stared at me, brush in hand; for once she looked taken aback.

'When fucking?'

'Yes.' I was trying not to be insensitive; trying not to smile.

She slinked over to me, dangerously crawling across the bed and spread herself over my groin,

'You bad man,' she whispered, 'but I love you.'

Lily took my hand as we left her room and I followed her down stairs. Susie was hanging about in the kitchen again.

'Hey it's the newspaper man,' she said as a couple of guys checked me out, 'Lily's just nuts about the newspaper man.'

The two guys were salivating at Lily. It didn't feel good.

'You fucked the *red*,' one of the guys said grinning, 'cool.'

I grabbed him by the neck of his t-shirt; his eyes widened; he could only have been about twenty.

'Cunt.' I growled, my nose pressed against his, then I threw him back against the table.

Lily re-claimed my hand and we left the house. I had a peculiar feeling in my gut. I had a feeling of being out to sea; drifting; drowning.

'J,' she said as we walked, 'I love you.'

I stopped and studied her; she looked tired; young; vulnerable.

'Lily,' I brought her closer to me by those lovely dainty shoulders, 'why did that guy say that back then?'

'Why should it bother you J?' she walked away from me; I quickly caught up.

'You're complex.' I said.

'You've always known that.'

'Did you fuck him too?'

She stopped walking; her eyes were watering. *I shouldn't have said that.*

'It's because I won't fuck him, or any of them.' We joined hands again and carried on walking, 'even Lauren wants to fuck me.' She looked at me, 'I do a lot of things J, but there are two things I don't,' I was interested to hear this, 'women and sharing.'

I started laughing; *I love her.* I picked her up by the waist and spun her around. She was crying out, laughing, her hands gathering the air. I brought her back down and we kissed,

'I love you,' I whispered over her mouth, 'I love you madly.'

'Jefferson,' she cupped my face between her hands, 'When you said I didn't belong, what did you mean?'

What did I mean?

'Well, you're Lily Ellen aren't you; the girl with her own rules; the free spirit who runs free; you're wild; you're fresh; you're...well, life.'

'J, do you think we belong together?'

I smiled; resting my forehead against hers, nodding,

'Yes, I think we probably do.'

Les Deux Amoureux (the two lovers)

So, Lily and I are lovers, but more than that, I'm amazed at how frighteningly quick an attachment has formed, a bond created, and now I don't want to be without her.

'I know what I want,' we were stood outside the Hummingbird Bakery; she has pink cup cakes on the brain, 'I want every colour they've got, so I can divulge tonight.'

'Cupcakes and Champagne?' I tightened my grip on her waist, holding her from behind; she held my arms snugly around her; she's delicious.

'Yes,' she laughed, turning in my arms, 'you asked how I'd like to be spoilt, and that's it.'

'I was thinking more of a 5 star Hotel in Paris, dinner at Claridges, a Chanel purse or a Valentino dress.'

'For now J, cup cakes and Champagne.' And she winked over her shoulder and went inside.

After stocking up on cup cakes, I took Lily to dinner at an Italian in Notting Hill called Ripe Tomato.

'I'm having dinner with James and Helena Allen-Tait tomorrow night; I want you to come with me.'

'I'd love to.' She said picking up her red wine, 'will we be allowed to be affectionate?'

She's cute.

'Sure will Honey.' And I squeezed her hand across the table.

I ordered another bottle of wine, and the more we talked, the more I learnt about my lady.

'I'm a real redhead you know.' She grinned; she is so naughty.

'Cuffs and collars sort of give it away *Belle.*' I smiled.

She also confessed that her "crush" on me began after reading an article I'd written on Henry Miller almost 7 years ago.

'You struck me as a man who wasn't afraid of danger,' she said, 'a man who liked desire, but wasn't afraid to love as well.' She looked at me, 'that's rare you know.' Then she started laughing, 'you were also a man who dared to write about redheads, I loved that, honest I did, especially that line about *"plunging in and out of the red stuff"*; I found it fascinating.'

'Just once Lily, everyman is at liberty to fall in love with a stunning redhead.' I winked at her and our hands tightened.

She also confided that despite how she portrays herself at times, she isn't just a "literary freak" and she does dabble in the odd bit of chick lit.

'It's been known,' she smiled over the rim of her glass, 'Marian Keyes is hilarious.'

I now know her favourite actress is Audrey Hepburn, and when she was growing up, she wanted to be a ballerina,

'But I got carried away writing stories.' She said over coffee, 'it drove my mum mad, but it never stopped me falling in love with the ballet in Paris.'

And then she confessed this,

'Before you, I'd never been in love.'

'No?'

'No.' and she started laughing. 'Is that difficult to believe?'

'Well, it's just, you're on fire Lily, you're like the rawest, most passionate person I've ever met, how could you not fall in love?'

'Like Anais Nin,' she said softly, 'I need a man who isn't afraid of what or who I am, and yet still has the guts to treat me like a woman.' she leaned over the table slightly, 'J, ever like this?'

I took her hands; glanced at them, then into her eyes,

'Never like this.'

We headed back to my apartment talking about Paris.

'I went out to Louveciennes,' I love it when she talks like this; she's pure inspiration, 'I stood outside Nin's house, imagining the illicit days and night's she spent with Miller,' she looked at me, 'I know you can never glorify an affair, but sometimes there's no where else to turn is there?'

I leaned her against the apartment door and cupped her face,

'Stay close to me Lily, and I promise you it will be beautiful.'

I poured Lily Champagne and placed a single pink cup cake on a plate. She was lying on the lounge floor on her stomach, legs kicking behind her reading Ian Hamilton's autobiography of J.D Salinger.

I hovered for a moment, watching her, this most fascinating little lady, and I couldn't remember being this selfless or this, well, infatuated, this in awe of a woman in my life.

'For my lady,' I said sitting on the sofa, 'champagne and cup cakes.'

Lily was laughing as she sat up; legs crossed. She suites this life with me, even with Rachmaninov as background distraction.

'Thank you J,' she took the flute and the plate, 'you're amazing, do you know that?'

She flatters me; I adore it.

We tapped glasses and I wondered how long I'd got her, after all, I still don't really know what she does with her free time; she remains an enigma.

'I like this place J,' she said twisting her head around the room, 'it's very you isn't it; sophisticated, elegant and refined.'

'Elegant?' I couldn't help but smile.

'Yes,' she looked right at me, 'Jefferson is elegant; I like that a lot.'

'You describe me as a much better person than I really am.'

'No J,' she got to her knees, 'you are that person.' She sat back down, 'do you think anyone would miss me if I never went back to Chalk Farm?'

'I don't care if they miss you,' I said, 'they're not worthy of you; you deserve more; I'd like you to stay here. With me.'

'I'm not worthy,' she grinned, 'but I like being here with you J; it feels right.'

'It is right.'

What the hell am I saying? She's still Luke's girlfriend and I'm trying to convince her to move in with me.

She tilted her head, watching me as she drank her champagne; she was all those things she said about me; so much more than I am.

'J's been in love before.'

'Never like this.' I was quick to retort.

'How many times?'

'Just once.'

'Gracie Miller.' And she smiled, but I didn't want to talk or think about anyone that might get in the way of this Heaven.

'Never, ever like this Lily.'

'You prefer youth J?'

'I love YOU. Lillian Mills.' I said sitting beside her on the floor, 'your freshness, your intelligence, your depth, beauty, sexiness, open-mindedness, filth, honesty, passion, rawness, strength, trust, creativity, charisma, kindness, vibrancy...' I took a breath, 'Lily,' I was on my knees in front of her; 'I just want you.'

Her eyes were watering; she looked a little stunned; a little, overwhelmed,

'Jefferson,' she said softly, removing my specs 'I love your idea of this girl,' she kissed me once, 'always see me like this.'

I lifted her in my arms and she folded hers around my neck. We didn't take our eyes off each other. I laid her on my bed and we kissed; gentle; sexy, languorous kisses, because now the fury and urgency of fucking had been fulfilled for today, a new opportunity has arisen, I get to make love, and I get to do it with Lily.

With Debussy as our musical backdrop, Lily lied on the bed watching as I lit the fragranced candles on the mantelpiece.

'Lilies?' she asked; she knows; she always knows.

'Tiger lilies.' And we smiled.

I placed the champagne on the bedside table and lay beside her. We clinked glasses again and sipped, never taking our eyes far from each other. I'm not afraid of this intimacy; I breathe it with her.

Taking her glass I put it with mine and watched as she lay back. Brushing her scarf to one side I lifted her fragile arms and smoothly removed her vest. Her hair tumbled across the pillow; I have to be careful not to just fuck her, because seeing her like this, I know this fever never dies.

I unfastened her jeans, slipping them and her panties from her legs; stunning legs, discarding them to the floor.

'You make my head spin,' I whispered looking down at this most wonderful sight, 'you do this stuff like no one else does.'

'I want to be naked Jefferson,' she said arching her back for me to unfasten her bra, 'I want your skin against mine.'

I threw off my sweater and unfastened my jeans. Her eyes burned into my groin. I was big tonight. I watched as she unhooked my jeans and jocks, pushing them to my thighs.

'You...' her eyes are brimming with fire, '...make me so full it hurts.'

'I don't want to hurt you.'

'I need to feel you inside me; every bit, even if it makes me scream, oh J,' her insatiability has risen, 'let's be bad; so bad...'

I kicked away my underwear. Lily was watching my dick and balls. She reached beneath, juggling them, I groaned; my cock quivered and I almost collapsed.

She slid beneath me as I knelt on all fours. She took my balls into her mouth in turn; I threw my head back, crying out. I could hear her suckling, savouring them. It made me crazy.

I watched her pretty girly fingers curl around my dick. I held the wall in front of me as she started to rub, her mouth now between my thighs, licking, biting, kissing my perineum.

'Oh Christ!' I hollered as she pried open my ass, licking the length of it, still rubbing my dick.

My eyes were watering; the intensity in my cock at bursting point. I flinched as her finger pierced the tiny hole of my ass; she slipped in and out gently, rubbing my dick with her other hand, my balls back in her mouth, and if I come, I'll shoot in her hair, oh God, I want to see it, my sperm swimming through the auburn sea.

Still rubbing, she let go of my balls, aching and taut, they hung like weights. I whimpered as she opened my ass again and stuck her tongue into my hole. I swallowed; I'm struggling to keep my balance;

she makes me giddy; rubbing my cock, rimming my hole. *Oh Jesus, Oh fuck*, I wailed, squirting sperm over her belly and tits and still she fucks my cock with her hand, raising herself to capture every drop of milk, and there's buckets of the stuff, gushing down her belly to her cunt.

She slid her delicate fingers into the sticky substance, massaging her clit, as on all fours I watched. She rubbed faster, harder, her hips thrusting to meet desperate fingers, I want to kiss her but I can't reach, and then, oh my god, she hits it; she shoots; and I swear to god, if I never fuck again; I will never forget this moment. The most erotic moment of my life.

'The naïve part of me wishes Nin and Miller had married.' Lily was laying between my thighs in the bath. I've been reading to her for the past half an hour, I want do this with her for the rest of my life. 'I know she saw him as weak and everything, and I know he was a selfish man, but their unrestrained passion strikes a chord don't you think?'

I nodded with a smile,

'The trouble with Miller was he had a habit of falling crazily in love.' I said, 'but I do think Nin was probably the greatest love of his life.'

After, what can only be described as "devastatingly erotic" sex, I ran us a bath, complete with honey crème bath and let Lily get in first. I washed her hair, poured her more champagne, and later joined her, and we've been here ever since.

'J?'

I put the book to one side, lay my head against the back of the bath and closed my eyes,

'Yes little lady.' I said.

'When are you next going to Paris?'

I raised my head and smiled; she was washing my arms with a sponge,

'When are you free?'

She curved as much as was permitted, oh how can I live without that smile,

'I'll make the time,' she lay her head back against my chest, 'I have to.'

I couldn't sleep. There was something on my mind and I knew it was on hers too, but neither of us said anything. I've been watching Lily sleep for about an hour now; her red splendour spread wildly across the white pillow, her shallow breathing, her beautiful body partially exposed amid ruffled sheets, a pink nipple brushed against soft cotton, so elegantly slumped like only a girl can, and maybe if I didn't want her so much, maybe if I didn't need her in my life, I might let this guilt in, the one that's been banging obscenely inside my head all day, instead I find myself plotting and planning how to convince her to give him up;

to come to me. To be mine.

'Jefferson?' Lily was stirring, delicately twisting in the bed to face me, 'keep me warm.'

I love this about her; this soft side; her vulnerability and innocence (although she'd hate me thinking this), and that divine femininity she's started to reveal to me; the femininity that is so clearly present in her writing, and as I curl around her, and we hold each other tight, I wonder what might happen to us; I wonder if we'll ever make this work.

A Love that makes Life Drunk

Regrettably when I woke, there was no Lily. I vaguely remember her kissing me goodbye, but I couldn't open my eyes. I sat up somewhat dazed, and pulled the hair from my eyes, there was a note on the bedside table; she has beautiful handwriting.

"My J,

Sorry I couldn't stay and wait for you to wake, but I have a shift at the restaurant.

Listen, I need to tell you I love you so much. J, as a lover I can't put into words the strength of your passion and what it does to me. Do you remember at my party when you said I had officially met someone who could match my passion, well J, you are a man of your promise, of your writing, a man with a deep desire who isn't afraid to love and I am no longer afraid to love you back.

Oh J, I still can't believe we finally did it, it's so much more intense than I imagined. I knew it would be passionate, but I didn't envisage how powerful the bond would be and how quickly it would evolve. J, what should I do? How should I tell him and when? These questions plagued me all night. I hate doing this to him, but I can't help it. I thought about ringing him in the early hours, but I think I need to say it face to face; surely that's the least I owe him?

Anyway, I can't think of the consequences right now, the "what happens next", I'm a one day at a time kind of girl, and I need to stick to it otherwise I'll go insane. Listen J, I feel wretched about this, but I want you more, but hey, I'm sure I'm destined to go to hell anyway! I wonder, do *reds* ever go to Heaven – no, they just feel and taste like it!

Got to go; I love you madly,
Lily Ellen xx

I lay down holding the letter; had it ever been this good; had life ever tasted so fucking sweet; Lily, beautiful smouldering Lily Ellen. "*This isn't just about you Jefferson*", no, Joe, I thought, this is about Lily and I; a love that makes life drunk.

To: james.allen@msn.com
From: jjhowie@msn.com
Subject: Dinner tonight

James, I have a friend I would love you and Helena to meet. Her name is Lily Mills; she's studying for a Masters at the University of London, but she's also an unpublished writer and she's brilliant.

I've been helping her edit her most recent work but I would like you or Helena to cast a critical eye over it before I give it to Henry. Lily isn't aware I've approached you yet. I've attached a copy of the first chapter; let me know what you think,
Regards,
Jefferson.

To: jjhowie@msn.com
From: james.allen@msn.com
Subject: Dinner tonight

Jefferson, my friend.

Many thanks for Lily's work; I read the brief synopsis you wrote, I figured it was more Helena's genre than mine; she's reading it avidly as we speak.

I will be discreet this evening about Lily's work, until you tell me otherwise. I look forward to seeing you, and meeting your friend,
Kindest regards
James.

To: jjhowie@msn.com
From: lily.mills@virgin.net
Subject: My J.

Good afternoon J,
It's now, (just looking at my watch), 4.37pm and I've just got back from work.

Listen Jefferson, I've been going crazy thinking about you today. Thinking about all the times we've been in the same room over the last 12 months wondering why I kept you hanging on for so long; I can't help but think we've wasted so much time, because now I've let go I feel so unbelievably liberated I could scream out of my bedroom window (see, I am crazy! I'm laughing; it's amazing!)

J, do you remember Christmas just gone? Look, I'll be honest, when you turned up with Bella Lewinsky I was gutted; she was so beautiful (and blonde! Oh J, how could you!) and she was so into you, it was in her eyes.
I don't know whether it was the envy, but I wanted you so badly that night, watching you move so elegantly around your parents' kitchen in that charcoal suit and white shirt; untucked with no tie. I'd noticed you'd grown your lovely dark hair a little longer; I adored how it tumbled into your eyes. Oh J I love your eyes, with or without glasses, I love touching your long dark luscious lashes that blink when you're perplexed and those sexy thick eyebrows, J has smiling eyes; he has naughty eyes.

J, I think about your body all the time; your broad shoulders, your toned arms and thighs, oh, your thighs, and your ass, all toned and muscular with a fine sprinkling of dark hair. Oh I love that you are so tall, especially against me, and I love the slight curve of your belly, I want you as you are Jefferson, you are a man of experience, I like that; I want it. I'm not envious of the sex you've had in the past because it makes ours superior.

Listen J, your armpits do crazy things to me, (you know this), I want to kiss them, suck the hair between my lips whilst fucking myself, or even better, whilst you're fucking me, either with your penis or your fingers. I love your perfectly cut nails, clean with almost feminine qualities about them, watching them running up and down my thighs, my belly, my breasts. I adore the scar on your right hand.

I've been thinking about how full you make me. I love watching you grow, how the head of your penis bursts from your shaft, so thick and solid. You go so deep it hurts, but you know I can take it J, will always take it.

I love seeing sperm on the end of your penis when you pull off the protection. How I wish you could come inside me, it seems such a waste. I think about it a lot you know, how it would feel to have you naked inside me, to feel that twitch as you come, soaking me with your seed. Oh how I hate this *safe* thing sometimes, how it is a barrier to free sexual expression – but it's a price we pay in this life, and I am afraid to deviate.

Oh my J, you are so sexy, and the way we fuck is pure erotica, and I want more of it, always, everyday and night, Oh J, I wish you were here with me now, I'm open you know, ripe, ready...

I swallowed. I had two choices. I drive over to her place, fuck her senseless, or rather, Lily fuck me senseless, because that's exactly what she does, or, I write her a filthy e-mail back and tell her just what's on my mind, what's been on my mind from the moment she walked into my life.

To: lily.mills@virgin.net
From: jjhowie@msn.com
Subject: A LOVE THAT MAKES LIFE DRUNK

Darling Lily,

Oh Lily, I'm going to say and describe things in this letter that may surprise you, but after reading yours, I have to; I've got to tell you.

Lily, you are my woman, and not a day has gone by in the past 12 months that I haven't thought about you for some reason.
Now listen Honey, when Luke first brought you here to meet me, I was astounded by you. I'd heard you were beautiful, but nothing could have prepared me for when we met; is it any surprise that every Sunday from that day on, I haven't been able to take my eyes off you, making excuses to talk to you, dropping by the writers circle every week, or Holborn Library to catch you working, or a quick drink in the restaurant; any opportunity to tempt you, because that's what I've been doing Lily; tempting you.

It didn't feel good seeing Luke's hands on you that day; or to hear him talking about you; you see honey, my mind is too vivid; it felt like a betrayal.
Lily, I turn 38 soon, and my darling, you're just 25, and yet with you, this interdependence, this connection, urge, craving, desperation, is making me realise how fast time is passing us by.

I shouldn't have waited; I should have taken you then, before it became so complex, and Lily, as for the likes of Bella, all I can say is, until you I was just filling time; there were lots of Bella's and Madeleine's but never, ever Lily, and now I've got you, I want to keep you.

Lily, will you grow tired of me? Now it might feel novel that I'm so much older than you; more experienced, but with age you'll mature, you are unique now, what will you be like in 5 years time? Everyone wants you, they'll want you even more later, but as long as you love me how you love me now, this will never break.

Lily, you are splendour; you are delightful; beautiful, demure, tiny, cute, sexual, dangerous; from your enormously sexy freckles to your sweet tasting cunt.

I must go now, and later I will show you everything I'm feeling, but right now my head is too fucked...
I love you completely, madly...
J xxx

Ps. I've given your work to Helena Allen-Tait. I hope this is OK.
X

Pps. Our union is sexual freedom itself Lily, but like you, I too find this "safe" thing restricting at times, but I will never ask you to "deviate" XX.

My intention was to buy Lily a gift, but I ended up buying a lot more than one. Realistically, I could have spent hundreds of pounds on her, but I thought I'd better reign myself in, after all, I don't yet know how she feels about gifts.

With just a couple of hours to go before picking her up for dinner, I carefully wrapped the presents and left them on the bed. I enjoyed a slug of whiskey and buttoned up my blue gingham shirt. I wondered what Lily would make of James and Helena; don't get me wrong, I'm not worried, Lily knows hundreds of people in London, probably more than I do, she socialises regularly and appears unfazed when she meets new ones, I guess I just want her to embrace my world.

After casually ruffling wax through my hair, I cleaned my specs and checked my face for shaving nicks. I was rushing earlier and caught myself beneath the chin. Appearance has always been important; now more than ever.

I sat on the bed and laced my shoes. I'd had another e-mail from Luke and it lowered my mood slightly. From what he'd written, Lily seems more like herself (ironically, from the first night we slept together), but he still thinks she's being distant. He said for once in his life he'll be glad to get back to the UK so he can put things right. It made me wonder what he's been writing to her, and how emotionally it must be making her feel, because the interesting thing is, for all the hours of talking Lily and I do, we rarely mention his name.

I got up and shook out my dark pin stripe trousers. I was going to put this to the back of my mind for now; my time with Lily is too precious, besides I have Champagne in the fridge, complete with olives or pink cup cakes, whatever the lady desires, and in the morning, she'll have the finest coffee served with croissants and scrambled egg (her favourite, cute eh?), and tonight, I will be introducing my world to Miss Lillian Ellen Mills.

Breathless

As my cab pulled up outside Lily's place, the front door was slightly ajar. I could hear voices, but not hers. I was just about to get out, when the door opened, and my chest tightened.

'Hey J,' she ran elegantly to the cab, so I got out and opened the door for her, 'you smell beautiful,' she whispered brushing past my arm.

I sat beside her. I couldn't take my eyes off her.

Now, as a rule, I'm not very good at describing women, but I'm going to give this a go, because to miss out on this beauty would be scandalous.

Lily's fiery mane is parted in the middle, sleek, glossy and draped around her bare delicate shoulders; it positively glistens against her skin. She's wearing clear gloss on her lips giving her a sensual pout, (she does wear make up; natural stuff that "enhances" her, sometimes I can barely tell she's wearing it), and since she's grinning at me and holding my hand, which is laying in my lap, I've now got a huge hard on.

Right, let me focus again. Her freckles are subtle and graceful, and her eyes, ocean blue against her light sun kissed skin. She's laughing at me because I can't speak; because I can't stop staring at her; she has laughing eyes; she's happy; I love her happy; I want it for the rest of my life.

I have never seen Lily look so dazzling, and this evening, she has blown my expectations through the roof. The pastel yellow of her dress is stunning. There are no straps, just flimsy chiffon clinging to the erotic curve of her breasts. Lily has quite full breasts, but they remain pert (I know she is a 32C because I asked her – I can't help myself). The dress tapers in at her tiny waist and back out again on those luscious hips. It gathers in layers around her knees, and now that she's just crossed her leg at the knee, I can see she is wearing flat silver sandals.

‘Come ‘ere.’ I dragged her into me by her waist and we kissed. One of those deep, delicious kisses that should be the prelude to making love; the ones that go on and on, the ones that turn your stomach upside down, the kind where you take in their saliva and relish it like a good wine. One that leaves you breathless.

‘Mr Howie,’ she whispered, her lips tantalising mine, ‘you kiss very well.’

‘Madam,’ I kissed her again, ‘I am crazy about you.’

I got out first and took Lily’s hand, assisting her from the cab. She did this life so well I wondered if she’d lived it before.

‘I didn’t mind that you gave your friends my work,’ she said as we walked to the front door, ‘I’m flattered.’

‘I believe in you,’ I said cupping her face between my hands, ‘completely.’

I was about to ring the doorbell, when she took my hand and looked up at me,

‘J?’ There was desperation in her voice; it unsettled me, ‘I love you.’

She’d definitely had contact with Luke.

‘I love you too Honey; madly.’

She smiled, then nodded, immediately relaxing,

‘I’ve been looking forward to this all day,’ she said as I rang the doorbell, ‘I told my Dad about it on the phone, he says he’s read James Allen, he’s the crime writer isn’t he?’

‘That’s right.’ I kissed the top of her head; I sensed she was a little anxious, not that I blamed her; we were in Chelsea, standing outside a flawless three story townhouse, which I wouldn’t like to hazard a guess on the price, and she doesn’t even know these people and yet I’m taking her to dine with them, knowing that the food will be the finest, and the drink alone will cost as much as my suit.

Helena opened the door (yes, they do still open their own door incase you’re wondering). Helena is thirty five; she married James when she was a tender twenty four, and James a rather mature, but refined forty five. Ten years later, they are the most devoted couple I know, and Lily will pick up on this within minutes, and relax.

‘Jefferson,’ it had been a while since I’d seen Helena, ‘your hair’s grown,’ but she wasn’t really interested in me, she wanted the woman holding my hand. ‘Lily,’ she took Lily’s hand and squeezed, ‘I’ve been looking forward to this.’

‘I’ve just finished reading your book “*Interdit*”,’ Lily said nervously, but deliciously, ‘it took my breath away.’ Helena caught my eye and we smiled.

Inside, I could see Lily silently absorbing her surroundings. In fairness, their house is spectacular. The white minimal interior with just a splash of colour; wouldn't look out of place in Harper's.

'Jefferson, my friend.' James embraced me briefly; he looks very distinguished at fifty five. 'And Lily,' he took her hands and stood back, admiring her, 'pleasure to meet you.' And he kissed her on both cheeks.

'It's lovely to be here.' She gripped my hand. I squeezed it back.

Drinks were served, and Helena ushered Lily away.

'We ladies have more important matters to discuss.' Helena smiled and I winked at Lily before she disappeared.

'So,' James and I sat in the drawing room; this is James' room, he's had this house for years; written in this room for years. It reminds me of the days he mentored me; the nights I'd sit in here talking with him, crouched over a 30 year old Glenfiddich and a book. He was like a father; they are fond memories;. 'You didn't tell me Lily was your lady.'

I smiled and sat back in the huge high backed leather chair,

'She's not strictly mine.' I couldn't be dishonest to James, yet how unsettling that I found it so easy to do it to my brother.

'Ah, I see.'

'No, it's worse.'

'Go on.'

I gulped my whiskey and put it on the table. I didn't realise I was sweating so much.

'I met Lily through my brother Luke…' I said, 'she's…his girlfriend.'

James didn't flinch; he'd been through a pretty similar experience with Helena years before, maybe that's why I found it easy to tell him.

'Top up?' James lifted an 18 year old Glenfiddich Ancient Reserve and I nodded, 'how long have you been together?'

'Not even a week; but I've wanted her from the moment I set eyes on her.'

James smiled, then he started laughing, nodding,

'You went all out to get her then?'

'I've waited twelve months.'

'Painful.'

'Cruel.' And I smiled.

'And the lady?' James crossed his leg, 'how does she feel?'

I laughed softly; what a question.

'In a nut shell James, we're fucking crazy about each other.'

'So I see,' he laughed, 'so what next for you both?'

'The million dollar question hey?' I shrugged, 'I honestly have no idea.'

'Have you discussed it?'

'No, well, a little.'

'And Luke?'

'He's away in Australia; surfing.'

'Ah right, so it's easy at the moment then?'

'Too easy.' My gut ached talking about this shite. 'People will get hurt; I know that; but I want her.'

'You want her?' He raised a fatherly eye.

'For everything.' I dragged my hands through my hair; I didn't want to do this; to analyse it; I wanted to be back in our High Place; reading, talking, fucking. But this is so like James; it's like being a student again, digging into the depths of despair. 'Christ James, every fucking day I'm getting closer to forty. I've wasted so much time fucking about; I don't want to do it anymore.'

'Can you live with the guilt?'

'My need for her is much bigger.'

'Do you want to marry her?'

I looked up; Helena was standing at the door,

'Sorry to interrupt,' she looked very elegant in her signature black Chanel. 'Dinner's ready.'

I got up; my mood had dropped significantly.

'Listen Jefferson; people will judge you harshly, but I can't. You know my past; you know my hell, and you know my Heaven,' and he nodded to where Helena had been standing, 'I'll be here when you need me.'

Being back with Lily boosted me immensely. I sat down with her at the dining table and immediately took her hand; she was warm and I felt incredibly comforted. I love listening to her in female company, relishing every confession. I adore how she frees herself slightly to be more "girly". Maybe I should let her know she can confide in me about watching sunsets, about wanting a pair of vintage pink ballet shoes and how she envies her sisters life. Her freshness is beyond anything I have encountered before, and if I didn't know her; if I didn't know she was just 25, I would think her much more mature, and so the more time I spend in her company, the more I know I can't let her go.

'You will come out to Paris won't you?' James said before I stepped into the cab.

'Of course.'

'Will you bring Lily?'

'I hope so.'

'Listen Jefferson, I hope you get this sorted with as little hurt and upheaval as possible, and you know where I am right...'

'Thank you.' And we shook hands.

‘J?’ Lily turned to me in the cab, ‘thank you,’ she said touching my face gently, ‘for this evening; for every evening we’ve been together.’

‘It’s my pleasure Lily.’ And I took one of her hands and kissed it.

‘I told Helena about us.’

Now, this was a revelation. Lily is a private woman; she doesn’t discuss things like this unless she has to.

‘Oh?’

‘She doesn’t think I’m bad,’ she said gazing at our joined hands, then she flicked her eyes back to mine, ‘she says as individuals we can’t be blamed for who we fall in love with, and how we come to do it.’ She squeezed my hands, ‘just as long as we mean it.’

‘Do you mean it?’ I asked.

‘Of course.’ She looked a little sad; ‘J?’

‘Yes Lily?’

‘This is serious isn’t it?’

‘Yes *Belle.*’

‘I’ve never been in this situation before; you know, the unfaithful thing.’

‘I’m sorry.’

‘Luke e-mailed me this evening,’ *I knew it*, ‘he says he’ll come home early if it means we can sort things out.’

My gut churned.

‘Lily talk to me?’

‘Everyone will hate us won’t they; me, I mean, for what I’ve done. For hurting him, and your family.’

‘Nobody will not hate you Lily.’

She covered her face with her hands, but I pulled them away,

‘How serious is this J?’

I swallowed,

‘Serious enough for me to ask you to leave him and come to me, I can’t let you go.’

‘What if it’s infatuation?’

‘It’s not; I love you; I don’t say it lightly; I never have; you know that.’

‘I know,’ there was a sigh in her voice, ‘I’m sorry; I do trust you.’ She looked up at me, ‘Mr Howie, I am crazy about you.’ I smiled, making her smile, then we both started laughing; just gently. ‘This was always going to happen wasn’t it?’

‘Yes.’ I took her hand to my lips again.

‘And even if we promised never to see each other again, we wouldn’t be able to stop loving each other would we?’

‘No.’

‘Do I belong to you J?’

‘Do you?’ I said, ‘because I wonder whether a woman with her own rules allows herself to belong to anyone?’

She started laughing; but her eyes were watering,

'I don't want to live or breathe without you Jefferson.' She whispered, 'That's the only rule I follow.'

I poured Lily Champagne and sat beside her on the sofa.

'I bought these for you,' I placed the pink gift bags next to her, 'because I can, and because I want to.'

She handed me her drink, and smiling, she opened the first bag, laughing as she pulled out the pink satin Coco De Mer corset and peek a boo panties,

'I know about bad men like you Mr Howie.' she whispered running her fingers over the satin.

'So now you know it was for you.'

'I hoped.' She grinned.

'Was I that obvious?' And I kissed her, holding the satin between my fingers.

'It's in your eyes Jefferson, always in your eyes.'

She opened the next gift, an Agent Provocateur box. Her eyes lit up; confirming my decision.

'Oh my God Jefferson,' she was stunned; this made me happy, 'these are incredible.'

I watched the sheer pastel yellow fabric glide across her fingers; it matched her dress. I have imagined seeing her in these for months. Lily, in stockings; the full regalia, suspender belt and nylons.

Now, I could have gone for the most erotic range they had, and don't get me wrong, I did seriously consider it, but that's not Lily. Lily is a lady with assured panache, so when I saw the carefully hand stitched rose buds skimming the edge of the chiffon; it was hers.

'You bought the full set,' she gazed at me; disbelief in her eyes, 'Jefferson, this would have cost a fortune.'

'I can never put a price on this lady.'

She put the underwear to one side, got to her knees and sat astride me,

'Question,' she whispered, 'this dress, the corset or the nylons?'

I chose to fuck Lily against my desk, sleazy hands on pink satin,

'Do you know how long I've imagined this?' I growled.

Delicately tracing her tongue in circles around my nipple, she bit me; my legs almost gave way,

'Tell me J?' Our eyes met; *oh she's so naughty and I want to do such bad things to her.*

'From that first day.'

I tightened my grip on her silky thighs, so deliciously wrapped around my waist. She stretched her arms behind her, propping herself up, her head tilted, beautiful hair tumbling down her back – she's hot, panting, oh Jesus, her nipples have just popped over the corset.

She hollered as I sucked, gorgeous breasts bursting from my mouth; sweet skin seeping out like honey. I love her nipples, they grow in three layers when aroused; it's astounding.

After banging her hard, I slid my cock out of her cunt to see how wet she was; so I know how much she wants me. I pulled out completely, breathless, turned her around, bent her over and plunged straight back in from the rear as my hands cruise the satin.

'Fuck my ass,' I think I hear her say, 'J, fuck my ass.'

I fling her to her knees, then to the floor, crouch over her, smearing the juice from her cunt over the bud between her ass and slip a finger in and out. She squeals, bucking against my finger; God, she loves it, I love it, *I love her.*

She's lusciously wet now; she's ready. *Jesus*, she's holding her ass open for me. I steady myself in; she's whimpering; her body stiffens and I go in further, there, I grin, now she's full.

I steady her at the spine, playing with the pink ribbon, sweetly rocking her; she can barely move; ensnared by our lust. I'm going to come; I want to delay, but her ass is too tight, squeezing sperm from my balls, I whip out, rip off the johnny and rub myself over her back, grunting at the delight of watching sperm soak into pink satin.

“A lot of being Jefferson and Lily”

'Henry, there's been a change of plan for Friday.'

Lily was asleep; I don't think she slept much last night, I heard her get up a few times.

'I'm bringing someone with me to the bash,' I said leaning against my desk, captivated by the discarded pink corset on my chair, a stirring between my legs. 'Her name is Lillian Mills. She's a writer; she's also a very close friend of mine.'

After discussing the Costa Awards dinner arrangements with Henry, I went back to the bedroom. Lily was still asleep; curled up, hugging the duvet. I sat on the chair and watched her; I was thinking back to our conversation last night, the one about how she's planning to finish her relationship with Luke.

'I'm going to tell him I've met someone,' she said, 'someone I've accidentally fallen in love with.' We lay facing each other, 'I'm not going to say it's you though.'

'Lily, that's ridiculous...'

'No J, for now it's the way I want it, but I wish I didn't have to wait another two weeks to do it,' she said wiping her eyes, 'it makes me feel real bad inside.'

Watching her now, I know the extent of what she's doing for me; for us, and I made a promise to her last night; a promise that whatever happens, we will stay together; this will not break, and I guess by saying that, I'm committing myself to her for a very long time, so regardless of Lily's kind intentions, the inevitable is a ticking time bomb.

'J,' her eyes are closed but she's smiling; 'stop staring at me.' And she rolled over and started laughing.

'No madam,' I laid beside her, and immediately we cuddled up, 'I will not stop staring at you. Period.'

With her head on my chest, she gazed at me; she's very cute when she's just woken up,

'J, shall we hang out today?'

'Sure, what you got in mind?' I said stroking her hair.

'A secluded bar, a few drinks, simple food, talking, laughing, reading, writing, kissing, holding hands and a lot of being Jefferson and Lily.'

'*"A lot of being Jefferson and Lily"*', I liked it. 'Can I borrow that line,' I said brushing hair from the corner of her mouth, 'that's a good line; it'll work well in my writing.'

'You can have it for free.' and she started laughing.

'I have a proposition for you little lady, in return for your line, but also for strictly selfish reasons.'

'OK go for it.'

'Well,' I'd barely given this any thought; but already I wanted it badly, 'how about you stay here with me for a few days and then we can do a lot of "hanging out" together.'

She's staring at me vacantly; she thinks it stinks, shit.

'OK,' she said smiling, 'but I'll need to go back to Chalk Farm and get some stuff,' she said sitting up on one arm, 'is that alright?'

I could not believe Lily Mills had gone for it without a struggle,

'Right then madam,' I said before she could change her mind, 'we'll drop by your place, then grab breakfast at 5th View, maybe check out some books, then move onto Covent Garden where I know a secluded little number we can settle ourselves for the rest of the day.'

'J?' she climbed on top of me; Jesus; what a view. 'I love you.'

'I love you.' I whispered, 'completely...madly...'

I started revising my writing whilst Lily was in the shower, and since I've spent the last few days reading her work, I'm beginning to grasp why I'm consistently criticised for portraying women in a less favourable light; I'm beginning to see I've been blinkered by the sexual element; in essence, I've been focusing too much on body parts.

'Hey,' Lily came up behind me; I turned to see her wrapped in a white bath towel, hair dripping, smelling and looking like meadow flowers. I pulled her onto my knees and kissed her shoulder, she tasted pretty godly too, 'is this your new book?'

'Yes.' I said twisting the PC screen so she could see.

'Do you mind me reading it,' she looked at me and smiled, 'I know about your superstition.'

'You're different,' I said holding her at the waist, 'you're my inspiration.'

She smiled; tilting her head,

'What a lovely thing to say.'

'Well, it's true.' And I nodded to the screen, 'so take a look *belle.*'

I'm proud to have Lily reading my work; after all, her presence is pretty damn heavy in it.

'J,' she said turning to me, 'can I say something?'

'Sure.'

'Please don't be offended,' she said folding a damp arm around my neck, 'but I thought perhaps you could show women in a bit of a better light sometimes.'

I smiled; I couldn't help it.

'Look,' she said cupping my face, 'I fucking love your work; I always have; I think you're a genius and I wish I could write like you, but I've only been blessed with what I've got, anyway,' she looked back at the PC, 'I think we can help each other; if you're not too proud.'

Now, if it had been anyone else but Lily; my ego would definitely have taken a bashing; but I trust her; she loves me unconditionally.

'OK, I'm listening.'

'See, as you probably know, I can't write about a man for toffee,' she smiled, 'and since you're brilliant at it, let me help you with women, and you help me with men.'

'You mean I can write about Lily and her free rules?'

'You can write about how I fuck you if it fits.' we started laughing, 'OK, so you hate the idea don't you?' she said somewhat deflated, 'you're thinking, "who the fuck is she to question me when she isn't even published", but in all honesty J, with the exception of Gracie Miller, your "ladies" have been a little, well, not that deep in personality,' she grinned, 'so surely your research is slightly flawed?'

'That's a very polite way of saying the women I've dated are "shallow".' I smiled.

'I didn't want to sound rude, but yes.'

'So what does that say about me?' I laughed.

'That sometimes you don't care who you fuck, just as long as you do.' She stifled a smile.

'Ooh Lily Mills!' I picked her up and laid her on the bed; her laughter gives me such a buzz, 'Are you calling me "easy"?'

She giggled cutely as I tried to grab the towel from her,

'Yes!' she screamed out laughing, 'J, stop it!'

'Ah, so Lily is ticklish I see.'

'Jefferson, no! Please!' she was wriggling all over the bed, until her towel came loose and I whipped it from her. She looked up at me, smiling, breathless, and beautiful.

'Lily,' I said quietly, stroking the damp hair from her face, 'I'm not altogether proud of myself for some of the things I've done in the past, but I can't change it.'

'That's not what I meant,' she shook her head, 'I don't care about that stuff,' she had her arms above her head, hair strewn sexily across my pillow; 'we've all done things we'd rather not think about.'

I raised my eye at her,

'I do sometimes wonder Lily,' I studied her vivacious eyes, 'about you; who you've fucked; how many? Where?'

'Listen,' she smiled, 'the last time I told a boyfriend any of that stuff, he held it against me.'

God, she excites me.

'Would you tell me?' I feel on dangerous grounds.

'Ask yourself, would you tell me?' she said slightly more seriously, and I wasn't sure what I was getting into here.

I leaned over and whispered in her ear. We stared at each other. I saw her swallow. Then she started to smile; then she was laughing, head back, her body quivering beneath mine. It felt lovely; she was liberating me immensely and I will always be grateful for that.

'Jefferson Howie, you bad man.'

She cupped my face and we kissed, then she whispered gently in my ear, and I almost choked.

'Jesus Christ,' I thought my eyes were going to pop out of my head.

'I'm always safe though,' she sounded a little wounded, 'I mean, nearly all the time,' I know what she's trying to say, 'accidents happen right?'

'Lily, I think anyone who's been as sexually active as us, will make a *faux pas* at sometime.'

'Even you J?'

Now, this is where our age difference was going to matter.

'Let's just say, for an intelligent man in his early twenties, I wasn't always too clever.' I linked her fingers above her head, 'But I wised up quickly.'

'I really love you, you know.'

I smiled, brushing the hair tenderly from those anxious eyes, I think it's her way of saying she trusts me.

'Let's take our time Honey; there's no rush, and certainly no expectations, isn't that the joy of fantasies?'

And there you have it; I officially have no secrets from Lily. Now that's what I call serious.

Susie was hanging about when we arrived back at Lily's. I wondered whether this woman did anything else with her time other than sit about in this goddam stinking kitchen. Actually, I wondered if she ever left the house.

'Oh here they are, the old marrieds.' Susie was lighting up a cigarette; she looked awful; she looked like a junkie. 'Your mum's been around looking for you.'

'When?' Lily was sorting through the post piled on the table.

'This morning.' She said, 'so I told her you were probably with the newspaper man; I said I haven't seen you for days and I think you've moved in with him.'

I felt Lily's heart stop.

'What did you really say?'

'That's what I said.' Susie spilt ash on the table, so she blew it everywhere. 'OK, so I didn't say the moving in bit, but I did say you'd probably be with the "delectable Mr Jefferson Howie." Susie shrugged, 'anyway, she said give her a ring; she hasn't seen you for days.'

'Join the fucking club.' Lauren skulked in. She had track marks on her arms; I hated this place, but I hated the thought of Lily being here even more.

Lily slipped her hand into mine and I gently pulled her in the direction of the stairs. She followed me up, and I closed the door behind us. She leaned against it; she looked big time pissed off.

'Just ignore them,' she said grabbing her suitcase from under the bed, 'they're jealous of you; they both want to fuck me; they'd do it together if they could; one night I woke up and found Lauren lying next to me, she had her hands down her underwear; I almost threw up.'

That most definitely did not turn me on. In fact, if you had the tiniest tingle of arousal, let me tell you; Lauren is dirty in its purest form. Her hair is greasy and she has at least three inches of black re-growth. Her skin is grubby and she is covered in blackheads. Her make up is a week old and she is incredibly pale. Today she is wearing a white string vest with a green bra beneath it. She smells as bad as she looks, believe me, the thought of her fingering her cunt beside Lily, is one hell of a bad dream.

'Lily?'

She was packing her clothes; jeans, t-shirts, skirts, bras, pants, I couldn't take my eyes off them because they were hers.

She looked at me,

'Yes J?'

I went over and took her hands,

'Pack as much as you can,' I had no intention of letting her come back here, 'books, CD's, your writing, clothes, anything that's important to you.'

'OK,' she started packing again, 'you hate it here don't you?'

'I hate you being here.'

'It never used to be like this,' she said going to the book case, 'until Lauren met Jake,' she looked at me, 'he's a dealer.' She stopped packing and sighed, 'J, what are we going to say when people ask why I'm staying with you?'

'Just that,' I said, 'that you're "staying" with me for a while.'

'People are not going to believe that,' she sat on the bed and covered her face with her hands; she took a deep breath and I sat beside her, 'I should just stay,' she said, 'I'm barely here anyway.'

'No, you are not staying here.'

'Well I'll go to mum and dads then; just until I sort myself out.'

'At least let me have you for the weekend?'

We looked at each other and started laughing; she was nodding, then she wrapped her arms around me and I held her tight.

'Your *High Place* is becoming *Louveciennes,'* she leaned her forehead against mine, 'the place where Mills and Howie meet.' We kissed, we had to. 'The place where Lily and Jefferson shut themselves away from the rest of this bad fucking world.'

'Would you like that?' I asked stroking her hair and tucking it behind her sweet ear.

'Ah, *oui.*' She whispered.

'Soon *Belle,*' I kissed her again, 'very soon.'

We arrived back at my apartment and I gave Lily freedom to organise herself. Despite having a cute pink Apple laptop I offered her unlimited access to my PC when I'm not working. She stacked her books on the floor beside mine, so I told her she was welcome to put them on the bookshelf; so she did, even if it was only for a few days.

'We've got two of each book,' she smiled slotting them in place, 'cool hey?'

And it was.

I emptied half my wardrobe for her clothes and shoes, and cleared out a drawer for her underwear and smaller items. She stacked her writing and studies in a corner in the office, so I cleared a space on a bookshelf and placed her folders and research in a careful pile. If Lily was going to be staying with me, I wanted her to feel welcome; I didn't want her living out of a suitcase and the more I thought about that fucking junkie hovel, the more my gut churned that she'd ever lived there at all.

'J?' Lily came out of the bedroom; she was wearing a pair of vintage jeans rolled at the knee and a white hooded sweater and those sexy butterfly sandals; she dazzles me. 'Where should I put my laundry?'

'With mine.' I said admiring her hair; with the sun behind her like that; it blazed like a sunset. 'In the bathroom.'

I'm having an out of body experience again; me, lying on the sofa reading, Lily pottering around in the bathroom organising her laundry. Has Lily moved in with me?

'What do you want to do about food?' she was holding a pile of clothes, 'take out; eat out; eat each other?' And she winked.

'Second and last,' I grabbed her around the waist, clothes flying everywhere; she cried out laughing as I pulled her onto the sofa with me. 'Lily Ellen is a beautiful lady.'

'Jefferson James is so handsome I rub my eyes every morning I wake up next to him.'

See what I mean; she does everything so much better than me; she's amazing; it's no wonder I'm so much in love with her.

We decided on Gili Gulu on Monmouth Street. I love Japanese and I know Lily does too. I pulled on a v-neck maroon sweater and sat on the bed to tie up my shoes. I could hear Lily on the phone in the next room.

'No, he doesn't mind at all; he's being really lovely to me.' I guessed she was talking to her mum. 'Well, Lauren's being a pain in the ass; the house is a mess and they've been taking my clothes when I'm not there.' She added. 'Yeah, Jefferson's really cool, and he's got stacks of books I can use for my studies; honest mum, I'm fine, please don't worry.'

I went through to the lounge. Lily was sitting cross legged on the sofa still talking on the mobile; as weird and uncool as this may sound; it feels like she's been living with me for some time. I winked at her and she blew me a kiss. *I love her, I love her madly.*

Having the opportunity to dine with Lily is wonderful, because she is such fantastic company. We ordered a beer and started talking about the Arts bash tomorrow night; (Lily is a little nervous because she doesn't know what to wear; but I have an idea – a surprise for her), then through food we chatted about her Masters, ("*I wish I'd never started it; it's so damned time consuming*"), then we touched on my current novel, ("*It's crude and filthy*", I said, to which she replied, "*all the things we love then*" and winked), then about Livvy and Tom and the farm ("*I'd love that life*", she sighed, "*tranquillity and stability*"). We salivated over sex talk, ("*J, can I strip for you?*" and "*I don't usually swallow; but I can't help it with you*"); then about each other ("*The uninhibited lady is so adorable*" (me on Lily) and "*I love the way your mouth twitches into a smile; it's incredibly sexy.*" (Lily on me), so by the time we got back to the apartment we were well overdue a fuck.

'Great fucking is an art.' Lily smiled as she took me to the bedroom. She'd lit the candles but the blinds remained open. 'Lay down J.'

I did.

I watched her standing at the window. She lifted her sweater and pulled it over her head, her glorious hair tumbling swiftly around her shoulders, partially covering a white cotton bra. I glanced at my dick struggling against the front of my jeans. She'd seen it too, I knew she'd be eager to watch it unfurl.

She unfastened her jeans and they fell to her feet and she elegantly kicked them to one side.

'I want to be the best fuck you've ever had.' She whispered.

'You already are.' And I meant it.

I shifted myself to the edge of the bed. Lily threw up the blind; there was some sort of party going on in the opposite apartment; if they were to look over, they'd see everything.

She slinked between my legs,

'Undress me J.'

I unhooked her bra and slipped it from her slender arms and gazed up at her. She had her eyes closed; her mouth open a little. I tossed her bra to one side and drew her in by her ass, prying my fingers into the crevice and she flinched. I popped a nipple in my mouth and tugged her panties to her thighs. I cupped her sex in my hand, running two fingers between her lips until she was dripping. I pierced her harshly with two fingers; oh I love how she whimpers, and despite how many times I've fucked her, she remains tight.

I dragged her panties off and started to undress myself, but she stopped me.

'Just take your penis out and let me fuck you.'

Lily mounted me. I leaned back on my hands to support us. The window was open; the blinds up; she was crying out freely, arousing me beyond belief. I gazed between our legs, my cock was glistening; her cunt, scarlet. *Oh Jesus*, she's coming and the harder I suck her tits, the more fiercely she rides, *Holy fuck*, she's coming again and she's taking me with her, *oh Lord* I'm coming and she's still fucking me, milking me for everything; well she has everything; mind; body and soul.

'Oh Lily,' I could barely grasp my breath, 'don't stop fucking, it's still coming.'

I snapped my eyes open; I was seeing stars. Lily was still astride me but I'd collapsed back onto the bed. She was smiling; that cute smile when I know she wants to tell me *she loves me.*

'Jefferson?'

'Yes Lily?' I stretched my arms above my head as I admired her.

'You're the best fuck I've ever had.'

And after what she'd whispered to me earlier; I was pleased to hear it.

Red Dress

When I finally got out of bed, Lily was already working on her laptop at the dining table. She was surrounded by books, papers, an empty coffee cup and half an eaten croissant, and was currently wearing just my sweater from last night.

'My J,' she smiled, got up and came straight over to me, 'I was just going to make some fresh coffee.'

I lifted her up and she wrapped herself around me,

'What a sight to wake up to.' And we kissed.

'Likewise,' she kissed me again and I put her down, 'I needed to get a few things finished before this afternoon,' I had my hands on her bare ass, 'then I must go to town and buy an outfit for this evening.'

'Actually Lily,' I took her hand and led her to the sofa, 'I want to buy you something to wear this evening.'

'Are you serious?' She stared at me in such disbelief, I wondered if anyone had done this for her before, and if they haven't, fucking shame on them.

'Yes,' I laughed hauling her onto my lap, 'I'm serious.'

'Well that's very kind of you.'

'No it's not,' I squeezed that peachy ass again, 'I want to do it because I think you're amazing.'

She twinkled,

'Will you come with me?'

I shook my head,

'Buy exactly what you want; cost is not an object,' I love that smile, 'and then tonight, you can surprise me.'

'Leave it with me.' Did I mention she was naked beneath my sweater? 'You won't be disappointed.'

I was staring between her legs; she has the most beautiful cunt; I love her cunt, and she knows it.

'Lily,' we looked at each other, 'I love you.'

With tenderness I only associate with Lily, she cupped my cheek and I covered her hand with mine and we linked fingers,

'*Je t'aime* J.' she whispered over my lips, '*beaucoup.*'

I'm writing like a Trojan at the moment which isn't a surprise since I'm spending most of my time with Lily. I've also been analysing her portrayal of men, and my portrayal of women and come to some interesting conclusions.

See, when I read Lily's "women"; they're strong, sexual, and intelligent, with a hint of softness (much like the lady herself), but when I read mine, they're empty sexual parts, sent to take cock and nag. When I read Lily's take on men, they are soft, forgiving and unselfish. When I read mine, they are powerful, sexual and unforgiving.

I sat back and folded my arms. We needed a balance. Women aren't always strong, sexual and intelligent, and men are not always powerful and unforgiving, but Lily is right, my portrayal of women is totally off beam; a stereotype I've naively fallen into.

OK, so some of it does come down to individual writing styles, but it's also about attitude, to which Lily has opened my eyes; but ironically when I think of my relationship with her, I am the men she describes: soft; forgiving and unselfish. Has Lily succeeded in "moulding" me? Or is it "*just Lily*"? Unhelpful recollections of her and Luke over the past 12 months spring to mind, and I wonder again whether I can keep her.

These lonely thoughts make me desperate; make me want to text her; call her; something. She's a genius and I can't lose her. I start dipping into "*Henry and June*"; she left it on the bedside table, open on the page she was reading last night. There's a passage underlined in pencil, it unsettles me, so I phone her, asking her to explain it.

'It's research for a piece I'm writing,' her voice is sweet and happy, 'I've been trying to work out whether Nin was really jealous of Miller's whores.'

After we said goodbye, I received a text from her.

"I have conquered a man least conquerable." (H & J, pp199)

She smells my fear. I text her back.

"You know how men feel after they have had a woman. They want to kick her off the bed. With you it remains heightened afterwards as before. I can never get enough of you. I want to marry you..." (H & J, pp219)

She text me back with this,

"I crave [J], only [J]. I want to live with him, be free with him, suffer with him...I partake his curiosities, his desires...I think his thoughts. Everything in us is married."

I am soft over Lily; I am forgiving with Lily; I am selfless with Lily. This overwhelming emotion is far crazier than it was with Gracie. With Lily, it's rich and complex; and I mean it when I say I want to marry her, I do, even though it sounds fucking crazy.

Someone rang the intercom.

'Jefferson,' it was Joe, 'let me up fella?'

I wandered into the kitchen to start coffee, when he appeared.

'You are alive then?' Joe has been trying to get hold of me; time with Lily is precious.

'Coffee?'

'Sure.' He pulled out a stool. 'So, what's the crack?'

'Same.' I said. 'You?'

'Florence is back tomorrow.'

'Can you manage to keep yourself out of mischief until then?' I smiled at him over my shoulder,

'More to the point fella, can you?' Joe nodded to the pink lap top and books on the dining table, then the butterfly sandals by the sofa and the white hooded sweater on the back of the chair.

'Lily's staying for a few days.'

'Fuck off,' he laughed, 'I bet you've moved her in you *sleazy bastard.*' I smiled; he knows me too well. 'So what's happening then, you know, you and Lily?'

'Like you said, I'm a *sleazy bastard.*'

Joe shook his head; I sensed disappointment; it didn't feel good, but I wasn't going to let her go.

'Jesus fella, how you going to explain this one?'

'I have no idea.' I handed him a coffee, 'I don't know how I'm explaining it to myself.'

'You've fallen for her haven't you?'

I laughed a little,

'You could say that.'

'Christ, she's so young, or should I say, you're too old.'

'We connect; age has no part in this.' I smiled.

He's pondering; I honestly believe he can't get his head around this; for the record, I don't think many people will.

'But...he's your brother; doesn't that feel like... double treachery?'

We looked up as the front door clicked open.

'Hey,' her smile immediately lifted my mood, 'sorry,' she said glancing at me then Joe, 'should I come back later?'

'No,' I winked at her, 'come 'ere.'

She was holding a couple of bags. I went to take them from her, but she shook her head,

'Surprise remember?' and I can't believe what I did next, I kissed her; right infront of Joe, like I'd forgotten, because I had.

'Lily, you've met Joseph before haven't you?'

'Yes,' she smiled, 'hi.' And they shook hands.

'Good to see you again Lily,' Joe was at least keeping his dismay under wraps. 'Jefferson said you're staying for a while?'

'Yes,' she said putting her bags on the sofa, 'the place I've been living in was, well...'

'Undesirable.' We looked at each other and smiled; I suddenly wanted Joe to leave.

We watched as Lily headed towards the bedroom with her bags.

'You two are smouldering.' Joseph was gazing at where Lily had been standing, he was laughing, 'what the fuck does she see in you?' he shook his head; smiling; I don't expect anyone to understand; fucks knows I don't.

'I'm taking her to the Awards tonight.'

'Is that wise?'

'I want her to come with me; they'll be influential people there that I want her to meet.'

'Be careful not to forget yourself,' he warned, 'they'll be a lot of people there who know you.'

'J?' She dazzles me in that pink playful beach dress, 'do you mind if I...?' and she pointed to her laptop and books.

'Carry on,' I can't stop staring at her legs.

'Right folks,' Joe gulped back the espresso and got up, 'just a fleeting visit; enjoy yourselves this evening,' he looked at Lily; her dress had risen slightly, he was leering at her thighs; I didn't like it much, 'nice to see you again Lily.'

'Yes, you too Joseph,' she glanced from the screen and smiled, 'take care.'

I saw Joe to the door.

'She's lovelier than I remember.' He said grinning, 'you old dog.' And he nudged my arm.

'Like I said,' I was feeling quite narky, 'can you keep yourself out of *enniu* before Florence arrives back?' He stared at me; bewildered, this speaking French thing is rubbing off, '"*trouble*" Joe,' I repeated in English, 'keep yourself out of trouble.'

He patted his nose with a finger and left. I closed the door. Glad he was gone. When I arrived back in the apartment Lily was leaning against the dining table biting her bottom lip; I've noticed she does this when she's feeling, well, dirty. She threw a foil wrapper at me; I caught it, and she laughed.

I shoved her against the table and ran my hands beneath her dress, ripped off her panties, lifted her onto the table, pulled her legs apart, whipped down my joggers and plunged into her. She squealed, so I held her legs above my shoulders as she lay out, and slammed into her. Her cunt juices were gushing, I could see a smattering on her thighs. She rested her calves on my shoulders and I rubbed my fingers in her wetness. I put them to my nose, then into my mouth. Her pupils were huge; I think she likes it, despite the frown. When she gets like this, she makes me fuck her ass and I love it.

She lay a hand on my stomach so I stopped fucking her, and steadily, she began thrusting, like she's the one fucking me. It makes me crazy and I'm going to come. She yanked the zip at the front of her dress, her breasts spilt out and she started flicking her nipples, so I bit them hard and she gasped, ah, how I adore her vigour as she squashes my head to them.

She shoved me away and got up and I watched in awe as she bent over the table and dipped her fingers in and out of her cunt, smearing it around her lovely ass. I did the same, both our fingers dipping in her cunt like chocolate, buttering her cavity so I can fuck it.

'Oh J,' I love fucking her ass, 'come in me this time.'

I managed two measly strokes before I shot my load up her. She grabbed my hand, cupped it between her sex and started rubbing against my fingers. She managed slightly more strokes than me before she came, and I swear I felt her come ooze onto my fingers. She's so juicy, and I love playing with her cunt when she's this wet; when she's just come.

'You have conquered me,' I whispered breathlessly, 'now there's no turning back, for either of us.'

As I waited for Lily to come out in her evening attire, I was thinking about the conversation we'd had earlier after brutal sex. We were lying on the floor, cuddled up, gazing at each other in that way we do,

'I want to tell him now that it's over; I want to ring him up and tell him today so I can be yours.'

'You are mine.' I said stroking her hair.

'Totally yours; so it doesn't feel like I'm betraying you when I answer his e-mails.'

'Lily?'

'Yes J?'

"Epousez moi?"

Asking Lily to marry me in French made it easier, but even so, my heart was pumping so fast I felt a little, well, drunk; see, I've never asked that question before.

The bedroom door swung open disturbing my earlier thoughts. I sat up. My chest tightened. I tried to cough but the palpitations made me queasy. I stood up. She's grinning; she knows she fucks me up; she loves it that I'm like this; like putty.

She pirouetted towards me, parading her luscious body, consenting to my hungry eyes. Oh fiery red hair with a dangerous dress of red silk and chiffon, clinging to the curve of sensual breasts, small straps exposing delicate and beautiful shoulders. Red ribbon accentuating her fine tiny waist, and kicking out sexily at her hips, chiffon cascading to her knees. I drool over slender calves wrapped elegantly with pink satin ribbons, her perfect feet sat prettily in pink heeled sandals; she is a sexual ballerina.

I know I'm being rude, but I can't stop gawping at her; her hair falls like satin around her shoulders, curling gently on the ends. Her lips are full and glossy. Her freckles; cute and dangerous.

'Am I good enough for the elegant Mr Jefferson Howie?'

OK, you may think me feeble; you may think I'm insane, but I dropped to my knees and clung to her waist, my head taut to her belly. She stroked my hair and I squeezed the life from her.

She got to her knees and we hugged, then kissed; furious kissing. I slid my hands beneath her dress; Jesus, no panties.

'Like your book J,' she whispered, 'the night at the opera.'

She climbed onto me, unfastening my trousers, immediately liberating my incredibly stiff cock, then mounted me. I momentarily thought about a rubber, but this exquisite friction blinds my judgement, and now she's coming, lifting her dress, compelling me to watch her cunt convulse around my cock, so I shoot with her, right into her womb, squeezing those ballet shoes, their sensual ribbon tantalising my fingers. Oh, this is obscene; this violent pleasure, *but I love her; I love her so much,* my girl in *la robe rouge.*

My Lily

There is something arousing; something animalistic and something quite satisfying in knowing Lily is wearing no panties beneath a dress everyone is admiring, unaware that an hour ago, I emptied myself inside her, to which I am sure there will be residue, shrouding the soft delicate walls of her cunt; yes, mine and I'm relishing every moment of it.

'Henry, meet Lillian Mills.'

He swooned; I knew he would.

'Lillian, pleased to meet you.'

She gently shook his hand,

'Hello Henry.'

We circulated for a while, drinking Champagne, until I no longer wanted to share, so I escorted her to our table. She was drawing attention from a number of directions, men and women alike. It appears I'm not the only completely dazzled by Lily Mills.

I poured her more Champagne, revelling in this feeling, but, oh no, someone's coming over and he's looking at Lily, now me, smiling; it's Eliot Hansen, *damn.*

'Jefferson,' I have never seen this man unhappy, 'good to see you mate.'

We shook hands vigorously, or rather Eliot did, and I feel I should introduce him to Lily since he hasn't taken his eyes off her; (see, she can even dazzle a happily married man).

'Eliot, this is...' I glanced at her and she winked at me, and I just can't help myself, '...this is *my* Lily.'

'Well "*My Lily*",' Eliot smiled taking her hand, 'pleased to meet you.'

She knows his work well; in fact; she is a huge fan, which is ever so slightly weird for me since Eliot is married to Gracie.

'It's amazing to meet you.' She gushed, and my stomach sank.

I studied Eliot with Lily; he's handsome to the extreme; he's young

(28), he's sexy; confident, northern (Manchester) and a fucking brilliant artist, and he's shaking hands with *My Lily*.

'Lily's a writer,' I said hearing Pride in my voice, 'contemporary women's fiction.'

'Cool,' to my relief Eliot took his hand from Lily's, 'you should meet my wife, she's a writer too.' This guy has so much energy it unnerves me, 'you might know her?'

'I know her work well,' Lily smiled, 'I attended a few of her workshops at the University a few years back; she's brilliant.' I had a feeling it took Lily a lot to say that.

'Wow,' Eliot nodded like a dog, 'small world.'

I saw Gracie standing with her agent, and when she saw me, she started to make her way over. Lily saw her too, painfully squeezing my hand; she has absolutely nothing to worry about; History is history.

'Gracie honey,' Eliot took her around the middle, well, as much as he could since her bump is huge, 'This is Jefferson's lady Lily, she's a writer.'

'I'm not published though,' Lily shook Gracie's hand; I think she's struggling with this, 'Jefferson's helping me revise.'

'Well you've got the best man for the job,' Gracie smiled at me, and I nodded, then she turned back to Lily, 'what a stunning dress.'

'Oh... thank you.' Lily gripped my hand tighter; it hurt. 'How long do you have left?' and she nodded to Gracie's swollen stomach.

'Four weeks,' she sighed, 'it feels like I've been pregnant forever.'

I stepped back from the conversation for a moment. I was thinking about Lily. Lily with my baby inside her. I swallowed. I promise I have never had these thoughts before, and now it's a possibility, I want it, and like everything I feel with Lily, I want it *badly*.

'Jefferson?' I came back to the conversation. Gracie was standing beside me; Eliot talking with Lily. 'Jefferson are you there?'

I managed a smile,

'Miles away,' I'd been staring at Lily.

'So I see.' Gracie smiled with a raised eye; 'can't blame you,' she said, 'she's beautiful.'

Gracie and I are able to talk like this; able to stay friends, because, well, she's a kind and generous woman, it wasn't her fault she was in love with Eliot and not me, and knowing the situation Lily and I are currently in, eerily I'm able to empathise.

'How are you Gracie?'

'Tired,' she smiled, 'fat; pissed off, shall I go on?'

I started laughing,

'I think I get the idea.'

'Anyway, I'm trying to stay excited; we've just finished the nursery and changed the car and now it's a case of waiting for this little girl.' And she patted her stomach, but I was watching Lily again; I was being completely rude I know; but I couldn't help it, 'So,' Gracie glanced at Eliot and Lily, then back to me, 'she's different for you isn't she?'

'Yes.' I grinned. 'She's unique.'

She laughed,

'That's very noble of you Jefferson.'

I adjusted my specs,

'We've known each other for a while, but we've just started to become a little more than friends.'

'You're smitten?' Gracie was studying me; I didn't like it.

'I guess I am.' I said, 'she's a genius and I'm confident in a few years she'll be one of the most innovative writers of our time.'

She smiled,

'What a lovely thing to say.'

Eliot re-joined his wife, and I re-claimed Lily. I leaned over, gently brushed her hair from her ear and whispered,

'I love you.'

She winked in reply.

During dinner, I wanted to ask Lily to move in with me. Earlier she told me she liked her clothes beside mine, her books stacked with mine, her toothbrush in my pot, and I told her I adored her underwear on my radiators (!), but more than any of those, I treasure waking up beside her and even though it's only been 24 hours, I don't want her to leave me. I guess I'm becoming a cuckold insecure old man, or maybe, to quote one of my own novels,

"...captivated to the point of insanity; there is no turning back; it's happened; all the others were stepping stones to this; to her; to Ellen." [Extract taken from my current novel entitled, "Red"]

After introducing Lily to some influential people in the fickle and fucked up world of publishing, I wanted to leave, and I sensed she did too.

'J, forget the cab, let's just walk home.' she slipped her hand to my ass, she's crazy tonight; full of Krug; full of life; full of me, 'let's play.' Lily's "play" makes me giddy, but I want it; want it all the time.

We held hands back to my place, kissing and laughing. I picked her up and we sat on a bench, her luscious legs wrapped around mine, her arms grasping my neck. We kissed, one of those delicious lingering kisses that makes me want to screw her, and for a moment I think she's going to, but instead she adjusts her dress and we kiss again.

I watch her dance and spin; her dress a mass of chiffon around her waist, revealing her luscious strawberry blonde cunt, her cute ass and silky thighs, so I go to her, backing her against the stairs in the apartment block. She whispers that I'm naughty; she's drunk; I want to fuck her hard.

She shoved me away, bent over and raised her dress. Her ass opened, so I quickly unfastened my trousers and thrust them and my briefs to my thighs. My cock throbbed; I could feel come bubbling in my aching balls. She dropped her clutch bag, the contents spilling at our feet, she claimed a rubber, and ashamedly, I was disappointed.

She reversed onto my cock, and I glided in like silk.

'J, don't move.' she whispered.

So I didn't, and she fucked me against the wall, her hands supporting herself on the stairs, repeatedly slamming against my dick over and over as I watched her cunt juices coating my shaft.

I was pretty close to shooting, but I spun her around and yanked her legs apart and quickly stuck my head beneath her dress and started to eat her; every bit of her, jutting my tongue in and out her cunt, drinking her juice, whitewashing my mouth and nose, savouring the fragrance of her fresh ripe sex.

She was getting a little crazy, grabbing my hair between her fingers, slamming my mouth against her clit; I was biting it, flicking it with my tongue. Jesus, she's fingering herself, and putting it into my mouth; I feel like a king at a banquet, a cunt banquet, drinking the finest come of all.

She started whimpering; legs so wide I could have climbed inside, but I kept sucking until she came again, then she jostled me to the floor, the rubber was hanging off; our eyes locked, our breathing fierce against the silence of the hallway. I swallowed as she whipped it off and mounted me, fucking me hard until I shot my come deep into her womb, but I'm insatiable so I lay her back, open her legs and drink warm sperm from her cunt.

Lily's watching me. I can feel it. I want to open my eyes and see her smile; her sexy bed hair, her satin shoulders, those freckles, but I also want to wallow in this feeling; this bizarre and secure feeling that for once in my life, someone feels like me.

I resign and open them. Her smile chokes me. She's lying beside me in the bed, sat up on one arm. I look at her closely and I know she's been crying.

'I got an e-mail.' She said.

I swallowed.

'Luke?'

She nodded,

'He's coming home early.'

'How early?'

'Tuesday.'

I sat up. Two days. OK, I was going to be cool about this. I had to be.

'I'm going to meet him at the airport,' her eyes were watering. 'I'm going to tell him.'

I pulled her into me and she held me tight; she was crying.

'This won't break Lily.'

'But it means I've got to leave you, move back to my mum and dad's for a while,' she leaned her forehead against mine, 'just until it's done.' I don't want her to go, but I understand, 'because I know he'll come straight to you.'

'I know he will.' It took me back to Joe's "double treachery".

'And I'll understand if you change your mind about me,' she rubbed her nose sweetly against mine, 'he is your brother.'

'Lily stop,' I closed my eyes; I didn't want this; I didn't want her to give up on me, 'I love you.'

'I love you.'

We started kissing; gentle, soft sweet Lily Ellen kisses, but it quickly dissented into something urgent, until I had her on her back, gliding inside her, but instead of our usual acrobatics, I took her tenderly and now I know; this is serious; she belongs to me; I belong to her, but all I can do is wait.

Lily's mum was standing at her front door. Her eyes narrowed in on me; she knows everything. I could feel it.

'Hello Jefferson.'

'Hello Mrs Mills,' I said putting a box of Lily's books on the doorstep so I could shake her hand, 'good to see you again.'

She didn't reply. That confirmed she knows, and she loathes me for it.

Last night, Lily and I had agreed after Luke's announcement that she should stay with her parents for a while; even though she'd only just come to me.

'Not too long though.' I said as we lay in the bath together this morning.

'That's impossible,' she smiled looking up at me; those dot to dots working their magic, 'can't stay away from my J for long.'

Lily came up behind us carrying her lap top and satchel,

'Hi mum.'

'Your room's ready love,' she said kissing Lily on the head as they met in the doorway, 'your dad's in the garden.'

That was one person I didn't mind if I never met again. I doubted I'd ever be perfect son-in-law material as far as they were concerned; not that I blamed them; I wouldn't like me very much either.

'I'll bring in the rest of the boxes.' And I made myself scarce by going back to the car.

Unloading the boot, I thought about why Lily's parents potentially detest me. It could be the fact I'm 37 and she's just 25, or that I've been sleeping with their daughter knowing she's in a relationship with my brother; I imagine it's both, topped off for good measure with the vulgarity of my novels and my occasionally arrogant and pretentious column.

'J!' I looked up to see my beautiful girl hanging from an upstairs window, 'where are you?' she was laughing, 'I miss you!'

She's crazy; a crazy risk taker, but seeing her glorious auburn halo blowing in the breeze, her laughing eyes; I have no choice but to go to her.

'So this is your little girl's room?' I said entering a room no bigger than the one she'd left in Chalk Farm, although this one was immaculately preserved.

'Yes J,' Lily took my hand, 'my little girl's room.'

I smiled; she's good; too good on times.

'You do realise your parent's think I'm the devil personified?'

She started laughing, letting me go,

'And that's before they know about the nylons, the butt plug and the *sperme.*'

She was giving me a tremendous erection.

'Where shall I put these boxes?' I was desperately trying not to notice Lily getting to her knees and sliding her case beneath the bed, her denim skirt rising, panties revealed: polka dots, oh Holy Christ! Then she looked up, hair shaping her face, eyes so blue I wanted to dive into them, cheap yes, but if you could see them, you'd know what I mean.

'Just stack them in the corner thanks.'

I hovered over the photos on her window sill. There was a silver framed one of her mum and dad, arms wrapped around each other, it looked like Livvy's farm, I recognised the barn in the background; there was also a wooden one of her and Livvy from a few years back, Lily was probably about fifteen, and alarmingly one hell of a cutie, so moving on, I found this,

'When was this taken Lily?' I held the pink plastic frame between my fingers; I couldn't take my eyes off it.

'I was three.' She smiled getting to her feet and coming over to me, 'have I changed?'

I started laughing,

'I hope so otherwise I'd be in prison by now.' I looked back to the picture; the shy, red haired girl sitting on a chair holding a bunny *and I love her madly.* 'Your hair looks similar.'

'I suppose it does,' she looked at it with me, 'and the freckles...'

We gazed at each other in that stupid way we do; but we can't; not here; what the fuck am I thinking? I had palpitations as Lily quietly shut the door. She closed the blinds and took off her panties. She unzipped me and leaned me against the desk. I closed my eyes; she was on her knees, her mouth wrapped around my dick, sucking away at it like a lollipop. I looked down, her hand busy beneath her skirt, I was going to come but she withdrew and I thought I heard footsteps, except this time it wasn't Susie or Lauren, it could be her mum, even more scary, her dad.

I stared at her. The footsteps had disappeared. She leaned over the bed and displayed her wet cunt from the rear, and I hoped to God she wasn't going to ask me to fuck her ass because I'm too loud. She opened the lips of her cunt and I plunged straight in. She cried out, so I covered her mouth firmly with my hand and fucked her. She squirmed beneath the force of my body, muffled screams beneath the palm of my hand but oh, how I enjoy this brutality.

I trapped her with my other hand, pumping in and out, over and over, my hand still covering her mouth, her head back, I could hear footsteps again, but I couldn't stop, I was going to come, oh fuck, I am, I'm coming, but there are footsteps again and I freeze, but Lily carries on fucking me and I lose my head, and my orgasm has barely finished when I grab Lily from the bed wrench her skirt back down and pull up my jeans. We looked hot; we looked like we'd been fucking. I combed my hands through hair; they were shaking violently. I slipped my specs on and the door knocked.

'Lily love,' Jesus, it was her dad, 'do you need anymore help?'

Lily was grinning at me; I've never met anyone like her.

'No thanks dad,' she called back, winking at me, 'we're all done now.'

The footsteps disappeared, and I breathed out.

'We should not have done that.' I could smell my fear, 'not here; your parents place...'

'I'm sorry.' She smiled and took my hand, 'Am I *too* bad sometimes?'

I sat on the bed and covered my face with my hands. I hadn't noticed how badly this thing was fucking me up. I thought it would be simple: I love Lily; I want her, and OK, she's with my brother, but he's young, handsome and cool, he'll find someone else in no time; but it wasn't quite working out like that, because I hadn't contemplated how much in love with Lily, Luke is, and it's only now that I'm loving her, do I realise the strength of her allure.

'I save all the best loving for you J.'

I looked up to see Lily sitting at her desk, she seemed a little wounded.

'Sorry?'

'I want you to know I've never been like this with anyone but you.' We gazed at each other, 'and I know you sometimes wonder if I'm too much for you; if you can keep me.'

'Yes I've thought about it.'

'J,' she sat down beside me and we held hands, 'let's get out of here; go somewhere together; Paris, wherever you want, I just want to be with you.'

I cupped her cheek with my hand and she closed her eyes. That was reassurance enough for me.

The apartment felt empty, something I'd feared. I miss her; for the first time in my life, I miss someone. Miss them so badly I want to cry. It's dark; it's cold and it's so fucking lonely and my head is throbbing.

I looked at 3 year old Lily. She gave me the picture you know, she knew I was taken by it, and she was right, I don't know why, I just wanted it, and right now it was a much needed friend.

Lying out on the bed, I noticed Lily had left her "*Henry and June*" on the bedside table, along with her butterfly hairclip and Fossil watch. I picked up the book and flicked through it. Lily had read this book so many times she knew her favourite passages from the top of her head. I've never been a huge Anais Nin fan, but after getting to know Lily, she's changed my mind, like she's changed my mind about so many things.

Embracing the book and the photo, I closed my eyes. Her mum had been quite hostile towards me when I left, but I think it was more to do with her anxiety over Lily than the suspected affair we're having. I can understand that; Lily's free rules frighten me sometimes.

'Jefferson,' her mum called to me as I was leaving earlier, 'I have a fair idea of what's happening here, but please, she's just a girl...'

'She's a woman Mrs Mills; an amazing and beautiful young woman; she has a mind of her own and I go with whatever she wants because that's how much she means to me.'

'She's a novelty to you because she's young.'

'I love her for everything she is and everything she isn't.'

She stared at me as though I'd lost my head; she's right.

I got up from the bed, taking "*Henry and June*" with me. I had no idea what Lily was doing right now, maybe she was at one of her parties, maybe she was hanging out with her junkie friends, maybe she was studying, or maybe she just might be thinking about me...

To: jjhowie@msn.com
From: lily.mills@virgin.net
Subject: I miss you

My J,

It's been less than four hours since you left me, and I miss you terribly. How can it be that in just 7 days I can't function without you? I don't like this feeling; it's alien to me. When Livvy first met Thomas, she was like this, all lovesick and lonely and when she wasn't with him, she was talking about him, and when she was with him, she said it still didn't feel enough. I feel like that about you Jefferson, but I didn't understand it back then and now I need to be close to you all the time.

These walls are caving in on me, I feel like coming to you, to our *Louveciennes*, our *High Place*, fuck everyone else and what they think, these things happen right, people do fall in love, even if others think it's wrong. Oh, J, let's run away, let's just go, take me to Paris, let's live a dream, let's talk in French, love in French. Let's make love all night and wake up and drink coffee and eat croissants in bed, then make love again before venturing out into the streets where we can sit in cafes and bars and talk about books and writing, where we can dance in the streets, laugh, kiss and hold hands, J we can be free, we can follow our own rules, our made up rules, because since you, I can't even follow my own anymore.

Listen J, what I said before, about us getting married, well I don't need to think about it, I will marry you, let's spend our life together, get old together someplace amazing. I love you more now than I ever have.

J, when my friends at University hated you, I defended you, I wanted to be you because you are that much of a genius, and now that I'm loving you, that I know you, I feel proud that I delved through the hype, the reputation, the critics...

Now listen J, I know you're not perfect, I know your flaws, I have them too, we all do, but you suit me, we suit being together, it works...
Oh J, I miss you; miss you like an idiot.

Lily Ellen xxxx

To: lily.mills@virgin.net
From: jjhowie@msn.com
Subject: I miss you

Darling Lily,

"...terribly, terribly alive, pained, and absolutely feeling that I need you...But I must see you: I see you bright and wonderful...you will understand; you must understand. [Lily] stand by me. You're all around me like a bright flame. [Lily], by Christ, if you knew what I am feeling now." Henry and June (pp68)

Lily, my love, I miss you. It's true, I have never missed a woman before, not in the way I miss you. You've got me doing crazy things like touching your hairclip, your watch, reading your book, putting your forgotten panties, (the black lace ones with the ribbons either side), to my nose, finding your scent and breathing in, almost grabbing my coat to come and get you.

Listen Lily, I'll be honest when I say that when we brought your belongings to my apartment a few days ago I had every hope that you'd stay with me permanently. I want you here, you suit being here, this is our place, I realise this even more now because it's so empty without you, God, I'm lonely Lily; come to me now, let me breathe you in, make this place come alive again; God I crave you, I love you...

Now Lily, I'll make you a promise, we will marry, you will be my wife. We'll do it in Paris. Soon. I won't wait, I've waited long enough. Wear white; I've imagined you like that; so demure, so elegant, a lady, my little lady. I want to stand at your side, take your hand, draw you in, and whisper that I love you, my *femme.*

Will anyone ever believe this? Do I even believe this? Just 7 days ago you were so far out of my reach I never imagined that we'd love as much as we do, that we've seen and done the things we do, oh Lily, let me join up your dots, let me drink your mulled wine hair....

Forever your J xxxxx

Luke

I was in bed, 3 year old Lily propped up against my lamp, and that's when it happened.

I sat up and checked the clock; it was after two thirty in the morning. I tossed back the covers and stuck my head out of the window. *Fuck.*

I dived over to the bedside table, threw my 3 year old Lily into the drawer beneath Salinger, and grabbed my joggers. My fucking heart was pounding. Millions of questions and mixed up emotions made my head throb. Does she know he's here? Has she told him? I quickly checked the apartment for signs of Lily; nothing except a few books, which I doubted he'd notice.

I was pulling on a t-shirt as I reached the apartment door; my hands shaking, my eyes delirious.

'Hey Jefferson mate.' He was glowing. *And I've been sleeping with his girlfriend.*

'Jesus Luke, what you doing here?'

'What sort of a fucking welcome is that?' Luke laughed; he'd already grabbed me around the neck, hugging me in that macho way he does. I realise now we are so very different. 'I grabbed an earlier flight,' I felt like I had a hangover but I hadn't touched a drop, 'but since mum and dad would throw a bender if I turned up at this hour and with Lily being back at her folks, I thought I could grab a bed here,' he looked at me as we stood in the kitchen, 'just for the night?'

'Of course.' I managed to smile but this felt much worse than I'd anticipated.

'Look mate,' he said throwing his back pack down by the breakfast bar, 'sorry about it being so late, just took the opportunity,' he was radiant; my stomach churned. 'I've got to see my girl.'

I swallowed. How easily I'd forgotten.

'Cup of tea?'

Luke started laughing,

'Hey Jefferson never changes; cup of tea? Sure.'

I filled the kettle. I wanted to look at him but it was difficult. He threw himself on the sofa. My brother. My little brother. The one who'd followed me around aimlessly when I was sixteen, the one who wanted to be just like me, the one who asked my advice on everything, yes Joe, you could call this *"double treachery"*.

'Have you spoken to Lily?' I had to ask.

'I'm gonna surprise her tomorrow,' he'd taken off his sweater, the muscles in his sun kissed arms made me anxious. 'Gonna whip round to her folks in the morning.' He got up and came over to me; he had a question; I could feel it. 'JJ, I need some advice, you know, about Lily,' he was getting tongue tied; this was bad, 'being away from her for so long has made me realise, well...that there's no one like her, and being 28 now, maybe it's time.'

'Time?' My back prickled with sweat.

'Yeah, to get serious.'

'You're going to propose?' I heard the shock in my voice; I hoped he hadn't.

'Steady on JJ,' he laughed, 'I just meant "get serious", maybe rent a place together, see how things go, and shit yeah, if it's great, I'll ask her and we'll get hitched.'

I reached for two cups. I needed to speak to Lily. Desperately. Luke was on the floor rifling through his back pack.

'Is Lily the getting married type?' I asked.

He turned and grinned at me,

'Come on Jefferson, what girl could resist this?' and he pointed to himself.

'So, this "getting serious" issue, does that mean you've managed not to stray from Lily?'

He stood up. He was a handsome fucker, I'll give him that.

'Look, I've been a cunt in the past right, but not with Lily, OK, I thought about it, being away and stuff, choking the goose isn't always enough when you've got the most gorgeous girls knocking on your door, but hey, Lily's cool right, she's, well, she's Lily.'

My Lily.

'You mean to say, you managed not to fuck about all those time you were away?' I was trying to make myself feel better; it wasn't working.

'Yeah.' He grinned, 'proud of me JJ?'

'You could say that.'

He took the cup from my hand and we went through to the lounge,

'So, how's my girl been? I hear she's blossoming under my big bro's wing.'

'Lily's been, well, amazing.' I put my cup down; my hands were trembling, 'so, you came home early for Lily?'

He shrugged; the tea burnt his mouth.

'Just got a feeling you know. She's been dead weird with me.'

'Maybe she's under pressure with her studies?'

'Nah,' he tried again with the tea, 'there's something I just can't put my finger on.' Our eyes met. I swallowed. 'Hey JJ, can I ask you a personal kinda question?'

'Umm...yeah, sure.'

'I always tell Lily I love her right, cus I do, but she's never once said it to me, I mean, I'm cool with that right, she's a free spirit and all, I've always known that, but I just wondered...'

My chest was tight. I was tired and had palpitations. I wanted Lily. I needed Lily.

'I can't tell you what's on her mind,' lie number 1, 'but it doesn't mean she doesn't.' lie number 2.

'Yeah, I suppose.' He looked at me again, 'should I stop saying it, you know, make her think I'm not as keen as I say I am.'

He'd got it bad; I felt even worse.

'Say it if you mean it. But you've got to really mean it.'

'Yeah,' he pondered, then he looked at me, 'you didn't see anyone hanging around her did you?' he held his hands firm around the cup, 'you know there's a few guys that wouldn't mind getting their fucking grubby hands on her.' He stared at me; I hoped to God my eyes weren't as revealing as Lily always tells me they are. 'Those fucking parties man,' he said shaking his head, 'I hate it when she goes to them, freaks me out.'

'Susie and Lauren are frightening that's for sure.' I still shuddered at the track marks and fingering episode.

'Yeah,' Luke was nodding profusely, but smiling, 'got to agree with you on that one.' He sipped his tea, 'anyway, thanks for persuading her to move outta that joint, she wouldn't listen to me.' He smiled into his tea, 'she thinks a lot of ya, you know,' but then he looked right into me, 'you know, I once thought she'd like you more than me, you being a writer, and all, that "elegant refined" stuff she likes.'

I swallowed.

'But I haven't got a physique that could match yours.' And we both grinned. 'Look, I'm gonna crash if that's OK, I'm totally fucked.'

'Sure.' He nodded.

I gathered together a couple of blankets and a pillow and handed them to him. He was wearing just his boxers, jeez, what Lily sees in my body compared that, I have no idea, but I'd be forever grateful.

I closed the bedroom door. I felt a little calmer than I had earlier, but I still needed to speak to Lily.

'Jefferson,' she sounded tired; that same sweet voice I hear every morning; it soothed me, 'are you OK?'

'Need you Honey.'

I knew she was smiling,

'Need you too J.'

'Lily,' I was careful to keep my voice down, 'I need to tell you something.' Silence; so I carried on. 'Luke's here; he got an earlier flight. He's staying the night... then he's coming to you.'

More silence.

'J, I love you.' She said.

'I love you Lily.'

'I guess this is it then?'

That didn't sound too good, but I knew what she meant.

'I'm waiting for you; thinking about you; loving you all the time.' I closed my eyes lying out.

'J your e-mails are so beautiful.' There was a sob in her voice, 'I print them out and read them over and over...'

'I want to come to you.'

'I wish you could.' She was crying. I wanted to go to her.

'Est-ce que je peux vous voir demain?' I am such a selfish fuck it's unbelievable; already asking if I can see her tomorrow.

But she was laughing through her tears. I love her; she understands me.

'Oui, je t'aime Jefferson.'

'Thank you,' I had her worn copy of "*Henry and June*" by my side, 'Lily, listen to me...

"I love you. I go to bed now – it is too painful to stay awake...I am hurt to be alone. I need you...Shoot with me. Wrap your legs around me. Warm me."

To which she whispered,

"...my [Jefferson], the man I love tremendously now, too much, dangerously."

Journal

Luke left for Lily's folks place about ten minutes ago. To be honest, despite feeling secure in Lily's love, I felt a twinge of nausea watching Luke leave the apartment with his dark floppy surfie hair, sharp blue eyes, cheeky smile and lean muscular physique. He carries himself well; he's confident, and his swagger in those jeans makes me wonder.

I've decided to wait to hear from Lily. I have no idea how or when she's going to do this, so I'm giving her all the space she needs, and since I figured it could be some time, I thought I might as well get my head down and write, but I had an e-mail from Lily, with an attachment. It was sent at four thirty six this morning.

To: jjhowie@msn.com
From: lily.mills@virgin.net
Subject: Journal.

My darling J,
Read this; immerse yourself in it. It's all for you. It's part of a journal I've been writing for years. I've pasted some of the extracts about you. I love you. Lily Ellen xxxx"

3 Nov 1999

I have just read a man. A man I think I like. He is arrogant; self assured; a little pretentious, but I like him. I like his writing style. He's a journalist. His name is Jefferson Howie.
Stevie gave me today's Independent. He said I should read this particular column,
"He's a pretentious wanker", he said, "but he knows his stuff."
It was an article about "Tropic of Cancer" by Henry Miller, part of The Independent's "Looking Back" series in the Arts Section:

"The self assurance of Miller's work is unparalleled...He was a man living on the edge of vulgarity in an ignorant and censored world, where he recklessly immersed himself in the seediness of bohemian Paris...to know he acted on what he wrote, makes his work even more compelling; a world of whores, debauchery and infidelity, and it is this, entwined with clever fiction, that creates such an intensely rich and cocky autobiography..."

7 March 2002

I've just finished reading "Lost Without You". Gracie Miller is a brilliant writer. The way she captures Eliot on paper is graciously intense. Their self destructive love and frighteningly passionate fucking sessions make me want a love like that. I wonder how Jefferson feels when he reads this; I wonder does it stir him; I wonder whether he smells his own fear...

22 May 2002

I saw Jefferson Howie today at the University. He'd been in the audience at Gracie's lecture. He is so handsome and elegant...I saw him standing with her in the corridor. She was talking to some students; he was by her side wearing a dark suit and a long black coat. He looked a little awkward; a little, well, like he didn't belong. He brushed his hair from his eyes and looked up; I caught his eye and we smiled briefly before I headed past to meet Annie...

28 Sept 2002 [The Evening Standard, 27 Sept 2002]

"Gracie's New York Bound"

"Bohemian writer Gracie Miller is set to take New York by storm after being invited to lecture at Colombia University.
Gracie, 25, who has sold over a million books nationwide, will fly out for three days, with long term boyfriend Jefferson Howie.
The New York lectures coincide with the release of her greatly anticipated third novel "Under the Weather"...

10 October 2002

I read in the Standard that Jefferson and Gracie have split up.

18 April 2003

Went to Eliot Hansen's Roundhouse "Eva" exhibition with Jude. I saw Eliot standing talking with Gracie and some guy in a black suit. Jude told me off for staring at Eliot, I said I was just interested in a man who inspired 3 novels.
I wondered if Jefferson Howie might turn up, just to be controversial.

4 May 2005 [Taken from "Paris" Journal]

Went to Café de Flore for my usual breakfast. Bought a copy of the Independent, I was having one of those days when I crave to read English.

I see Jefferson Howie's still writing his column; I take comfort in this...he hasn't lost his ability to inspire. I wonder what he's been up to, this most elegant man with his dark floppy hair and retro glasses.

20 June 2005 [Newquay, Cornwall]

Today I met Luke... I still can't believe his brother is Jefferson Howie. At first I thought he was winding me up, until he swore on his life. I couldn't stop laughing; it's so surreal. I think he thought I was crazy or something...

I'm excited and nervous about meeting him. There are so many things I want to ask him but I don't know where the hell to start. I think Luke felt a bit dejected because I kept talking about how brilliant Jefferson is,
"Hold on babe, forget JJ, what about me?" he said.
I just smiled because they are so totally different; I would never have put them as brothers.

30 June 2005

I've been having weird thoughts about Jefferson Howie, like, how does he smell, (I imagine he wears an expensive cologne; I bet he is divine), how does he talk, (deep; confident; masculine), how does he smile, (sexy; handsome) what will he wear (signature dark suit; no tie). Will the confident Howie I've read in his novels show himself, God I hope so.

I know he's tall, I read somewhere he's about 6ft 2, I like that; he'll make me demure and feminine, but I think my mind and my writing are too masculine for him to want me. His women are usually quite delicate, I think he likes to be in control, I couldn't give him that, but I could give him the best fuck of his life.

Last night I felt bad. Fucking Luke was good, but everytime I closed my eyes I was thinking of Jefferson and when I came I had to stifle the words. Luke is simple in his approach to sex; he likes to fuck on top; he feels weird about me taking over, but I want a man who can say "cunt" and relish it. I want a man who can say "I love your cunt" and mean it. I want a man who loves his sperm as much as I do.

8 July 2005

I have just met Jefferson Howie.
He is a man who writes. He is a man who drinks champagne. He is a man who thrives in his High Place, he is like me.

He was wearing a dark suit (no jacket); he was sharp, refined, elegant, and effortlessly sexy. His white shirt tails were hanging carelessly over his trousers, his dark hair had fallen casually into his dark brown eyes protected by black rimmed rectangular glasses. He was clean shaven; fresh skinned. His sexy side burns, elongated and chic. His feet crossed at the ankle. Noble shoes; square toed. Black. I've never felt attracted to a man this much older than me before. J is almost 37. He's experienced. I want that. He makes my skin tingle.

Just as I thought, he smelt divine. He was tempting me. It's in his eyes. He wouldn't stop looking at my hair. I think he likes it. He likes my breasts too, I wonder if he imagines putting them in his mouth. I'd like to kiss him. I think he'd like to kiss me too. I wonder if he'd like to fuck me as much as I would like to fuck him.
He talked gently to me about my writing. He was compassionate. Much kinder than I imagined. I loved the way his mouth twitched into a smile. His skin was smooth despite being slightly toughened, and his laughter lines made me happy. He is a man who can laugh, I like that.

I noticed a scar on the front of his right hand. Luke told me it was from a surfing accident when they were kids, it happened during one of their many holidays to Cornwall. I wanted to kiss it. I loved his long fingers, his clean neatly trimmed nails. He turned, his ass is tight, I want to fuck it. He leaned over the desk to talk to me; he was flirting. I flirted back even though Luke was beside me, oblivious.

I looked between his legs. His balls were tight against his trousers. I wanted to follow the curve with my hand, my fingers, my mouth, my tongue. I wondered about his penis. I imagine him deep. I want him to fuck me until it hurts.

I told J I have defended him to my friends. I think he was impressed but he wouldn't let on; I liked it. His arrogance made me angry but at the same time he thrilled me. He is a man who's not afraid to take risks for something he wants. He is a man who can lust and love, like me. He understands.

When we said goodbye, Jefferson winked at me, I was on high alert. My body was in a fever. Luke is relishing in this, yet it's his brother whom he has to thank. I have a feeling; a small feeling Jefferson Howie likes a girl. But I must hold back. I have to. It will pass. Luke is kind; he is good, I must stay focused...

Jesus Christ. I looked up from the PC. So much wasted time. So long of wanting Lily and her wanting me. Why did I hold back? Why didn't I take her then? I wanted her, she was right. I looked back to the PC, reading greedily. She is a genius. *I love her; I love her so much.*

21 August 2005

Sunday lunch. Struggled to keep my eyes off Jefferson. He was sat opposite me. Our eyes kept meeting. I wished they wouldn't; eventually we ended up smiling at each other. His foot touched mine beneath the table, our eyes met again and he grinned – he is wicked but I am in raptures.

1 Sept 2005

I am totally alive! This has been the best night for a long time. Jefferson turned up at the group tonight. My face must have been a picture as I looked up and saw him. He nodded to Jon (I know they are friends), sought me out and sat beside me on the bench.

'How's it going?' he whispered, and I swear I closed my eyes and sighed at him being so close, he smelt beautiful.

'Good.' I turned to him; his eyes twinkled; he is incredibly handsome.

I couldn't concentrate, not with him being this close. Leanne kept looking at him; it made me feel bad inside. I've brought J's writing up in the group before and I know Leanne has a thing for him; she kept staring at me too, because J keeps looking at me, and I can't help but catch his eye.

After wards, I thought about asking him if he wanted to go for a drink, but I couldn't, but he did offer me a lift home, and being alone with him in his car was way too much for a girl like me...

8 Sept 2005

I anticipated the group. No J today.

15 Sept 2005

I didn't expect to see J at the group because I knew he was in Manchester on business, so when he arrived in the last quarter, I couldn't believe it!
'How was Manchester?' I said as he sat beside me.
'OK,' he smiled; he was wearing jeans and a white shirt with a white and grey striped jumper; I adore his intellectual look. 'How are you?'
I love those glasses; he is elegance personified.
'Good thank you.'
'Need a lift home?'
I pondered; there had been mention of having a drink with the others,
'Yes; thanks, that's very kind of you.'
'No problem.'
Jon was getting annoyed with us; it felt like we were surreptitious lovers; I liked it.
'That's a very cute satchel you have there,' he whispered, 'the real McCoy?'
'Yes,' I smiled; I think I looked too happy, 'I found it in a boutique in Camden.'
'It's very you Lily.'

We didn't talk long in the car, J was tired after his journey. We said goodbye and I hovered at the door watching him in the car; I would have liked to ask him in; I'd have liked to fuck him.
It looked as though he was watching me too; I wondered what

he was thinking. I wanted to run to him; he was staring at the steering wheel, then back at me, and I thought for a moment he was going to get out, but Lauren pulled open the door; she was pissed. J put his hand up to me and drove off. I have a pain in my gut and it won't go away.

6 Nov 2005

Sunday lunch. J was watching me again. Ever since he started attending the group, we've been watching each other even more.

When I got up to help Alex clear the table, his eyes followed me the whole time. I dared to look at him, we smiled. I sat back down opposite him and his calve brushes against mine. I looked up. He held my gaze. We shouldn't. I wonder if he's playing with me...or am I playing with him?

Jeremy was watching. I tried to turn away from J, but his gaze is too intense. My insides were churning.

At the table, we talked quietly between ourselves. J was focused on me; I was trying to be good – I promise, but I couldn't help imagining his expressions as he fucks; I wonder how he sounds, especially when he comes; I hope he's loud; I wonder if he'll want me wide open or legs beneath his. I'm falling...really falling, someone help me...

15 Nov 2005

It's cold. I love being on the farm when it's this cold. I wrapped myself up and imagined all sorts of stuff.
I fed the chickens this morning and watched the cows' breath in the air. I love this time of year.
I started thinking about my J. I wondered if he turned up at the group last night. I wondered if he was disappointed that I wasn't there.
I've started to miss him, well; at least I think that's what it is. A nagging, lovelorn feeling in my gut and my head hurts; sometimes I don't even want to speak. Livvy leaves me alone; she knows me.
I've been talking about J a lot recently, barely mentioning Luke,
'So, this thing with Luke's older brother,' Livvy said last night as we sat in the kitchen, 'bit more than a crush I sense.'
'I'll get over it.' I hoped I sounded convincing.
'He's on your mind though?'
J is always on my mind.

29 Nov 2005

Snow! We have snow! Chaos all around; London is a crazy place to be when it snows, it's rare we get it here. I've been sitting at the window all afternoon imagining walking through Hampstead Heath with J, both of us wrapped up, holding hands, talking; we'd stop for a drink, some food, and then head back to his apartment; he'd look after me, wrap me in his arms to warm me; we'd drink champagne and lay together. A sweet innocence before a lustful storm.

11 Dec 2005

Sunday lunch. Talked to Jefferson about how much I like his apartment. I've been there a few times now with Luke, I always stand at the window; I love people watching. Jefferson usually offers me Champagne and olives. He knows I like it. He knows I've done it before. He knows a lot of things without having to ask.

I usually help him with the drinks and aperitifs; it's my excuse to chat with him in the kitchen; we don't talk about much, just surface things like, my study; parties; the writing group, that sort of thing, but then Luke comes in, and grabs me like he always does. I know I frown, and I feel bad because J sees me do it, and yet I feel torn between these two men, but like a magnet to just one...

I want to be alone with him. I sense he wants to be alone with me too. I've tried several times, and so has he, but we've never quite managed to pull it off. I couldn't sleep last night, thinking about seeing him today. He looked so beautiful: brown moleskin trousers and a crisp multi-coloured shirt with the tails hanging out. I desire him more than I have any other man, but I should stop making it so obvious...

I think J looked up my skirt tonight; I hope so, I did it for him. I was wearing pink satin panties; J writes about panties all the time, I want him to enjoy mine, I hope they made him hard.
I lay alone last night. I put a finger inside myself; it wasn't enough. I used a dildo, fucking myself in front of the mirror, oh I was wet, soaking...

I have a tremendous erection. My jocks are around my ankles. She arouses me with such intensity that to wank isn't enough. I want her.

Want her cunt. Want her cunt juices. I want to fuck her ass hard, then her cunt.

I froze. Hand around my dick. I turned to the mobile. It was ringing. I jumped up and grabbed it, almost tripping over my trousers. But it wasn't her. It was Jeremy. I ignored it; he'll leave a message if it's important.

15 December 2005

J came to the group today. He crept in, nodding to Jon and sat beside me. I couldn't concentrate; his fragrance is divine. I wanted to ask him to have a drink with me, but I think that might be too much...

I glanced at him as Jon waffled on; he turned and looked at me and we both smiled. I wanted to look away but tonight he held my gaze and I could feel myself blushing; no man has ever done that before. I blinked and looked away; my stomach was in knots, I don't know what this feeling is, it's so weird to me, I'm churned up most of the time, and I can barely eat. I told Susie this morning and she laughed,
"You're in love you daft cow; it's that ass Howie isn't it?'"
"Luke?" I frowned.
"No, the other one," she laughed, "the newspaper man."
J offered me a lift home. I wished the journey was longer; we arrived back at Chalk Farm too quickly. I tried to think of a reason to keep him talking, but I didn't need to, he'd already turned off the engine.

We talked for hours (over 2 actually!). J turned on the heating and gave me his jacket; I breathed in his aroma and he smiled at me; he knows and I don't care. He is so beautiful, and in this light, he takes my breath away. I wondered if one kiss would do any harm, but I know one kiss would probably lead to a lifetime of fucking.
I now fear the worst.

26 Dec 2005 – Boxing Day (Luke's parents)

I am afraid to admit it, but I am in love with Jefferson. He was kind and attentive today, and I didn't mind that he was with Bella, because he followed me around for most of the day.

J and I talked for hours. Luke couldn't get a word in and Bella was furious, I heard them arguing in the hallway; I heard her say my name, J defended me, "Lily is a very interesting young woman and I enjoy talking to her..." but Luke doesn't notice a thing, not even the way Jefferson watched me through dinner, or how I watch him as he talks, or how he finds me wherever I am or how we launch into conversation like we've just stopped talking. I love talking with J; he's wonderful. He is the first man I have ever loved...

My phone was flashing. Jeremy had left a message.

"Listen JJ, there's some shit going down at the house and I figured you'd know all about it.' I heard him take a breath, 'Mum's really upset, but thankfully she hasn't mentioned your name.' He sighed, 'Jesus fella, I hope you're serious about her, because the mess you've left is not a pretty one. Catch you later."

I immediately dialled directory enquiries,

'Brown's Hotel, Mayfair, please.'

I quickly changed into a pair of jeans and pulled a black cashmere jumper over my shirt. I slipped the remaining pages of Lily's journal into my over night bag, and hailed a cab.

I kept checking my mobile. Nothing. I hoped she wouldn't go to the apartment, chances are Luke would be on his way over. I just wanted to hear from her. It's rare I worry over a woman as much as I do Lily; she's wild, she's free, and there are still things I don't know about her, but she's done this enormous thing so we can be together and I'm not about to back out, infact, I'm in deeper.

I nodded to the doorman at Brown's and declined his offer of help. After checking in, I went straight to the bar, downed a double whiskey, found a table and got out Lily's journal.

31 Dec 2005

New Year party at Jefferson's.

Luke's been grumpy all day because he doesn't want to go to J's, he wants us to go into town and get pissed with Dan and Ben again, but they bore me. They talk about girls like they're surf boards and it fucks me off. I told Luke that too, but he just laughed like he always does. I used to admire his ability to laugh things off, but now it just frustrates me. I think he knows it too, which is why he eventually agreed we'd go to Jefferson's,

"What's so fucking good about my brother,' he laughed, 'I love him and all, but he's a bore Lily, it'll be all champagne and fucking canapés, and as for that bint he goes out with, Christ..."

I've chosen my party outfit carefully. Jefferson only sees the "girly" side of me, and although I sense he likes it, I want him to see the other side of me too. I've decided on a black skirt, black ballet pumps and a black polo neck. I'll wear my hair down and curled on the ends and clip the fringe to one side, because I know for sure J loves my hair. Not sure if it's the colour or the style, but he commented on it at Christmas, without going into detail. I think he has a fetish for reds; I like it. He would never be disappointed to have me...

I feel slightly nervous about the party because of how I feel about J, also, Bella's going to be there, but I'm not envious of her, she is one of Jefferson's many ladies. I don't believe he loves any of them, he needs to fuck, he is insatiable, like me; fuck on a "needs only" basis.

1 Jan 2006

Hungover. Sick. Tired. In love.
Last night Jefferson followed me around again. I think Jeremy noticed, and his friend Joseph. They kept watching us. J didn't seem to care; he was pissed; he made me laugh. I wanted to kiss him; I very nearly did.

As soon as Luke and I arrived at his party, Jefferson took me to one side; his eyes were all over me, I think he wanted to say something but he didn't. He showed me the rare JD Salinger writings he'd bought. He said he wanted me to read them before him,

'I'm very interested in Lily Mills,' he said, 'her mind of course.'
He poured me champagne and told me I'd been on his mind when he bought the olives. I told him I liked his suit, but he just smiled and nodded in appreciation. Luke took my hand, dragging me to the lounge. He didn't suit being there, I didn't suit being with him. A little later Jefferson caught my eye as I sat on the floor admiring his CD collection,

"Lily Mills likes The Beatles?"

"I'm more of a Stones fan, but yeah, I don't mind.'
He told me I have rules of my own; free rules. He's said this before but I'm not totally sure what he means.
When he wasn't following me, I followed him. Discreetly courting each other in a room full of people I didn't know and didn't care for. This man; this most elegant man who occupies my mind all the time, who I now want more than anything, was pouring me more champagne as the countdown to the New Year began. I wanted to be near him. I wanted to beable to hold him and kiss him at midnight. I knew this would be my only opportunity – and excuse.

Luke grabbed me first, kissing me full on. Jeremy managed to prize him off and we hugged, laughing gently at Luke's keenness. I looked for J; he was with Bella, but he was looking over at me, nodding his head; summonsing me with his eyes, I went to go to him, but he got caught with Joseph; then he held his hand out for me, I went to take it, but Joseph's self-important wife grabbed it instead. Defeated, I felt a hand on my arm, I turned hoping it was J, but instead it was the creep who'd been staring at me all night. I shook my head and went to the kitchen. I wanted vodka.
"Happy New Year Lillian."
I turned to see my man leaning against the breakfast bar, smiling at me.
"Happy New Year J."

I went to him; he met me half way. He folded his arms around my waist with mine around his neck. My feet left the ground for a moment and I closed my eyes. His face felt good in my neck; I think he was breathing in my perfume.

I withdrew from him, feeling his reluctance, and maybe if Luke wasn't in the next room I would have felt a little more confident. I buried myself into him again and he whispered something, but I couldn't hear. We were dangerously close but he was warm and smelt divine; My God, he is so beautiful I could look at him forever.

He gazed at me through heavy eyes, his mouth moved in and so did mine, but inches apart, I couldn't do it, so instead he kissed my cheek, catching the corner of my mouth and I closed my eyes and gripped him firmly, and he understood.
"Happy New Year." He whispered in my ear, 'lovely Lily Mills.'

4 Jan 2006

I had to speak to someone; I rang Livvy.
"I'm in love with Jefferson."
"I know,' she said kindly, "I've known for ages."
"Oh Livvy, I don't know what the hell to do."
"How do you feel about Luke?"
"He's not right for me," I said truthfully, "if he thinks about it, I'm not right for him either."
"And Jefferson?"
"I think he likes me too."
"I have a bad feeling about this Lily," she said, "I don't want you to get hurt."
"I know, it's a risk, but I just don't know what else to do."
"Hold back?"
"I've been holding back for six months." I was crying, "I want to stop seeing him but I can't."
"You're going to get yourself into trouble Lily."
"I'm already in trouble' I sighed, 'deeper than you can imagine."

6 Jan 2006

Alex told me Jefferson and Bella have split up.

12 Jan 2006

J came to the group again. He is becoming a regular. It was on the tip of my tongue to ask him for a drink. He sits so close to me, knotting my stomach. I felt his thigh against mine, he does it on purpose. We looked at each other and I wonder how he imagines fucking me, because I know he does.
Oh, I'm feeling insatiable at the moment; I fuck everyday, sometimes twice, if not Luke, myself, it's not enough; never enough...

22 Feb 2006

I've been re- reading Jefferson's novel "Gallant". He is a bad man (I'm laughing!) He gave me a copy before its release last summer. I asked him to sign it for me, he laughed and said it felt weird to sign a book for me, but I justified it by saying since he is a genius and I'm learning from him I'd be honoured, so he did, he signed it, "Lily, just once, everyman...J xx". Anyway, this is my favourite line for today:

"She's one hell of a good fuck, and thinking about the way her cunt sucks in my cock, makes my balls ache...",

I'm laughing again; only my J could get away with that. Actually, I wonder if he really does speak like that in bed. The thought makes my body tingle with sordid delight.

26 Feb 2006

Sunday lunch and Luke is away in the US. J was wearing brown cords and a black polo neck. He looked like a bohemian. I was wearing a dark denim skirt and red skinny rib polo neck. I think if a stranger had walked in they would have assumed J and I are together...

The more I see him, the less I can disguise my feelings. He is the same; he takes risks to be near me; we stood in the kitchen and talked for ages, Alex came in and eyed us together; she sees it, I know she does; it frightens me; but I just can't stop.

19 Mar 2006

Sunday lunch. J has been talking to me about Paris. We talked about his time there, and about my translating. He wouldn't let anyone interrupt our conversation. He was focused on me today, more than usual. I don't think anyone else noticed. I think it stirred him when I spoke in French.

He talked about his writing and how he listens to Debussy. I want to know everything about his writing; I'd love to be by his side when he creates. J said he'd like to read my work, but I don't think he's ready for the real Lily Ellen Mills just yet.

1 April 2006

I saw J in Waterstone's today with Madeleine. Thought I'd better not go over. They didn't look very happy. He saw me as I was leaving, I could see he was on his way over, but I waved instead and headed out of the door. My expressions are too revealing.

16 April 2006

Easter Day. Lunch with Luke's mum and dad. Luke talked about my birthday party. I wanted to invite Jefferson. Luke said it would be cool. I didn't think J would want to come, not all the way to Stow, but he accepted without hesitation.

23 April 2006

Sunday Lunch. I spoke to Jefferson about the Hotel arrangements for my party. He said he'd already booked himself in. I was amazed at his keenness. When I told him I was surprised he was coming, he thought I meant he was too pretentious. It made me laugh. I don't think he has any idea of how I feel about him.

He started asking questions about me. He's never done that before – it felt lovely. I mean, we talk about books and writing all the time, but never ourselves. He wanted detail and I was happy to give it to him, although I wasn't quite sure if he was humouring me until he said "...you have officially found someone who can match your passion." Despite him not intending it to mean the obvious, I thought it, and I think he did too; and he's right, because the more I get to know him, and the more I let myself love him, the more certain I am that this man can more than match my relentless burning passion.

I was on my third whiskey. I had a head on. I was fucking buzzing. Shrouded in Lily; in her love. She is genius. This wonderful woman. Her words are more evocative, more profound than I ever imagined; this journal alone makes her a prodigy. I want her, right now, in my arms.

'Would sir like another drink?'

I looked up. The waiter was signalling to my empty glass. I smiled, nodded and handed it to him. My mobile started ringing.

'Lily?'

'Where are you?' she sounded the same. *I love her madly.*

'Looking for you.' I laughed; she understands. 'Get a cab; come to Brown's in Mayfair, I'll meet you at the entrance.'

I turned off my phone and slipped it in my bag. For at least one night I wanted her all to myself before this fucking thing blows up in our face, because we both know it will, it's just a case of how and when.

My unforgettable night with no ordinary redhead

Now listen, before Lily, I was most definitely not this damned soft. OK, I do have it in me, I blame dad for that; his obvious devotion to mum is still on display after almost forty years of marriage, but I swear, when that cab pulled up outside the Hotel, and the concierge opened the door, I wanted to cry.

Her auburn halo grabbed my last breath; glossy and slinky as it wafted gently around her shoulders. I ran my eyes over that body, so stylishly dressed in black trousers clinging provocatively to slender thighs, and a black vest that embraced her deliciously full breasts and delicate waist. The crest being a teasing pink and black scarf looped elegantly around her neck, and black ballet pumps.

She saw me and dropped her bag and yes, get this, I ran down the stairs and picked her up. She grabbed me around the neck and wouldn't let go, even when I tried to gently prize her away, and then I knew she was crying.

'Come on Honey,' I whispered, 'let's go inside.'

The doorman took her bag and I smiled and nodded for him to leave it in reception. Lily loathed anyone seeing her crying, least of all strangers. I was going to protect her from that; it was the least I could do.

I gripped her hand and we looked at each other; she's beautiful despite slightly swollen eyes; she will always be the most beautiful woman to me.

'Miss me J?' she sounds like *My Lily*. She is My Lily.

'More than I can tell you.' I dabbed a stray tear from her cheek with my thumb and I took her to the bar. I ordered Champagne.

'Do you mind if we don't talk about it just yet?' She sat down on the chair I'd pulled out for her.

'Of course not.'

'I would have called sooner, but mum and dad...' she shrugged, 'you know...'

'I understand.'

'Anyway J,' there; a little twinkle in her eyes again, 'I'm all yours now.'

I felt a twinge in my stomach; hadn't she always been mine?

'Thank you.' I whispered.

'No,' she smiled linking her fingers through mine, 'thank you.'

I ordered more champagne, and realised Lily and I had been talking in the bar for almost 2 hours.

'Lily?' I said taking her hands across the table, 'I want to give Henry your Journal.'

She shook her head,

'No.'

'Lily, it's a masterpiece.'

'It's just a load of clumsy words.'

'That is so not true,' I squeezed her hands, 'you write beautifully; the way you wrote about me, about us is exquisite, honest Lily.'

'I'd have to censor it.'

'No way.'

She looked from our hands and into my eyes,

'Are you serious?'

'Of course I'm serious, and I'd love to see the full Journal.'

She started laughing; shaking her head,

'Never.'

'Why?' I grinned, guessing her apprehension has something to do with the content.

'You don't need to see it J, there's stuff in there that's very delicate.'

I so badly want to do this for her.

'Please Lily, I will be open minded, I am a journalist remember.' And I winked.

She shook her head again,

'I don't believe we can be open minded when we're so intensely involved with each other.' I'm pushing her patience, I know, 'even we couldn't ricochet that kind of pain and jealousy Jefferson.'

'OK, I understand.' And I did. I think. 'Let's compromise,' she tilted her head and looked at me; *I love her so much*, 'let me give Henry the chapters you sent to me?'

'What about the content?'

'I'm honoured. I want to quote it in my own work; I want to review it in my column, I want to do a feature on you,' I held my hands up signalling a headline, "Meet Lillian E Mills, the most innovative writer of her generation."

Lily was laughing; she looked happy; I'm always happy with her.

'I love you Jefferson.' she spoke so softly, and I knew she was hurting, so I kissed each hand in turn, 'OK Mr Howie,' she smiled, 'give it to Henry.'

I got down on my knees and held her hands,

'Thank you,' my voice was so soft I almost didn't recognise it, 'for making my life drunk.'

'Pleasure is all mine.' Her eyes were watering.

'*Non, c'est le mien.*'

I watched Lily through dinner. Captivated by her elegance, her sophistication, her precise posture. I am envious of the men who ogle her, intrigued how women admire her.

She is energized about Henry reading her Journal. She tells me there are other entries she didn't e-mail; fantasies she'd had about me; risks she'd taken to get close to me; I liked it; I wanted it; it aroused me. I know nobody like her.

I love her laughter. She laughs a lot, but in a shy demure manner. I have a feeling she doesn't like to show her teeth, but those teeth are wonderful; I've touched them and felt them traveling deliciously over my skin. They are strong and seamless. Just like her.

I'd arranged for a few luxuries to be set out in our room, a bottle of Tattinger, fresh strawberries with dipping chocolate, fresh oysters, and green queen olives. I poured us a drink and we tapped glasses. Lily eyed me over the rim of her flute; she is so incredibly beautiful and so deliciously gorgeous, I want to eat her.

She gushed over the room; how exquisite it is, and how she imagined staying somewhere like this with me.

'The kind of place Mr. Howie belongs.' She whispered.

'The kind of place you belong with me.' I took her hand and the strawberries and led her to the bedroom.

She pushed me back on a chair and circled me, provoking me wildly with lustrous eyes. Debussy played in the background and I could smell her perfume, but I wanted to smell her cunt.

'Let's be bad J?' she whispered putting down her drink, 'let's do something we'll always remember.'

'I remember everything.' I took her hand in an attempt to sit her on my knees, but she laughed and playfully withdrew.

With eager eyes, I watched her dip into her bag and take out a Polaroid camera. I swallowed; my cock bursting at the seams. She circled me again holding the camera; she handed it to me, lied against the desk, her glorious hair falling against the dark wood. She was laughing. *I love her.*

'Take a picture J,' she brought her head back up; her eyes directly on mine, 'be bad.'

'Strip for me,' it wasn't a request, 'lay back; open your legs. Wide.'

My dick hurt to be restrained so I unfastened my jeans and freed myself with a heavy sigh. I opened my legs, Lily had her mouth open, watching my dick throb to attention. She glared at me; pupils dilated; smiling, her lips wet from licking them. She is insatiable when it comes to my dick and balls. She'd eat them if she could.

She whipped off her vest and threw it at me; I caught it, put it to my nose and breathed in. Her breasts are ripe, her sexy nipples poking through the sheer fabric of a black bra. She turns around, I can see her reflection in the mirror, directing her ass my way. Carefully she unfastens her trousers, slipping them over her rear, the crevice divine through the chiffon of her panties; I want to fuck it.

She kicked off her trousers and staring at me in the mirror, she slipped her hand down the back of her panties and began rubbing the tiny bud between her ass. I took a photo. She hitched her panties to her thighs and opened her legs. I took another. Then she dipped a delicate finger into her cute kitty and began fucking herself. I took another photo. Then she smeared the juices between her ass and gently pierced the bud with her finger. She was in ecstasy. I was in *red* Heaven.

She began pumping her finger in and out of her ass, fast, then slow. I took a photo. I got to my knees, pulled open her cheeks and sucked at her ass hole; she cried out. I stuck my tongue in as far as I could; bad yes, but oh God, she makes me like this. She pushed me away; I was on my knees. She handed me champagne and I drank it; she drank too, then tipped it down herself, the bubbles trickling provocatively between her breasts and down into her belly button. I took a photo.

She unhooked her bra and threw it and her panties to one side. She was sitting on the edge of the dresser; arms back, legs up and wide open. I can see inside her gash; her white ecstasy juices. I got between her legs and licked it from her inner lips, swallowing with pleasure. She tipped champagne over her cunt and I lapped it like a dog.

I lay her scarf between her breasts and covered her cunt. Legs open, head back, breasts out. I took a photo. She nodded to the bowl of strawberries. I smiled, dipped one in chocolate and fucked her cunt with it. I ate the strawberry, satisfying a hunger and then dived in to ravish the chocolate around her hole. She bucked swiftly against my mouth, she wanted to come but I wouldn't let her.

I dipped my cock in the chocolate and ordered her get to her knees and forced it into her mouth; she took it. She sucks like no one I know, and I have to stop her; I fear I'm going to come. She got up and pulled the pink satin corset from her bag. I fastened it for her. I can see she's rubbing her clit in the mirror. She turned around, got to her knees and gazed up at me; her delicious breasts spilling over the top of the satin; her hair; Jesus, her hair, shaped around her face. I took a photo.

She took the camera and unexpectedly mounted me on the chair. I howled; there's violence in my voice as she fucks me; too late, my balls are too heavy, I'm coming, Holy fuck, I'm coming; oh Lily's withdrawn, she's on her knees, there's fresh sperm pumping from my cock, she's taking a photo. I lay back in the chair; delirious.

The only time I wish I was a woman is when it comes (excuse pun) to orgasms. I wish I didn't have to wait to get hard, even though with Lily it only takes a short time, but even a moment is too long when I want to fuck her. Of course it helps that Lily is genius with her lips and tongue, but it helps even more when you're watching your girl standing naked, save a suspender belt, one leg up on the Chaise Longe, fastening the belt to nylons. I take a photo.

'J?' she is dangerously innocent my Honey. 'Make love to me?'

I banged Lily against the desk. That's what she wanted. She wanted to watch me fucking her from behind in the mirror. She was getting off on it big time; I'd never seen her like this before; drooping eyes, open mouth, dribbling. I pulled out of her; my cock glistening with creamy, sweet smelling cunt juice, I turned her around, ripped open her legs, forced them down against the dresser and took her, making sure I was rubbing her clit just so, and believe me, she went off in seconds, I'd never seen her come like this before; all that built up passion and desire from our foreplay.

Oh, look at my Love, she's crying. I rock her in my arms and she squeezes me. I whisper over and over that I love her, I want her, that I need her, and she tells me I'm the most amazing man she's ever met.

Lily's washing my hair. I'm in the bath, her by my side; I can't describe this feeling.

'J?' she was washing the shampoo away with a sponge.

'Yes Lily?' I had my eyes closed, but I could see her in my minds eye.

'Do you mind if we talk?'

I reached for a towel and rubbed my eyes. I helped her in the bath and grasped her loosely between my thighs.

'I told him I'd fallen in love with someone.' She laid her head against my chest; I gripped her at the waist, 'I told him I never meant it to happen, but now it has, I can't live without that someone.' She sank deeper into me, 'he said he guessed something like that had happened.' She twisted slightly and we looked at each other, 'he wanted to know who it was.'

'Lily I'm so sorry.' Feeble I know, but I didn't know how else to help her.

'He asked me if I'd ever loved him,' she said, 'I had to tell him the truth, and I think that hurt him more.'

I tried to forget this was Luke we were talking about. My brother. My little brother. It made things slightly less painful.

'Lily, I need to tell him.'

'No,' she shot me a look, 'not yet, it's too raw.'

'He will find out, and soon.'

'I know.' She sounded upset, 'I just wanted this one night.'

I hugged her; rocking her in my arms; the water a blanket around our bodies,

'My unforgettable night with no ordinary redhead.' I whispered.

Lily giggled as she sank into me,

'You like my hair don't you J?'

'This hair,' I ran my nose through her wet hair and breathed in, mumbling into the auburn velvet, 'is like Heaven on Earth.'

'J?' she sounded surprised, 'you've never told me this before.'

'Ah Lily, you are smouldering auburn, a delightful vision that captures my breath everytime I see you. The allure in your eyes, the fire in your words, the passion in your voice, I want you, every damned bit of you; your delicious body to your genius brain, and it's so much stronger now than it was a year ago and much more complex, oh Lily,' she was sat astride me as I gazed up at her; her down at me; her eyes watering, 'I'm smitten with you. I love it that you're a free spirit in theory, my homebird in practice, I love running free with you, I don't want to abide by the usual rules, I want yours, your made up ones. I want to follow you... Lily?' I lay a hand on her face, 'run with me?'

'Yes.' She whispered.

As I took her mouth deeply, she mounted me. We didn't stop kissing all the time she was making love to me; yes, Lily making love and it's so delicious; so adoring. She came softly, panting tenderly through our kiss; we have never been like this before, I guess we're turning a corner, but I'm ready; ready for life, for this love, a love that makes life drunk.

60 Days

I took a photograph of Lily as she was sleeping. I have a friend, Jez, an artist whose niche is portraits, I'm going to ask him to commission one using this photograph.

After my unforgettable night with Lily, I left her outside her parents' house. I told her I'd ask the driver to stop a little down the road so we'd be out of sight, but she insisted I take her to the door,

'You're not my dirty secret Jefferson.' She winked.

I was relieved to hear it.

As we kissed goodbye, I felt her reluctance and I hope she sensed mine, but we immersed ourselves in the thought that tomorrow night we'd be back together; we had a party to attend.

As the cab pulled up outside my apartment block, I wasn't surprised to find a visitor sitting on the steps.

'Been waiting long?' I approached Luke, mindful that I had at least 10 extremely raw photographs of Lily in my bag.

'Bout an hour.' He looked like shite. 'Been away?' and he nodded to my bag.

'A bash in Brighton.'

When I'd finally turned my mobile back on after dropping Lily off, a barrage of phone calls awaited me; the burden of being the eldest son. First Luke. Then Mum, then dad about mum, then mum about dad, Luke again, then Jeremy.

'Just needed to talk to someone.' Luke threw himself on my sofa, 'she never loved me you know,' he said, 'not ever.' He tossed his head back and shut his eyes, 'for over a year, she never once loved me.' He turned to me sitting beside him, 'and then some fucking geezer turns up and she falls in love. How?' he shook his head, 'she must really fucking love this guy or something,' he shot me a look; I froze, 'I hope to fuck I never find out who it is.'

'At least she never lied about loving you.' I interjected.

'Thanks JJ, is that an attempt to make me feel better?'

'Sorry mate.' I got up, 'beer?' OK it was early, but I guessed he was going to be here for some time.

'Sure bro, why not.'

I listened to Luke for over two hours. Two solid hours of listening to him talk about Lily, and it hurt. It hurt more than I can tell you, because Luke didn't just talk about their relationship, he went into detail; vivid detail, even though I'd told him I didn't want to know.

'I even fucking stood by her when she thought she was up the duff,' there was anger in his voice now another hour had lapsed. 'I mean, come on, she forgot to take her Pill, how fucking careless is that.'

'Well maybe you should have kept your fucking dick in your trousers.' I retorted. 'You're responsible as well.'

He shrugged, reminiscence of the teenage Luke.

'Maybe.'

'No maybe about it, if you're old enough to fuck, you're old enough to face the fucking consequences.'

'OK, jeez, I was just saying.'

Official; he never deserved her; bitter or not.

'I understand you're feeling bad about all of this, but put it into perspective, yesterday you loved Lily, you respected her...'

'What a fucking waste of a year that was, all those birds I could have shagged.'

I wanted to put my fist through his head.

'Thank yourself lucky you had her at all.'

'What?' he frowned.

'You're fucked off because you've been dumped.'

'It's not just that,' he said, 'I loved her you know, really loved her.'

'You barely saw her.'

'It worked for us.'

'It obviously didn't.'

'Listen JJ, I know you're trying to help, but you don't know Lily like I do, her crazy ways and stuff, you don't know how it worked for us.'

'Maybe I don't.'

He sighed defeated, then slugged back his whiskey.

'Look, did she ever mention anything to you, you know, about this guy?'

'Nothing.' Even if he was being a prick, I was being a bigger one.

'And you honestly have no idea who it could be, not one of your fucking fancy writer friends you've introduced her to?'

'No.'

'And you didn't notice anything different about her?'

'No I didn't, she was just the same with me.' I gulped my whiskey, 'anyway, what good would it do knowing who he is?'

'Are you kidding JJ?' he laughed and a chill trickled down my spine, 'revenge is fucking sweet you know.'

My mobile started ringing. It was Mum.

'Where have you been!' I held the handset from my ear, 'your phone's been off all night.'

'Hi Mum.'

'Is he there with you?'

'Yes he's here.'

'Is he coming home?'

I looked at Luke,

'Mum says are you coming home today?'

He shook his head. He was pouring more whiskey.

'I'm crashing with JJ!' he shouted.

'Is that alright love,' Mum said, 'I'm worried about him, he's acting strange.'

'Dented ego Mum.'

Luke was steadily getting more pissed. He couldn't hear a word I was saying.

'I'm so sad about all of this, we all love Lily dearly, she's wonderful; she was part of the family.'

'Things happen for a reason,' I said in the hope of building a foundation for when this volcano erupts, 'no one's to blame.'

'No, I know, it's just that we'll miss her.'

I waited for Luke to pass out drunk on the sofa before unpacking my bag in the bedroom. I sat on the bed. I love these pictures. Every fucking one of them. I opened my bedside table, took out an envelope and slipped them inside, along with my lovely 3 year old Lily. I sealed it and slipped it inside my copy of *Catcher in the Rye.*

My clothes were drenched in Lily. I wanted to speak to her. I miss her terribly, yet remain haunted by visions of her and Luke in his Camper van on the beach; her and Luke in the toilets at the Electric Ballroom with someone banging on their door, of her and Luke on the kitchen table at that junkie pit she used to live in and my head pounded.

I went through to my office and switched on the PC.

To: jjhowie@msn.com
From: lily.mills@virgin.net
Subject: Everything with you is wonderful!

My lover; my J,

Less than ten minutes have passed since I left you and already I have to write. I know he's probably there with you now, so I can't even call you up, but I want to, I'm struggling to hold myself back.

Listen J, last night I reached new heights; relinquished new things – all because of you, because of how much I love you.
Please J, hold on, I know you might hear some things that may hurt, but I'm yours, all yours like I've never been anyone's girl before, and never again. Oh J, if you leave me now, I'll never love again, I know it, I couldn't, you've taken every single bit of me, I'm covered in Jefferson Howie; he burns inside me, deep inside me.

Parallels to Nin and Miller make me afraid Jefferson, like now, I'd usually be sitting at the PC writing my novel or my Journal, instead all I can think about is you, writing to you, and thinking about when I'll next see you, Oh J, you give me such a rush, an excitement I've never known before. I cannot lose you.

I have your photograph propped up against my bedroom lamp. Have I ever told you, you have the most beautiful eyes? Yes? I thought so, but you do.
I love you,
I love you,
I love you.
Lily Ellen xxxx

I wondered how long we'd have to keep this love a secret. See, I've been living the dream with Lily for almost 2 weeks now and OK, that isn't long, but as Lily said to me last night, if we consider my writing and her journal, our thoughts, our exchanges and our meetings, we've been together for just over 12 months, but now I'm tired of the hiding. I want to start making plans, yes, grown up plans, like asking Lily to move in with me, introducing her to my friends and acquaintances, going away for weekends, holidays, meals, parties, galleries, awards, lectures, everything "Jefferson" I want Lily at my side.

To: lily.mills@virgin.net
From: jjhowie@msn.com
Subject: 60 Days.

Lily Ellen, my love,

60 days. 60 days in Paris to be filled enjoying an espresso and a baguette (or a pink cup cake for *ma belle epouse*!), or a luscious red wine in a corner bistro on the Left Bank, sitting on the edge of the Seine in each other's arms...
60 days you ask? That's all we need to apply for a marriage license.

Lily, will you marry me?

I drifted off for a while in my chair; when I woke, my mobile was bleeping. I picked it up.

"Yes. I will marry you x"

Halle- fucking-lujah!

'Henry?' I balanced the phone beneath my chin, fighting the papers on my desk to get to Lily's journal.

'Jefferson, I've been trying to get hold of you.'

'I've been away,' I said locating it, 'Henry listen, I'm going to e-mail you something.'

'I don't have time for this Jefferson, you know that...'

'This is something you have to see, I beg you.'

'You, beg?' Henry laughed, 'this must be good; what is it?'

'Remember Lillian Mills from the Costa Book Awards?'

'What about her?'

'Well, I've read her work and she's amazing...'

'I'm not looking for another client at the moment...'

'Henry, I'm just asking you to cast an eye over it.'

He sighed; fucking agents, they're all the same.

'Just send me a few pages...'

'Done.'

After e-mailing several pages of Lily's work, I got on the phone to James Allen.

'Jefferson my friend.'

'James, how the devil?'

'Good, and how are things with you?' I know what he's referring to.

'Lily's with me now.' Is it cruel to smile through someone else's misery?

'Ah, I see.'

'James, can I ask a favour of you and Helena; it's quite a big one I'm afraid, just until I can get something sorted.'

'I'll help if I can.'

'Lily and I want to marry in Paris. We need a place to stay for a while until we can apply for a license.'

'Consider it done.'

So there you have it; that's how serious I am about Lily. I've asked her to marry me, and she's accepted. We want to do it in Paris, and we'll be staying at James and Helena's apartment in Montparnasse; what happens after that I have no idea, but one thing I am sure of, is neither my family or Lily's will be attending our wedding, but I guess that's their decision.

To: jjhowie@msn.com
From: lily.mills@virgin.net
Subject: Exile

J,

Quick note: Mum is furious. She found your photo in my room and she's angry at the way I'm brandishing it about. I told her I love you, and that I'll go anywhere with you. She said it would be over her dead body and that "a man like Jefferson Howie is no good for you" and I laughed and said "A woman like me is no good for a man like Jefferson; he is good, I am bad." This made her really angry. She called Livvy, but she already knows how much I love you. She says I can stay on the farm with her if things get difficult. Mum called us "scheming" but she's just hurt because for the first time in my life I didn't confide in her.

Listen J, when you marry me, can we do it on a boat cruising the Seine; can I wear white; will you wear your black suit? I can barely wait.
I love you
L xxxx

To: lily.mills@virgin.net
From: jjhowie@msn.com
Subject: Exile

Darling Lillian,

I am sorry for the grief you're having, but please don't give up on us. I'm here, desperate, waiting...

Ah, my Lily Ellen in white, I struggle to catch my breath at the thought, yes, I will wear black; I will sail along the Seine *avec mon epouse.*

Listen Lily, I've arranged for us to stay at James and Helena's apartment in Paris until we can apply to get married. I know this is huge for you, more than it is for me because of your family, friends and studies. I understand if you change your mind.

Lily Honey, I am happy to marry you wherever. I have visions in my head; they help me sleep. Lily, when Luke leaves, I will come for you.
I adore you,
J xxxx

Jeremy turned up as Luke was about to leave. I really didn't need this bullshit.

'So this is where you've been hiding?' Jeremy said.

'Hanging around with JJ is cool,' Luke grinned, nodding to the empty bottle of whiskey on the lounge table, 'he looks out for me don't you bro.' and he slapped me on the back.

I avoided Jeremy's gaze.

'Jeremy's right Luke,' I reasoned, 'you have to go back home sometime.'

'I'm cool.' Luke was calm; it was freaking me out, 'anyway, some of mum's tomato soup and I'll be back with the programme.'

After Luke left, I sat on the sofa with my face in my hands.

'Were you with Lily the other night?' Jeremy plonked himself beside me.

'Yes.' I uncovered my guilt.

'We were all trying to get hold of you.'

'I didn't want to be interrupted.'

'Jesus Christ Jefferson; she'd only just dumped him!'

'I don't care,' I stood up; the walls were starting to cave in around me; I just wanted to go to her. 'Look, it's done OK, I'm sorry it's happened like this and I feel like shite,' I glared at him, 'but I love her; I won't give her up.'

'Even though it'll kill mum and Luke to find out what really happened.'

'Mum will get over it and with Luke, it's just a young boy's ego.'

'You callous bastard.' He spat.

'Yeah, well, nothing new there then.' I stared out the window and took a deep breath. 'I don't expect anyone to understand or sympathise,' I turned to him; the sun was hurting my eyes, 'I am not taking this lightly. I didn't mean it to happen. Honest.'

Jeremy sighed; this burden was too much for him; I knew it would be.

'I'm trying to understand,' he said, 'I'm trying to see that you and Lily fell in love and you couldn't help it, and I do, really I do, but I'm struggling with the idea that for the past 2 weeks you've been sleeping with Lily knowing she was Luke's girlfriend for almost a year.'

'Well that makes two of us then.' I sat down and we looked at each other.

'So what now for you both?' he said.

'We're staying together,' I said firmly, 'we'll take each day as it comes; we're prepared for it to be difficult.' I shrugged.

Jeremy let out a sigh and covered his face with his hands,

'I feel like shit because I know,' he said dragging his hands down his face, 'I feel like shit because I could see what was happening months ago and never stopped it.'

'Believe me Jeremy,' I said, 'you wouldn't have stopped this happening.'

He managed a small smile,

'No, I suppose not, you both had that stupid "in love" gaze in your eyes the moment you met.'

I chuckled, but quickly turned a little more serious,

'I am in love with her Jeremy; I wouldn't do this and not believe this is where my future lies.'

He gazed at me,

'I know,' he nodded, 'so, will you guys just keep a low profile for a while?'

'I guess so.' I shrugged.

'In all honesty though JJ, you could wait a year to disclose this and it'll still receive the same hostility, bitterness and anger as if you tell them today.' He was right, of course. 'Anyway, I didn't come here to lecture you,' he seemed quite upset, 'it's just that it's all a bit surreal isn't it, you know, you and Lily...' our eyes locked, 'Christ,' he gasped, 'you're not going to run away together are you?'

I didn't answer.

To: jjhowie@msn.com
From: lily.mills@virgin.net
Subject: Paris

J, my love,

I'm so happy you've made arrangements with James and Helena for Paris; and please don't worry about me, I've already requested to defer my studies, I wrote the letter this morning. I see you as my future J, I'll do anything I have to, to make this happen, so please, make all the arrangements you need to, because I'm right here and I'm all yours, my beautiful Jefferson James.

Listen J, Luke text me, he wants to meet up but I said no. He says he's been staying with you and that he spent all night talking about me. I feel sick in the pit of my stomach at the thought of what he said. I can't help what I've done in the past, and I hoped you'd never have to hear those things, but J, please, I love you, my body is yours, everything I have is yours to share with me for a very long time.

I look forward to tonight when I can be with you again, having to stay away from you is unbearable, it hurts so much. Oh J, let's run away to Paris soon, very soon.
I love you wildly,
Lily Ellen xxxx

Ps. I have attached another chunk of my Journal for you to read.
PPs. Let's be bad tonight x

To: lily.mills@virgin.net
From: jjhowie@msn.com
Subject: My Lily

"[you] will always be the virgin-prostitute, the perverse angel, the two faced sinister and saintly woman"

I LOVE YOU. Thank you for being you. xxxx

Lily's "Happy Ever After"

This evening I love Lily more than I ever have, and tonight I'll be showing her my world, my little lady.

I'd arranged to collect Lily in a cab from her parent's house and right now her mum is eye balling me from the front door. I waved knowing she wouldn't wave back, and that's when I saw Lily, my darling girl, dressed in an outfit I am already imaging slipping off. She is so innocently sexual it's frightening.

I opened the cab door for her and we kissed briefly. I wanted to run my hands beneath the white, pink and red floral chiffon sat at her knees; to slip my fingers beneath the flimsy ruffled sleeves clinging provocatively to her delicate shoulders and arms. I want to tie her hands with the tantilising red ribbon beneath her breasts, but mostly, I want to fuck her wearing just these silver buckled sandals; I'm guessing Gucci, sexy and stylish yet extremely elegant.

'Evening J.' She winked.

I'm delighted she accepted my plea to buy her an outfit for this party.

'Good evening Lillian.'

As the cab pulled off, we launched into one of our deep sexy kisses. I ran my hand beneath the fragile fabric of her dress and raised her leg slightly so I could feel those buckles against me.

'I think...' she whispered running her mouth over my neck and to my ear, '... J likes what he sees.'

I closed my eyes at the feel of the heel rubbing my ankle.

'Oh indeed J does.'

Did I mention she has her hand on my tremendously stiff dick, rubbing it through my trousers? Actually, she's unfastening my zip, *Holy Jesus*, she's just slipped her hand inside my jocks. I closed my eyes, then opened them, the cab driver hadn't noticed. I haven't come since our night at Brown's; it could be messy,

'J?' she mumbled into my neck, 'when we get to the party, can we fuck?'

'Yes.' I gasped, 'please,' and as quickly as she'd started; she withdrew, leaving my balls aching so badly I didn't think I'd beable to walk.

'I've been imagining your sperm all day,' she winked, 'fantasizing about where I want it first; cunt, ass or mouth.'

Jesus; she makes my head spin.

'They'll be enough to fill all three.'

'Oh J,' I love this fever, 'my ass, please.' Ah yes, the reason I say what I do, because I love fucking this woman's neat ass; it's tight; it's lewd, it's the utmost in coition.

I have a finger inside Lily. Her dress has risen, and she's disguising our actions with her mirrored handbag. I gently withdraw my finger from her cunt and put it to my nose. We stare at it. She's urging me to taste, but I put it to her mouth instead and she closes her eyes and takes it.

'I will always be the virgin-prostitute, the perverse angel, the two faced sinister and saintly woman...' She's gazing at me rather intensely, '...and I love you.'

'And I love you.'

The party is being hosted by an acquaintance of mine from the Arts Council, Tobias Long-Fry. I've worked with him for almost ten years and yet we still only meet at parties. Tobias is forty five; married to Fleur and they have two children: Adela and Arabella. They live in a huge manor house near St Albans and the party is a "thank you" to all those involved in the ongoing development of Cuckoo Farm; it's also for the benefit of the Press to generate further promotion; pure Long-Fry.

As Lily and I walked the steps to the front door, I could already hear the chit chat of socialites. I grabbed two glasses of Champagne from a passing tray and spilt a little down my white shirt. I wiped it away. Lily was holding my hand tight. There is a limit to her confidence, and mine.

I saw Joe and he waved us over.

'Jefferson old man,' He shook my hand, but he wasn't looking at me, 'and Lily.' He announced as though she was an old friend, 'good to see you again.'

'Hello Joseph.' Lily's hair is completely radiant against the luster of her dress, immaculately parted in the centre with slight curls around the bottom; she is like a pre-Raphaelite painting; she is Francesca to my Paolo. 'Good to see you too.'

'He must have bribed you.' Joe chuckled; 'to be seen out with him in public.'

Lily laughed gently,

'I think I bribed him,' she squeezed my hand, 'what woman wouldn't want to be seen out with Jefferson?'

I grinned at Joe and he shook his head at me,

'Jammy bastard.' He was drunk.

'Jefferson Howie.' Florence. 'How the devil?'

Florence is older than Joe by five years. She is a well bred Chelsea girl; with an attitude to match.

'Florence,' I said kissing her hand courteously, 'how was Portugal?'

'Good thank you Jefferson.' She was staring at Lily despite having met before. 'Lily isn't it?' I think she's checking her out; I'm not surprised.

'Lily goes out with Jefferson's brother remember?' Joe added "helpfully".

'Not anymore.' I chipped in before this went any further.

'Oh, I see,' Florence raised a judgemental eye; I loathe it when people do that, 'well, they do say "keep it in the family".' And she did that awful goddam guffaw.

Lily was uncomfortable. I could feel it. She was trying to break free of my hand but I wouldn't let her. Her eyes pleaded with an unfamiliar frown; she's loathes these people as much as I do.

'Good for you,' That was Joe's attempt to laugh off his wife's inappropriate but unfortunately usual attitude, 'well done Jefferson,' he nudged me, 'lucky you.'

'Lucky you?' Florence glared at her husband, 'I think you should make that your last one, don't you?' And she nodded to his almost empty glass of what smelt like whiskey.

Lily tugged on my hand again. I was not going to let her go.

'Jefferson?' she said firmly under her breath, 'do you mind?'

I let her go; helplessly watching her stride across the room towards the garden.

'She dumped him then?' Joe whispered in my ear as Florence talked to Tobias, 'for you?'

'It wasn't as sleazy as that Joe.'

'I bet it was,' he laughed, 'you've been screwing your brother's girlfriend, and look at her Jefferson, she's just a girl.'

I looked at a man I used to call my friend; he wasn't usually this obnoxious, maybe Florence was right, maybe he should make that his last drink.

'Lily is a woman; an intelligent, innovative and beautiful woman.'

'I take it Luke doesn't know about the "love triangle"?' he grinned.

'No.' I was losing patience.

'Mads is here you know.' Joe nudged my arm again, 'steer clear,' he leaned into me, 'a woman scorned.'

That was all I needed.

I made my way through the room, nodding and smiling to acquaintances until reaching the garden. Lily was sitting alone on a stone bench watching the fountain. I observed her from a distance.

This is unlike her; she doesn't get fazed by ignorance and arrogance; she rises above it, but tonight, well, I guess this whole situation is taking its toll.

'Lily honey?' I sat down beside her. There were candles dotted around the garden, folk sitting at tables drinking champagne and eating canapés. It was a warm night with a slight breeze. Lily's hair blew gently; her curls make her an angel. She looked at me, 'I'm sorry about Joe, he's pissed, and Flo, well, I can't apologise for her, she's always that awful.'

She smiled and took my hand,

'It's not that J,' I could see the candlelight in her watery eyes, 'I just feel bad that's all.'

We hugged and I buried my face into her hair and breathed in. As long as I have her, this life will remain as wonderful as when she holds me.

'Lean on me Lily,' I whispered stroking her hair, 'let me look after you.'

She sank her forehead into my cheek; her nose rubbing gently against the tip of mine; I love this intimacy; I wouldn't dissolve it for anyone.

'One day they'll all forget about this won't they?' She said softly.

'I hope so.'

She nodded; her eyes dropped to her feet,

'They will try and break us won't they?'

'If I were a betting man....' I couldn't lie.

'Then I'm sorry for them,' She raised her head until our eyes were level, 'that they'll never feel like this.'

I smiled; that's my Lily Ellen.

'They'll never know what it feels like to be drunk 24/7.'

Lily started laughing; I love her laughter; her happiness; I need it.

'My J,' she rested a hand on my cheek, 'a man who makes life drunk...'

'Lily, be bad with me?'

She smiled; now I'm really talking her language,

'Toujours.'

I've been watching Lily from across the room for some time. After screwing her in Tobias' bathroom (one of five I'll add), she appears to have come out of herself. She's enjoying talking to new people, laughing and listening, but frequently catching my eye and winking.

'Who. Is. That?' Joshua Dunbar, Journalist with the Daily Telegraph sidled up to me like the sleaze he is, 'what a scorcher.'

I turned to him, but Lily caught my eye again; we smiled; she was in conversation with Grace Oswald, a lecturer at Kings College.

'That is Lillian Mills.'

'Hey,' he nudged my arm, 'looks like you're in there.'

'I hope so,' I grinned with pleasure, 'she's my fiancée.' I nodded, and left him to pick up his jaw from the ground.

Someone took my arm, it was Joe again,

'I've been trying to think who she reminds me of.'

'Who?' I grabbed another passing glass of champagne.

'Your Lily.' He nodded over to her; I looked at him; leering, 'the naked redhead you've got stuck on your fridge.'

I glared at him; I couldn't decide whether to laugh and agree, or put my fist through his mouth, instead I walked away shaking my head.

Despite the hiccups at the beginning, the evening was turning out to be quite splendid. Lily has succeeded in making acquaintances for herself, and with that, her confidence has soared; I am proud to say I'm with her, and not just because she's beautiful.

I left Tobias by the French doors and headed back inside to find my lady, and that's when I saw it; Lily with Madeleine.

I kept my distance and observed. Lily is so effortlessly elegant, so beautiful, and so gracious as she smiles and nods, humouring a woman I know is out to cause trouble; but I have no desire to hear the content of their conversation; I know Lily isn't fazed by petulance; she abhors it and I feel safe in her love; I have no insecurities, we will continue to be tested, that is the down side of our fate.

'Champagne Mr. Howie?' Lily was back at my side; she is buoyant.

'Thank you Honey,' I tapped her glass with mine and slipped my arm around her waist as we gazed stupidly at each other, 'you are so incredibly beautiful Lillian.'

'Thank you Jefferson,' she appeared a little taken back; she shouldn't be, I tell her everyday. 'It's because you make me so happy.'

I swallowed, pleased with myself, and she grinned, showing her teeth; those lovely teeth, for the first time, no longer shy.

'Lily?'

'Yes J?'

'I love these teeth,' I clasped her jaw between my fingers, and she started laughing,

'I know you do,' she smiled, 'the bites mark down your back and between your thighs are testimony to it.'

She had me now.

'Not unlike the bite marks on that luscious ass of yours then Miss Mills.'

Yes, I confess; I can't help myself when it comes to Lily's buttocks; they are so damned peachy; so delicious, I have to bite them, either playfully when we're lying together, or as I'm fingering her ass hole; it makes her come in seconds flat; no kidding, it's astounding.

Madeleine caught my eye as I drew Lily close to me. I shut my eyes to avoid her gaze; impossible.

'I thought I should come over and say hello since you've been avoiding me Jefferson.'

'Hello Madeleine.' I said with firm politeness.

'Lily was just telling me you're going on a trip to Paris.'

'That's right.' I grimaced, holding Lily tight to me.

'Well bravo,' Madeleine raised an eye at me; it was fair to say she was pissed off, 'it seems you take great pleasure in fucking two people over for the sake of your dick,' I wished this woman would disappear, but I'd let her say her piece if it made her feel better, 'your own brother Jefferson, tut tut,' I hate that malicious smirk, 'wouldn't it be a great shame if he was to accidentally find out about your surreptitious behaviour.'

I watched with vomit in my throat as she waved over her shoulder. I simply couldn't discount anything where that woman's contempt was concerned.

'I'm sorry about that,' I sighed, 'she's well, let's say, not taking the news too well.'

Lily smiled,

'You're wicked Jefferson Howie, do you know that?'

'But you love me right?' I said softly.

'I love you left and right.'

Lily and I wanted to spend the night together. We knew it was a risk; Luke was still at large, and the possibility of him turning up was fairly great, but still I helped her into the cab, and still I kissed her outside my apartment. We held hands to the front door, and we kissed again on entering. We went to the bedroom, undressed each other, made love, and fell asleep, and I woke in her arms a little while later.

'James and Helena will be in Paris the week after we arrive,' I said playing with her beautiful hair, 'it's quite a spacious apartment, so we'll still have plenty of time alone, don't you worry.'

'J, after we're married, what would you like us to do?' Lily was propped up on one arm looking at me, 'would you like to come back to London? Stay in Paris? Buy a country house, have chickens and eat scrambled egg?'

We laughed, but I sensed a degree of seriousness in her last option. I know she's keen for tranquility and that she adheres to her sister's life, but she remains vague about what she really wants from life.

'What would Lily like?' I said.

'You always turn it back to me.' she laid out on her back; glorious hair tumbling over the white pillow and my shoulder.

'That's because Lillian, you are the most important person in this relationship.'

'No I'm not,' she sat up; she seemed surprised.

'Yes you are.' I smiled, 'Lily, I'm thirty eight soon, I've done so much and seen so much, now it's your turn; I want to do whatever you want.'

She leaned over and kissed me; such divine perfume.

'Why?'

'Because I'm in love with you.'

She's studying me. Usually I loathe it when people study me, I don't want them second guessing my thoughts, it's too frightening, too personal, but with Lily, her eyes are soft and candid, she's not trying to work me out, she just muses.

'Can I tell you something?' Her voice is melodious; I sense the mood she's in.

'Of course.'

'I'd prefer to write it down if you don't mind.'

'There's a pen and paper in the drawer.' And I nodded to the bedside table.

When I woke, the sun was oozing through the slats in the blinds. Lily was asleep. She was lying in my arms, head on my chest, her arms around my waist, legs thrown over mine. With care, I unfurled her arms and slipped from the bed. She shifted about slightly, quickly silenced once becoming comfortable in the fetal position. The urge to cry is growing familiar.

Pulling on a pair of joggers, I sat on the edge of the bed. I pulled my hands through my hair then rubbed my eyes. I don't know what time we fell asleep last night, but it was late. I got up and closed the blinds tighter, then stroked Lily's hair amorously, noticing the papers on her bedside table. I picked them up. There were quite a few of them. Taking them, I went to the kitchen and started to read.

"Lily's happy ever after."

"J, I'm telling you this because you are the only person in this life I trust.
See, I'd been wondering for some time what would happen if we collided. Would it just be immense sex or "quelque chose beau". J, it is both.

Jefferson, when I think of you, I see a refined and elegant gentleman. When I read you, I think the same. Your writing inspires me as much as you, the man. Our relationship is based on the passion of our writing, our animalistic fucking, our exquisite love making, the intense way we talk to each other, the beautiful way we perceive and believe in each other, and so J, the following extract is a girl's dream, this girl's dream, completely uncensored. Forgive me."

I'm not proud of myself for falling in love with my boyfriend's brother. No one sets out to hurt people, which is why I believe with even more fervent that I, Lillian Ellen Mills, belong to Jefferson James Howie. This is the reason I strayed, the reason why I will marry him.

With J, I am myself; I am free, but caught, I am wild, but tamed. J runs with me and I love that. He talks of following "my rules", which I find endearing, because our rules are exactly the same, it says so in our work. People will dig at the disparity of our ages, but they fail to see it makes this relationship so rich and gracious.
J lets me fuck in any way I like without question; he is so like me. We need each other. We want each other, and I thank God we have each other.

From the moment I met him, my heart was never the same. My passion was fuelled, my sexual yearning, inescapable. I lapsed into a fever, sometimes I couldn't breathe in his presence, fearing I'd die if he didn't touch me, if I didn't touch him.
With J, this craziness makes sense. For years we were apart, for years we didn't know each other, for years Lily yearned for Jefferson, and he hungered for her. How can that be wrong now that they have found each other?

J, listen, when we marry, I will wear white. Satin, like a ballet dancer. I will be graceful, demure and beautiful. I will look up when we take our vows and see a man I will grow old with.
Take my hand J, glide a ring on my finger, and let me be "Lillian Howie" for life, but always your "Lily Ellen" in bed.
I loved it when you said,
"When I write about you, I will have to write about you as an angel. I cannot put you on a bed." (Miller)
And you love it when I quoted you back as I prepared food for us in your kitchen,
"Let me play at being the wife of a genius." (Nin)
Well, I don't have to play anymore.

J I have contemplated Paris, of living in the city, where we can fulfill our lives as perverse lovers fucking in alley ways, drinking

red wine in restaurants, dancing in the streets in a red dress and no panties, sleeping between pink satin sheets.
I have thought about espresso and croissants every morning, of roaming the café quarter with you, of talking, reading, writing; going to the ballet, the opera, and art galleries.

I have thought about a house in Louveciennes, sentimental over a love affair that happened over 70 years ago, but then I'd be living out someone else's life. A life that perhaps doesn't suit me or you. A life that belongs to the two people who brought us together, but whose destiny was so different to ours.

I have thought of London. Of your apartment, of me moving in, of us making a life in Covent Garden, but I'm not sure a London bachelor hub can accommodate 3 children and a wife!
J, listen carefully now. I will go anywhere with you, do anything for you. I want to make you happy always, but you asked me "what does Lily want?" Well J, Lily dreams of this:

Of a house in a field. A house made of reclaimed brick. A house with a farmhouse door and a fireplace to accommodate a huge roaring fire for cosy autumn/winter days and nights. A home brimming with our books; shelves filled with our work, of muddy shoes by the back door after a walk in the hills, of seeing our breath in the air as we return on a frosty day. Of seeing you wrapped up, of feeling your hand in mine.

J, I dream of a home. Our home, where I can look out of the windows and see trees and sky; breath in fresh air, feel alive, run free! A place where I can write beside you, or be near you. Where we can hide away in our "High Place". I dream of a boudoir bedroom brimming with texture: fur, cashmere, velvet, cotton, and chiffon. I dream of that way you look at me everytime you see me.

Oh J, I dream of sex. Of brutality. Of exploration, of experimenting further with you; breaking new ground, pushing the boundaries, just you and me.

I want a garden. A field. I want trees and flowers; I want good wine and fine foods. I want to cook, I want to sit down with you and clink glasses, smiling as you open another bottle because we haven't finished talking. Of you laying me out on a fur rug infront of a blazing fire and making love to me. Of candles in the bath, of baking bread and scrambled egg in the kitchen, of cooking on an Aga, of feeling autumn leaves billowing carefree around my face as I collect eggs for us. Of washing your hair in the bath, of watching you sleep by my side, of making you happy.

I see myself with you at prestigious Awards, at dinner parties, pretentious Mayfair parties, on breaks in London Hotels, decadent weekends in Paris dressed elegantly by Chanel, Prada and Valentino. Of having friends to stay with us. Of birthdays, of Christmas'. I dream of a real Christmas tree with twinkling lights and silver stars and us opening presents before breakfast.

Oh J, I dream of a life with you, so ask me that question again, "what does Lily want?", Well Lily dreams of all of the above, but would feel just as rewarded to have you, just you, just us, for a very long time."

Exile

After reading Lily's beautiful testimony, I needed to go out urgently; so I left a note on her bedside table as she slept. When I arrived back the apartment was empty; Lily's belongings had disappeared, only a cup by the sink and my note were evidence that she'd been here at all.

I picked up my mobile. I'd forgotten to take it with me. There were several missed calls, all from Lily. I put down the small gift bag and sat down on the sofa. A strange uneasiness surrounded me.

'Umm, J,' Lily's message sounded a little weird, 'I, umm,' and she was crying, 'look, I never said anything to him, I thought it was you at the door so I answered it, I'm really sorry,' she was sobbing, 'I just forgot...' she hiccupped; there was bile in my throat, 'he knows, not sure how, but he was so mad, going fucking crazy at me...J, I'm going away for a while, but I love you; always love you...'

I shut my eyes as my head hit the back of the sofa. I swallowed vomit. I got up. I needed to find him. To explain. I left the apartment. My mum thought I'd lost my head as I barged in asking "is he here?" Then to World's End, that place he hangs out, then to Jeremy's, to Ben's, to Daniel's, nothing. He had completely disappeared.

I dragged my sorry ass back to the apartment. I was going to Lily. She didn't say where she was, but I had a fair idea. I ran upstairs to find my door had been forced open. I took a breath and stepped inside.

'You fuck!' he grabbed me, thrusting me back against the wall, I slumped to the floor trying to get up, but he climbed on me, Jesus Christ, he had one hell of a whack on him; my specs fell to the floor. 'I trusted you, you're my brother for fuck's sake, you're a liar, an absolute fucking liar!'

Fuck, he smashed me in the side of the face, my cheek burned. I hurled him back by his jacket and he collapsed face down. I grabbed him by the ankle, but he jumped up and hit me in the mouth with his foot, I touched my lip, blood, a fair bit of it too.

'Luke listen to me, I...' Holy Christ, right in the eye, I slumped to the floor, my head sore from where I'd fallen the first time; my eye was throbbing, 'just let me explain...'

Luke stood over me. His face was raw. I couldn't remember seeing him like this before.

'You and your whore,' he threw something at me, photos, loads of them tumbling all over me, 'deserve each other.'

'Don't call her a whore.' I managed to sit up; I wiped the blood from my nose, it covered my sleeve.

'From those photo's, she's nothing but your dirty whore. I wouldn't want her after seeing those.'

I grabbed his leg, yanking him down and leapt on him, I was beating him around the face and ears. He turned me over, walloping me in the stomach. I was gulping for air, he let me go, both of us breathless, a mass of blood and cuts. I caught sight of 3 year old Lily. *I love her; I love her madly.* He's hurt, but I won't let him say those things about her.

I dived at him again, punching him in the stomach, he curled up, I went to him, I didn't want this, he smashed me in the face with his knee catching my chin, I slipped down the wall, slumped in a heap, he stumbled to his feet and spat on me,

'Brother?' he wiped the blood from his mouth; it was all over the floor, 'I wouldn't piss on you if you were on fire.' I watched from the ground, grasping my stomach as he snatched the cup and launched it at the kitchen wall. It shattered into a thousand fragments. 'I know about the e-mails too; I know about everything.'

I lay down and closed my eyes. I heard the door slam; I flinched. Somehow I managed to drag myself to the sofa. The gift bag was still on the table. I pulled it to the floor and the red velvet box tumbled out. I opened it. The single diamond solitaire, distorted through salty water.

I looked at what I was clutching in my other hand. A picture of Lily. 3 year old Lily. *My Lily.* I grasped that and the ring to my chest and slumped back down, sobbing like a child, curled up as tight as I could, and if I never take another breath, I will never regret my time with her.

I sat beside my suitcase on the bed and dried my hair with a towel, careful to avoid the tender areas, and believe me, there were plenty of them. I couldn't believe it had happened like this. I just wanted to explain. To try and spare him just a little pain if that was possible. Who was I kidding, as far as brothers go, I'd committed the ultimate betrayal. I know Luke, he won't forget and he'll probably never forgive.

Before showering I tried to call Lily but her mobile was switched off. I didn't leave a message. I wondered what Luke had said to her; how he'd done it; did he hurt her? I know of course who told him, I knew by the look in her eyes last night that she'd been serious. Joe was right; a woman scorned and all that. Anyway, I'm not trying to say I didn't deserve it, I just think Luke and Lily should have been spared. Madeleine was my mistake, not theirs.

Tying the towel around my waist I finished packing my case. I wasn't sure whether Lily still wanted me after what had happened, I was quite sure she would, but even so, in the light of everything, I wasn't confident.

I inspected my face in the mirror. I had one hell of a shiner. The purple bulge on my cheek didn't look too clever either, not to mention the split lip. My ribs were sore and I was sure they'd be plenty of bruising over the next few days, and when I'd been drying my hair, I found a lump at the back of my head. I guess I got what I deserved; I'm not looking for sympathy.

I placed the photos in my case. I didn't want anyone touching them again. He'd found all the e-mails too, the ones I'd printed off to use in my writing, even the ones about getting married in Paris, so when Luke said he knew everything, he really did.

I called home and Dad answered; when I asked to speak to Mum, he said she wasn't feeling well and was having a lie down. Mum didn't "*do*" lying down.

'JJ, it's a little difficult at the moment...umm, your brother's just come back and well...look, call later OK.'

'Dad?'

'Yes JJ?'

'I'm sorry.' I swallowed.

'I think deep down son, we all knew what was happening, we all could have stopped it.'

'No dad, nothing could have stopped it.'

After lacing my trainers, I took my case and headed to the lounge. The gift bag was on the table. I hesitated for a moment, then took the box from the bag and slipped it into my pocket. I folded "*Lily's Happy Ever After*" and slid it into the front of my case.

It was raining. It started just after I got out of London. I wasn't sorry to see the back of the city, these days I never was.

I was thinking about Lily's Journal. Her masterpiece. I was thinking about a lot of things. I turned the radio down in favour of the rain. I love listening to rain, like Lily loves tuning into storms, even though she's afraid of them.

It was dark. I wondered if Lily would come for a drink with me, or whether she'd prefer to stay at home. I'll do whatever she wants. I'm hers now; I belong to her.

I saw signs for Stow. I carried on down the road and into the countryside again, following the same route I did for her 25th birthday party.

The rain was grave. It was difficult to see. I thought I saw something in the road. I slammed on the breaks; it was nothing. The car behind me sounded its horn, I carried on. Adrenalin pumping.

I turned right onto a dirt track. I could see lights ahead. Lights I anticipate will take me to Lily. I got closer. The lights more vivid. There was smoke coming from the chimney. It warmed me. I pulled up outside the gate and steered my car to where there was a space. It was still raining. Someone was standing at the door but I'd turned off my lights. I ran to the door. It was Livvy.

'Is she here?' I was soaking, but the rain was a comfort. 'I need to see her, please Livvy?'

'I couldn't stop you even if I wanted.' She had a compassionate, accepting smile as she opened the door for me. There were muddy shoes on the mat. I smiled. *I love her so much.*

I took off my specs and dried them on my shirt. It felt like I hadn't seen Lily for days and yet this morning we were laying in each others arms. So much had happened since then.

'Come in Jefferson,' Livvy smiled as I brushed the wet hair from my face, 'I'll get the little lady for you.'

I smiled, hovering awkwardly beside the dining table. I took off my tank top. It was wet.

'Nasty eye you got there,' Livvy's husband Tom nodded to my face, 'need it seeing too?'

I shook my head; it throbbed.

'It'll take care of itself thanks.'

I can't explain how it felt seeing Lily again; to know she still wanted me, and by instinct I held my arms out and she ran to me, she actually ran to me, so I picked her up and she wrapped herself around me. I sat her on the edge of the table; she was crying. I tried to swallow mine, but I couldn't.

'You came,' she whispered; ours noses touching, her hands on my face, mine on hers. We kissed, my lip stung; I didn't care for pain. 'I couldn't be sure.'

'Wild horses.' And I smiled.

'I'm so sorry,' Lily ran a gentle finger over my lip, my cheek, my eye. I flinched, wincing with pain. 'I want to make you better.'

'You already have.'

I slid a tear from her cheek with my thumb then took her mouth. Wholly. Pain and all. I wallowed in her saliva, comforted by its sweetness. I ran my tongue over her teeth, her chin, her neck. She sighed and held it back for me. I breathed in her perfume, it reminds me of infinity.

'J?' She whispered.

'Yes Lily?' I rested my forehead against hers and closed my eyes; I'm so tired, I just want to fall asleep with her.

'I never got the chance to ask what you want from life.'

My head is drowsy against hers, but she's holding me up. I feel secure in her love. I will not let go.

'A house in a field...' I rasped, *'A house made of reclaimed brick. A house with a farmhouse door and a fireplace to accommodate a huge roaring fire...'*

Lily was stirring home made soup on the Aga, vegetable soup she told me Livvy had made yesterday from the vegetables grown on their land.

'So, Lily dreams of an Aga?' I was sitting at the well used rustic dining table when Lily turned and grinned at me. She is so beautiful, and so authentic in those jeans and sexy pastel yellow vest revealing gorgeous breasts and dainty shoulders.

'J is laughing at me.' She smiled still stirring.

'Not at all,' I got up; I had to touch her, 'until this moment I couldn't really place you here.' I wrapped my arms around her tiny waist, leaning my head against hers. I love sinking into her, she's warm and safe. 'Now I can't see you anywhere else.'

'Sorry to interrupt,' we turned to see Livvy standing in the doorway of the kitchen; I held Lily tighter, 'we're off to bed now; the fire's still going, can you make sure the guard's on before you come up?'

'Of course.' I answered for us.

Livvy smiled; she understands. She's probably the only one who does.

'Goodnight both.'

'Night Liv.' Lily said.

And I put my hand up to say goodnight. Tom nodded to us as he followed his wife and I did the same.

Lily had prepared chunks of crusty bread for the soup, and as we sat together, we started to talk.

'Debussy?' I smiled as we listened to the music. 'I'm impressed.'

'See how much you've influenced me J?'

'So Lily,' the soup was delicious, 'tell me about your "happy ever after"?'

She looked up, spoon midway to her mouth,

'Well,' she mused, putting her spoon down, 'it's just that, this is a home you know, it's real, a bona fide home with depth and texture, with everything out of place, it's like organised chaos, oh I don't know,' she sighed, 'I struggle to put it into words.'

'I've bought a book for you.' I reached into my case and carefully took it out, ensuring it remained flat.

'There's a marker in it,' I handed her the "*Letters of Anais Nin and Henry Miller*", 'open it Honey.' I whispered.

I watched uncertainly as she opened the book. I swallowed as she picked up the diamond ring between her fingers; she was trembling. I pulled the chair back, and got to my knees,

'Lillian,' I felt a little foolish, but her smile soothed me, she doesn't think I'm stupid, dirty or a cheat, she sees me in a way I'm not sure I wholly deserve: a genius, refined, elegant; but she makes me those things and I so badly want to be them, 'will you marry me?'

Her eyes were watering, but she was nodding,

'Yes I will.'

I took the ring and tenderly slipped it onto her finger,

'Believe me when I say this will never break.' I squeezed her hands between mine, 'Stay close to me Lily, and I promise I will make it beautiful.'

Her arms swathed me. It hurt as I sank into her, but she alleviates my pain.

'You do realise by doing this we're committing ourselves to a lifetime of exile.' She whispered.

'I embrace it.'

I love Lily's laughter.

'I love you J.'

'Lily Ellen,' I put my hand on her face, 'your allure is addictive, don't ever change.'

'Jamais,' her French is delicious, 'Never.' Her English, just as charming.

Lily's hair is beautiful as she hovers above me. I can see the flames from the fire in her eyes as she lays me out, cautiously lifting my arms so she can remove my t-shirt. I close my eyes; I'm struggling to breathe as she runs her dainty finger tips over my chest.

She takes a nipple into her mouth, flicking it with her tongue, dragging her teeth over them in turn. My dick is straining for freedom; her sexy allure is exhilarating. She tugs on the zip of my trousers, drawing them and my jocks to my thighs. My cock springs free and she smiles. I have no idea what she wants to do with me. She is in control. It's how I want it.

She kisses me; sweet Lily Ellen kisses across my ribs, nurturing the bruises, healing me. She travels articulately to my navel. Her mouth hovering over my dick; it's throbbing. It wants her. I want her. Instead she looks at me, leaning over my partial nakedness and tenderly kisses the contusion around my eye. She laps at it, kisses it, runs her mouth over it. It's sexual agony; I want to fuck her, but this adoration, this love, prohibits me, oh I worship her.

She licks the cut on my lip and kisses me, then my cheek, doing the same. I'm motioning beneath her. I feel like a woman seduced by a man,

'You are a sexual angel,' I whisper, 'you are wonderful.'

'Would you like me to behave like an angel?' her mouth is running gently down my chin to my neck; I lay it back further; she takes it.

'You are forever the *two-faced sinister and saintly woman* and I love you.'

The flames snarl as Lily removes my clothes. She remains fully dressed over my nakedness but I feel no vulnerability in her care. She has her head between my thighs, her auburn halo spilt across my groin like glowing embers. I touch it, rub my fingers through it. I groan as she takes my balls into her mouth and holler as she pries open my ass with her finger and effortlessly fucks me, for she is immense at this.

She releases my balls, biting my thighs, this wouldn't be the first time I've come without her touching my cock; it's insane. Oh Christ, oh no, I am, it's coming. She stretches back my foreskin and I manage to raise my head to see sperm spurting from the tip, dribbling down my shaft like hot lather. Lily laps at it, loving it; I feel like I'm going to cry.

It oozes from her mouth as she gazes back at me, I wrench her over me and take her mouth licking every corner, eating my own come from her lips, oh I want it, every bit of it.

I sit up with her astride me; I can't help this brutality; it engulfs me. I rip off her vest and devour her breasts, biting down on her nipples as she begs me to stop, I shove her back, pull off her jeans and panties, slam open her legs and fuck her cunt with my mouth. She thrusts up to meet me, my *perverse angel, my virgin-prostitute.*

Her arms lay above her head, I'm holding them there; I want to be hard again, solid, so I can fuck her. Instead I turn her over onto all fours; the fire blazing beside us, we are sinners in hell.

I pull her buttocks apart and assault her ass hole; licking, biting, jutting my tongue in and out. I stick a finger in her kitty, whilst fucking her ass with my tongue. I'm hard again, I turn her over; she opens her legs wide, her chest is red, her nipples ripe and sharp. I plunge into her and she hollers, arching her body in pleasure, I fuck her cunt and don't stop until she's coming, feverishly coming, and as we collapse, sweat slicked and breathless, we look at each other, and she grins wickedly,

'Jefferson,' she pants, 'you are one hell of a fuck.'

And I laugh, because I was thinking exactly the same about her.

I'm lying in bed with Lily thinking how much I like this room, it's endearing; it's very Lily Ellen. I think it's the beams on the slanted ceiling and the low cottage like window.

'This is a cute room.' I said.

'You think so?'

There is a sheet of delicately embroided muslin concealing us from the outside darkness, the only light is a string of flower shaped fairy lights draped around the window.

'Cute like you.' and I snuggled into her, making her giggle.

Furniture is sparse. A wardrobe, a chest of drawers and a desk fitted into the corner. I love this bed though, with its harsh iron wrought head rest, and bulky white duvet covered in pink butterflies, shielding us from the countryside chill. Lily has her legs thrown over mine, she does that a lot and I love it, it shows she's comfortable with me, that she trusts me.

I turn to her; she's smiling at me, now she's giggling again making the bed tremble, it's all very cute. I roll her over, and she wraps her heavenly body around mine.

'How does it feel to be in exile?' I kiss her neck, she's sensitive; it makes her giggle more; she warms me immensely.

'I'm using this time to be incredibly selfish with you.' we rubbed noses like some innate mating ritual. 'But seriously, I feel relieved.'

'Did Luke hurt you?'

She shook her head,

'I think he was in shock more than anything,' she said, 'he pushed me a little, then he went crazy, searching drawers and stuff, I tried to stop him, but I couldn't, I'm not sure whether he found anything...'

'I'm afraid he did.'

I saw her swallow,

'The photos?'

I nodded,

'And the e-mails.' I propped myself up on one arm, 'now you can see why he almost bludgeoned me to death.'

'Oh my God,' she gasped, 'I'm so sorry Jefferson.'

'I've no regrets.'

I took her hand, pressing my palm against hers. It's so demure against mine; I love it. I dragged my fingers down hers, a fingertip grazing her engagement ring.

'Lily, talk to me?'

There were tears in her eyes as she stared at our hands,

'Mum won't speak to me and Dad wants to but he thinks he's betraying mum,' she dabbed her eyes with the duvet. 'She says she's disgusted by my behaviour.'

I held her head to my chest and embraced her, rocking her until her body eased and sank into mine.

'Mum's disowned me too.' I smiled as she glanced up at me,

'This is my fault Jefferson...'

'No Lily,' I was firm, 'this is the sort of thing people do when they're hurt, like this,' and I pointed to the carnage on my face. 'Lily, I want you to come back to London with me.'

'I thought you might.' She left my arms and laid on her back, drawing the butterflies up to her neck, 'I'm afraid to go back,' she turned to look at me, 'I don't have anywhere to go, I've deferred my studies, I've probably lost my job, my friends are junkies and now I'm relying heavily on you.'

'I want you to rely on me, we're getting married for God's sake.'

'I know, but, you've got to understand this is new to me, and as much as I want it, I still need to adjust.'

'Lily, the reason we need to go back to London is because I'm going to sell the apartment.' She shot me a look, 'if we want our house in the field, the one with reclaimed brick and a huge fireplace, then we've no use for a "*London bachelor hub*".' She grasped my hand, 'In life, I choose you.'

'What about Paris?' She has beautiful eyes; alert; focused.

'Do you still want to go?' I said.

'I'd like us to get married there.'

'If that's what Lily wants, that's what Lily shall have.'

It's at times like this, I realise Lily is young. Not in a childish manner, but emotionally, because there are tears dripping down her cheeks and saturating her pillow, but she still won't take her eyes from mine, and I won't let go of hers either.

'I can't wait to go to Paris.' She said softly.

'I know *belle,*' I caught her hand and put it to my mouth, 'only two more weeks of living in exile.'

'I just want to be with you.' She whispered.

'You got me.'

She started crying again,

'Mum and dad know we're here.' She dabbed her eyes, 'Mum's angry with Liv about it, she says we've been colluding.'

'Like I said Honey,' I tucked her hair behind her dainty ear, 'people do and say things when they're hurt.'

'Do you think anyone will ever forgive us for this?'

I kissed her forehead and smiled,

'We just fell in love Lily, remember that.'

She laughs so gracefully, even though she's crying. She makes me want to hold her, protect her, make all this mercilessness evaporate. I will, I promise.

'We're not as depraved as they say though are we?' her seriousness faded and she winked at me; *I love her so much,* 'well, OK, so maybe between the sheets we are a little naughty.'

I propped myself up on one arm. I love this time with her and I realise if we were not in "exile", this fervor, this surreal intimacy might not be happening, well, not as swiftly anyway.

'A little naughty?' I smiled, 'would madam like to elaborate?'

'Madam would much rather show the elegant and refined gentleman what she means.'

The restless butterflies cover us; the muslin flutters and dances daintily around the open window, the fairy lights shimmer sexily over her divine and goddess like body and I immerse myself into her sweet velvety honey.

'Lily Ellen,' I whisper knowing she's sleeping beneath the butterflies, 'Just once, every man is at liberty to fall in love with a stunning redhead, and she's changed my life, so thank you.'

I've never been in this situation before. I've never been in a relationship where you love someone so unconditionally, with every breath you have, that you're saying and thinking all kinds of unfamiliar things.

For me, this isn't an obsession or infatuation, it's love in its purest form and I know Lily feels the same. We believe in each other, in our love, our future and our work, and as I watch Lily sleeping, I can't imagine my life without her.

"I've never said it before as strongly, but listen now, I love you madly. You've got me, you've got me..."

Louveciennes

Lily and I are in exile.

We've been on the farm with Livvy and Tom for just over a week now, but regrettably, next week it must come to an end. We'll return to London, but with the hope of leaving for Paris soon after.

I've tried calling Mum again, but apparently, (so Jeremy informed me), I'm the "devil alive", so, nothing new there then. Dad's still being coy and Luke, well, in the same conversation, Jeremy told me he's taken himself off to Cornwall to "surf, fuck and forget about the whore". I bit my lip. It hurt. There was blood. Jeremy apologised, I told him he didn't have to be so brutal.

I spoke to Joe and he confirmed what I suspected about Madeleine, and get this, she actually went to my parents' house and told Luke in person about Lily and me. I didn't even know she knew where my folks lived and I certainly didn't consider my "relationship" with her to be so serious as to warrant such possessive and bizarre behaviour, but there we are, it was done.

Lily hasn't escaped the backlash either, infact, she's suffering more than I am. She's been having a few intense conversations with Livvy from what I've seen and the little she's told me. It appears her parents are being totally irrational, insisting Lily removes her belongings from their house as soon as possible. Tom's agreed to do it at the weekend; I wanted to help, but for obvious reasons Lily talked me out of it, but I'm furious at the way they're treating her.

See, I don't think there was anything manipulative or malicious in how Lily behaved, we couldn't help the over lap, Christ, we'd been containing it for the best part of a year and OK, it doesn't make it morally right, but fuck that, life isn't simple, and just to confirm that, she also lost her job. I hope I'm worth it.

Anyway, my girl and I have embraced our exile, by taking time out to experience country life after so long of living in the City, and so far, I'm having the finest time. We quickly found "our place", a Hotel called

'The Grapevine', or more specifically the 'Gigot Bar', a gorgeous cozy bar complete with a roaring log fire, where we've become rather fond of an exquisite mature red from their extensive cellar, accompanied by a dazzling selection of tapas.

During these selfish days and nights, Lily and I have spent our time filling the gaps. It's what most people call the "getting to know each other" stage, which seems a bit crazy considering our situation. But I love it; I love how we delve into literature and analyse our beloved writers, and how easily I forget Lily is just 25 because she's so rousing when she converses. Before her, I'd never dated a woman with whom I could totally be myself, and what's more delicious, I get to take her home at the end of the evening and make love to her – what more could I ask for?

We've also started planning our future, talking about how we see our lives once we're married, and I'm delighted to find Lily opening up to me in a way that is rare for her.

'I want to cook for you, drink with you, bath with you, hang my washing next to yours, buy you gifts, read your work, watch films, listen to music, have a party, paint, write, sing, dance and hours of disinhibited sex with *mon mari magnifique...*' She laughed.

'Say that again?' I snuggled up her; the fire beside us couldn't have been more appropriate.

'Say what again?'

'"*My husband*" in French.' I kissed her lips, 'it turns me on.'

She started laughing again; she had a hand on my knee.

'*Mon Mari, Mari, Mari!*' Ah, how her laughter fuels me.

'God woman, I love it when you speak French,' I buried my face into her neck, she was giggling, folk in the bar were staring but we didn't care, 'oh Jesus my name is J. J. Howie and I am a very bad man.' I whispered.

'I hope you didn't spend too much money.' She smiled.

'On what?' I asked.

'On therapy; it obviously didn't work for you.' And we started laughing.

No kidding, since being on the farm, Lily and I have been fucking like teenagers. You see, Lily's excited by the barn, and so far we've fucked each other brain's out everyday in there, sometimes at the risk of getting caught too. She's insatiable, and I go on satisfying her because I'm gratefully following her rules.

See, Lily lures me (OK, I don't need much persuasion); she purposely wears a skirt; guides me to the deserted barn, pushes me back onto a hay stack and mounts me; she simply wants to fuck me, and I'm happy to oblige, because seeing her sticky kitty around my cock as I lift the front of her skirt, her tender young breasts bouncing before my eyes, I am having the most incredible orgasms, and topped off for good measure, Lily has a thing for my sperm.

Honest, she's getting it everywhere. She's drinking and pumping me dry. Everywhere she can get it, she will. I sometimes watch with wonder, because in my experience a lot of women wouldn't be too happy about having a man come without warning on her face, in her ears (!), her feet, her belly button, down her back, her armpits (!), and my personal favourite, her hair, but Lily, well, she's special, and right now, as I'm lying on the bed watching her work, I am completely in awe of her.

See, for me, it's Lily's soft femininity, combined with her masculine desire to fuck that makes her unique. When I think about her sexuality, her sensual and sometimes ingenuous nature, I don't believe Luke understood her at all and he certainly didn't understand her sexual desire. His imagination didn't stretch that far. He wouldn't have satisfied Lily for long even if we hadn't met.

'I have met in you Jefferson,' she whispered to me last night in bed, 'a man who fulfills and more than satisfies every one of my urges.'

Because for Lily, fucking isn't just about having my cock in her cunt, her ass or her mouth, it's about the extreme sentiment that goes with it, something I think a lot of men struggle with, and OK, I'm not always clear what Lily wants, her mind is complex, but I match her passion, desire and lust, but most of all, her love and it's because of this, I have no anxieties about Lily straying from me.

As I watch this beautiful woman, I know I have someone who understands my work and my lifestyle, someone who accepts my past and shares my interests. Someone I get drunk with and stay up with for hours talking. Someone I plan with, someone I tell my most wicked thoughts and who doesn't judge me, but instead makes me act them out. We love, we share, we belong together and sometimes I think if I didn't see anyone in a day but Lily, I would still live a happy and full life, that's how I know she is the woman I will grow old with. There is no more looking, no more passing time; she's here; I've got her; finally.

Although it wasn't totally our kind of thing, Lily and I had been strolling in and out of the antique shops around Stow. We stopped for a drink in a bar on the main street, and then grabbed lunch at a quaint country pub over the road, the type you'd expect from the Cotswold's; beams, a fireplace, wellies and a sheep dog. We enjoyed a plate of local mature cheddar and stilton, crusty bread and local made chutney, and then ambled onto the main square where we stumbled upon an estate agent.

OK, so we've looked in a few of these windows over the last week. We've even been in, spoken to an agent and left with details, but there was something different about this one.

'Shall we?' I nodded to the door and held out my hand for her, she took it smiling.

'Oddington is a typical and quaint Cotswold village,' said the agent, Jonathan, 'and this house has been beautifully renovated using Cotswold style stone to fit in perfectly. It's detached, five bedrooms plus a study, three bathrooms, a two bedroom converted coach house and 5 acres of land and a paddock.'

Lily looked at me, her eyes were watering; I squeezed her hand and Jonathan continued,

'The house has spectacular countryside views, and there's an orchard adjacent to the garden.' I glanced over the photographs again, crazily enough I was thinking about chickens for Lily. 'It's literally down the road from Stow and there are excellent schools close by...' he looked at us again, 'do you have children?'

'No, not at the moment.' I smiled.

'Well, OFSTED can provide details when appropriate.'

Jonathan told us the kitchen has a cream Aga and slate flooring, and there's a mezzanine overlooking the vast hallway and entrance. He said there are beams in all the rooms including the stairway and as the garden is south facing, we'd see the sunset every night.

'There's a claw foot bath with shower attachment in the master bathroom, a magnificent brick fireplace in the lounge and stable doors on every room.' He drew breath, 'The front door is traditional farmhouse and the garden is very well established as you can see from the photos.' There was also a lot of ivy and wisteria creeping up the front of the house. It really was quite charming.

Lily nudged my arm and ran a finger beneath the asking price. I wasn't concerned about the cost, all of the above came to what I'd paid for the apartment in Covent Garden.

'Shall we take a look?' I winked.

'Do you mind?' Her eyes were twinkling; my beautiful little lady.

I turned back to Jonathan, a nubile guy with a little charm,

'When's the earliest we can view?'

'I think this is it.' Lily pointed to a small dirt track. 'Is that smoke?'

I slowed down as we rumbled over the muddy track. It was smoke.

'It looks like they're having a barbeque.'

We drove on until the dirt track turned into a driveway. The farmhouse gate was open so we drove through.

'Oh J,' I turned to Lily's fragile voice, 'it's stunning.'

She was right. It was awe-inspiring. Slamming the car door, I went around and took her hand. I turned back to the road, the farmhouse was quite set back, exactly what we'd hoped for.

The subtle blend of traditional meets contemporary was enchanting. As beautiful as Livvy and Tom's farmhouse was, the 'oldness' of it made me feel a little oppressed, but this conversion was a masterpiece that suited both Lily and my requirements.

We walked around the side of the house, hit by a stunning glass and timber extension. Lily squeezed my hand; I squeezed it back. We could make out part of the coach house Jonathan had described, but there were quite a few mature trees disguising it, there was also a double garage, built to the same period and style as the house, and the view across the countryside was absolutely breathtaking, and on a glorious day like today, Mr. Witchell was guaranteed an offer.

We made our way to the front of the house where smoke continued to billow. The vendor had offered to show us around since he was home. Lily rang the door bell, then dragged her hand down the farmhouse door and when she looked up at me, I winked at her.

'Ah, Mr. and Mrs. Howie.' Jonathan had told us the owner was a builder by trade, and had bought this derelict farmhouse five years ago, then completely gutted it, renovated it, and bought a small holding. The small holding had gone, leaving land to do whatever we desired. 'Come through.' He said opening the door for us, 'we're just having a bit of lunch out the back.'

As we went through to the garden, we saw what he meant by "a bit of lunch" and also where the smoke was coming from.

'Innovative barbeque.' I smiled nodding to the home made outdoor cooking device.

'The wife abides it,' he had a throaty laugh, similar to someone who smokes fifty woodbines a day, 'but me and the kids love it.'

So I could see, as four well fed children dressed in shorts and dresses danced merrily around a make shift table covered in a blue gingham table cloth. It was disguised by plates of every kind of barbequed food you could imagine.

'Glass of wine?' We turned to the patio to see who I presumed was Mrs. Witchell, holding a bottle of wine, 'there's plenty.'

I looked at Lily,

'Sure,' she smiled, 'thank you.'

Whilst Mrs. Witchell poured us a glass of wine, "Lionel" started showing us around the garden. He talked about the vast patio his company laid four years ago, and how one set of French doors leads to the sitting room, the other into the study. We gazed out over the colossal lawn to the trees; I was dreaming about the sunset.

'I'm not sure how much you know about orchards,' Lionel said, 'but it comes into bloom in the autumn, my wife can tell you more, she loves the bloody thing.' Lily squeezed my hand, 'and if you look beyond the trees through there, that's the converted coach house, we use it as a self contained unit for guests.'

Mrs. Witchell handed Lily and me a glass of wine,

'The trees act as a barrier,' she said pointing right across the garden, 'over there is the paddock and just over there,' she said pointing somewhere to the left, 'is where we had the small holding, but we just didn't have the time so we sold the stock.'

I admired my little lady; I know that expression, she's awe inspired.

'Are they vegetables over there?' Lily said appreciating the vast area of what looked like over grown weeds.

'Yes dear,' Mrs. Witchell smiled, 'it's a little run down because we've been using the seasonal veg in preparation for moving, but I'm afraid we didn't bother planting anymore.'

'Why are you looking at selling?' I said after sipping my wine.

'We want to build our own,' Lionel said, 'we've bought a plot of land in Stroud.'

That's good; maybe a quick sale.

'Get a move on Lionel,' Mrs. Witchell said shoving him a little, 'they've come to see the house.'

I squeezed Lily's hand, and we looked at each other. I folded my arm around her shoulder and kissed her head. Her hair smells sweet and fresh. She suits this air. I suit being with her.

I explained to Lionel and Jo, we're currently living in London and getting married shortly.

'The city loses its appeal.' I said truthfully.

'What do you both do?' Lionel guided us down the corridor from the patio and towards what I knew was the kitchen.

'We're writers.' I announced.

'Writers?' Jo seemed quite taken by that, 'should I know you?'

'Maybe,' I smiled politely.

'Jefferson also writes for the Independent.' Lily said a little proudly.

'Ooh, famous then?' Jo linked Lionel's arm, nudging him

'Not "famous" as such.' I smiled.

'Yes you are,' Lily said quite seriously, 'he's had five novels published and he's writing his sixth. He's brilliant.'

'Lily's just got herself an agent,' this was true, I just hadn't told her yet, 'so watch this space.'

Lionel and Jo gawped at us. OK, we did sound a little geeky I suppose, but then we are each others number one fan.

We followed, but Lily held me back slightly,

'Agent?'

'Henry,' I was elated to be telling her this, although I had planned doing it over dinner tonight, 'he left a message this morning.'

'Oh my God,' she covered her mouth with her hands, 'are you serious?'

'Deadly.'

This house was made for us. For Lily. For me. Everything about it is *"a lot of being Jefferson and Lily"* and she feels it too. From the striking log fire and chunky mahogany beams, to the bijous study that will be our *"High Place"* with its attractive French doors blessed with an explosion of red and pink roses draped prettily around the frame. To the logs stacked on the patio outside the French doors, to the sitting room, the orchard, the Aga, the cobbled floors, the spiral staircase, the circular window at the top of the house where the early morning sunlight radiates, to the boudoir dressing room in the master bedroom.

'Lily?' I said as we arrived back at the car.

'Yes J?'

'A house in a field. A house made of reclaimed brick...' I drew her into me, crushing her, holding her face to mine, 'is this what Lily's dreams of?'

'It's our *"Louveciennes"*,' she whispered, her nose pressed against mine, 'a real home.'

'Then it's yours.' I picked her up and she laughed out loud, luscious legs wrapped around my waist as I spun her around; she's holding her arms out like she did that first night I asked her to come to me, and *I love her; I love her madly.*

Back from Exile

Our offer on "Louveciennes" had been accepted and my apartment was currently up for sale, something else that had majorly pissed everyone off.

'Have you honestly thought about this JJ?' Jeremy said during lunch at the Wolsley, 'It's a huge commitment.'

'No more than when I bought the apartment,' I said, 'anyway, I'm tired of the city.'

'It all seems so sudden, you know, you and Lily, now buying a house together...'

'It's not sudden.' I retorted.

'People are just looking out for you JJ.'

I started laughing,

'No, people just don't want Lily and me to be together.'

'Now you're just being paranoid.'

'Maybe, but do you blame me?'

*

To: jjhowie@msn.com
From: luke.howie@yahoo.com
Subject:

CUNT

*

So far, we've had a good response on the apartment. We've had a few viewings, some I've done, and others by Lily, but I've noticed we receive a more positive response when Lily's around; and unsurprisingly it's usually from the male species,

'As long as we get a sale who cares?' she laughed as I sat on the bed watching her undressing for bed, 'anyway,' she slinked over to me in a pair of delicious pink chiffon panties, 'this,' she ran her hands slowly down her luscious body, 'is for you only.'

'Then come 'ere,' I pulled her onto me by her waist, 'and prove it to me.'

And by Christ she did, because I swear to God, my balls are the size of raisins and my asshole aches.

Another week passed and still no sale. I'm not usually like this, anxious, but I want "Louveciennes" badly, and if we lose it, well, I'll never forgive myself.

'J?' Lily turned from the PC as I sorted through my mail, 'I have an idea, about the apartment.'

Lily told me she wanted to "change" it slightly.

'A woman's touch you mean?' I smiled sitting on the edge of the desk.

'I'm not talking pinks and flowers, I just think we should give it a little more... femininity.'

Without hesitation, the answer was yes. So that's how we spent the afternoon, trawling around the shops, picking up pieces that might inspire a sale. The following day, I was having lunch with Joe, and then meeting Henry, Lily said this would give her the time and space to "do her bit". I was happy leaving it in her capable hands.

Lunch with Joe was tedious. He repeated what Jeremy had said to me a week ago about selling up; so I made my excuses and met Henry in Daisy's Deli. The intention wasn't to discuss Lily or her work, but it wasn't long before we were.

'So this is what, or should I say "who" has been on your mind lately Jefferson.' Henry poured us both a glass of red; how appropriate. 'I must say, Lily is a bit of a contradiction of herself if you understand my meaning.' Of course I did; I'm living the dream. 'When you meet her she's demure and graceful, but by God, in her writing, she's, dare I say, *racy* at times.'

I started laughing,

'She's immense, and she's a genius; her novels could easily have been written by a man. That's why she's so fresh, she's moving away from chick lit, it's a whole new genre Henry.'

'I suppose it helps that you're the main character.' Henry raised his brow at me, 'aren't you a little...uneasy about it becoming public property?'

'Not at all,' I said truthfully, 'I'm very proud to be featured in such a masterpiece.'

'Steady Jefferson,' he smiled, 'I have to convince someone to publish it first, I mean, it is extremely explicit for mainstream.' Henry's food arrived; I adore Daisy's mozzarella and sunblush tomato ciabatta.

'People love a true story,' I said, 'and I must say, the way things are going, it'll be a novel in itself.'

'How do you mean?' he raised his brow again.

'Never mind,' I picked up my wine, 'look, Lily and I have discussed the content and yes, I guess having our sexual exploits in print for people to read is a little, well, risqué, but I love her, I'm not ashamed of it, and neither is Lily.'

Henry was eyeing me,

'You've gone soft Howie,' he smiled over the rim of his glass, 'I think I like it.'

I smiled and leaned forward,

'Look, you've read it; it's verging on Avant-garde, people just don't write like that anymore.'

'That's why I'm concerned about finding a publisher.' He said.

'I think you're wrong,' I scoffed, 'it's endearing.'

'What about the feminists...'

'Oh come on Henry, that isn't an excuse, Jesus, they've been sending me death threats since "*Northern Road*"...'

'Yes, but the publishers I would usually approach with literature such as Lily's are predominantly feminist, take Virago and The Women's press...'

'In her journal, Lily brilliantly describes the complexity of her feelings and the conflict going on in her mind, of falling in love with me whilst being with my brother, it portrays her as a strong and sensual woman, it's something to be proud of, not ashamed of, this is something only a woman could write, we should celebrate it.'

'You've got me in a corner haven't you?' Henry sat back in his chair holding his wine, 'I can't promise a substantial advance though.' He said, 'people will eye this with caution...'

'And excitement.' I grinned.

'What are you looking for Jefferson, blood?'

'She's just looking for recognition Henry.'

'Huh, that's what they all say,' he smiled, 'anyway, I'm intrigued,' he said, '"*Ellen*" in "*Red*", is she based on Lily?'

I started laughing,

'Everything I've written in the past 12 months has been inspired by Lily.'

He shook his head laughing,

'You do realise the publicity and controversy this Journal might bring you and Lily.'

'Everyone has sex Henry, well, almost everyone,' I grinned, 'it's just some of us choose to write about it as well; some of us are incredibly inspired by what we do away from prying eyes.' I knocked back my wine, 'we're steadily breaking through the taboo.'

And my Lily Ellen is leading the way.

The meeting with Henry over ran, and then I went to Carluccio's to pick up olives, bread, cheese and a bottle of Champagne. I text Lily to tell her I love her and that I'm on my way,

"J, I need you terribly – absolutely x x x"

I'm happy she's missed me too.

On opening the apartment door, I could hear Pachelbel's Canon in D, Lily's favourite. I left the food bag on the breakfast bar; I needed to find my girl.

'Lily?' I called.

Her changes to the apartment were subtle yet miraculous. Small pieces placed stylishly around the kitchen: plants, fresh herbs, lemons and limes in a wire bowl, cool espresso cups articulately positioned beside the machine. A tin of Illy, a Bodum salt and pepper set, a chrome can for olive oil, a bottle of red. The wine rack was full, and a small glass bowl bursting with purple tulips sat elegantly on the breakfast bar. I don't think this place has ever looked so "lived in" or so chic.

I went to the bedroom. She wasn't there. I think she's playing one of her games again. Then I noticed the room, the sexy fur throw lain languorously at the bottom of the bed, deep red velvet and fur cushions against white bed linen. A fur rug by the side of the bed, a jar of red roses on the dresser, glass tealight holders. There was a framed picture of a Degas nude above the bed, subtle white lights around the bed stead.

I want to find her. I went to the study then to the bathroom; I could smell ylang ylang. I opened the door, delightfully confronted by candles, and bubbles' covering what I know to be completely delicious,

'Hey J,' Lily was holding a glass of champagne, there was one waiting for me on the side, 'come join my dots and drink my mulled wine hair.'

Lily has given me further extracts from her Journal. I've been reading them whilst she studies at the library. She's chosen to work at the library because although she is the hardest working person I know, she finds me a serious distraction. Take yesterday for instance, she was in the study working and I walked in after having a shower, and OK, it wasn't accidental, but I pulled up a chair and asked her what she was working on.

She stared at me, nostrils flared; fervent eyes crawling over my skin. I wasn't wearing my specs; she likes to gaze into my eyes. She kissed me. She's like that, impulsive, she does it a lot in restaurants and at the supermarket; I adore it.

She sat on my knees, wrapped her thighs around my waist and started kissing me, her hands raging through my hair. She took my neck, and I threw off my towel, she raised herself, rucked her panties to one side and mounted me. We went at it for a few frantic minutes until we were coming. It was unreal.

So, today she left early.

I tried working for a couple of hours but quickly got bored. The thing is, I've become used to having Lily near me, so when she's not here, I feel a bit, well, lost I suppose, which is perplexing coming from a man who spent most of his days alone, anyway, how quickly life changes. So, I lied out on the sofa, and started reading the journal.

"August 18

Attended a dinner with Jefferson hosted by The Chartered Institute of Journalists. It's the first time we've been out publicly since being forced into "exile". I told J I was nervous. I was worried photos would be taken and people would accuse us of "rubbing their noses" in it. J made me laugh, he said he "didn't give a fuck", it made me feel better. He changes my mood so quickly. No one has ever been able to do that.

J bought me a dress. A most beautiful and elegant, pink chiffon dress all the way to my feet. He says I was born to wear Chanel. I wore it with silver heeled sandals and a pink satin clutch bag.
He kept touching my ass. He knew I was wearing a pair of flimsy panties because he watched me put them on. I don't think he realises the extent to which he makes me wet. I could feel the moisture as I walked. I tried to control it, but his fingers were supple, graceful. He rubbed a finger teasingly up and down my crevice, and I wanted to open my legs to him.
He made delicious comments about my nipples. He said he imaged them pink and ripe beneath the fabric. He told me he had a "tremendous hard on". After the publication of my Journal, we will no doubt become a source of entertainment for some people, and maybe even the subject of voyeurism for the more perverse.

I was proud to be beside Jefferson this evening. He is so elegant in a tux. His hair draped with sophistication onto his forehead, his glasses giving him a gauche edge. I saw women looking at him; admiring him; wishing they could have him. Jefferson is prestigious and elegant, he works brutally; men admire him; women want him. I don't fear these women; I never have.

He barely left my side all night. We both like it like this, a desperate need to be close. People started commenting on it, they said we looked "happy" and "content", most people were kind, some not so, J reassured me, that's all I need.
We drank Champagne and I talked to Roberto Dacks about D.H. Lawrence. He was amazed I spoke with such passion for someone so young. He tried to guess my age, he said "twenty"; I laughed, he was trying to flatter me. I felt Jefferson's hand on my ass as Roberto flirted with me, and I felt safe. I wanted to take him home.

A pretty lady with brown hair accosted me on my way to the toilets. She asked after Jefferson. She introduced herself as Lydia Wimberley. She dated Jefferson briefly just after his break up with Gracie Miller. She is a Journalist with the Daily Telegraph.
'I heard a rumour,' and she took my hand and eye balled my engagement ring. I can't imagine J to have been satisfied by a woman like Lydia, 'I guess it isn't a rumour.'
'No.' I took back my hand.
'When's the big day?'
'Soon.' I smiled politely; I had to remember she is a journalist.
J gets concerned by episodes like that, he wonders sometimes. He shouldn't worry, I am safe in his love.

August 22

I didn't tell Jefferson, but I tried calling mum today. She wouldn't speak to me. Dad had sympathy in his voice. He asked if I was keeping well, and was Jefferson looking after me. I told him J is amazing, that he is a good man. Dad didn't say anything, although I sensed he wanted to. Then mum came on, it took me back a little, she wanted to lecture me again, she said I'd "let her down"; she thinks I've made a "show" of myself, "parading" around with a man who so obviously needs me for his ego. She hung up on me. I laughed, but then I cried.

August 23

J and I went for dinner at The Ivy. It had been booked for ages. I adored the Risotto. J had the sea bass. We polished off a bottle of Laurent-Perrier.

Through dinner, J felt frisky, rubbing his leg against mine, whispering across the table how divine my tits looked in my lemon fitted vest. I kept him hanging on; he finds it "delicious". We wanted to fuck in the alley close to our apartment but the paparazzi were out because Kate Moss was rumoured to be dining tonight. Instead we went to his car and he fucked me dirty. After he'd come inside me, I dipped a finger into my sex and scooped it out; I put it in my mouth, J couldn't take his eyes off me, he says he'll write about it.

August 24

I didn't feel that great today. Not sure whether I'm just hung over or my period is due. I worked in the library for most of the day, but my head was sore and my belly ached. When I got home, J was waiting for me. He'd laid the table and there were candles and music.
'Sit down Honey,' he said holding me at the waist, 'I have something to tell you.'
I was slightly nervous to be honest, especially as he got to his knees. I felt scruffy in my jeans and t-shirt beside my elegant beau in trousers and a shirt,
'We've had an offer on the apartment.' I love his smile. 'Asking price.'
'Who?' I was bursting.
'The couple you showed around yesterday, it seemed they adored your pink cup cakes, they found them very "cute".'
That made me laugh. We celebrated with linguine and champagne.

August 25

I felt bad again today. I didn't drink much last night either. I fell asleep early too. I think J wanted to make love, but I collapsed in a heap on the bed.

I've been working like crazy today and I have a meeting with Henry later. He wants to discuss "the future". J told me not to expect much of an advance when Henry finds a publisher, but I

couldn't give a fuck. It's all surreal to me anyway.
J and I talked about "Louveciennes". I love lying out with him on the sofa; I adore how he lovingly strokes my hair. I wonder if he realises the way he looks at me. I hope he knows how deeply I love him.
Now that we've sold the apartment, Louveciennes has become a reality. We've been holding back slightly to avoid disappointment. I asked J if I can have chickens. He laughed,
'I've taken it as gospel that we will,' he said, 'I've taken the liberty of asking Leigh where she bought her chicken house from; she called it an "Eglu".'

We talked about our wedding. I want a quiet one, and Jefferson agrees. Neither of us are ones for fuss or bullshit. J said he sees our marriage as a "seal", but the thing that excites him most is, he's found the person he's going to spend the rest of his life with.

August 28

Dinner party at Leigh and Thomas' house.
We looked through their wedding photos. They got married in Devon on a beach called "Hope Cove". She wore a simple white satin dress and had bare feet. I wonder whether Paris is too decadent for a girl like me...

J fingered me hard beneath the wisteria; he was reminiscing about the first time we crossed the barrier in this garden. I couldn't be quiet so he covered my mouth with his hand. It excited me even more. I unbuttoned my shirt, and pulled down my bra, J bit my nipples as I rubbed and flicked them; they were swollen; it made me come. J whispered that I have the sweetest come and lapped it up like a puppy.

We couldn't get home soon enough. I pushed J against his apartment door and took out his penis. He was like rock. I studied it. He is big; I am a very lucky girl. I glided his foreskin down the shaft in slow simple motions. He was in agony. His head was back, his mouth open. I licked the head like a lollypop, wetting it to masturbate. I saw his pre-come juice seeping through the eye. I licked it. I tore off my panties, turned around and slammed my sex over him; he cried out.

He held my hips, rocking impatiently. He bent me over so my fingers almost touched my toes. It hurt; it was too deep, but I wanted it, it's the only way I can satisfy this desire, this filthy lust.

J shot all over my back and whilst he rubbed his cream into my skin, I fucked myself with two fingers."

August 30

I can barely believe I'm marrying Jefferson Howie. I can barely believe I'm getting married at all. When I think about it, I can't believe this is happening to me that such an amazing man should fall in love with me.
I keep looking at my ring. I don't tell J though, he might think I'm crazy! I love watching it sparkle in the sunlight; it makes me smile.
I've found a wedding dress: satin and ruffles; J will adore it...

I've lost the dates for my period. My belly's been aching again. It's starting to wear me down. I'm tired too, and this headache is rotten. I wonder if I'm doing too much, between studying and trying to arrange a wedding I guess I might be...

Got an e-mail from Susie this morning. She said some guy called the house late last night asking for me. He was drunk. He called me "that whore". I guessed who it was.

Livvy called. Mum went to see her at the weekend. Tom accidentally told her about us buying "Louveciennes". Mum got upset. She says I never tell her anything. How can I when she won't speak to me. Oh Christ, my stomach hurts. I hate this! I hate this!

Lily was crouched over the desk typing furiously; her cheeks a delightful pink from concentration. She didn't notice I'd come in until I put a cup of tea at her side,

'Hey my J,' she always has a smile for me.

'How you feeling?' I pulled up a chair.

'Fine, why?'

If I hadn't read her Journal, I wouldn't have picked up how she's feeling; she's very good at disguising things when she wants to.

'Your stomach?'

She picked up her tea and sipped,

'Better thanks.'

'Can I get you anything?'

She smiled showing me her exquisite teeth,

'Just you.'

I stroked her cheek,

'Did your period come?'

She shook her head,

'Imminent though.'

I kissed her forehead,

'Good,' I said softly, 'I don't like to see you feeling unwell.'

Lily sat on my knees and folded herself around me,

'You won't ever think I'm too young will you?'

I gazed at her, wondering where this had come from.

'Too young for what?'

'To be with you?' Her sincerity made me anxious.

'You're absolute,' I whispered, her face grasped between my hands, 'the disparity in our ages will never be an issue.'

'Honest?'

'Yes,' I laughed kindly; she's pensive; I know these moods. 'You suit me Lily Ellen. I suit you. That won't change, I have no doubts about that.'

Her body eased and she folded her arms around me. In her embrace I am safe but she has something on her mind and for that, I'm not sure whether I feel quite so protected.

The Second Most Important Person in my Life

I've discovered there are two entries missing from Lily's Journal. I'm alerted to this because it's unlike her to give me incomplete work; she's compulsive when it comes to being organized, and in light of her dark mood, there is a peculiar nagging in my gut, so I read the before and after entries in an attempt to make sense of this misdemeanor.

"September 2.

It feels and smells like autumn. I walked through Neal's Yard earlier, leaves billowed aimlessly around the fronts of the cafes. There's a smell in the air that reminds me of being a little girl, it's like burning leaves, I like it; it makes me think of being warm and cosy sitting by the fire in "Louveciennes", of being with Jefferson, talking with him, trying to tell him...

The last two mornings have felt cooler. I've been leaving J in bed and bringing home croissants and coffee. I made him breakfast and we talked and loved for hours, even though we should have been working. I long to be there, our sanctuary in the country, I will settle there. Feel more complete. Won't worry so much...

J wonders about my mood but rarely questions me. I want to tell him, but I'm afraid. I've only just got him, I don't want him to leave me. I will have to do something soon, he's going to notice one way or another.

We're due to go to Paris at the weekend, for 2 months before we get married, but I'm not sure I want to go. I'm safe here with Jefferson. It seems an age ago that we made the pledge to marry in Paris. I wonder how J will feel if I change my mind. He's not a demanding man, he gives me so much in a way no one else ever has. He's there when I need him, it feels as though he's the only one I have now.

Oh I feel bad again. Was ill after dinner. I lay on the bed after Jefferson left to meet Thomas, I didn't want him to see me looking like this.
I tried to call Livvy. No answer. I tried again. Tom said she'd gone to town so I left a message for her to call me back. She did, but Jefferson was next door. I don't want him to hear.

September 5

Henry: "If I had the means today and I asked you to come away with me for good, would you do it?"
Anais: "...But if there were no June and no Hugo, I would go away with you, even if we had no means."
Henry: "Sometimes I wondered if it was a game for you."

I had a feeling in the pit of my stomach. A feeling I can't explain. I put the Journal to one side. She's trying to tell me something; a cryptic message hidden amongst powerful words. I have no idea what it is.

After two quick espressos, I'm having an adrenalin rush. I'm pacing; a million things spinning around my head. Has Lily changed her mind? Did she ever love me? Was this a game for her? Has the novelty of the older man been fulfilled, only to be discarded? Maybe if I didn't love her so, if I didn't want her so badly, I wouldn't be marching aimlessly inside these four walls, and let her go.

I sat down on the sofa in an attempt to get a grip. I told myself the missing entries were a mistake, that Lily's been under the weather for a while, and her parents aren't helping; we're going through a fairly stressful period, and waiting to move house and location is a lot for a couple to cope with, albeit one who have been together for such a short period of time.

I strode to the study and rummaged through her unfinished work, eyes hungrily eating her words, but nothing.

I heard the door. My heart was thumping in my chest. I leaned against the desk to compose myself, waiting for her to appear.

'Sorry I'm a bit late,' she's been crying; my heart sank, 'I stopped by at Carluccio's.' and she held up a bag; I think they were olives.

'Lily?' My feet were stuck to the floor; I have no idea what's going on here, but it feels serious. 'Are you alright?'

'Of course.' Her smile is feeble; not good.

'You would tell me if something was bothering you,' I said with hope, 'I'm always here for you.'

'I know.' She dropped her head; my back prickled with sweat.

'I read your Journal today.' She looked up at me, 'there seems to be some missing.'

Her silence deafened me.

She opened her satchel and handed me a file.

'I'm not proud of myself for not being able to tell you,' she sniffed, 'like you Jefferson, sometimes I find it easier to write it down.'

She turned to leave but I gently grabbed her hand; I've never known her pull away from me before,

'Where are you going?' My head was in bits. 'Lily, what the hell's going on?'

'It's huge Jefferson; too huge even for you I think.' She left the room, I called her back,

'Let me decide how vast this is?' I was sick in my gut.

She nodded and left me. I sat down at the desk, the papers trembling. I have no clue as to what's going on here, but from Lily's reaction it feels bad.

"September 3

Sick again. I was so tired that as soon as J left the apartment I went back to bed. I'm totally zapped and have no energy, and to top it off, I've lost my concentration.

Oh how I love J. Oh how I wish I'd taken more care with him. I know what people will say, what they'll think, that I did it on purpose, but I didn't, why would I, I don't want to lose J, but I know I could. I know he could so easily walk away from me for doing this. Maybe Luke's right, I am a "dirty whore". A dirty whore who will rot in hell.

"It" won't even let me wallow in self pity. I'm up again, throwing up. I cleaned the toilet crazily before J got back. I've picked up his concern. He says I'm "distant". He doesn't plague me with questions though, and he doesn't bother me for answers, but I sense his concern. Oh I wish I could change this!

When I finally rose from the dead, my stomach felt bad. It's swollen so I rolled over onto it, keeping it warm. My breasts ache too. They're sore and heavy, have been for weeks.

To comfort myself, I tried to imagine when, where and how we did it, to try and feel some joy, but I'm so frightened and so lonely and yet J lies right beside me. I cuddle up to him and he cuddles me. I love the way he lays his head on my chest and snuggles down

into me. I stroke his hair and whisper the words to him. I want him to hear, to secretly be awake.

Livvy rang me again. J was out. I started crying. I felt like a right fucking idiot for getting so upset. Livvy's going crazy with worry. She asked if I've told Jefferson yet, she says I must, but I can't because I don't want anything to change, that I've waited so long for him, the most beautiful man I've ever met, and now I'll lose him.

Livvy's angry with me for thinking like this, she says I didn't do this on my own and I'm talking sentimental bullshit; she's right of course. She says I shouldn't be worried, that Jefferson is a gentleman and that he adores me, she says he'll understand.

How can a stick change someone's life so quickly? The stick doesn't know I'm just 25. The stick doesn't know I love Jefferson so much I truly believe I'd die for him, but will now probably lose him. This stick doesn't know J and I aren't always careful when we make love and that I haven't been taking my Pill for almost two months because I kept forgetting to make an appointment; but what this stick does know is I'm pregnant. 99.99% positively pregnant..."

I looked up from the Journal. "*99.99% positively pregnant*".

"September 4

I found my diary; it was hidden beneath my studies in a box I packed when I left Chalk Farm. I checked my dates. It's been 2 months since I had a period. How can I be that fertile? Maybe it's not me, maybe its J's who's fertile...no, it'll be me for sure... That means, in the first month of us sleeping together, I got pregnant. I'm laughing but I shouldn't. I must be in shock. I'm feeling really frightened and weird. Not sure I want to do this; I'm scared and feel alone. What would J want? I don't even want to ask him. I want to slip out and do something immoral..."

Why am I smiling so much whilst Lily's crying in the lounge? I attempt to stifle it, reminding myself she's sore and confused. I'm smiling again, disguising my delight with a hand, but when I see her sitting cross legged on the sofa, her hands covering her face sobbing, my smile evaporates and a weird thing happens to me, my eyes fill up.

I go straight to her.

'Lily?' I whispered, 'Lily look at me?' she shook her head, 'Lily I love you.' she uncovered her face, 'you don't have to be frightened, lonely, or confused.' A tear fell from my eye and landed on her knee, 'I'm almost 38, in truth I thought my time had passed.' She has striking eyes when she's been crying.

I claimed her hands, crushing them in mine. I watched her, the most worthy person in my life, 'I want the second most important person in my life,' I swallowed, 'who is being carried by the most important person in my life more than I can ever tell you.' Lily's staring at me, blinking; I can see relief and a little surprise. 'You thought this was a game for me?'

'I sometimes wondered.' She whispered.

I seized her face with my hands, my lips hovering over hers; it's delicious,

'So,' I smiled, 'who exactly is the most fertile?'

And thankfully, she smiled.

OK, let me talk about this colossal thing that's happening to me and Lily.

Lily is pregnant; 9 weeks. Nobody knows but us, and Livvy. Lily's frightened and apprehensive, and me, well, it hasn't fully sunk in, but I have to say, inside I feel pretty damned honoured, and before you ask, yes, I did momentarily think it could be Luke's, but Lily put me straight, she said they'd been absolutely no sex with him before he left,

'I was on a period,' she said, 'believe me J, I've done my dates a thousand times.'

So, as I admire Lily sitting at the desk typing away, I see Lily plus one. She'd feel weird knowing that, so I keep it to myself, but as I watch her, reaching for a book, flicking through the pages to find what she's looking for, I feel warm inside because Lily's having my baby, something I truly believed had passed me by, and had I not met her, it might well have.

Last night, after this huge thing whacked me right around the head, we spent most of the evening talking about it.

'I've sort of known for about two weeks,' she said as we lay together on the sofa, 'my cycle is usually really accurate, but I lost track after we started sleeping together.' I stroked her hair, she looks tired. 'I didn't realise just how much "undisturbed" sex we were having.' she smiled.

Lily confided in me she's useless when it comes to taking the Pill. She mentioned the "scare" she'd had with Luke just before Christmas, and how it pretty much frightened her into remembering.

'Getting pregnant was my number one scare,' she said, 'and even though I've always got other protection, I still took the Pill, I even started carrying it in my satchel,' she laughed, 'not very elegant hey?'

But when she took her last one, she just never gave it another thought, (just as I often didn't give it a thought when I was coming inside her), which she feared I would think made her "callous" and "lazy",

'That's why I was so scared to tell you,' she said, 'I didn't want you to think I'd trapped you.'

I started laughing; girls live in such a strange and wonderful world sometimes,

'You really have no idea do you?' I whispered, 'how I feel about you?'

'A little maybe.' Oh that girly laughter.

'Do you want to tell your parents?' I said.

'No!'

I didn't ask her why, or try and persuade her otherwise, Lily's an intelligent woman; I trust her.

'Do you want to tell yours?' she said rubbing dainty warm feet against mine.

'I'll go with whatever you want.'

'Do you mind if we just keep it to ourselves for a while?'

'Of course I don't mind,' I said leaning my head against hers as it sank into my neck, 'whatever you think best.'

So, standing here now, in the doorway of the study, watching her work, I love her so much but I just don't know how to tell her.

She leaned over to the bin, and I thought, "There's my little lady with a baby inside her"; stuff I didn't think would bother me, and I guess until it happens, you don't know how you'll respond.

'J stop staring at me.' She grinned without looking up.

I laughed and went over to her, she turned around and opened her arms and I took them,

'Lily Ellen,' I whispered as she kissed me, 'I love you.'

On my knees and looking up at her, she stroked the hair from my eyes and smiled,

'Jefferson James is so beautiful; I wish I had a camera right now.'

I grinned,

'Knowing how lethal you are with that thing, I'm glad you haven't.'

As expected, this mammoth news has changed our plans. Paris is off by mutual consent, and if I'm honest, I'm not disappointed. The sale of the apartment is going through pretty quickly as far as property is concerned, and "Louveciennes" is closer than we originally thought.

'J?' Lily was sitting astride me on the study floor; she's incredibly agile, managing to wrap herself around me at any time in any position, she says it's because we're made for each other; cute.

'Lily?' I tightened up my grip.

'I'd quite like to get married before I have a bump.'

I looked down at Lily's currently iron flat stomach; whoa, I hadn't thought that far, 'will you fit a baby in there?' I grinned.

She started laughing,

'I don't have a choice.'

'So, what's on your mind Honey?'

'Well, I was thinking how lovely it would be to get married on your birthday.'

'Sounds good.' But Lily never stops thinking, so I know there's more to this. 'Anything else?'

'How about doing it at a registry office?' Lily, coy? Now that's rare, 'I mean, I can still wear my dress and everything...'

'Sure.' I'm easy as far as this is concerned; I just want to marry her.

'I also thought we could have the reception at "Louveciennes?" I adore those excited eyes, 'we'd keep it very low key, nothing fancy, just *a lot of being Jefferson and Lily.*'

She uses that line because she knows it's a cert.

'See, I remember talking to Leigh about her and Thomas' wedding, she said she did all the flowers, food and decoration herself with a bit of help from her sisters.' It's fair to say, Lily's given this a lot of thought, 'you know what Leigh's like, her house is amazing and she does all that stuff herself.'

I listen to Lily and wish she wanted something more. I don't tell her, but I'd love to marry her in utter decadence, to see my princess walk down a red carpet isle, because she's so wonderful, so beautiful and so absolutely the finest part of my life. I want to give her everything I can, because she deserves it, but if Lily wants us to be married in a registry office with a home made reception at our farmhouse, then she can have it, but the little she does want, I will ensure she has the absolute best.

As you can imagine, a few things in our life have changed, but with Lily, one thing remains a sure bet.

I'm lying on the sofa watching her (pretending to be reading the newspaper) because she's currently wandering around the apartment in a pair of extremely cute red and blue polka dot panties and a delicious white vest that is clinging to spectacular breasts, but the cherry on the cupcake is those cute pink lambswool bed socks (I know, please don't ask, I just do right.).

'J?' she called me from the kitchen. I wanted to follow her in, bend her over and fuck her.

'Honey?' I called back; I have one hell on a hard on.

'Did you see the read up for "Cabaret" in the Standard?'

'I did,' I said folding the paper in half and throwing it on the floor, 'I'm glad you've persuaded me to go.'

Lily came back to the lounge. My gorgeous Lily; My genius Lily, the woman who has a baby inside that belly. She's smiling, no, make that grinning, she knows; she can see it on my face; *I am such a bad man, and she loves it.*

'J?' she stood in front of me, brow raised; I'm lying down with a tent in my trousers. I gaze up at her, running my free hand between her legs. 'J is feeling bad?'

'J is always feeling bad with you madam.' I sat up and pulled her onto me by her waist; she is so dainty and I know she gets sick, and feels tired, but she gets so incredibly wet, and when I finger her, the juices are thick and white on my skin, and I just have to fuck her.

'Lily honey,' I said huskily, 'lambswool against silky skin makes JJ a very bad man.'

'Then come join my dots and drink my mulled wine hair and show me just how bad you can be.'

I'm waiting for Lily outside Holborn library. She's right, there is an autumnal feel to the air; it's cooler and the breeze is brisk.

I draw the collar up on my coat and breathe in. Lily loves autumn; she adores going outside late at night to take a quick breath, and again early in the morning to pick up fresh croissants; a stolen chance to immerse herself in the smells and sights that inspire her.

There she is, my girl, so effortlessly cool as she carries her books, her satchel strapped around her body. She is divine as she strides towards me; her hair tied back in a sleek tress and so sassy in grey trousers, matching waistcoat and black skinny polo neck, complete with cute white pumps. I love her like this.

She drops her books and leaps into my arms as though she hasn't seen me for days, infact it's a little over 3 hours.

'Jefferson, will you marry me?' she laughs as I put her feet back on the ground.

'I sure will.' And we kiss because we're off to meet with the Superintendent Registrar at Marylebone Registry office to give notice of our marriage.

After our meeting with the registrar, I had a call from Jeremy. I'd left him a message earlier to call me back.

'Lily and I are getting married,' I announced as we headed to the Underground, 'I want you to be my best man.'

Silence; then everytime he tried to speak, he was tripping himself up all over the place,

'Married? When?'

'My birthday.'

'JJ, that's less than 6 weeks.'

'Yes, I know, so will you come?'

'Umm, well, yes, of course I will,' he was delirious, 'do Mum and dad know?'

'Yes, but they've declined the invite as expected.' I would have been amazed if they'd accepted.

'Mum's still sore, but she might come around.'

'Perhaps,' Lily was smiling at me, so I winked, 'anyway, I'll call you in the next few weeks, let you know the arrangements.'

'Hang on JJ, where are you planning on doing this?'

'Ceremony at Marylebone; reception at our place.'

'Is it big enough?'

I started laughing,

'Jeremy, it has 5 bedrooms and a two bedroom coach house...'

'Oh, the farmhouse.'

'Yes.' I was still laughing.

'Right, very good, I'll look forward to it.'

"September 8

I'd put it off for too long. I had to tell mum and dad about me and J getting married. Actually, I have to tell them about both things that are happening right now but it's so hard.

I spoke to Livvy about how frightened I am, she was so lovely, saying she'd come with me if I wanted, I thanked her but said I should do it on my own.

I went to the house after leaving the library. Dad was at work and Mum almost closed the door in my face, but she changed her mind when she saw me crying.
I told her I needed to talk to her about something important. She just stood there, so I told her in the best way I could that J and I are getting married,
"You're pregnant aren't you?"
I wanted to tell her, honest I did, but I couldn't get the words out,
"No, we just want to be together."
"Then why the urgency?"
"We don't want to wait; we love each other."
"Oh Lily, why are you doing this, you're so young, you have so much to see and do, what about all the plans you made."
I don't know why mum dislikes Jefferson so much. I think it might have something to do with his "reputation" even though she knows

of mine...
'I love him Mum.'

I read her mind, she thinks it won't last and yet she forgets so easily the grief and bullshit she and dad went through when they got married, and they were a hell of a lot younger than me. Why do parents do that? I know they want the best for their children but you have to trust them. I so hope I don't do that when I'm a mum, I don't think I will, I wouldn't want my children to feel as grave as I do right now..."

I filled up my glass with red wine.

I've been thinking about going to see Lily's parents. Their hostility doesn't bother me, but what does, is the way they're making her feel. OK, I've only met them twice, but I don't think they'd behave the way they do if they realised Lily's not as resilient as they obviously think she is.

They have a whole new life to look forward to, but they'll miss out if they continue to push her away, I know they will; see, Lily might be hurting, making her seem fragile, but inside she bears a mighty strength, and if they don't move on from this, from the unpredictableness of life, they will lose her and their grandchild.

"J's loving is immense. He is like a Trojan. I came back from the library last night. He was waiting for me. I went to him like I always do and he picked me up. His arms were warm but his mouth was hot, and as he laid me back and sank his burning wet penis inside me, I forgot all about the bad stuff and immersed myself in the man I call J..."

"I had an e-mail today. I didn't tell J, not because I didn't want him to know, but just because I'm tired, and when I talk to him, I want it to be worthwhile. It was from Luke; he's being cruel again. He says he kept one of the photos that J took of me and he's going to post it on the internet. I'm not sure whether I believe him. He's still very upset and angry with me, in fact, he says he hates me more than anything or anyone. He blames me for this. He says Jefferson is weak when it comes to "a good fuck" and that since I'm such a "useless slut", J will get bored once he's all fucked out. It hurts to hear that. It hurts a lot..."

I got up; pacing. I wanted to jump in my car, drive to Cornwall, hunt him down and hold his fucking head under the surf. I didn't give a fuck for his hurt or his anger, he will not say those things about Lily, he will not make her feel like this; but more than anything, I will not have my parents or her parents thinking like him.

'JJ?' Dad answered the phone, 'it's late.'

'Is mum awake?'

He couldn't deny it; I could hear mumbling in the background,

'Ur, well...'

'Dad, just put mum on the fucking phone will you.'

Dad knows how angry I am about what's happening, how juvenile and ridiculous everyone is acting, and I've let it go until now because in essence, how I conducted myself whilst Luke was away is unforgivable, but this is where it stops.

'It's late Jefferson...'

'Mum, listen to me,' I could tell by her silence I'd shocked her with my firmness, 'this hypocrisy makes me vomit, this pathetic self pity, this "holier than thou" bullshit that's getting stuck in my throat; your youngest son is not an angel, and I have never professed to be one and if I discover through any means that anyone, and I mean, ANYONE has been saying things about Lily, I will not be responsible for my actions. Stop fuelling Luke and get it out of your head that this love with Lily is wrong, it's no different from you and dad and don't you dare use the disparity in our ages as an excuse, it's bollocks,' I took a quick breath, 'Lily and I are getting married, we will be a family, and we will live and work in our new home, but I swear, if you continue this feud, you will never be welcome in my home again.'

Dad came on the telephone. I knew he was angry with me for shouting at mum, but I continued to lay in to him,

'If they'd made you choose between Mum and me, what would you have done?'

'It was different for us JJ, your mum was pregnant.'

'Well here's news dad, so is Lily.' And I hung up.

Now I was more wound up than before. I stormed into the bedroom and threw open the bedside drawer. I grabbed the Brown's photos and counted them. There didn't appear to be any missing, but it didn't ease my fury. I rang Luke's mobile. It went into answer phone. I considered leaving a message, but I had to see him face to face, so I hung up. This would have to wait.

I checked Lily. She was sleeping on the sofa. Feet curled up, her head resting on a cushion. I stroked her hair softly and kissed her forehead. I wrote her a quick note, then grabbed a cab to Camden.

Her father opened the door. He just stared at me gormlessly, he was in shock I think, then he looked behind me.

'She's not here.' I announced.

'Where is she?' he snapped.

'Do you care?'

'Don't get lippy with me,' he stepped out of the door, but I didn't back away, even as he squared up to me, 'why are you here, it's late.'

'I want you to stop hurting Lily.'

I could smell his breath; hot tea,

'You're just after what you can get, taking advantage of my daughter's good nature.' He laughed; I didn't like it, 'you must think your bloody ships come in, look at you, you're an old man.'

'Jim, who is it?' Her mum appeared at the door. 'What the hell are you doing here?' she's unstable this woman, she's freaks me out with her frantic eyes. 'Where's Lily?'

'She's at home.'

'Home?' She screamed right in my face, 'With you? That's not a home, it's a place where you can live out your sleazy fantasy with my daughter.' She took a breath, 'I've never heard so much shite.'

'I have,' I raised an eye at her, 'everytime you make Lily cry, everytime you refuse her calls, when you slam the door in her face, or tell her she's made a mistake and she'll have to lie in the bed she's made, how you won't come to her wedding because you think I'm using her, will get bored with her, how you pump her with bullshit about my "reputation", how you call her "careless" and "stupid", well let me tell you both, I'm surprised you've had as many chances as you have, you've hurt her so badly, neglected her so much, you don't deserve her.'

'Don't you dare speak to me like that, you gobshite, you don't really know anything about Lily.' She dug her finger in my chest; I didn't appreciate it, so I carefully pushed it away.

'Be angry with me; hate me, I don't care, but you should be ashamed of yourselves, abandoning your own daughter because of one lousy mistake, a mistake that's turned into something beautiful...'

'Piss off.' Her dad shook his head dismissively, 'you poncy git.'

I smiled, backing away; I'd said my piece.

'I feel sorry for you, that you'll miss out on the rest of her amazing life.' I said calmly, 'and it will be amazing, I promise.'

As I walked away, her mum continued to scream obscenities at me, but regardless, I still felt relieved, because a few miles away, there is a lady waiting for me, one who loves me unconditionally and inside that wonderful woman, grows a child, one we created, but one all these people will miss out on. The second most important person in my life.

"Mr. and Mrs. Howie"

We have a moving date. The end is in sight, and I have honestly never seen Lily so excited. She is now 11 weeks pregnant, and finally the sickness seems to have disappeared, so we can immerse ourselves in planning the wedding and getting used to the idea of becoming parents.

'Boy or girl?' Lily grinned, sitting opposite me in Arbutus.

'I honestly don't mind,' I smiled taking her hand across the table; I love her happy; I love her. 'Either would be great.'

'I'm nervous about the scan next week,' she gripped my hand; it wasn't the first time she'd said this to me, 'it's all real then isn't it, I mean, I know that sounds a bit crazy, but, because we can't see anything yet, it doesn't feel like there's any thing there.' She makes me laugh, but I know what she means.

'I've been thinking about names again,' her eyes twinkle, '"Miller",' she announced, '"Miller Jay".'

'"Miller Jay"?' I deliberated, 'it has immense significance that's for sure.'

'But do you like it?' Huge eyes; such beautiful blue eyes gaze at me.

'Yes, I like it.'

She started giggling,

'What about a girl...you choose?'

In all honesty, I hadn't thought about it, that's how weird and new this is for me. I didn't have a woman's ability to think of the millions of things that come with having a baby. I just want him/her, that's all.

'Well,' I mused, 'I adore "Lillian".'

'No J,' she sighed smiling, 'we can't.'

'Yes we can, she'd love to be named after her mum, she's a wonderful woman you know.'

'OK, let's compromise,' she smiled, 'how about, "Anais Lillian."?'

'I like that compromise.' And I winked at her.

So it stuck. If we have a boy, he'll be "*Miller Jay Howie*" and if we have a girl, she'll be "*Anais Lillian Howie*". Now I know it's for real.

We'd put our work on hold this week to prepare for today's big move, and in case you're wondering, the answer is no, I am not sentimental about leaving this apartment, especially now it's empty.

'J?'

I turned from the window to see my girl standing in the doorway.

'Come 'ere.' I held my hand out and she took it,

'Are you alright?'

'Never been better.' I folded my arm around her and we hugged.

'I promise our new home will be even better than this.' She gazed at me with gorgeous eyes; I want to swim in them.

'I'm not sad Honey,' I said truthfully, 'I'm not one for regrets, I know we're doing the right thing.'

Lily squeezed my hand as I closed the door for good. Yes, there'd been alot of great times; alot of being Jefferson Howie, but the memory that shines the most is her, *my Lily*, of her walking into my life on a beautiful summer's afternoon and completely blowing my world apart; the sun on a redhead's hair is like Heaven, and by God it still is.

'Are you going to say goodbye?' she said softly.

I smiled and kissed her lips,

'I don't need to Honey.'

See, I'm about to enter a new stage in my life, and as I glance at Lily's reassuring hand in mine, and we arrive in the open, she's right, autumn is almost here, the perfect time to move to the country.

"October 3

Let me show you our baby. I know it's not called a "baby" yet, but to me he/she is (attached is the Polaroid from the scan we had last week). It was the most immense but weird feeling when we saw our special friend in there, with their cute button nose and perfect spine, it was so beautiful, so small, but as real as me and J.
I didn't cry though, but J and I did look at each other in that way we do. I wanted to laugh because I still don't believe this is happening. I'd love a bump just so people know I'm having a baby, because now we're are at "Louveciennes", I'm embracing life, I feel safe now, safe and protected. I no longer feel afraid of what's happening to us.

J is wonderful. He knows just what to say and do. He's there when I need him, and he leaves me when he senses I need to be alone.

I don't need to be on my own much though, I mean, I even work beside him; it's more the times when I've been talking to Livvy about mum and dad, or when I think about our baby and how they've chosen not to be part of our life; that my dad won't give me away at my wedding, and my mum won't be there to tell me I look like a princess.

It still hurts, but Jefferson's my man, and we have our "special friend" who will come and live with us next April; that's my family now.

Livvy's been amazing. She comes around a lot to see us, bringing pumpkin and apple pie, or quince jam. I'd like to say I'll be as good a housewife and farmer as Livvy, but I just don't think I've got it in me. I will be a truly honest, faithful and good wife, but J knows the mind of a writer...

We have chosen bedroom three as the nursery because it looks out over the orchard. Livvy told me I've started preparing too early, but J said I could do whatever I wanted, and that sometimes it isn't always empowering or exciting to follow superstition. I love him; I love him so much; he is my soul mate; my kindred spirit, everything I have is shared with him; he has me; every bit of me..."

I look up from Lily's Journal and watch her through the window. She's dancing in the orchards, her auburn halo billowing freely about her face. I can see her breath in the air. She's been picking apples from the floor, I know she chops them for the chickens, and then picks more from the trees for us. I am endeared to her free spirit, her found soul, and I'm forever grateful I have been allowed to see this, to be part of it.

I went to the sitting room and put another log on the fire. I've surprised myself how easily I've embraced this life, and how quickly this house has become our home, Lily and my first home together.

'J?' Lily was stood in the doorway smiling at me, her cheeks flushed, her eyes, brilliant; she is such a beautiful creature. 'Do you fancy eating out tonight?'

I held my hand out and she came to me,

'I was hoping I'd get you all to myself, you, me and that.' And I nodded to the snarling flames, licking the log I'd just thrown on.

'Then you got me.' She whispered.

She unfastened her coat and got to her knees. She lifted her arms and I removed her jumper, her glorious hair cascading down her back, competition for the lustrous flames. She unhooked her bra and swiftly threw it to one side. Yes, another thing I am passionate about: pregnancy swelling. She thrust her breasts into my face and I scoffed at them. She drew away from me, frowning, searching the room, she's looking for something, I sense her dissatisfaction.

She pulled her jumper back on,

'Lily?'

She held a hand out and I took it. I followed her out the French doors and we ran to the orchard. It's dusk and the air is crisp. She falls back among the leaves taking me with her; she's laughing, throwing her arms above her head, *I love her so much*, My Lily, who even in pregnancy, remains the most sexually charged, and resolute person I know, for which I'll be forever grateful.

"October 6

Tomorrow I marry Jefferson James Howie.
I went to Livvy's today to try on my dress for a final time. She said I looked like an angel. She said I will make Jefferson proud and I said I try my best.

We're all heading to London later. We'll be staying at Brown's. J and I are staying together tonight, even though people say it's bad luck. In the morning, Livvy will help transform me into a bride, and J will go to Jeremy's. We'll meet again at Marylebone.

At the moment I feel calm, although last night I was nervous, actually, I was very nervous, I think the realisation that I'll be taking vows with J, and that we'll be married to each other, made me a little overwhelmed, especially considering everything we've been through, and are still going through; but from a selfish point of view, I cannot wait to get that ring on J's finger; now for that I am proud.

Leigh has been amazing. She has almost single handedly arranged the wedding décor for us. We opted for an autumnal theme, just something simple but effective. A marquee with heaters has been set up in the garden, along with oil burners and pretty glass tealights, and there'll be aperitifs beneath the white twinkling lights in the trees and orchard. Later, there'll be a four course dinner in our dining room, which I decorated last night. All it needs is for the candles to be lit and the food and drink served.

Our guests will meet us in London tonight: Leigh and Thomas, Jeremy, Joe (no Florence!), Livvy and Tom, Helena and James. I have chosen a simple menu, which is organic and locally produced

in the Cotswold's, so I hope it will adhere to everyone's tastes. J says it looks "marvelous", so that's enough for me.
If everything goes to plan, tomorrow's menu should go something like this:

Aperitifs, followed by:

Starter:
Pumpkin soup with Moroccan flat bread

Main:
Wild mushroom risotto sprinkled with parmesan and pine nuts and served with herby rustic bread and seasonal vegetables

Desert:
Pink cup cakes decorated with an edible red rose petal (part of a seven tier cup cake stand that will hold 49 handmade cup cakes! – this is instead of a traditional wedding cake).

Followed by a selection of locally produced cheeses with hand made biscuits and coffee.

Drinks:
Cristal, red and white wine; elderflower cordial (for me!)

I looked at our wedding rings last night. I'm happy we chose platinum. I can't wait to see Jefferson wearing a wedding ring, women all over the world will mourn, but I will celebrate! He says the opposite, he says he's approaching 40 and that he thankfully lost his title as an "eligible" bachelor a long time ago,
"Whereas you Lillian, you will be missed." And I said,
"You are a man that makes life drunk – you will always be missed."

I was out in the orchards today, dancing again. I felt a quiver in my belly. I stopped, it happened again. I ran inside to Jefferson,
'Do you think it's the baby moving?' I said.
'I don't know,' he said laying his hand on my stomach curiously, and then we looked at each other and started to laugh. I will never forget it."

*

To: jjhowie@msn.com
From: luke.howie@yahoo.com
Subject:

CUNT

*

Today I married Lillian Ellen Mills. It was my 38th Birthday. Lily wore white. I wore black. It is a moment I will never forget.

'Mrs. Howie?'

Lily turned to me. She's smiling as we travel home in a limousine. I'm drinking Champagne, Lily has orange juice with hers.

'Yes Mr. Howie?'

'Do you know how much I love you?'

'Well, I couldn't possibly say.' She winked.

I adore Lily's kisses. They are heady and intoxicating. I didn't notice the journey back to Louveciennes, I was pre-occupied talking to my wife, yes, I have a *wife.*

It was a simple, yet elegant service. I chose the music, "Cavatina" by Stanley Myers, and even with Jeremy as my best man, I felt more nervous than I thought I would, until she appeared, a *genuine spark of the divine fire,* a vision in heavenly white chiffon, mulled wine hair sleek and glossy upon petite uncovered shoulders, elegantly curled on the ends and clipped gracefully from her eyes; I now know it was a diamond heart.

It was Livvy who escorted this remarkable woman to me; delivering her to a life I promised will be beautiful. I stand by it. We gazed at each other; I was counting her freckles. I have learnt they are subtle in the autumn, but they are there, and I can most definitely join them up.

Lily carried a posy of pink roses, with a red satin ribbon sensually holding them together, it matched my corsage. I clasped her demure hand, so soft between my fingers; I felt it tremble a little. I repeated the vows and slipped the band onto her finger; she returned the gesture.

We are husband and wife.

A small crowd had gathered outside, but Lily and I didn't notice much, we were locked in an embrace; she tasted delicious. Her perfume intoxicating. She cried out, laughing as hundreds of pink rose petals showered us. She raised her dress oh so gracefully as we walked, and I noticed her shoes. Silver heels. Magnificent.

Photographs were taken; we modeled, we smiled, we kissed, we whispered, then joined our friends to enjoy the celebration of our union. Our limousine awaited us, so I took Lily's hand and we kissed again before I helped her inside, then joined her; the driver opened a bottle of Cristal and we drank.

We were the last to arrive at the farmhouse.

'Oh look, they've got a fire going.' Lily pointed to the smoke billowing from the chimney; fair play to Jeremy, he'd been thrown into this, bewildered by what was happening to his family, and yet today, he'd been there for me as my brother,

'It's your wedding day,' He'd said earlier, as we waited for the limousine to pick us up, 'everything aside for this.'

He was a man of his word, he'd even got a fire going for Lily.

I helped *my wife* out of the car where we were greeted by our friends. Thomas popped open another bottle of Cristal and poured everyone a glass. It was a little cool in the breeze, so I folded a pink cashmere wrap around Lily's shoulders and she snuggled into it. We headed to the marquee, where Leigh and Livvy had prepared an aperitif of fresh strawberries with warm chocolate from a fountain, tomato and stilton miniature pastries, sundried tomato ciabatta and gordal olives.

We wandered inside to the dining room, admiring the delicate décor; the wooden table laced with branches of red berries from our garden, and ivy cleverly entwined around the branches. Tea lights in demure glass holders conscientiously placed on the table; a square glass vase in the centre, brimming with an eccentric array of seasonal fruit and flowers.

The antique chandelier was fitted with white candles; all alight. It offered a tranquil luminosity as I sat beside Lily and we smiled at each other.

'Happy?' she said as the others talked amongst themselves.

'I'm very happy.' I took her hand and kissed it; my ring firmly on her finger. 'Thank you, because I will never forget this birthday.'

Our guests took their seats, and not for the first time since being with Lily, I was completely in awe of her; of this life we've created; a life that makes us drunk.

My Genius Pregnant Wife

Witnessing my wife's subtly changing body has become somewhat of a fascination. See, Lily has always been so slight; a tiny wasted goddess with magnificently satiated breasts, so when I arrive back from meeting Henry in London, I find her sitting crossed legged on the sofa with the fire blazing; floor covered in books, papers and her story board, and that's when I notice her disappearing waistline.

'What?' she self consciously glanced down at herself, 'what are you laughing at?'

'I'm not laughing,' I tugged her open waistband, 'what's all this then?'

She sighed deeply, and when our eyes re-met, she was grinning,

'It seems to have happened overnight,' she said lifting her jumper to show me a cute paunch, 'I don't know where it came from.'

'Must be the country air.' And I winked at her.

We sank into the sofa together, and OK, we've only been married 4 weeks, but I adore being married to her, it's the best thing about my life.

'How was London?' She took off my specs and stroked the hair from my eyes, and I know it sounds crazy, but she makes me nervous when she stares into my eyes so intently.

'Dirty and busy,' I said tracing a fingertip over her freckled nose, 'I just wanted to be home.'

'Well, you're back now,' she smiled slipping my specs back on, 'and I haven't eaten yet so shall I put something on for us?'

'Sure.' We sat up, and I remembered the old Evening Standard article Henry had given me. 'Well we've already made it into the papers,' and handed it to her, 'journalists hey, what a bunch of fuckwits.' And we grinned as Lily unfolded the newspaper on page 7,

"Pretty In Pink"
– Journalist and author weds girlfriend in quiet London affair.

Words: Marlene Sawyer
Pictures: Jason Leigh

Prestigious journalist and author Jefferson Howie, yesterday married his girlfriend Lily Mills, in a quiet ceremony held at Marylebone Registry Office.
Howie, 38, author of "Grey Rain" and "Northern Road", met beautiful Lily, who is just 25, whilst she was dating his younger brother.
Scandal amongst their respective families sent the couple into hiding at their plush home in the Cotswold's, but they appeared together in public yesterday after taking their vows with nothing but jubilant smiles for photographers.
They appeared "really in love", said a by stander, "he couldn't take his eyes or his hands off her!"
Auburn haired Lily, who is currently studying at the University of London, wore a pretty couture Amanda Wakeley white satin and chiffon dress with ruffled shoulders and hem, teamed with silver Gina heels and Jane Packer bouquet, made entirely of pink roses and tied elegantly with red ribbon. In place of a traditional headdress, stunning Lily opted for a demure diamond Chanel grip to clip her free flowing hair from her eyes.
The handsome groom remained sophisticated in a Saville Row black suit, no tie, and white shirt, with a single pink rose on his lapel.
The newlyweds left Marylebone in a chic silver limousine, followed by close friends and family, to celebrate at the couple's £1.5 million country retreat. It's rumoured they'll honeymoon in Paris.

'How do they find out this stuff?' I love her laughter; it's contagious.

'Numerous possibilities.' I took back the article; she'd looked so completely beautiful that day.

'But how do they find out so much detail?'

Welcome to the world of Journalism.

'Joe, Florence, Luke himself, who knows, who cares.' I was still chuckling, 'maybe even Henry; anything for a bit of publicity.'

'Well, there we go,' she smiled, sexily stretching out, 'people know as much about us as we do.'

I admire Lily's ability to not take this shit too seriously.

'Ah, well, you're wrong aren't you,' I lay over her; I like this belly, it's cute, 'because they don't know about our little friend inside here.'

Lily kissed me; *I love her madly.*

'Do you think that's why I got that letter from mum and dad, because they'd seen that article?'

'They knew we were getting married.'

'Yeah, I know, but actually seeing it in the paper must have been a bit weird.'

I have to play this carefully; she rarely talks about her parents these days, but I know she misses them.

'Do you want to give them a call?'

'No.' she swallowed, 'no thank you.'

I let it rest.

'How about we grab a bite to eat then,' I gently blew on her belly as I got up; it sent her into raptures, she was trying to tell me something but she was laughing too much, 'what?' I was bewildered.

'It moved; do it again!'

So I did,

'Anything?' I looked at her.

She shook her head, but then her eyes grew wide and she started giggling,

'There! It happened again!'

As you can guess, it was pretty late when we finally had something to eat, but what the hell, I'd had an amazing night thanks to my endearing wife and our energetic baby; folks, it does not come any better than that.

"November [extract written as a continuation, as Lily missed a few days]

We stayed over in London last night for a party in Mayfair, one of J's friends from University (now a banker!). It was the first time some of his friends and acquaintances had seen him since we got married; of course, they were more surprised to see I'm pregnant. OK, I'm not massive (yet), but I have a bump, a "cute" one as J calls it. Anyway, I have lost my waist and so any outfit with a waist band is immediately ruled out and trying to find something glamourous and comfortable has been a fucking nightmare, and it won't stop at tonight, because J's social calendar is already full from now until the New Year (I have to get a grip on this quick!)

Anyway, considering the party was Mayfair, and there were going to be quite a few people there who J had known for years, I wanted to make an impression, be "a good wife" (ha ha!), so I chose a high neck printed silk dress with a green trim by Kenzo. J was with me when I got it. The assistant was very kind, she could see my situation and recommended a seamstress to "take out the waist a little", (her politeness made me laugh inside!) so that's what I did, and I have to say, I was very pleased with the results, and yes, I did decide on 3 inch heels, (just to prove something to myself I guess), I thought they gave me a more polished edge, and Karen Millen shoes are just gorgeous. I am still lucky enough to be a slight woman with just a bump and boobs!

At the party, J kept whispering to me, bad things, filthy things, getting me aroused. He spent most of the night with his hand on my ass and people noticed. He said the green of my dress looked beautiful against my red hair; he kept putting his nose to it; touching it.

He seemed so happy tonight, introducing me proudly. I think he's surprised people who have known him since his late teens, people who thought he'd never "settle down" or "have a family".

'How wrong you can be,' he laughed as Sol, one of his friends questioned him about us, 'how absolutely wrong.'
I know people look at us and "discuss" the difference in our ages, but J and I are comfortable with it, in fact, we adore it. People will always make the assumption that a man does better out of a relationship with a younger woman, but actually, the experience and confidence from being with an older man, far exceeds anything else I have experienced before, so I stand by this; I'll always stand by my J.

I feel like I've been here all my life, at Louveciennes with my husband, yes, my husband, which still sounds weird to me, especially when I look at him, my J. My J who sends me flowers every Friday because he knows I like it, and because he likes "my happy"; pink roses, always pink. I love him so much.

Livvy and Tom joined us at the weekend and we had a brilliant bonfire night. J and Tom made a fire out of waste from our garden and we even had fireworks! Later we enjoyed baked potatoes cooked in foil on the outside BBQ, hot dogs and tomato soup made by Livvy. I had to endure endless mugs of tea and hot chocolate, whilst the others devoured red wine.

I have to admit I was worried when we first moved here that I wouldn't beable to take J's heart out of London, but I'm happy to say he's embraced this life as much as I have. In fact, it feels much richer and varied, something I know Jefferson feels too.

Today we went for dinner at "our local", the Horse and Groom. J told me the Chianti was immense, I only had a sip but I'm looking forward to over indulging next April! We went to Daylesford to the farmshop to pick up bread and gordal olives (my absolute favourites), and then took a brisk walk around Moreton; J laughed because I danced through the leaves, he says I'm a ballerina (I say I'm a rather clumsy pregnant ballerina!). We talked about Paris, and made plans to go there soon.

Recently we've been spending a fair bit of time in London. Usually we stay at Brown's or crash with Leigh and Thomas. I do enjoy it, but living this lifestyle is so much more like hard work when you're pregnant AND sober.

We went to that party in Mayfair last weekend, then another mid week in Primrose Hill, which I didn't mind because it was hosted by one of the charities J is involved with, but then I spend most of the weekend completely fucked out. J feels bad that I get so tired, especially when he catches me stifling a yawn (!), he's started insisting we leave early, he says it's all the excuse he needs to be alone with me.

He's so lovely, my man, because when we got back to the hotel, he ran me a bath, and washed me down, watching my bump in amasement. He tells me how beautiful I am, I wish I could see what he sees.

J's just told me about a function we'll be attending in December. It's an evening dinner held by the Arts Council in Covent Garden. I don't mind going, infact, I feel quite overwhelmed when I do go to these places because J's so well practiced, so effortless and so very handsome, and it's at times like this I realise how influential, and how intelligent he is.

I'm still nervous about going though, see, I've got a bit of a belly now, so what I'll look like in December, I dread to think. Sometimes I get a bit embarrassed by the bump because people stare and I find myself turning to an angle where it's not quite so obvious – I'm only just getting used to it myself.

J gets frustrated when I tell him I'm not keen on getting bigger, he says he adores it, and feels very proud and fortunate. Infact, the more visible it is, the more excited he gets. He says my bump makes him feel warm inside, which I find very sweet. Actually, sweetness aside, J's being very bad at the moment (which I am completely immersing myself in), it seems my changing body is arousing him and although we don't fuck as brutally or as often as we did, we still fuck good.

** I have a meeting with Henry tomorrow; I have no idea what it's about."*

"November 13

Meeting with Henry at The Wolseley. J came with me.
Henry has found a publisher for my Journal! Even now as I write I can't believe it. I'm completely bursting inside. I almost screamed when he told me, (well, actually on the train home, I did), Jefferson laughed hard, I love him like that.
Hamish Hamilton, a subsidiary of Penguin has accepted it; I'm amazed, Me, writing a piece of non fiction, I can barely believe it, I've always been a fiction girl, I never imagined it would be my Journal that would get me published. There are eerie parallels to Anais Nin here. J picked it up too.

They've offered an advance of £50 000 plus a second edition. I've never earned that sort of money in my life. The first edition will be entitled "The Jefferson Journals" [OK, not hugely inspiring, but Henry sort of pushed me into a corner on it, I wanted something a little more provocative, like "A Genuine Spark of the Divine Fire" – J always says it to me – but I think Henry wanted to maintain control].

Anyway, Henry says if I re-think having my early Journal's published, the fee could rise by twice as much if not more and with the royalties, well, who knows, I may make my living as a writer after all.
Only problem with this dream is, I hate the early Journals. J's read parts, but there's so much stuff in it that makes me nervous, I mean J is not a jealous man, but some of those entries are not meant to be read by my husband.
He understands, but says I should edit those parts out and anything else I'm uncomfortable with. My only concern is it'll lose its fluidity, but I suppose that's what Henry's for. I will start working on them next week."

I'm watching Lily. Actually, I watch her all the time and she knows it, but does nothing to discourage me. We're like that you see, we just can't take our eyes off each other, and if you think a "tiny" issue such as Lily being pregnant stops us from being wicked; how wrong you are.

'J?' She comes to me swathed deliciously in a white bath towel, 'will you dry me down?'

I sit on the edge of the bed with Lily between my legs. I slip off her towel and it tumbles to her feet. I look up at her; she's grinning; she is a bad girl sometimes. I run my hands up and down her glorious body to find she's bone dry.

'J?' She says softly,

'Yes Lily.'

'Will you oil my bump?'

Lily is a lady who takes care of herself; I have seen this even more since she's been pregnant.

I light the candles and switch off the bedside lamp. She hands me the oil she uses on her stomach and breasts and I rub it oh so soothingly into her creamy skin. Her eyes close, but her mouth opens. She has given me a sexual license and I know I can do anything to her.

'I adore you,' I whisper, running my mouth where I've oiled, 'I love this body, these changes, oh Lily, you're wonderful.'

And as I make love to her, the stars shimmer through the window, and I think of her, *my genuine spark of the divine fire.*

December 4

"WE'RE HAVING A GIRL!"

I love this picture. ["Polaroid" scan photo of our baby]. *Today J and I went for my 20 week scan (although I'm 22 weeks). I can't believe how much bigger everything looks, and she was moving about like crazy, we giggled loads as we squeezed hands and tried to get to grips with what's happening to us.*

We made the decision weeks ago we didn't want to know the sex, we wanted a surprise, but seeing her swishing about on the monitor, we changed our minds. We were told it's 95% accurate. On the way home, we were so excited, we talked about her all the way.

'We're having an "Anais Lillian",' J sounded quite choked as we left the clinic, 'Jeez Lily, we're having a girl.'
J's ecstatic, because although he didn't mind what we had, I think he was quite excited at the idea of having a girl, a "little Lily" he said. Already I'm thinking of pink! Lots of pink! Friends said we've spoilt it for ourselves, but we laughed it off, it's still going to be a surprise because we have no idea what she'll look like. Knowing she's there is enough of a surprise for me. I love her so much already.

December 8

** Arts Council Dinner – Covent Garden Hotel.*

We left Louveciennes early this morning to get to London in good time. Don't get me wrong, I love London (especially since we've moved to the country), but now I'm getting bigger, the craving to stay closer to home is increasing. I haven't told J, I don't want it to hinder his job, anyway, I've coincided this trip with Christmas shopping and seeing the Christmas lights, because last week it hit me, this will be mine and J's only Christmas together, come next year we'll have a nine month old baby with us; weird and amazing in one. I told J, he laughed and squeezed my knee; he gets excited about things like that.

I like this hotel. J and I used to meet here sometimes after I'd been to work or he'd had a meeting. It's kind of cosy, and yes, kind of expensive. Someone took our cases and J took my hand and guided me to the lifts; he couldn't stop grinning, a real giveaway he had something planned.

As we reached the first floor, I wished for a moment I didn't have a bump, because despite choosing my "day" outfit carefully (black cord A-line skirt (maternity – of course – hideous panel at the front!), a fitted black v-neck jumper with a white camisole underneath and calf length black boots. My hair parted in the centre, loose, clipped to the side), I still managed to feel dull against the few women we passed in the corridor.
'Where are we going?' I was looking for a place to hide.
'Here madam,' and he stood infront of "Tiffany's Library", 'I've booked it for us, for you lovely Lily, for afternoon tea.' And I loved him just a little bit more.

Our room was divine. "Cosy and Regal", J called it, and I agreed. After traipsing around London Christmas shopping I was fucked. (J had been in a meeting all afternoon regarding future Arts projects in England and Wales). My feet were hurting and my back ached and I still had to get through tonight.

I lay on the bed, propped up by gorgeous firm pillows and stared at my dress hanging on the wardrobe. When I ordered it, it seemed like a good idea. I was tired of feeling dreary and fat and thought a sexy Julien McDonald couture slip dress would give me a glamourous and sophisticated edge, but looking at it now, I just don't know if I've got the balls, and if that isn't bad enough, I

thought 4 inch silver Choo's would be a good idea too.
'Lily?' J laid by my side, 'what's the matter?'
'This.' I said pointing to my swollen belly, 'and that.' And I nodded to the dress.
'You're going to look beautiful, you'll stun everyone, they won't beable to take their eyes off you.'
'But that's the problem,' I said turning to him, 'I don't want people to look at me.'

I feel sorry for Jefferson, he tries, really he does, and OK, he has limitations being a man and all, but he'd do almost anything to make me feel good, but I'm afraid he'll never win, not whilst I'm pregnant.

I stepped out of the shower. J had just finished shaving. He smells lovely.
'Come 'ere Deanna; Miss May 1972.' Comparing me to a Playboy centre fold is actually quite a compliment at the moment, 'let me join your dots and drink your mulled wine hair...'
And he did; right there in the bathroom. He amazes me because I can't possibly imagine how he finds fucking me a turn on looking like this. I kept the towel around me, concealing the obstacle to my sexiness, but watched as J buried his head between my legs, and no kidding I came in seconds. Maybe, just maybe he will win this battle...

'Let me admire you, my beautiful wife.' J was sitting on the bed waiting for me. He is divine in a black tux; I adore those square toed shoes; he is a true gentleman and I love and desire him more everyday.
He put his hands out and I took them, 'my own private centrefold.' He kissed each hand in turn, 'let me appreciate you?'
I twirled for him, imagining I looked like the "old" me; the Lily Ellen he fell in love with.
'You are magnificent.' He whispered.
The silver and pink beads, and diamonds shimmered elegantly in the table light. I know my breasts are gorged and despite initially being embarrassed by them, I've decided to try and love them as much as J does!

My legs still look slim though, which is just as well since the dress stops mid thigh, (but I have to admit I copped out of the 4 inch heels and opted for my flat silver roman sandals instead). My arms remain slender, and with my "Deanna" hair (long, centre parted with a wave going through it), for a woman who is almost 6

months pregnant, I've done everything I can to woo my husband, and I think it worked.
'My Lily,' J whispered as he took my hand and opened the door, 'you astound me.'

People stared as we entered the dining hall. Some were aghast with amasement, others couldn't wait to find out who I was. Everyone congratulated J on our marriage,
'And a bun in the oven too,' some guy called Rupert said, 'well done chap.'
'Fuckwit,' J whispered to me, 'public school boy.'
At dinner I sat beside a kind lady called Rachel Gillingham, she's married to the playwright Benjamin.
'You are the most gorgeous creature,' she said as we talked, 'positively beautiful, tell me,' she was looking at my dress (breasts in particular), how do manage to look so completely ravenous, when I was 6 months pregnant I looked at least 9!'
I'm sure she was just being kind, but all the same, it was a much needed compliment.
She was intrigued by my Journal. She said she loved memoirs and diaries, but had never read one written by someone she actually knew.
'You are brave,' she said topping up my water, 'but well done you, one for us girls hey?'
And again I wonder whether I'm doing the right thing."

"December 10

Part of article published in the Independent on Sunday Arts Review (with picture of me and J.)

A CAUSE WORTH SERVING?

– Influential Arts Council members dine to discuss the future of Arts in the UK

Senior members of the Arts Council gathered at the Covent Garden Hotel this week to discuss the future of the Arts across England and Wales.

After pejorative reports that millions of pounds of public money is being misspent on state of the art buildings, the government has ordered a review of its campaign to promote and provide creative recreation and opportunity for the public.

In some parts of the country, Arts centres are closing before they've even opened, resulting in fewer opportunities and negative reactions from local communities to whom these centres were designed and built to support.
Amongst members, Journalist and Author Jefferson Howie, who has remained a keen and passionate supporter of the Arts in the UK, defended the decision to carry on pushing these projects forward,
"..it's clear that in the past we've thought too much about innovation and architecture, whereas this remains important, it is not a priority." He said after the meeting, 'however, these projects remain crucial to aspiring artistes and we will not give up our campaign, we will merely alter them to re-work the balance..."

"December 18

I'm only writing about this because it's hurting me. I can't talk to them, and I can't talk to J. I simply can't open up to anyone about this. I would enclose their letter but I've destroyed it. J knows it was from them, but he didn't question what I did; he understands, even though I know he'd do things differently.

My parents want to get back into my life, but I don't want it. During a time when I desperately needed them, they weren't there for me and I'm finding it hard to forget. See, they've had a trigger, a bit of a wake up call; they know I'm pregnant.
OK, so people might find it a little cruel that I never told them, but they chose not to have me in their life anymore, they made me choose, and I chose Jefferson, I have never, and will never, regret that.

When I found out I was pregnant, I swore Livvy to secrecy, even though she hated it, and even though she nagged me to tell them, I couldn't, and now, after the Independent published our picture, it's there for the world to see, and now they want me back.
Mum said in her letter she was "shocked" and "ill" at seeing me. She said she had no idea. She said I looked "so beautiful" and "grown up".

OK, it's not the first time they've tried to contact me, but usually it's to have a go about something. Before it was about getting married, then the house, then deferring my studies and now it's about not telling them I'm pregnant, needless to say, I haven't responded to any of their letters or voice mails, or any messages they've given to me through Livvy, and this one is no exception. They will never know how much they have hurt me. Never."

I stopped reading the Journal and went to Lily. She was laid out on the sofa reading. The fire was searing; a log snarled. It was cold outside and it looked as though we might have snow. I took the book from her hands,

'Get your coat and boots.' I said.

I took her hand and lead her to the garden. I smiled at her confusion. I started running with her towards the orchard, she was laughing, dancing, and then we slowed and hugged, lingering in our snug embrace amongst the winter bitten trees. I rested my mouth upon her ear and whispered,

'Stay close to me, and I promise you I'll make it beautiful.'

A Most Beautiful Naked Lily

Remember the photograph of Lily I took at Brown's during "my unforgettable night"; the one I intended asking Jez to commission? Well, I'm on my way back from London after collecting it, and Lily has absolutely no idea.

You see, my little lady is just under 6 months pregnant, and it's evident; and the evenings we've talked, Lily's confided she's finding her changing body more difficult to accept than she imagined. She says when she looks in the mirror, she can't identify with the reflection, and therefore, she thinks I can't either.

What I try and tell her is, she's incredibly beautiful in everyway, and I love her even more for this amazing thing she's doing, and as shameful as this comment might sound, she's even more of a woman to me now. I find her obsessively sexy and my infatuation with *the redhead* continues; but I'm not completely sure she believes me.

Anyway, I'm giving her this portrait as a Christmas present to remind her of how magnificent she is (or "was" in her eyes); it's all the proof she'll need.

When I arrived back, I was in eager to see her. When I left her this morning, she was feeling quite morose, her parents had been in touch again but she's still refusing contact. Even Livvy's tried, but failed. I try not to interfere, Lily knows I'll support her whatever she chooses to do. I know she's hurting badly, and for a woman who usually forgives easily, I can't begin to imagine the colossal damage her parents' rejection has caused her.

My parents on the other hand are arriving tomorrow. Yes, I know, something you never thought you'd see, well, me neither, but after a few weeks of intense discussions with dad over the phone, we appear to have "healed" our rift; Mum though, she's a harder nut to crack, but I want to try.

Of course, they know Lily's pregnant, (most people do after the Independent article, oh and for the record, I received another rather unpleasant e-mail from my little brother, but I didn't tell Lily), but until they actually see her pregnant (especially mum), it's just conversation, especially for dad, God bless him, he hasn't got a clue, he didn't have an idea when we were growing up and 38 years later, he hasn't changed a bit. Anyway, I've confided in Lily many times that I miss them, for whatever hurt they've caused us and she feels the same.

'I understand your parents' hurt and anger,' she said last week over dinner, 'I mean, it directly involved two of their sons, but my mum and dad, well, I'll never understand what they did.'

I left the portrait in the car, and walked up the drive to see Lily, well, actually, I saw our bump first, then my beautiful lady, mobile under her chin cutting off branches of holly. She was wrapped in a black tweed coat (buttons unfastened at the front – adorable) and a pink cashmere hat, her heavenly hair draped around her shoulders. She hadn't noticed me yet.

'I know they're worried,' she said on the phone, 'but they had loads of chances to see me when I was living in London, and now because I'm pregnant they want to know me again.'

I gathered she was speaking to Livvy.

'Maybe,' she continued cutting off more holly, 'but just because they're ready to forgive, it doesn't mean I can forget.' I don't like seeing her sad. Lily Ellen doesn't do sad, but with all this shite going on, I've noticed her doing it a lot.

I stood beside the pink Eglu; the "ladies" had put themselves to bed. Lily turned and saw me, she smiled instantly and I swear the sun came out.

'J's back,' she said walking over to me, 'I'll speak to you tomorrow, yeah, love you too, bye.'

She put her phone away and ran to me, and as much as I could wrap my arms around her, I did, actually, I picked her up and spun her around a little, she is not too pregnant to avoid my affection.

'My J,' she is like my 3 year old Lily, 'I missed you.'

'Missed you too Honey.' Oh, Lily's kisses do crazy things to me. 'Everything alright?' I dared to ask as we strolled back to the house.

'Well you know mum and dad are staying with Livvy and Tom for Christmas,' she said as we went inside, 'well, Livvy "suggested" they come over to us for a drink in the evening.'

I gripped her hand; she was cold.

'Why don't you give it some thought?' I said cautiously.

'The thing is Jefferson,' this was serious; she rarely calls me "Jefferson", 'even if they do come over, I don't think I'd know what to say to them, and anyway,' she pulled her hat off, her glorious hair was sticking up slightly; she looked very sweet, but I wouldn't tell her now for fear of being stabbed with holly, 'I fucking hate the way they've treated you.'

'I'm tougher than I look.' I helped her take her coat off; she was wearing that lovely blue Fair Isle tank top, don't ask me why, I just do OK?

'Yeah,' she grinned sitting astride me on the sofa, her mood seemed much lighter, 'you are tough aren't you?' As she kissed me, her hair brushed against my cheek and my skin tingled with delight.

I rubbed my hands up and down her thighs in black trousers,

'Lily?' I said softly, 'despite what you think about yourself, how you see yourself, you remain so effortlessly elegant that even now, sitting here, I want to fuck your brains out.'

She started laughing, lifting her arms, her eyes begging me to undress her, for which I wasted no time in doing. We moved to the floor, the rug; the flames of hell at our side. Oh she is magnificent...

'Hey J,' Lily was standing at the Aga; I could smell she was cooking scrambled egg, and there were Christmas songs coming from the lounge; *cute*. 'I found this amazing quote this morning,' I went to her, folded my arms around her and sank my nose into her neck; she giggled; I love her just a little bit more than before I got up. 'It's from *"Anne of Green Gables".'*

I wonder how long she's been up; she looks fresh whereas I still feel tired. These dark mornings are a drag.

'I'm intrigued.' I said.

As she turned off the eggs, I admired her; she was wearing pajama bottoms that no longer fit her waist, but that she pulls beneath her bump, believe me, this woman puts a whole new emphasis on being pregnant. She is delightful.

She pushed me gently onto the chair behind, and sat on my knees, arm draped around my neck, and proceeded to tell me only people with red hair really know what trouble is.

I smiled; I like these sexy games,

'Right,' I held her by her legs, 'I have one too.' I said, 'it's from Jeeves and Wooster.'

She was laughing,

'Go on then?'

'A lady with red hair, can be wickedly dangerous.'

She folded both arms around my neck,

'But I know J adores danger.' She whispered.

'But I never realised what "danger" was until I met you,' I tucked her hair behind her tiny ear, 'and now I can never go back.' I kissed her, 'my very own centrefold.' And after seeing Jez's portrait of my wife, that's exactly what I have, *A most beautiful naked Lily.*

On opening the door to my parents, I had a weird but pleasant feeling in my stomach.

'JJ.' Dad hugged me, well, a pat on my back in that father-son way. 'I see married life is doing you well,' and he nodded to my slightly expanded waistline, 'it happens to us all at some point lad.'

Hum, not exactly what I wanted to hear.

I opened the door wider to see mum striding towards us,

'Well don't just stand there,' she said shaking her head at me, 'give me a hand Jefferson.'

I smiled, because after six months of living with this hostile relationship, mum remains just as I remember her as I was growing up. Dad winked at me and I headed outside to help with the luggage.

'Well, well,' Dad said hovering in the hallway, gazing up at the mezzanine, 'nice house JJ.' He admired the beams, 'very nice house indeed,' then he looked at me, '£1.5 million I read in the paper.'

I shook my head at him, smiling as I took his coat; he never changes,

'Lily's in the kitchen,' I said hanging up mum's coat, 'go through.'

Now I know this reunion will be especially weird for mum and dad because the last time they saw Lily she was (a) with Luke and (b) not pregnant. Now she's with me, married and pregnant; a lot can happen in a few months, that's all I can say on the matter.

I stood back as mum and dad entered the kitchen. Lily looked nervous; she looked young and *I love her like crazy*.

'Hello.' I saw her swallow.

Dad went straight over and hugged her, then he looked at her swollen stomach and patted it gently; he was beaming,

'I see you've got a belly to match his then,' he nodded to me, 'but at least you've got an excuse.'

Lily's eyes were watering, but she was laughing as she held my dad, and I have to be honest, I was quite choked.

Dad stood aside and let mum through. She couldn't take her eyes off Lily, Lily then the bump, and then back to Lily. I could see my girl didn't know what to make of it, but then mum thrust forward and tenderly took hold of her and they hugged as tightly as the bump would allow; I think mum was crying, so I nudged dad and we headed to the lounge.

'So,' Dad took the single malt from my hand and I sat beside him, 'you look happy JJ.'

'I am.' I heard Pride in my voice, 'more than I can tell you.'

He nodded,

'Good, good, I'm glad, well, we both are.'

I had to raise an eye at that,

'And mum?'

Dad started laughing, he'd already gulped his drink; it must have been the journey with mum.

'What do you think son,' he said softly, 'you saw her out there, she's missed you both like hell, stubbornness you see JJ, it doesn't always pay.'

'Heard from Luke?' I couldn't keep ignoring it, despite the sad fact we'll probably never speak again in this lifetime.

'He's in Hawaii for Christmas and New Year.'

'Hawaii?' I topped up his glass, 'Surfing?'

'Got a lady out there,' he said, 'met her at some competition or something,' dad shrugged, 'it's put a smile on his face for now anyway, I'm sure it's just temporary, you know Luke.'

Yes I do; very well actually.

I looked up to see my wife, yes, *my wife*, coming in with my mum. Mum had her arm linked through Lily's chatting away as though they'd only seen each other yesterday.

'Oh JJ, what a beautiful Christmas tree.' Mum was gawping at the 8 ft fir tree beside the fireplace, magnificently decorated by my little lady, (twinkling white fairy lights and silver stars). 'Oh I do love the traditional decorations.' Mum was like a kid in a sweet shop, 'oh and look at that, and oh Lily, your garden...' mum had her nose pressed against the French doors, 'Oh I must see that in the morning.' And so it went on: wedding photos, scans, a tour of the house and so on, and finally, when I lay down beside Lily, for the first time since mum and dad arrived, I had her to myself.

'Hello.' I smiled as she lay her head on my pillow with mine, she often does this; she's so endearing.

'Hello.' She put her hand on my cheek; I put it to my mouth and kissed it.

'That wasn't so bad was it?'

'I've had a wonderful night.' She smiled, 'do you think we've been forgiven?'

I laughed softly,

'I think so.'

'Your mum was quite taken by the wedding photos wasn't she?'

'So she should be.'

'And the scans.'

'It's their first grandchild so be prepared.' And I kissed her forehead. 'Lily?'

'Yes J?'

'I have something for you.'

She propped herself up on one arm, stroking hair from her eyes,

'Oh?' she grinned, 'go on, you've got me now.'

OK, so I only have one more day until I can officially give it to her, but I don't want to wait, I'm following Lily's rules remember.

'Our "unforgettable night" at Brown's?' I said slipping out of bed and going over to the wardrobe,

'With "no ordinary redhead"?' she's laughing; it's lovely.

'Yes.' I said carefully taking the 6ft by 5ft portrait from the wardrobe, currently covered by a sheet of canvas, 'well, now it certainly is unforgettable.' And I whipped off the cover to reveal my beautiful redhead; my own sexy centrefold. 'This is for you Lily, all for you.'

Now, let me tell you, seeing Lily (currently dressed in a white vest clinging very cutely to her bump and those floral pajamas bottoms), sitting on the edge of the bed astounded by her portrait, makes me one very happy man.

She looked at me, then the painting, then back to me with watery eyes. She got to her knees and touched it, the oil on canvas.

'Oh my God,' a rogue tear slid down her cheek, 'you've taken my breath away.' And I had, because she was holding her chest trying to take gentle breaths.

'I asked Jez to commission it for me,' I said leaning it against the wall then sitting beside her, 'from a photograph.' She looked at me, 'I took it the following morning.' I folded my arm around her and we kissed, 'see Lily Mills, to me you are the most stunning woman, then, now, always.'

We looked back at the painting. It was seamless, it could be a photograph.

'You can see my nipples,' she grinned, 'I hope no one else but Jez saw this.'

I laughed,

'Don't you worry about that Honey.'

'They're quite nice nipples though aren't they?' she's smiling at me, my little lady.

'They're exquisite nipples.' And I kissed her hand.

'He's made me look quite beautiful.'

'You are beautiful Lily.'

I brushed the stray tears from her eyes with my thumb and she snuggled into me. I rested my head against hers and closed my eyes. Last Christmas I was lonely, last Christmas I knew for sure I'd fallen in love with Lily, even though we were both with other people, but I could never have anticipated, that 12 months on, I'd be here, in this incredible house, with my even more incredible *wife* who is pregnant with our first child.

'I thank God I followed your rules,' I whispered, 'that I ran with you.'

'We ran together.'

I smiled; she's right.

'Our rules?'

'Our rules.' And she winked.

My Mistake

I woke up alone with the exception of *a most beautiful naked Lily*, and wallowing in the warmth of this huge bed, I could smell food; I could hear laughter too. It's Christmas Eve, I thought snugly, and my folks are still here.

I dragged my sorry ass to the edge of the bed wishing I hadn't drunk that last whiskey with dad. I pulled on a pair of joggers and a sweatshirt and made my way downstairs to a sight that melted me.

I watched silently from the kitchen door, as "my centre fold" prepared breakfast with my folks: Mum, setting the table, dad cutting bread and Lily stirring at the Aga. The back door was open and "Ellie", one of our chickens, was scratching about on the outdoor mat; yes, crazy I know, but I wouldn't change it for anything.

My eyes wandered back to Lily; she was wearing a black wrap around dress and black ballet pumps, her hair sexily braided; she looked delicious. She was sharing a joke with dad. Actually, dad in particular has a soft spot for Lily, (as have most Howie men!) and watching him put his arm around her shoulder, laughing, I'm grateful for this moment, a moment I feared would never come, but with this visit I'm optimistic we've started to put the past behind us, and I wonder whether the time has come for Lily's parents to do the same, given the chance.

'JJ!' Dad saw me, 'come in son, we're having porridge, then a full English.' Can you guess my Dad loves food?

I made my way over to Lily and we hugged, then kissed, and she looked into my eyes like she always does,

'Tu as de beaux yeux, tu sais.'

I adore Lily telling me I have lovely eyes,

'Merci belle.'

Mum and dad were also sharing this moment with us, but that didn't deter Lily, nothing much did, and the small matter of having my parents in the room whilst we flirt is not something that worries her. Mum and dad on the other hand, well, I sensed their awkwardness.

'So, do you think you'll get back out to Paris?' Trust mum, I knew she'd be the first to break the intimacy, I could feel the discomfort killing her.

'I hope so,' Lily slipped her hand to my ass; I think dad saw her, 'but I want my figure back first.' She smiled rubbing her belly with her free hand, because right now she's rubbing her other hand over my ass and I have one hell of an erection which is not good in these joggers.

'Oh you'll have no problem getting that back,' Mum said admiring my wife's (my very naughty wife's) beautiful body, 'all you've got is a bump, from the back and the front you look exactly the same.'

I could see Lily was pleased with that, but something I wasn't entirely pleased about was not being able to get her alone to fuck her, and now that she's running her finger gently between my crevice over these joggers, it's making me crazy.

'Shall I pour the porridge?' Dad never "poured" porridge, he could obviously see what was going on; I think I'm going to have the leave the room in a moment to cool down.

'Yes,' mum agreed, 'let's all sit down together, that'll be lovely.'

'Umm,' I was trying to think of a way to excuse myself, 'I'll join you folks in a moment.' I smiled and nodded and headed to the toilet in the hope my erection might go down, but as I was closing the door, I felt a hand grip my arm, 'Lily,' I was trying to unpeel her, 'what are you doing?' But she was locking the door behind us, pushing me back against the wall.

'Shhh,' she said putting a finger to my lips, 'just be quiet.'

And right there, she got to her knees, pulled my joggers to my thighs, and Jesus Christ!

We took my parents to The Grapevine in Stow, where we tucked into a Christmas dinner in La Vigna Brassiere before they had to make their way back to London. When Lily and I arrived home I watched her on her knees placing my folks Christmas presents beneath the tree and I wondered again about ringing Livvy, so when Lily said she was going for a soak in the bath, I seized the opportunity.

'Does she know you're ringing?' Livvy said.

'No.'

'Is that a smart move?'

'Absolutely not.' I smiled, 'But I want to do this for her, because I know she wants it, she's just afraid.'

'Well, you know her mind at the moment, so if you think it'll work then let's give it a go.'

Truth is, I'm not convinced at all, in fact, I'm wondering now as Lily lies with her head on my stomach and we watch the fire calm, Christmas carols in the background, whether I've made a mistake.

'Happy Christmas!'

I woke to see Lily bouncing around the room (well, sort of, she was holding her bump with two hands; it's all very cute), 'J, look,' she said pointing to a pile of presents I'd secretly placed at the bottom of the bed, 'he's been.'

Did I mention my girl adores Christmas? Well she does; in fact, she's so excited by it, our house has become a grotto, but a very stylish and sophisticated one of course. So, for most of this week, my wife has been making mince pies and mulled wine – alcoholic and non-alcoholic, wrapping presents, driving me insane with Christmas songs, and collecting winter vegetables from the garden to give to Livvy to cook us up a treat,

'I have my limitations J,' she purred at the time, 'besides, I never said I was a domestic goddess.'

'No,' I said pulling her into me, well, as much as I could, 'you're simply "a goddess".'

As Lily organised breakfast I prepared a fire. She's been dreaming of this moment since we moved in, opening her presents in front of the fire, and as promised, I will make her life with me beautiful, and just to make it a little more wonderful, I've gone all out to completely spoil her with gifts.

I watched as she placed the breakfast tray on the table. There was a pot of tea, two glasses of Bellini, warm crusty bread, various cheeses, pickles, ham, pork pie and butter; my mouth was watering.

We opened our gifts beside the Christmas tree, fire blazing with a frosty outlook across the garden. Lily was so excited, making it officially the best Christmas I've had since I was a kid and mum and dad bought me a Chopper, because, you see, Lily does that, she's so vibrant, so alive and so happy that I can't help feeling her joy too.

In fairness, she gave me some amazing gifts, amongst many, an iPod, a Paul Smith sweater, black Prada jocks (for her benefit as well as mine; she says they make my dick look "luscious when hard" – she is unruly), a Cartier steel travel clock, and a leather case for work (my current one is falling apart) and in return, hold your breath, I gave her a diamond and white gold Tiffany watch and diamond earrings, a Chanel handbag, leopard print ballet shoes (she's been admiring these for months now), "Bunny" bra and matching panties from Agent Provocateur (for when she's no longer pregnant), and a black set designed for pregnancy,

'I took advice on this one,' I said as she opened it, 'I always want you to feel as beautiful as I see you.'

OK, I could go on, because I really did blow a hell of a lot of money on my girl; but it's only money right, and now I have her, I want to spend it on her; on my wife, because I enjoy it, and I have no regrets, because right now Lily is wearing her new AP underwear and I'm admiring her.

She feels self conscious because she knows I'm taking great delight in running my eyes over every delicious inch of her body, and as crazy as this might sound to a man who hasn't seen a pregnant lady in such an attire, she is, and will always be, my *virgin-prostitute*, my *perverse angel*, my *two-faced sinister and saintly woman*, my beautiful Lily Ellen.

OK, so let me tell you about this mistake I think I've made, because I've checked my watch and it's just about to happen. See, when we first moved into this house, we decided we'd have a quiet Christmas. Lily anticipated being "big and fat" and with not being able to drink she knew she'd find dozens of guests consuming copious amounts of alcohol a little, well, frustrating, so, despite an invite from Livvy and Tom (no way was she accepting, not after discovering her parents would also be there) and from Helena and James, we stayed true to our decision and remained at home, our *Louveciennes*, and right now, it's seven thirty, we've had dinner, indulged in way too much food, and Lily's staring at me because the door bell has just rang; and I swear, there's vomit in my throat.

'Who could that be?' I'm not surprised she sounded concerned; we live way out in the sticks and its Christmas evening. 'J?'

I think I looked guilty.

'I'll answer it.'

See, when I watched Lily and my folks in the kitchen together, laughing and talking, it warmed my heart, and so if we can do it with my parents, we should beable to do it with hers.

'I'll come with you.' She said taking hold of my hand.

Together, we went to the door. I peeped through the spy hole; our guests had arrived.

'It's Livvy and Tom.' I said knowing she was going to ask.

'Livvy and Tom?' She frowned.

I unlocked the door, praying in my head this would be alright, that this idea of mine was going to work.

I pulled open the door; two more faces had appeared and they were staring at my wife, no, let me rephrase that, they were gawping at my wife, then my wife's bump. Lily grabbed the door and slammed it shut.

'What the fuck are they doing here?' she was spitting fire; my heart sank, 'I told Livvy no! No fucking way, I can't fucking believe she's done this,' she was raging, pulling her hands through her hair; crying, 'why would she do this; she knows how I feel!'

The door bell rang again.

'Let me get it Lily...'

'No!' she screamed. 'Leave it!'

I went to her,

'Listen,' I said softly holding her by the shoulders, 'we did it with my folks, we can try with yours.'

She scowled at me,

'What the fuck is going on J?'

I closed my eyes and took a breath; I couldn't lie to her,

'Look, it wasn't Livvy's idea it was mine...'

She slapped me. Hard. Right around the face. I guess I deserved it.

'You fuck.' And she ran from me.

My face was stinging. I put my hand to it; it burned. She has one hell of a hand on her that's for sure. I heard her running upstairs and then the bedroom door slammed. I shuddered; I had to face our "unwanted guests".

'She's a bit upset.' I said.

'But you said she'd be fine about it.' Livvy sighed.

'I said I couldn't be sure.'

'Can we see her?' It was the first time her mum had spoken to me in months; it was quite surreal.

'She's gone to lie down, now probably isn't a good time.'

'I knew this would happen,' Livvy sounded frantic, 'I knew she's act like this; we should never have done it!'

'We had to try.' Tom said, thankfully thinking as a reasonable human being, because I was feeling seriously out numbered.

'I'm sorry you've had a wasted trip.' I said feeling my face burning up.

'Can we stay?' her mum's frenzied glare frightened me, 'see her when she's calmed down?'

'I think you might have a long wait.'

'We'll wait.'

I was getting annoyed.

'You should go; she's very upset.'

'I want to see her.' Her mum stepped forward as though she was going to come into the house.

'No.' I put my foot out to stop her entering.

'She's our daughter.' Her dad said; shame they hadn't thought about that before.

'Yes I'm aware of that, but it's Lily's decision whether or not she wants to see you.'

'So why did you bring us here?' her dad demanded, 'knowing she'd get upset?'

That was it; I snapped.

'Because I just fucking thought I was doing something right by you people for once, now please, leave!'

Tom smiled briefly at me as they walked away, and I nodded to him as the others mumbled between themselves, and if ever I had hope of being accepted into her family, I'd completely blown it, and now, well, that was nothing compared to facing my wife; that my friend was going to be a feat in itself, but I have every confidence we can work through it, because that's what we do, because I love her; I love her madly and it's just an argument right, it's not our first and it won't be our last, but as I climbed the stairs to our room, the pain in the pit of my stomach was telling me something different, and I don't mind admitting, I was afraid.

In my ignorance, as I opened the bedroom door, I expected to find Lily curled up asleep or perhaps sobbing gently, however, she wasn't, she was actually sitting on the edge of the bed looking more alert than I'd seen her for some time.

'That was one hell of a slap Lily Ellen,' I was trying not to take this seriously, because I had a horrible feeling it was the opposite, 'Fair play to you.'

'Jefferson help me to understand,' her voice was soft but focused, 'because I feel like you've betrayed me.' She looked at me; her words pierced me like a knife, 'you're the only person in this life I really trust, and I can't believe you'd do something like this.' She wiped a stray tear from her cheek, 'I feel really disappointed.'

I swallowed the huge lump in my throat. She could call me a cunt, a fuck, a bastard whatever and I'd take it on the chin, but to have her tell me she's "disappointed", well, that's grim.

'I'm so sorry,' I sat beside her; she flinched and moved away slightly. I had bile in my throat. 'I wanted to do something magical for you.'

She glared at me and I realised I'd never seen her like this, and now I know just how much I've hurt her.

'That was not magical,' she spat, 'that was gruesome.' She got up; I wanted to follow her,

'Where are you going?' I called.

'To work for a while.'

'But it's Christmas evening.'

She turned and looked at me with an unfamiliar frown, and now I fear I may have lost a little bit of her love,

'I need to work.'

I watched her leave, for ages staring at the spot where she'd been standing. I felt a sudden sense of loneliness and my eyes prickled. I swallowed that damned lump again and lied on the bed. I closed my eyes, tears trickled down the side of my face. I'd made a mistake, one I wished I could take back, a mistake I never intended to make.

A Letter to Lily; a Plea to J

One thing I am grateful for, is Lily did eventually come to our bed. OK, it was late, very early hours I think, but I know her well, and I know she wouldn't retire from working until she'd finished what was required of her.

See, although I was in bed, I hadn't actually been asleep; I couldn't. I was trying to find words that would allow me to express to Lily how sorry I was for the mistake I'd made; how I'd completely misjudged the situation. I guessed Lily would be telling her Journal something similar, so I thought I'd try my hand at a bit of journal writing myself.

Ironically, I'd only just turned out the light when I heard Lily coming upstairs, the note book to the side of me, filled with "a letter" I'd written to her. If I'm being honest, it's the most prolific piece of work I've written for some time, in fact, I'd go as far to say I've never been quite so honest or forward in my writing; it's a fresh feeling for me, one I like; one I hope she'll like too. One I pray will make a difference.

My darling Lillian,

I want to tell you some things about me I know won't surprise you, but even so, I feel it is my duty to say them to you.

Lily, when I first heard Luke had met a special girl, I was envious. Of course, I hadn't even met you then, but I'd heard you were a writer and that you were beautiful; even dad sounded besotted. I have to be honest Lily, I hadn't been in a relationship for 3 years before I met you, but I was looking, as shameful as you might find that, because after years of cheap glorified sex I wanted to find someone special, someone I could fall in love with, someone who would love me for everything I am, and everything I'm not.

Oh my darling, when you walked into my apartment last summer you snatched my breath. Not only were you incredibly beautiful with your exquisite centrefold figure and rapturous auburn hair, you were also a kick ass twenty something who provoked my conscious as well as my body.

See, I'd been wandering aimlessly Lily, from woman to woman, and as crude as this might sound to you, I was passing time, just waiting and not knowing when it might happen, and then you; and it was all over for me.

Lily, all those evenings I crept into the writers group, seeking you out, wanting to talk to you, confirmed to me how deeply attracted to you I was, and I sensed you might feel a little for me too, I wanted to push it as far as I could without us doing anything untoward, anything that might have gotten us into trouble; made us feel guilty; made us stop, so dropping you home every week became an event I looked forward to, an evening in which I took great delight in keeping you up late; talking to you, laughing with you, listening to you. Lily, so many times I wanted to ask you to dine with me, have a drink with me, always thinking of sleazy ways in which I could lure you to my place, Oh Lily, the thought of touching your velvet skin kept me awake for hours.

Precious Lily, you will never know how much I grieved that I couldn't be with you. How I wrote passionately about you, how you inspired me, how you made me happy, how I couldn't look or take any interest in a woman with you close to me. Yes, Lily, even Bella at Christmas and New Year, you were right with what you said in your Journal, about the New Year party, I did follow you; seek you out, notice your clothes, and yes, if you had of leaned forward and let me kiss you, I would have, even with Luke in the next room because I knew for sure I was in love with you, and selfishly Lily, if you had let me, I would have taken you and married you sooner.

Oh I have fucked Lily, you know I have, but from that June afternoon, every woman I fucked was you; but until I finally had you, until I finally had the privilege of opening your legs and looking inside your delicious sex I hadn't fucked at all. You're wonderful Lily, you are every kind of woman I can imagine would make me happy. How you do it I don't know, but you are Fire with your beautiful hair, the most perfect I have ever seen, you are smouldering and sexy, alluring and mischievous; you are cute and dangerous, you are free and caught; naïve and assertive, passionate, strong, delicious, elite, raw and fresh, innovative, kind, forgiving, generous and genius...

Lily, I don't think I have much to offer you, but what I do know is, the day you asked me if we belonged together, I knew then we did, but get this, I was afraid to tell you, I was so in love with you, I didn't know how I would manage the rejection if you didn't agree; you teased me Lily, and I took it even though it hurt sometimes, yes, me, "arrogant and pretentious Jefferson Howie" afraid of rejection from a woman!

My darling listen, the day we married, was the happiest day of my life. I took those vows with all of my heart because this is it for me Lily, I love you, I want to grow old with you, you are my family now; you're my life, this superb life I have is because of you, you make this a home, you and the second most important person in my life, because yes Lily, I had already imagined you having a baby, the night we saw Gracie and Eliot, I saw you there with a bump, can you imagine, even back then?

Lily trust me, please, I know I've done wrong by you, but you have me, everything I have belongs to you; I don't want to imagine not being with you, it's too painful, it brings bile to my throat. See Lily, when I saw you in the kitchen with my parents yesterday, how they loved you and wanted to be close to you, how they've embraced our marriage and our child to be, I wanted you to feel some of what I did; I know now it was a big mistake to be presumptuous about something you must think I know nothing about, and maybe so, but I do know their betrayal has hurt you very much, and for that I am truly sorry. Oh my darling, my sweet Lily Ellen, stay close to me; love me, and I promise you, not only will it be beautiful, but you will always be happy in my love.
I love you,
Truly,
Jefferson xxx

When I woke this morning, Lily was still asleep. Her magnificent mulled wine hair unruly across her face, her mouth slightly open. She was lying on her side, but facing me. At least she'd stayed the night, I feared she'd choose to sleep in one of the other rooms.

I gently stroked her hair and she shifted slightly. I know she doesn't sleep well at the moment, so I left her, pulled on my joggers and laid my "letter to Lily" by her bedside, and as I closed the door and headed downstairs, I wondered if I could turn this thing around.

I went into the study, and there on the desk was a pile of papers.

I eyed them curiously; I wasn't sure whether Lily intended me to read them, but there they were, staring at me, begging me to do it, and when it comes to Lily's work, I can't help myself.

J, my love,

I have to write about how I'm feeling right now; I don't think I'll regret this in the morning, but just in case, I love you Jefferson James Howie, I always will. This is my plea to you.

There are so many things I've wanted to tell you but I've either been afraid or haven't found the right time.

You see J, I'm not as perfect as you make me out sometimes; there are things I've done that I'm ashamed of, and others I'm quite proud, and if I tell you them now, you may understand my parent's actions and my desperation to avoid them.

Oh J, perhaps in hindsight, I should never have sent you those Journal extracts, then I wouldn't be feeling like this right now. You would never have asked me questions and I wouldn't have had to confront these early Journals again, which brings me to my plea, that you will read, and not judge me, but that you will love me as I am, for what I am, and if what you read hurts you, forgive me, I was just a girl, a girl seeking adventure; a girl who sometimes got it badly wrong.

I sat down on the sofa, the pages burning my fingers. This was something I knew I had to do, because regardless of what's contained in this Journal, I love Lily, she's my wife and she's carrying our child, I love her for her seamlessness and her flaws, but still, as I uncovered the first entry I could smell fear; she was just 16 years old.

September 9 1997

I saw him again today. He looked important in his work clothes yet really lovely, but I think I like the casual look better. He is so cool.
D, beautiful D, if anyone found out about this I'd probably be expelled, and if I didn't think he liked me too, I'd stop right now, but everytime I see him, he's looking at me, smiling and I just can't help myself...I can't eat much either and mum's moaning at me, saying I'll get too thin. Maybe D likes thin girls; maybe not wanting to eat isn't such a bad thing...

He walked past our table today in the canteen, I was sure he winked at me, so I smiled back and he did a double take, and nodded. My stomach went mad and I felt sick. He's so lovely, I feel like I love him.
Joanna was with me, she says all the young lecturers are like him, can't get enough of young girls and that I should watch myself, but I can't help it, that forbidden feeling, the butterflies in my stomach when I think about him...

September 13

James' Party. 7pm.

Oh My God. D was at the party. My belly hit the floor when I saw him. It turns out he's James' cousin. I hid so he wouldn't see me. I thought he might have a girlfriend, but he came with his friend Billy.

Joanna teased me, she said James told her D had been asking about me, I didn't believe her, why would he ask about me?
I hate alcohol, but I drank cider, my head felt a bit funny and I couldn't stop talking to people, even ones I didn't know. D was across the room when he saw me and straight away waved me over. My heart was beating really fast, it made me feel sick. I shook my head, I just couldn't do it, he's so much older than me. He shrugged and I regretted not going over, so I got another drink, trying to decide what to do, but when I turned around, D was in the kitchen with me. He smiled and said he understood why I was avoiding him – I doubted he did.

We started talking about college and I felt much better. He was really kind to me. He asked if I had a boyfriend, I said no. He asked me to dance, I said yes. He didn't do anything bad to me, I guess the place was crawling with people who could incriminate us, I mean, him.

I talked with D all night. A few other students from my English class kept staring and pointing, but D told me to ignore them. He said I was a very intelligent girl and that it's a pleasure teaching me. I wasn't sure what to say, so I said it was time for me to go home. He started laughing, but in a nice way and asked why I was leaving so early. I reminded him I was 16 – thought I should.

Oh D is so lovely. He makes me feel bubbly inside. When me and Joanna got back to hers, I talked about him all night. Joanna says he fancies me, I wish. I played the night back a million times, especially remembering how he touched my arm, how he moved it down to my wrist as he checked my watch...

September 18

D asked me to stay behind after class today. I was buzzing with anticipation all through class, I couldn't concentrate. He is so gorgeous. I was really nervous; I thought he was going to say something about the party – that I acted inappropriately.

It was strange being alone with him. It felt wrong, nothing like as nice as it felt the other night. I could see the fear in his eyes and it frightened me. He closed the door after the last person; my feet were stuck to the floor.
'Lily,' his hands hovered mid air as though he wanted to touch my face, 'did you have a good time the other night?'
'Yes thanks,' I said wondering whether I was in trouble, 'I wished I could have stayed longer.'
'I wished you could have too.' He smiled sitting on the edge of his desk, 'Lily?' My heart was beating really fast, 'listen, I know this might sound a little strange, but I wondered whether you wanted to go out some time?'
I thought I was going to throw up.
'OK.'
He smiled and reached for my hand; I let him hold it.
'What you up to Friday night?'
D asked for my phone number and gave me his. He said he'd pick me up somewhere neutral, Friday at 7. We're going to the cinema. He told me I should keep this between us – I'd already guessed I should.

September 30

I feel a bit weird tonight, there's a lot of stuff going on in my head and I can't talk to anyone about it. I hate being sworn to secrecy. It was nice though, I liked it, wasn't too sure I should have done it though, even though D was really lovely to me, you know, gentle and stuff. He seemed so big against me, like a real man – I don't suppose you ever know when you're really ready for it.
D said stuff that made me feel out of my depth. He said he loves my "bouncy breasts" and that even though it's my first time, I seem to know what to do,
'And do it so well.' He laid on me again. I closed my eyes, shuddering; it even hurt the second time.

He knew I was nervous about all of this, but he said he'd look after me and he did – he does. He said he can't help himself when it comes to me, that doing it with me is all he thinks about. He told me I was "beautiful" and that "sinning" with me has become an obsession. He said I wore pretty underwear and asked if he could keep my pants. I said my mum would miss them. He sort of went green and gave me them back.

Jesus H. Christ! Lily had an affair with her English lecturer.

I flicked through the next few pages, I wanted to be spared the sordid details (there were plenty of them – her inexperience didn't stop her immersing herself in this new found pleasure), however, the affair started to demise (for Lily) the following January, but for D, well, it seemed his obsession with the redheaded "sinner" continued.

January 15 1998

D stopped me after class; I told him I was late for Sociology. He asked me why I've been avoiding him, I said there was a rumour going around about us and I didn't want to jeopardise my studies. He said he hadn't heard anything, I told him he wouldn't – he's a member of staff.

He wanted to see me after college; meet up and go for a drink, I said I couldn't, I had work to do, but he didn't believe me, he seemed desperate, he sort of scares me when he's like this, he's becoming possessive and I'm not sure what to do, I mean, he's a handsome 27 years old teacher, why does he need to be around a 16 year old student – I have no idea...

I started laughing; this was so Lily, so my Honey; even then she was unaware of her allure.

I scanned the next few pages. Lily called it off a week after this entry and D did not take it well.

He's being horrible to me; I don't know how much longer I can be in his class.

By February, Lily had moved to another class, but the "*harassment*" continued. The interesting thing is, her entries start becoming a little more, well erratic, and if I know my Lily, she has something grave on her mind.

March 5 1998

I sat on the toilet for hours when I got home. I did everything Leanne said I should, even the hot bath bullshit, but nothing happened. I went down for tea and mum asked me why I'd been crying. I said I'd had a bad day at college. I don't think she believed me. I started thinking about knitting needles again. Oh I hate him; I fucking hate him!

I can't believe this is happening to me; how can I go to University with a baby! Mum heard me crying in the night; she said she knows there's something wrong, she begged me to tell her, it took her ages to convince me, but in the end I did, but I don't think it was what she expected...

Holy Christ!

Mum came in to see me; she said D was at the door demanding to speak to me; I said no. She told me I should tell him about the baby, I said he already knows, she looked shocked,
'He wants to keep it,' I sobbed, 'he wants to marry me.'
Mum started screaming; she said I'd made a right mess of everything, she called me "careless" and "promiscuous", I shouted back at her that I'd only ever slept with him and that I only told him it was someone else's so he'd leave me alone.

I've told mum I don't want it; I know she says it's my decision but I sense she wants me to keep it. D wants it; I hate him; he's made my life miserable; he has no idea! Me and mum are going to the doctors tomorrow. She says she has to tell dad...

There was heaps of the stuff. Pages on how the doctor made her feel ("*like someone dirty*"), how her dad almost beat "D" to a pulp outside his house; how "D" wanted to press charges until Lily's dad reminded him about underage sex (even though Lily was 16; he said he'd lie) and also for abuse of trust in his role as a teacher.

From what Lily wrote, it appeared D was in love with her and wanted them to be together, but she blamed him for getting her pregnant (she later revoked this; she blamed herself just as much for taking risks – she said she wanted the thrill just as much as he did) but at the time she hated him for "*ruining*" her chances of going to University.

Anyway, *My Lily* finally had a termination; she was almost three months pregnant. Her parents "*forced*" her to have counselling because they thought she would grieve, Lily wrote,

"I'm relieved it's gone; they're the only ones making me feel bad about it."

After the abortion, relations with her parents remained fraught, so when Lily turned 17, she moved into a shared house with three people she knew from the local writer's circle. This appeared to be the start of her rebellion.

At just 17 she posed naked for a series of paintings for some guy's Fine Arts degree. At 18 she got involved with a photographer, an American guy called Gerard who she met through "Bessie", and he took photos of her naked,

"But we did not fuck –it was just Art..."

A while later, the photos appeared in Gerard's portfolio, made public during a University open evening, but Lily stood by what she'd done; she said she was proud of them, (and why wouldn't she be, she has a beautiful body) – however, her parents were not impressed, and when they confronted her, she said,

"When I die I want to be remembered looking like I do on those pictures..."

Now, from what's written in the Journal, after her termination and the disastrous affair with "D", Lily had still only slept with a handful of men, and it wasn't until she turned 20 that her then boyfriend Ben, gave her a copy of Anais Nin's "*Fire*" from a Journal of Love, and that my friend gave way to her sexual licence, her "*awakening*".

"I no longer fear sex or intimacy," she wrote, *"I feel more of a woman now than I ever have; I want to see and feel so much more...I want to fuck like crazy..."*

With her new found confidence, Lily started going to parties; mixing with dissident bohemian writers, artists and poets, and "experiencing" fruits she never imagined existed. In between this, she wrote and studied and from the fire, arose a genius.

"I will dedicate my life to this..."

She drifted in and out of relationships, usually 'out' when sex became "*dull and uninspiring*". She started attending a writers group in Camden where she met a man called Stevie, an MA English Literature student, and also a bit of a mentor to her. He was in love with her; needless to say, she was not in love with him,

"Stevie is clever and kind of cool, and maybe if he was older and more experienced, maybe if he were a little more graceful and distinguished, he might be a man who could take me all the way..."

Stevie later introduced her to the writing of a "*pretentious wanker*" named Jefferson Howie.

"I have just read a man. A man I think I like."

I stopped reading; someone was standing in the doorway of the study. She looked tired. Her hair draped beautifully about her face, but there was no fire in her eyes; she was holding her bump. I recognise her as my Lily Ellen, and I love her.

I put down the Journal and reached out for her. Her bottom lip quivered; her eyes were watering; her hand like velvet against my palm, just like the first time we touched, and as she sat on my lap, and I stroked her face, she wouldn't look me in the eyes,

'Lily,' I whispered, 'forgive me?'

'You haven't done anything to forgive.'

'Last night?'

'Last night was about the strained relationship I've had with my parents since the abortion.' She wiped her eyes, 'cheating on Luke and being with you is just another way I've disappointed them.'

'Lily,' I prized her face until she looked at me, 'reading this,' and I nodded to the Journal, 'confirms to me what I've always known, that you are an astounding and brilliant woman.'

'A whore you mean...'

'No!' She makes me livid, 'you are a woman that makes life drunk, a woman who people crave to be close to, a woman whose opinion matters, a most beautiful, sensual and deliciously sexual creature.'

Lily wrapped her arms around my neck and started crying. I could feel that damned lump in my throat again. My hand slipped to her bump and I found myself soothingly rubbing it, over and over, and apart from when she asks me to smooth oil on her stomach, I rarely touch it, in truth, it frightens me; it moves, it has hiccups and jumps, but now I'm doing this, holding her and rubbing the palm of my hand over her bump, our bump, it hits me, Lily's having a baby, she's carrying in her beautiful body, my baby, our baby girl, something we created together during one of our many splendid sexual orgies.

'J?' she rested her nose against mine, I closed my eyes, I was crying, 'J, I loved your letter, you write so graciously about me and I'm not sure I deserve it.'

But I couldn't answer, because I couldn't stop sobbing, like an absolute fool, I was sobbing fiercely on her shoulder, leaving tear stains in her neck, on her velveteen skin. She held my head to hers, rocking me, stroking my hair. I held her tight; I feel safe, I feel warm, I feel loved, and I promise you now, I will never let this feeling go, I will not let Lily go; never.

'Lily,' she wiped my eyes with tender girly fingers, 'I'm going to give James Allen a call,' she kissed my cheeks; cute Lily Ellen kisses, 'I'm taking you away for a while.'

'To Paris?' I adore the fire in her eyes.

'Yes *Belle;* to Paris.'

Paris

'Jefferson my friend,' James shook my hand; it seemed an age since I'd last seen him, 'and Lily, my goodness,' it's fair to say my luscious wife is looking quite pregnant, 'you look beautiful.' And he took her hands and kissed them in turn.

'Thank you.' she smiled graciously, but if only James had heard her moments earlier, perturbed by her changing body and lack of flattering clothes, which I just don't understand, because she's wearing a black wrap dress that clings sexily to her curves and black calf length boots with a small heel. Her hair is sleek and glossy around her shoulders, the front held cutely to one side by a diamond butterfly clip (I also know beneath this dress, she is wearing black satin AP underwear and hold up stockings – delicious.).

So, to me, and of course, I am but a mere man, Lily smoulders. I touch her and she sizzles.

'Oh Lily!' Helena floated down the marble stairs and took my girl by the shoulders, 'oh look at you, oh my sweetheart, you look ravishing.'

I think this cheers her up.

Now, let me tell you, this is one hell of an apartment, and OK, I've been here many times, but Lily hasn't, and I know this evening, as we settle down in our boudoir together, she will write about it in her Journal.

'You have a beautiful apartment,' Lily said as Helena slipped her hand into hers, 'it's absolutely stunning.'

And it is, because although "baby pink" (Lily's words) is not my colour, in this Paris apartment, smatterings of it scream 'chic and sassy'.

We followed our ladies to the living room, and again, Lily gasped and sighed at the exquisite décor.

'Those French doors are wonderful,' she gushed, 'oh and there's a terrace.'

‘Come,’ James smiled as he opened them for her, ‘come and see the view Lily.’

Outside I know she'll be gazing across the incredible view of Montparnasse; I also know it will steal her breath away. During my many visits here, I've spend countless mornings and evenings sitting out alone with an espresso or a well matured red, reading a paper or a book; I intend doing those things again but with Lily by my side.

‘What do you think Honey?’ I slipped an arm around her and she looked up at me; she is beautiful, ‘how does it feel to be back in Paris?’

‘Oh J,’ she turned in my arms; our baby between us, ‘I wish we hadn't left it so long.’

I'd originally arranged with James that Lily and I would be in Paris for a couple of weeks. James said he and Helena were due back in England shortly but we could stay on for as long as we wished.

I haven't spoken to Lily about it yet, I know she's apprehensive about being away from home, but after the trauma of the early Journal and the ongoing feud with her parents, I thought I'd give her the freedom to immerse herself in Parisian life again, and then ask if she'd like to stay on.

See, since Boxing Day, after Lily read my letter and I read her Journal, we're closer than we've ever been, although I admit I remain stunned by the harsh reality she's been pregnant before, and I have to say, it has unsettled me a little, and now I'm experiencing that horrid termite called “jealously”, something I've acquired since falling in love with Lily, anyway it's something I haven't quite put to rest, but I will, in time.

Anyway, the affair with her English lecturer was not a shock and neither were the nude photographs, the paintings or her sexual adventures. My wife has lead a colourful life, and so she should, she's an inspiring and innovative woman, she should be free for the world to appreciate her, but we both know she belongs to me now – and no, I'm not a bigot, but I mean it in the most sincere and endearing way I can; see I belong to her too, with everything I own, so when she writes she is “*free but caught*”, that's what she is referring to.

‘I must say Jefferson,’ James urged me to follow him in the opposite direction to our ladies and towards his office, ‘your lady is extremely graceful.’

I smiled. It made me think of the conversation Lily and I had after I'd read the early Journal. She said there can be nothing “graceful” about a girl who gives her love too freely. I didn't believe her; I didn't she did either.

‘So, how's the book going?’ James offered me a chair.

‘Slow if I'm being honest, I think Henry expected me to churn it out in 2 weeks.’

'He's hounding you is he?' James smiled; he and Henry go back years.

'Oh yes,' I grinned, 'but I've been immersing myself in Lily's work.'

'Ah yes, the Journal.'

After talking to Lily in depth about her early Journals, she's agreed to consider giving them to Henry, she said I've only ever been her concern with regards to the content, and now I've read them, there's no need to hide anymore.

'When's publication?' James said.

'July time.'

'So this Journal,' James continued, 'I understand it contains a great deal of "personal" information about your relationship with Lily.'

I grinned,

'It does,' I said, 'and we've discussed it at length and agree the world needs to read it; it's a brilliant piece of work,' I sat forward, 'I always knew girl's were complex, but Jesus,' we both laughed, 'they make hard work for themselves sometimes.'

'Yes,' James nodded, 'too true my friend.' He finished laughing, and topped up my drink; whenever I drink with James I struggle to keep up; he is an ardent drinker. 'You know Helena was very excited when you rang, she's been desperate to see Lily.'

'Oh?' I was intrigued.

'You must have wondered Jefferson, about Helena and I, why we didn't have children?'

'On occasions.' I shrugged.

'We did try years ago,' he said staring into his drink, 'we had some tests,' he looked at me, 'quite intrusive things you know,' he smiled, a little sadly I thought, 'Helena didn't want IVF, she said if it wasn't going to happen it wasn't meant to be.' We were looking at each other, 'you are a very lucky young man.'

'I know.' I said softly, 'everytime I think of her, see her, or touch her I tell myself the same thing.'

'Helena simply adores her,' he seemed more his perky self now 'she reminds her so much of herself at that age, and I have to agree; I think it's the creative innocence.'

I smiled as I drank my wine; "*creative innocence*"; what a brilliant line.

'Lily's apprehensive about her work,' I said hoping I wasn't betraying her trust, 'was Helena the same?'

'Of course,' he smiled, 'what unpublished writer isn't afraid of their first publication, and something so niche as well.'

'Sometimes it's difficult to help her, to give her the support she needs in the way she needs it.'

James laughed kindly,

'I think that comes back to women being complex creatures Jefferson, all you can do is be there.'

'I am, well, I hope I am. In fact, I want to put my career on hold for her.'

'That's very noble of you Jefferson.'

'Not really,' I said looking into my glass, then up at James, 'she's a far better writer than I'll ever be, she's not a "trend", she's classic,' I smiled, 'in every way.'

We looked up as the door opened,

'Thought I might find you both in here,' Helena stood in the doorway smiling at us, 'Lily's keen to take a walk so I suggested we have a bite to eat somewhere, maybe *Le Pamphlet* or *Café de la Paix*?'

'Very good idea.' James said getting up,

'Is Lily in the sitting room?' She's heavy on my mind.

'I showed her to your room,' Helena smiled, 'she wanted to freshen up.'

I nodded and made my way to Lily, I opened the door rewarded with one hell of a magnificent sight.

'J!' she half laughed half shouted, 'shut the door!'

She was sitting on the chaise lounge in nothing but black satin panties and pale hold up stockings. She'd covered her breasts with her hands, her glorious hair cascading down her back. I went to her and took her mouth,

'I love you.' I whispered over her lips, 'you are so beautiful.'

'Even like this?' she slipped my hand from her bump and to the lace of her stockings.

'Especially like this.'

And so, I just can't help myself. Helena and James are waiting for us in the sitting room and I've just finished emptying myself inside Lily.

'Jefferson James,' she sounds so damned sexy, 'that was good non?'

I was still out of breath; her French accent makes me want to be hard again,

'Oh yes Honey.' I pawed those delicious breasts; she is a masterpiece.

'And since Paris is famous for unforbidden love and lust,' she stroked my jaw, 'we can have a lot of fun can't we?'

'I intend to *Belle*, don't you worry.'

As we arrive at '*Café de la Paix*', I have the urge to stay close to Lily. I grip her hand and she smiles at me, she knows my insecurities, her reassurance is all I need.

Earlier, after our moment of naughtiness, I laid on the bed watching her change into black trousers and a cute red polo neck jumper – it's cold outside and they're giving snow, and even in pregnancy, she's attracting attention, which I am encouraging her to notice. My insecurities are my problem, not hers.

As we sit and talk, I think about Paris. I'm remembering my heady days as a 22 year old. Back then, I made a promise that one day, when I was financially secure, I'd buy an apartment here, so far I haven't got around to it, but as I watch Lily elegantly sipping water from a wine glass and talking quietly with Helena, I'm doing my sums.

'Lily?' She turned to me, placing her hand over mine on the table. 'If we could,' I said softly, 'how would you like an apartment in Paris?'

No kidding, it was the most dazzling smile I've ever seen.

'That's a "yes" then?' I grinned.

I adore listening to Lily talk with Helena. They discuss "girly things", issues she doesn't talk to me about for obvious reasons, although I know she thinks about them. For instance, they've just arranged to book into George V hotel to use the spa. Helena says she goes there regularly and afterwards indulges in a glass of champagne and a macaroon. I want Lily to have those luxuries too.

They also talked about lingerie (OK Lily and I do this a fair bit but for other reasons), salivating over the exclusive boutique '*Fifi Chachnil*' which Lily has never been to.

'I always wondered what their underwear was like.' She said humbly, and from that moment on, I made a promise to myself that she will never go without again; I will make sure of it.

'Absolutely stunning corsets and baby doll negligees.' Helena said picking up her champagne flute. Lily caught my eye and winked; my chest tightened. 'If you desire satin and chiffon, this is your shop.'

Lily caught my eye again; she is wicked,

'I'd love to go there,' she said way too innocently, 'I just love satin; pink's my favourite.'

I almost choked on my red. I can't wait to get that corset back on her.

'We'll go there,' Helena smiled at me, then Lily; she's too good at this, 'pick you up some delights.'

We ordered more drinks and Lily had a delicious looking strawberry *mille feuille* and I chose a delightful *macaron*. As we tucked in, Lily talked to Helena about her Journal.

'What did your family and friends think when they read your work, you know, with it being so explicit?'

'Well, my mother wouldn't read it for years, in fact, I still wonder if she has,' she laughed, but I know Helena and her mother have a strained relationship, ironically because of her marriage to a man old enough to be her father, 'I believe if she had, she'd have had heart failure.' Lily was laughing; I was watching her, loving the way she holds her bump, 'and a lot of my friends still can't believe it comes from my head.'

'I wish I had fiction to fall back on.' I heard a sigh of concern in Lily's voice.

Helena smiled kindly,

'But they'll be seeing a sexy, vibrant and confident side to Lily Mills.' I couldn't have said it better myself. 'I'm so excited about reading it.'

'I have part of it with me,' Lily said putting her tea cup down, 'you can read it if you like?'

'Ooh could I?' Helena's eyes were hungry.

'Of course,' Lily smiled, 'but please,' and she grinned at me, 'don't read it when J and I are in the room, I'll absolutely hate it.'

We started laughing,

'Of course,' Helena said resting her hand over Lily's, 'I wouldn't dream of it.'

By the time we left the café, it was snowing. Lily held her arms out and smiled,

'Oh J, I wish we could stay forever.'

'We can little lady,' I said holding her face between my hands, 'we can do whatever we want.'

January 29 – Paris.

I can't believe how stunning the apartment is. Several times I've had to stop myself repeating the same compliments, because I just can't get over how gorgeous it is. When I first walked in, I couldn't speak.

My favourite is the lounge with its placid pink walls and huge velvet aubergine tub sofas. I adore the decadent ivory faux fur rug sprawled infront of the enormous marble fire place.
There are glass vases placed articulately on every table or window ledge, brimming with ripe pink and red roses. On the antique table there's a rare orchid that James bought for Helena, I can't begin to think how much it cost.

I love the risk of a black and white framed print of Audrey Hepburn, entangled with a polished oak floor, deep velvet burgundy draped curtains and antique chandeliers; it gives me a fever which I know J has picked up on.

Our room is no exception where beauty is concerned. It was made for me and J. The walls are pink like the lounge, the kingsize bed draped in pink satin sheets and mink coloured faux fur blankets. There are cushions scattered over soft pink pillows of all fabrics. I

ran my hands over them; it sent tingles down my spine. The room smells of camellias.

I unfolded the oak shutters and threw up the sash window. The snow billowed in making me laugh. J came over from the antique table where he'd been so elegantly reading Le Monde and enjoying a whiskey.
'Ah Lily Ellen,' he whispered into my neck, his arms tight beneath my breasts, 'how I love you.'
We've been speaking French to each other. He insists I teach him, and even after one day, he's so much better.
He has a very clear motive.
'Did you have a chance to look over those apartments I gave you?'
I've already fallen in love with one; a two bedroom ground floor apartment in St Germain. Cosy but bijou. The vendors are both interior designers and recently renovated it, it has that lived-in contemporary edge that both J and I aspire to. I showed him, and he nodded,
'I could have put a bet on you choosing that one,' he smiled sitting me on his knees on the chaise longe, 'I knew we'd choose the same one.'
Is it possible to love someone so much you would die for them? Discuss...

I waited until Lily was asleep before making the call from the sitting room.

'Yes, two tickets please.'

After hanging up, James appeared,

'Everything alright?' he said eyeing the mobile in my hand.

'Yes,' I said, 'it's a surprise for Lily.' I want to tell her; see her face; feel her excitement, 'two tickets for the ballet on Saturday night.' I smiled, 'she adores the ballet, but it's been a while since she's been.'

When I returned to the bedroom, Lily was shifting about on the bed. She used to love her sleep, now she dreads it, and I've got to say, trying to get comfortable with a huge bump at the front of you, especially with Lily's slight and delicate body, would be my idea of hell.

'J?' she sounded well pissed off, 'can you pass me those cushions from the chair please.'

I did as she asked and watched as she arranged the two cushions in a position where she could rest her bump and I don't know why, but I'd been thinking about that guy again, her English lecturer.

'Lily?' I sat by her side stroking her hair, 'can I ask you a question?'

'Sure.' She had her eyes closed.

'It's about "D".'

Her eyes flew open, and she glared at me,

'What about him?'

'I just wondered if you knew what happened to him.'

'Why?' She snapped.

'Well, you went into a lot of detail in the Journal about most things but not that.'

'At the time I hated him too much to want to write about him.'

'Did you see him after you left college?'

She propped herself up with four cushions, then took a slow breath,

'Yes.' *Fuck*, I was hoping she'd say no. 'It was a bit of a shock because I hadn't seen him for ages.' She was staring at her hands in her lap, 'I was at a party, someone I knew from Uni, it was my first year and he was there, but then so were loads of other people...'

'Did you speak to him?'

'I tried to avoid him...' she looked at me, 'but it seemed stupid after all that time.'

'Was he surprised to see you?'

'Of course,' she laughed, 'I was his nemesis; I guess he hoped he'd never see me again.'

'I don't believe that.' I squeezed her hand, 'he sounded like he was crazy about you.'

'J, this was years ago, do we have to do this?'

I'd got the bit between my teeth, Christ knows why.

'I'm just interested that's all.'

'I know, but it's making me feel uncomfortable.'

I got up and went to the window. I still wonder about Lily sometimes, the things she's done for someone so young,

'Lily?' It was starting to snow, 'did you sleep with him that night?'

Silence. I closed my eyes then opened them, I pushed open the balcony doors and a flurry of snow attacked my face. I breathed in deep; I felt alive.

'Yes.' She whispered.

I swallowed; closed the door and faced her,

'Because you loved him?'

'No, because I needed a fuck.' She was getting angry with me now, 'I'm getting up,' she said, 'I can't sleep and you're not helping.'

'Lily?' I took her arm gently and she stared at me, 'did it make you feel better?'

Her eyes were watering,

'It was something I had to do,' I watched a rogue tear glide down her cheek and explode on her lip, 'to exorcise a ghost.'

'And him?'

'Same reason.'

'How do you know?'

'Because that's what we agreed!' she pulled away from me, 'anything else you want to know; time, place, did I come? Or more importantly, did we use protection!' she glared fiercely at me, 'why are you doing this? Don't you trust me?'

'Of course I do.' I felt pissed off too, 'but it's something I need to lay to rest.'

Lily sat on the chaise lounge, and covered her face with her hands. I sat beside her and she laid her head on my shoulder.

'J?' we looked at each other, 'this sort of stuff isn't healthy.' She has a sweet frown, 'this sort of information doesn't help us, knowing what I did doesn't improve our relationship does it? I mean, all the times I've wondered about you, wanted to ask you things but haven't, because I know it isn't going to help us, it's going to do this – make us angry and jealous.' She held my face between warm hands, 'all those awards dinners and parties we've been to,' she said softly, 'do you know how bad I feel when I see women I know you've been with, or Gracie Miller for fuck's sake, I mean, God, we see her every fucking month at the Arts Club, how do you think I feel knowing she was the first woman you ever loved...'

'Lily, it was never like this, I promise.'

She smiled,

'Jefferson, I know that, but don't you think it hurts to know if Eliot hadn't come back, you would probably have married her.'

I covered my face with my hands then dragged them down my face,

'You're right, this stuff doesn't help us; I'm sorry.'

'I don't know what more I can do to reassure you Jefferson, I'm in love with you, we're married, we're having a baby...'

I dropped to my knees and took her hands,

'Let's move to Paris,' I whispered, 'let's leave our pasts behind; make a fresh start?' but she just stared at me, 'Lily?'

OK, so moving to Paris wasn't going to dissolve my insecurities, because that's what they are, mine, not Lily's. After all, she has to live with far more of my past than I do of hers yet she rarely mentions it. OK, so Gracie will always be an issue for her, but she lives with it, and I need to learn to do the same.

'Jefferson?' Helena was standing at the drawing room door; I'd been browsing through James' books, 'are you alright?'

'Of course.' I smiled. 'Lily's sleeping, we've done quite a bit if walking today.'

'Yes, she did say you were both going out, revisiting old haunts.'

‘*Shakespeare and Co.*,’ I smiled sliding a book back, ‘and *Gerard Mulot Patisserie*,’ I laughed softly, ‘Lily has a thing for pink cup cakes.’

‘Cute.’ Helena was staring at me; she senses unrest, this is so like her. ‘Tell me honestly,’ she said sitting down on the huge tapestry sofa, ‘do you find it difficult reading your lovely wife’s Journal?’

I took my time in answering,

‘Some pages I do tend to scan over, yes.’

‘James felt like that about “The Forbidden”’ (or “*Interdit*” as it’s more commonly known – Helena’s autobiographical novel of how she and James fell in love; it features pages of sexually explicit activities between Helena and her many lovers), ‘It was a difficult time, but we got through it – just.’

I sat down beside her. I wanted to come back with something profound and noble, but I couldn’t, in truth, the Journal hurts me, and the more I love Lily, the more difficult it is to read.

‘I don’t know what’s happening to me,’ I was trying to smile, despite the lump in my throat, ‘she’s my wife you know, she’s Lillian, my genius little lady and I hate imagining her lying there being fucked by some…’

‘J?’

I looked up at the door; *Holy fuck*.

‘Lily…’ I got up.

‘Can we talk?’ she was choked; pointing to the bedroom. I turned briefly to Helena who smiled with sympathy; pity I wasn’t sure I wanted.

The bedroom door was open and Lily was sat on the edge of the bed facing me.

‘You’re scaring me,’ she was rubbing her belly like crazy, ‘saying those things about me.’ She stood up, and then sat back down; I know this mood, ‘look, maybe I should go back home and you stay here for a while, sort your head out.’ She had hiccups; she was crying. I got to my knees infront of her,

‘No,’ I squeezed her hands, ‘I don’t want to be away from you.’

‘I don’t want to be away from you either, but this feeling between us at the moment is making me feel bad.’

‘It’s my issue Lily.’

‘And mine,’ she snapped, ‘because it’s me causing it!’

‘It will pass I promise you.’ I had a desperate feeling in my gut; it wouldn’t shift.

‘Listen J, there’s a few things I need to do back home.’

‘What things?’ I said holding her, sensing she wanted to leave, ‘why are you only telling me now?’

‘Being here has helped me make a decision.’

‘What decision?’

‘J, please, you’re hurting my hands.’

‘Lily, talk to me?’

'J let me go?'

'No, I won't, Lily, what decision?'

She was crying,

'That fucking Journal!' she screamed, 'I don't want it to be published!'

'Yes!'

'No!' she was enraged; I'd never seen her like this before; she ripped her hands away from me and went to the window, 'I never wanted it to get this far; it wasn't supposed to be read for entertainment, it's so personal, so private.'

'It's a masterpiece.'

She turned to me,

'For the sake of our marriage Jefferson, please, don't let it be published?' I stared at her; she was serious, and deep inside, I know her fear is real. 'You're more important to me than any publication, any career, any amount of money, I knew the Journal might be a problem for us, but I never imagined how much until now, until we were out of England, and OK, maybe this will blow my chance of ever getting published, but do you know what, I don't give a fuck, because I've found something else in life that inspires me, and he's standing right in front of me.' She swallowed; *I love her so much,* 'J please, for me?'

"Oh my Lily, how beautiful you are, looking at you this evening feeling proud to have you as my wife, knowing how lucky I am and how grateful I am to God. Oh how I adored watching you tonight, your eyes on "Le Parc", your dainty hand in mine, gripping with excitement and intrigue.

My dearest Lillian, in your black gown and silver shoes, your smouldering auburn hair and sparkling blue eyes, I want to tell you how my chest tightens when you wink at me, and how your modest charisma astounds me as I listen to you speak; your animation is awe inspiring; I have never met anyone like you.

This is so beautiful Lily, so gracious that I can barely remember anything that happened to me before I met you.
Today I reached new heights with you, holding your hand as we left the ballet, wrapping your pink cashmere cardigan around your shoulders and you asking me if we could drink coffee on the Left Bank,
"Let's pretend we're in 1930s Paris, surrounded by influential writers and artists talking intently..."
I love you for that; for how you transport me there immediately because you're passion is so vivid. Darling Lily, when I sat opposite

you tonight, and you laughed and talked about Nin and Miller, I know the sacrifice you've made for me, but Honey, don't you think we're already so much freer; so much happier?

Listen to me now Lily Ellen, I will make life beautiful for you, you will have no regrets about me, about us, we've waited too long, tried too hard, Lily, this love, the love we have between us, that grows by the second, is my life; it is a love that makes life drunk."

Pinkcupcakes.co.uk

February 16 – viewing of St Germain apartment, Paris.

Oh the apartment is beautiful. J laughed, he said I have the ability to see good in everything; he wasn't sure of the old wine crates being used as kitchen drawers and shelves, but he did love the cute wrought iron fire place and reclaimed iron radiators in the lounge. We relished in the beauty of the roll top bath and apple crates used for storage.

We had a glass of wine with the couple who currently own it. Sabine said she'd bought the 1940's French pendant lamp and brown leather chair from Les Puces and I said I loved the way they'd fitted the pieces into their open plan kitchen diner.
The contrast of the contemporary steel floor and recycled wooden cupboards really makes this apartment, and with a few select items from Louveciennes, it will be "a lot of being Jefferson and Lily".

Without prompting, Lily said she'd love to stay on in Paris, not that I was wholly surprised by her enthusiasm, because in the last few weeks Lily has embraced Parisian life, taking me with her.

James and Helena returned to England three days ago, leaving Lily and I to immerse ourselves in the luxury of their apartment, and I must say, we're having a ball.

'It's at times like this,' Lily said as we lay in the bath together (luckily for us the bath is king size – my wife is pregnant you know!), 'I wish I could have a glass of Champagne.'

I smiled; Lily often says this.

'Well, in less than 7 weeks you can.' I trickled water over her bump and she laughed, it also made our little lady start dancing again. Lily winced, she says it feels too weird to describe, but I can tell you, watching it is pretty damned freaky.

'J, I've decided to finish my MA.' She was softly rubbing a sponge over my arm; I love watching her girly hands; I'm hard and it's making her laugh, 'J, stop thumping me with it.'

'I'm not,' I was trying not to laugh, 'it has a mind of its own.' I buried my mouth into her neck, she's sensitive, it makes her giggle, 'but you're right, I think you finishing the MA is a great idea,' I said, 'I've been giving it some thought myself.'

See, what Lily's done for me, for us, is something I can never repay. She has given up her dream, her years of dedication, to be with me and since this is a genius wasted, I've been "collecting" ideas for her.

'Lily Honey?'

'Uh- huh.' I can tell she's got her eyes closed.

'Have you ever considered starting your own writer's group?'

'I have in the past.' She said, 'but I didn't think I'd be any good at it.'

'Lily, I think you'd be wonderful at it.' She twisted slightly to look at me, 'honest, you're brilliant in groups, I'm convinced inspiring writers will grasp plenty from you.'

'But I'm not published.'

'I know plenty of authors who started off running groups before they got into print.'

She lay back down, her luscious curves sinking into me,

'Tell you what I would love to do,' she said, 'an online forum; a place where people can chat about books, writing, study, anything really, as long as it's connected to writing.'

'It's possible.'

'But expensive.'

'Not an issue.' And I meant it.

'I wouldn't know where to start.'

'There's plenty of companies out there that get paid a fortune to do this sort of thing,' I said, 'and the rest you already know, honestly you've been doing this stuff for years anyway.'

She was laughing,

'Hey, I have an idea, how about I call it "pink cup cakes".'

Weird, but I kind of liked it.

'www.pinkcupcakes.co.uk.' I pondered. 'I think you're on to something here.'

'You have that much faith in me?'

'I have every faith in you; I believe in you more than I do myself.'

'What a lovely thing to say,' she twisted to look at me again, 'the only thing is, "pink cup cakes" sounds a bit girly doesn't it, it'd probably end up attracting just women.'

'Nothing wrong with that,' the ideas were rolling off now, 'make it an online forum for women writers only.'

Silence; Lily was pondering.

'Could I get away with that?'

'Fuck yes!' I laughed, 'come on Lily, you know women are published less than men, here's your chance to boost the ratings.'

Lily got out of the bath (well, struggled –she refuses to let me help her) and wrapped herself in one of James and Helena's huge feathery white towels,

'I really like the idea of the writers group.' She said.

'Do both?' I grabbed a towel from her hand and started to dry myself down; she's staring between my legs, but I'm determined to tie this up before she makes me fuck her. 'In fact, why don't you make them part of the same project, "pinkcupcakes.co.uk" – the online forum for women writers, and "PCC"– a local writers group for women run by women.'

I sat on the edge of the bath; Lily was drying my hair with a towel,

'J,' she said pulling the towel away; wow, what a smile, 'you are a genius.'

I took the towel from her and pulled her onto my knees,

'That was the easy part, I'm leaving the rest up to my wife, because she's the true genius in this family.'

February 28

I have had the most wonderful day with J. We had a table reserved at Café de la Paix in the winter terrace overlooking Boulevard des Capucines; it was incredibly beautiful watching the snow fall and settle.

After lunch, I wanted to take a walk, J was a little worried about me being in the snow, but he gave in when I said I'd hold on to him extra tight!
We popped into Laduree Royale where J salivated over the macaroons and I worshipped the cup cake! Needless to say, we came away with a few of each.

We walked over the Pont Alexandre III so I could take a look across Paris; it's such a stunning bridge with such an amazing view, this is something I used to do all the time years ago, but today, Paris looks even more spectacular with it's snowy covering.

I started getting tired, so we took the Metro and stopped off at the Italian deli on Rue Mouffetard so I could pick up olives, cheese and bread, and then we had coffee and a macaroon in the café next door.

When we arrived home, J ran me a bath and washed my hair. He's so lovely like that, my beautiful J. Afterwards, we sat by the fire reading – but my mind's been drifting – I'm feeling more and more anxious about giving birth...

March 2

Breakfast at Deux Magots with J. There was an event on, breakfast with books! We ate pastries, whilst selected extracts were read aloud by students from the University. I had hot chocolate. Deux Magots' hot chocolate is gorgeous, and there's plenty of it.
J and I discussed the PCC writers group, I would like to hold it somewhere like this, somewhere inspiring, J suggested the Gigot Bar in Stow.
'Roaring fires in the winter, serene sunsets in the summer.' He said, and I replied, 'I miss home.'
He smiled and squeezed my hand.

March 3

Visit to Chateau de Versailles, J got frisky in the Hall of Mirrors, but they did me no favours!!

Watching Lily at work is an inspiration. Honest, she is a Trojan, and since our discussion over a week ago when *pinkcupcakes.co.uk* was born, she has dedicated her free time to making plans, and whilst she's been focusing on that, I've started working on "*Red*" again.

See, in between, writing, talking, laughing, making love, going to the ballet, to galleries and restaurants, Lily and I have forced ourselves to get a grip on reality, because in less than five weeks, our baby will have been cooking on gas for 9 months.

'I have to be honest J,' Lily said as we sat in the drawing room where I'd prepared a fire, 'I don't think any amount of planning is going to prepare us for what happens next.'

I fear she is right, another reason why tonight is our last night in Paris.

After going out to *Louveciennes* this morning and standing outside the house that Anais Nin and Hugh Guiler shared in the 1930s; the house that frequented her lover Henry Miller, a place so significant to our love, Lily turned to me as though her work here was done (for now – this is Lily remember, and this is Paris),

'J,' she said softly, 'I think it's time for us to go home.'

March 5

After coming back from the "real" Louveciennes, J had a call to say our offer on the Paris apartment had finally been accepted. It was a little more than we wanted to offer but since we'd found ourselves in a battle with another buyer, J had got the bit between his teeth and it turned into a full on war!

OK, we're in bed together, but Lily's sleeping, and since I've been working on it for most of the day, let me tell you a bit about my novel, "*Red*".

I started writing it after meeting Lily. I'd been playing with the idea of a love story for some time but just couldn't make it work. It felt too crude; too cheap, a vital ingredient was missing.

It had been so long since I'd *felt* what it was like to be in love, I was finding it almost impossible to write about, and if I didn't believe it, how could I expect my readers to; that is, until a demure, but tough talking redhead swept me off my feet, so the least I could do was honour Lily, by dedicating my heroine, Ellen Spencer to her, with no idea I'd be lying with her now.

Right, so Ellen is the young student being taught by the novel's lead character Edward Myers, a University English lecturer. With gracious intentions, he nurtures her through a difficult period of damning grades and low self esteem, which results in her successful graduation.

After University, Ellen moves away from London, whilst Edward confronts his feelings. For a while it has a profound effect on the relationship with his wife, and despite working it through in his mind, he remains haunted by a desire that will never be fulfilled.

Three years on, Edward has left the University and is running a writing school in Andalusia. Here he has learnt to appreciate solitude among the peaceful mountains and valleys of olive groves.

As usual when his wife is back in the UK, he is dining alone at the local restaurant, when he sees a beautiful and demure redhead sitting on a nearby table. He recognizes her immediately.

He invites Ellen to join him for dinner and discovers she's been living in New York for the past three years, working as a journalist. She had recently moved back to London, which is where she'd read about his writing school.

The attraction between them is incredible and after three years of torment and regret, Edward sets out to embrace the one thing in his life that really matters, without thought of consequence.

Steadily and discreetly, they court each other and only on the final night do they unleash themselves in a frenzied session of brutal yet tender fucking. The torrent love affair continues on Ellen's return to London, where Edward finds himself under his wife's scrutiny as he travels back and forward from Spain to be with his young lover, and when the satisfaction of having her time and again doesn't rid of the infatuation; of his frightening obsession, Edward comes to a terrifying conclusion; he has fallen in love with her.

'You gave it a happy ending,' Lily mused as I spoke to her about it last night; I love her like this; the mind of a genius hey? 'That's rare for you.'

'I almost didn't,' I said playing with the ends of her hair, 'but I realise now, not all love ends badly; infact, love doesn't have to end at all.'

'It gets better don't you think?' Her smile dazzles me.

'It develops into something far deeper and much more complex than just desire.' I said truthfully, 'anyone who experiences it even briefly is very fortunate.'

'I did feel sorry for his wife though,' she said, 'it left a bit of a bad feeling in my stomach.'

'An illicit love that burns out of control will always leave chaos.' I smiled and so did she.

I turned back to my "pregnant centrefold" (I call her this because it makes her laugh); she's padded with cushions again. I stroked her hair lightly, I don't want to wake her, she barely sleeps as it is. I feel guilty that we try and pack so much into our days, I know she's uncomfortable and tired but she doesn't give up, although I sense it's because she fights it.

I closed down the laptop and reached for the latest entries of Lily's Journal. OK, so it's no longer going to be published (yes - Henry and Hamish went ballistic), but she still shares it with me, even though I don't ask her to. I think she finds the more intricate areas of her life easier to disclose when it's written like this, and in truth, I guess sometimes I understand it more.

You see, Lily pricks my conscience; she makes me think in ways a man isn't expected to; I don't know how she does it, maybe now I'm just more open to these things; maybe after reading today's entry, I realise I've ignored or simply not thought about the fact Lily has to give birth and how it's making her feel; the fact we're going to be parents and how it'll affect our relationship; our lifestyle, but more than anything, Lily's going to be a mummy, and I'll be a daddy; we're having a baby, and I'm not afraid to admit, I'm absolutely petrified.

"March 5 (continued)

Anais has been moving like crazy today. I keep thinking she's going to come early, and the fear of going into labour and being so far from home frightens me. J agrees and tomorrow we're going home, back to our lovely Louveciennes and even though I have adored being in Paris, I am looking forward to being in my own bed, with all my comforts around me.

I've been thinking a lot about giving birth recently. I haven't mentioned it much to J, mainly because I've been trying not to think about it; trying to ignore it I suppose, but after looking up some important facts on the web I so wish I'd gone for an elective caesarean – too late, but no way am I going to be a martyr, fuck it, I'm having every bit of pain relief I can get my hands on.

When I look at my bump I don't know how I'm going to get her out. I asked the midwife before we left for Paris whether she thinks she'll be big, she said she couldn't really tell, but that she wouldn't be huge. I wasn't comforted by this.

Now I have a new worry – what if I split so badly I need stitches? Oh Christ does this shit never stop! Is it not enough that I've put on 2 and a half stones, fear stretch marks, have a bad back, my feet are swollen, I'm too tired to fuck, my clothes are awful, I can't sleep, I'm constantly uncomfortable and now stitches! – I wonder if Anais will be an only child (sometimes I mean this – men will never understand, (not because they are ignorant shites, although I'm sure some are) but because until now, I never imagined I'd find it this difficult and I haven't done the worst bit yet!)

OK, so there we go, I've aired my shit for today, but another reason I'll be happy to return home is to make myself feel better about the hideous person I've become, by sitting in my little girl's nursery and reminding myself why it's all worth it – because inside, I know I wouldn't change a thing (OK, maybe not have put on quite so much weight – very bad idea living in Paris at 8 months pregnant – patisserie's are way too delicious).
You see, as soon as we found out we were having a girl, I started thinking about a nursery. Livvy told me back then it was bad luck to start organizing too soon, but I did it anyway, how can you not?

The thing is, buying a few toys, cuddly teddies and preparing a nursery is not really going to make a difference to how you feel if anything did go wrong (God forbid) and anyway, I wanted to immerse myself in the idea of J and I having a baby, because even now it's weird for me, it still doesn't feel real, even though we've had the scans and I have an enormous belly, but I don't think it will sink in until I am holding her in my arms (ah, what a lovely warm thought).

I looked up from the Journal, smiling, in fact, I have a lump in my throat, because I haven't really thought about it like that before, holding my daughter in my arms, Lily's right, what a warm and lovely thought.

Let me tell you about my little girl's room; J laughs at me because I go in there all the time, I even leave the light on in the evenings, just so she knows we're waiting for her; that this is the place she lives (although she seems perfectly happy living in the pouch at the moment!).

I bought some cute angel fairy lights from London before Christmas, because I've given Anais' room a theme. OK, cliché, but it's fairies, angels and ballerina's, although if I'm being honest, there's a bit of everything in there. I've even got blankets set out in her cot (white with embroided ballerinas on), and adorable "Jellybean" cats that guard at night. J put up a book shelf (in anticipation – I wonder since both her parents are writers!), and I've collected classic books along the way (Winnie the Pooh, Wind in the Willows and Peter Rabbit).

Often when I can't sleep, I go to her room and look through the drawers. I've bought her the most endearing sleep suits from a shop in London; one is white with ballerinas, another with fairies, and a pink one with white polka dots; and don't laugh, but I also bought a woolen rabbit coat because it was so cute.

I like to sit in the nursery chair and put my feet up, wrapped cosily in a brown pom pom blanket. Many nights J has found me asleep and brought me back to bed.

I love floating in there in the daytime when J is working. I stand at the window and look over the orchard; oh it is beautiful, reassuring me that moving away from London was the right thing to do. I stand back and look around the room, holding my bump, the bump that will soon become a little girl; our daughter.

I have to be honest, I haven't enjoyed being pregnant, but I haven't really made too much of a fuss about I either. OK, so I do moan to J sometimes, but anyone outside of us wouldn't have an idea about how bad I feel about my appearance, but that's something I'll work on once I've given birth, it's too close to worry about now, I'll immerse myself in J's compliments instead.

I adore looking at J; I watch him all the time, the way he moves around our house, how he opens a bottle of wine, how he sits at his desk, how he takes off his jumper or cleans his glasses, how he runs his hands over my body; he is divine, and I wonder whether he imagined his life would be like this. When I ask him, he says he loves his life and that he's very happy and considers himself to be very fortunate.

J's so warm as I cuddle him at night, he comforts me. Even after showering, he still smells like the J I met almost 2 years ago and that excites me so much. The other night, I was overwhelmed with desire for him and attempted to fuck him mercilessly, "forgetting" the small obstacle of having an 8 month bump in front of me; we still made love, but it was gentle; simple, Oh how it frustrates me, I so badly want to fuck him with a deep passion, I want him to fuck me hard, lift me from the bed, say dirty things to me, oh J, I want you more now than I ever have...

I laughed quietly to myself, remembering how Lily got upset about not being able to "*fuck you as I want*", and then she launched into a whole load of stuff she'd been fantasizing about doing with me when she's no longer pregnant. Jesus, she made my eyes water, and her idea of the Bunny Girl, well, that really did it for me.

I've been thinking about being a "mummy". I've decided I'm a sort of "accidental" mum, I'll be a day by day mum rather than an all embracing mother earth, I can't stop being Lily Mills, and neither do I want to, and yet I hate "yummy mummy" – the ultra glamourous mums who wear heels to push their children to the shops to prove a point, and just as hideous is "mother earth" – the ones who have those papoose things strapped to their front, all righteous and judgmental in the isles of IKEA; I don't want or need a label, I am Lily with a daughter. Men get away with it, I intend to as well (in theory of course because Society has the final word!).
Sometimes J and I talk about being parents. He says he's nervous and excited, but worries because he doesn't see himself as a good role model, but I don't see myself as a role model either, I think it just happens as they grow up, you think more about your actions and their consequences – already my thoughts are less selfish.
Sometimes I realise I have a romantic notion of what having a baby means, and inside I remain just a little bit afraid, but she's coming, and she's coming very soon..."

Maybe sooner than we think.

A Little Lady and Two Welcome Strangers

Ah, our Louveciennes, how I have missed you.

The drive from Waterloo was a long one, especially for Lily; she was tired and uncomfortable and despite grabbing some sleep on the train and in the car, she was still feeling bad, so I helped her upstairs and she lay on the bed. I closed the curtains and put some music on quietly, then covered her with a fur blanket.

'Just try and rest,' I said stroking her hair, desperate to hide my anxiety, 'and don't worry about anything but getting your head down.'

'J,' she smiled putting her hand over mine on her cheek, 'I love you.'

'I love you too Honey.' And I kissed her palm.

Inbetween writing and catching up with Henry, I'd been up a few times to check on Lily; fortunately she'd been able to sleep. However, when I went to get her up for dinner, I found her sitting on the edge of the bed, clutching her bump,

'Lily?' I got to my knees, breaking out in a sweat, 'what is it?'

'I think my waters have broken,' she showed me her wet trousers, 'can you call the midwife?'

I went into complete and utter overdrive; I was like a lunatic. Lily had gone over this with me so many times, she'd even written down the essential telephone numbers and pinned them on the fridge, yet I was still running around trying to find them.

'J,' every so often her face creased up, 'on the fridge yeah?'

'Oh yes, of course.' And before leaping down the stairs, I turned at the door, 'will you be OK for a minute.'

She smiled; her face creased up again,

'Yes...' She frowned; she was trying to breath in intervals whilst talking to me, 'Just hurry please.'

Fortunately, midwives are used to bumbling husbands who fall apart when their wives go into labour, so Jill knew exactly what I was saying when I called her, even though I think I was speaking another language.

Lily looked in a lot of pain. She had that strange TENS machine stuck to her back, which she said she hadn't fastened properly and would I help her. Honest, I was all fingers, but seeing her try to breathe through the pain and stay calm, I knew I had to get myself together; she needed me.

Lily was out in the garden when Jill arrived; she said she felt better in the fresh air. God, I love her so much, and I wonder how I could do this to her, I mean, Christ, she's so young.

I stayed downstairs whilst Lily was examined; she was four centremetres dilated; I think I understood; we'd been through it before, so she was still a way off, but even so it was still pretty good going. Lily had already told me she wanted to stay at home for as long as possible, she hates hospitals, and even though she's going into a good one, she's still afraid; but her suitcase is by the door, and she's physically preparing herself for something so huge, it makes me want a drink,

'Pour me one as well will you,' she managed between contractions, 'double and neat.'

'Ice?' I was trying to make her laugh.

She does,

'As it comes.'

We've been "warned", with this being Lily's first baby, it could be some time before Anais will make an appearance, and in this time, I've been bombarded with telephone calls. Joseph had rang to check progress, Livvy had been around, and Mum had called several times, (bless her) inbetween packing her suitcase to come up. Jeremy had rang after the midwife left, so I shared my crazy anxieties with him, and mentally felt more prepared for what was going to happen, even Dad called for a chat, but of course, there were two people noticeably missing and I wish she'd let me call them.

We've also been told Lily could be home pretty quickly after giving birth as long as everything is fine, so, to prepare, I have flowers on order (pink hybrid tea roses – what else?), vintage Dom Perignon chilling in the fridge and a present for my little lady (De Beers diamond bracelet) because she deserves it, in fact, she deserves all the best things in life.

Into the early hours and Lily was struggling, and now I wish I'd listened more at those damned ante natal classes. Jill came back out; Lily was now six centremetres dilated. She'd had gas and air, which made her a little giddy and she started laughing. I tied her hair back, wishing she'd go into hospital, it was making me anxious her being here like this, but she knows what she's doing so I just go with it, because I have absolutely no fucking idea.

An hour later, it's too much for her; she finally agrees to go into hospital. In the car she says to me,

'I've done my bit,' she stopped abruptly to have another contraction; they're frequent and close; I feel ill, 'now I just want as much pain relief as I can.'

I smiled at her in the mirror,

'No problem Honey.'

Mum and dad were in the waiting room; it was about five in the morning and we were all knackered. Still no sign of Anais, although Lily had an epidural, which had an amazing affect on her, she seemed much more like herself, she'd even been laughing and asking for something to eat and drink, but she was too tired and weary to see it through. I held her hand as she pushed again; it felt like she'd been at this for days; I was going out of my mind.

In between contractions, I reported back. Livvy and Tom had arrived,

'How is she?'

'Knackered,' I laughed, but I was so wound up I felt like I was on the ceiling, 'but she's in good spirits and the midwives are being great with her.'

'You look exhausted Jefferson.' Livvy smiled kindly, 'why don't you go out and get some air for a while.'

'No,' I smiled, 'thanks, but, I can't leave her.'

'Jefferson?' I turned to see the midwife, 'she's asking for you.'

My heart stopped. I didn't even look at the others, I went straight to her, the epidural was wearing off, she looked in pain again,

'J?' she winced and the midwife told her to push, to stop breathing through her contractions, 'J, do something for me.'

'What is it *belle?*' I squeezed her hand so tight I think I hurt her, oh fuck, another contraction; she pushed; she screwed her eyes up tight, gritting her teeth, I wanted to throw up. 'I want my mum and dad...'

After making that vital call, I returned to Lily. She'd decided not to have a top up epidural, she had gas and air and me to hold and squeeze. The midwives said she was doing brilliant, that she was fully dilated and soon they'd see the head. They examined her again; they could feel it was almost there. More contractions; more pushing, they could see the head. They asked me if I wanted to have a look, I pondered in horror, but Lily urged me, I did, oh My God, she's right there, my daughter,

'She's a red,' I was crying, 'Oh Lily.'

'Another big push now sweetheart,' the midwife said, 'come on now, another big one; let's get her head out.'

Lily told me I should watch, that I'd regret it if I didn't. Oh she looks so young; her hair wet from sweating, she's pure faced and I'm holding her hand helplessly, I am a bad man, how could I do this to her, but still I gawp between her legs, oh Jesus, I've never...oh Lord...

'That's it Lily, good girl, her head is out, now big push; well done, and another.' It looked like they were twisting the shoulders and now, another push. I encouraged her to push too and as she did, there she was; she was out; Jeez, she's long; she's, oh God, I don't know what to say...

Hands came from everywhere and there was one hell of a high pitched scream,

'You have a little girl,' the midwife said, but I wasn't sure I was conscious, but I must have been because I could see Lily's exhausted smile; oh my wife is so beautiful, 'a little redhead.'

The midwife brought Anais over and handed her to Lily. She was covered in gunge, but she had wide eyes and she was staring intently at her mum; her mum who I love so much; who I cannot believe has done this for me, gone through all of this; she is so brave, so special, so absolutely fucking everything to me.

I cuddled up beside her; she uncovered our little girl's face; I touched her hand tenderly; I was trembling. She's so tiny I'm afraid of hurting her. Lily wiped a tear from my cheek and we smiled at each other,

'My little girl,' I whispered, 'my perfect little girl.'

In the waiting room they huddled around me for news,

'Both are fine,' I couldn't stop smiling, 'Anais is a beautiful redhead weighing in at 7 lb 2.'

'Jefferson?' It was Laura Mills. 'How's Lily?'

I went over to her, leaving the others to celebrate amongst themselves; this was a surreal situation, but one I was no longer afraid of; they couldn't hurt us anymore.

'She's very tired,' I said, my hands deep in my pockets, 'but they're making her comfortable and she's already falling asleep.'

'And you?'

'Falling asleep on my feet,' I laughed gently, 'and I didn't even have to do anything.'

'I'm sure Lily would disagree,' she smiled warmly, 'do you think she would let us see her some time?'

'She asked for you Mrs. Mills, I'd say it's a sure bet.'

'Please, call me Laura.' *Is this a sign?* 'And Anais?' her eyes were watering, 'is everything alright?'

'She's beautiful,' I swallowed that damned lump, 'she's, well, she's perfect with huge brown eyes and a cute little nose.'

'Oh I'm so pleased,' she put her hand to her chest, 'We've been so worried, going out of our minds.' She wiped her eyes with a tissue.

'Your daughter is an amazing woman Laura; the most resilient I know,' I said, 'but she has a soft centre that isn't always obvious.'

I think I got my point across,

'She hides it well doesn't she?'

I smiled,

'Not so much these days,' I said, 'she's a little braver now.'

I looked up as someone thrust a hand at me, it was Lily's father, Jim.

'Congratulations.' I took his hand; it was a firm shake, like the first time we met. 'You'll need all the luck you can get now you've got a daughter.' And he winked and Laura nudged his arm, tutted, but smiled, and for the past year, there was me thinking Lily was just like her mum...

'J?' Lily had been drifting in and out of sleep for the past half an hour, 'J?' I stood up and took her hand,

'What is it Honey?'

'J, am I still your centrefold?'

I smiled and kissed her hand,

'Of course.'

'I look awful don't I?'

'You look beautiful.'

She started laughing; a fragile rasp and I stroked her hair,

'You're too kind.' She held my hand to her chest, 'how is she?' she turned her head to the plastic tank beside her.

'Sleeping.'

'She's so lovely isn't she?' she said, 'so tiny.'

'Lily?' she looked back at me, 'I'm so proud of you.'

She shook her head,

'It was nothing.' And she started to laugh, then she took a breath, 'are mum and dad here yet?'

'In the waiting room.'

'Did you talk to them?'

'We had a long chat actually,' I stroked her hair; her eyes closed, 'they're desperate to see you both.'

'I know,' she smiled, 'I'm just a little anxious that's all.'

'You don't have to be,' I said, 'I'll be right by your side.'

'Were they kind to you?'

I kissed her forehead; she's so cute sometimes,

'They were fine.'

'Good, because I wouldn't see them otherwise.' She looked up at me, 'I'd like to see them though.'

'Let me go get them then?'

'Oh I don't know,' she had her hand in the tank trying to touch our daughter's head, so I brought her closer, 'what do you think?'

'Is that a trick question Lily Ellen?' I laughed softly, lifting my head from her chest.

'Yes,' she laughed cupping my face between her delicate hands, 'OK, but stay close to me won't you?'

'Of course.'

I watched from the door as two welcome strangers sat beside my wife's bed. I sensed a little awkwardness at first, but only for seconds, because something important happened today, something that's eclipsed all hostility and bad feeling, and her name is Anais Lillian Eve Howie, and she is so beautiful, so tiny, and so helpless, and already I love her so much that I can barely remember what life was like without her. Without her and without Lily; two loves that make my life drunk.

Wife, Mother and Complete Tiger

I've been giving this idea a lot of thought since Lily had our daughter. See, I guessed this would happen; the next thing for her to start worrying about would be her weight, and 7 weeks on, guess what?

OK, so she's acquired curves, curves I happen to think are incredibly stunning, but for Lily, no, she absolutely abhors them, and continues to work extremely hard to shift them (regrettably for me), so in the meantime, I've come up with a way of making her feel sexy again, because she says she feels anything but.

So, remember "*my unforgettable night with no ordinary redhead*", well, I searched out those photos last night and unleashed my wife; my tiger, and no kidding, this morning, I ache all over.

'Don't complain, you got what you wanted didn't you?' she grinned, rolling across the bed to face me, her auburn hair spilling onto my pillow like velvet, her cherry nipples, sweet and attentive, her skin, fresh and young. She is Heavenly; honest, she is a centrefold.

'Lily Ellen?' I cuddled up to her; she touched my face with one hand because the other is fiddling with my dick beneath the duvet, see what I mean, complete tiger.

'Yes Honey.' Let me tell you, that was one hell of a purr.

'I have a suggestion.'

'Oh?' she has her mouth on my neck; I don't know how much longer I can keep talking.

'Those pictures...' oh Lily,

'Yes J,' she's teasing me; she's so naughty, 'cat got your tongue.'

Actually, yes, because right now, my tiger has her mouth over mine, kissing me like our early fuck filled days; she makes me wild.

I swallowed; she's going beneath the duvet; her tongue is quick and clever over my nipples and down to my navel; I have to ask this burning question; especially whilst she's like this.

'Lily will you let a professional photographer take pictures of you?'

She stopped and looked up at me; twinkling eyes in a gap in the duvet.

'Pictures?'

'Sexy pictures; for the purposes of Art.'

She smiled and shook her head,

'You've got to do better than that to get me to uncover again,' I think she's telling a fib, 'but let me think about it.'

And as she disappears beneath the duvet, I take hold of the iron wrought head board. Lily has my dick in her mouth, and I'm on such high alert after thinking about those photos I thrust forward, hitting the back of her throat, she gags briefly, but never falters, and just as she swallows (because she always does – "*can't resist your sperm J*"), I hear that familiar sound; it's our daughter, and it's my turn – bollocks!

No kidding, Lily has completely embraced her new role as *mummy* and considering she calls herself an "accidental mum", she is doing a blinding job. When we first brought Anais home, Lily confided in me she was worried about not being natural, (I have no doubt this notion was born from the pressure a few of the midwives put her under because she chose not to breast feed).

But I've been watching her, how she is with our daughter; the care and precision, her reasonable anxiety and knowing just what to do without panicking. She deals with things as they arise and the love she has for our Cutie chokes me. Don't misunderstand me, she doesn't smother or pamper her, she's just, well, sincere, and that sincerity is effortless, even after a broken nights sleep and colic filled days, Lily embraces it with confidence, whereas I, on the other hand, remain nervous of a sneeze or a jerky movement.

So, here I am, sitting in the study trying to work but instead I'm watching my sexy wife and my little girl in the garden. Anais is tucked up in her pram and Lily is pushing her through the orchard; she's talking to her; actually, she always talks to her, she even reads to her. She says you can never start too early.

Coming out of my work file, I went into Google. I need to convince Lily to go with me on the professional photograph idea. OK, she hasn't said no, but I'm aware of how she feels about her body at the moment, so it's going to take some persuading, and from an incredibly selfish perspective, I want the Bunny Girl I was promised, so I type in, "Deanna Baker 1972".

I walked out of the French doors to see Lily and Anais sitting on the patio.

'Hey J,' she sounds so much like my Lily Ellen I want to laugh, 'how's it going?'

'Good.' I pulled out a chair and took my daughter from her arms.

She's a beautiful little lady with thick auburn hair and chocolate brown eyes. 'Lily?'

'Yes J?' she's smiling; she knows me too well.

'There's something in the study I want you to take a look at.'

'Oh?' her smile disappeared, 'anything I should be worried about?'

'No,' I smiled, 'it's all good.'

I couldn't help grinning as Lily got up, and just for good measure I gently patted her ass as she walked by; she turned and winked at me, and if we didn't have the little lady with us, I'd have followed her inside; honest, I can't keep my hands off her, which was particularly embarrassing at the weekend when her parents were staying with us, because thinking they were in the garden with Anais, I grabbed Lily and held her against the Aga for a full on smooch, only to hear the back door open and surprise!

Anyway, I wonder what Lily is making of the file I left her, oh well Anais, we'll soon find out.

April 27

I have 2 words to say: "Deanna Baker".

The first time I came across Deanna Baker was in the heady days of "courting" J. (OK, so I wasn't supposed to be courting him obviously, but I was and I adored every wonderful minute of it!)

I was looking around his apartment, generally making myself seen so J wouldn't be able to take his eyes off me (hey it worked!), and there she was; J's pin up girl stuck on the fridge, and yet she looked alarmingly like me, so much so, I couldn't take my eyes off her. J looked a little embarrassed, not that I minded, at least I knew I was in with a chance because he obviously found redheads sexy and beautiful. Actually I remember asking if he found her beautiful, he looked me right in the eye and said, "She's...impeccable." I'll never forget it.

So, Deanna, the 22 year old Bunny Girl. It says here, she was working at the Playboy club in Denver when she appeared as a centrefold in May 1972 and the weird thing about this is, I could be her, we look so alike. Her hair is so like mine it makes me want to laugh. It's the exact shade of auburn, long, sleek and parted in the centre. She has subtle freckles and her build (was) identical to mine, OK, my breasts are a little fuller, but no one (except J) would notice. Anyway, J left a file out for me today; a file full of pictures of Deanna that he'd found on the internet; nude pictures, and I have to say, she is the most beautiful woman I have ever seen – I know that sounds weird because I've just said she looks like me – but I don't mean it in that way, honest.

Of course, I know why J's gone to the effort of finding these pictures; it's about me modeling again, and he doesn't think I'll do it, anyway, he didn't have to do this, I was going to do it for him anyway.

I looked up from the desk and watched J and Anais in the garden together. That's why I love this room so much, being able to see out onto our wonderful garden. I still smile in amasement when I think that J and I have a daughter, sometimes I'm still in awe that we're married, and yet just a year ago we were desperately trying to woo each other on extremely forbidden ground. Anyway, I'm getting distracted, because I'm mad about Jefferson, really I am, more now than ever, and so, what Jefferson wants, he gets; so it would be my pleasure to strip for him, and pose. His real life centrefold.

I've picked out my favourite photos, the ones I'd most like to imitate, and later I'll show them to him for approval. There were so many, I struggled to narrow them down. Anyway, the ones I chose go as follows:

1. *DB stretched out naked on a faux fur leopard print blanket, one leg lying elegantly over a matching pillow.*
2. *A close up. DB on her back on a bed facing the camera, her hair is partially covering her face, she isn't smiling, but she has pretty bright eyes.*
3. *DB in the dressing room at the Denver club preparing to change into her Bunny outfit, she is wearing just a dress but the back has been tastefully hitched up revealing a pert ass (J will love this one).*
4. *DB sitting naked in a window; there is rain on the pane. She is holding a flower to cover her sex (I will use a pink rose).*
5. *DB wearing full Bunny girl regalia.*

The following is a list of ideas I've come up with myself:

1. *Lily, naked in the orchard*
2. *Lily fastening a sexy bra in her dressing room (partial shot of breast and nipple)*
3. *Lily lying naked in a bath scattered with pink rose petals – important parts tastefully revealed.*
4. *Lily sitting elegantly on the edge of the bed tying up the ribbon on a pair of vintage ballet shoes; legs crossed at the ankles (need to find shoes!)*
5. *Lily in pink satin corset lacing the ribbon; shot will be taken*

from behind, revealing my ass.

6. *Lily completely naked, with her satchel strapped around her body just covering her sex.*
7. *Lily sitting astride a naked J as we look at each other in that way we do (my reward for doing this shoot! Ha-ha)*

Anyway, I'm going to tell J I'll do this shoot because these pictures will surpass any I've done in the past (except the very private ones of J and I at Brown's Hotel – these remain very special). I'm not quite sure what he intends doing with them when they're done, but I'm sure I'll have a lot of fun finding out,
Hey, quote of the day:
"Bunny Lily Ellen is born!"

I want to take Lily back to Paris. Since we bought the apartment in St Germain, we haven't stepped foot in. We keep threatening to take a long weekend, Mum and Dad will have Anais, and Lily and I get to play at being very naughty again, something I miss, but we just can't seem to find the time.

Anyway, since the whole "Bunny Lily Ellen" thing, I'm picking up strong vibes in Lily's Journal that she's looking for something fresh; some vibrancy in her life, in effect, she's inspired and needs to express herself, after all, it's been a tough couple of months for us, and I have to be honest and say our relationship (especially our sex life) has taken a bit of a bashing, what, with broken sleep, weight issues, dwindling confidence and sharing our time with a baby, things have been a little strained at times. I'm feeling slighter older, and my trousers are a little on the snug side, which everyone with the exception of Lily, keeps reminding me.

See, what I didn't bank on was how much of Lily's time our little girl would need. I assumed because we both work from home, we'd still get hours of talk and play, but with eight feeds a day, nappies, bathing and colic, it isn't working out like that, in essence, I'm having to learn not to be selfish, and let me tell you, it's the most difficult thing I've ever had to do, but the Sure Thing is this, I love Lily; am in love with Lily – she is every kind of woman I want and need; this will work.

So, to shake off my uncomfortable insecurities, I regularly read Lily's "*Happy ever After*" and immerse myself in this love, because like I said, Lily is every kind of woman. She's a woman who happens to be an amazing Mum, who ensures our Cutie is protected from all the bad in this life. A woman who makes mouth-watering scrambled egg and English breakfast tea in the mornings; who eats croissants and drinks espresso whilst feverishly reading *Bataille* on a street corner café. She is a woman who feeds chickens in the garden and collects eggs to bake cup cakes; a woman who wears the pointiest silver shoes I've set my eyes on, combined with the elegance of a silk scarf for dinner. She is a woman who writes through the night, and whom I have to carry to bed; a woman who fiercely loves me in every way I want and desire. Her level of ability is so, that I am completely overwhelmed by her, as she is of me. Together, we have a love that makes life drunk and I never want to be sober.

My Wife, the Contradiction

Lily's been talking to me about an idea she has for a novel, but with being mum to Anais, the launch of pinkcupcakes.co.uk next month and the PCC writers group beginning in June, she's had to put it on the back burner, but honest, it's genius, pure Lily Ellen.

It seems my pictures of Deanna Baker have inspired Lily more than I imagined. Not only has she dubbed her "the most beautiful woman in the world" (although I strictly disagree – that title goes to my wife), it appears Miss Baker (circa 1972) has my Lily boiling over with ideas for her new leading lady, for which she has been trying to research for the past few days.

'Bunny Girls,' she said over dinner, 'don't you think they're the epitome of classy sexiness?'

She makes me smile,

'*Classy sexiness*?' I said picking up my wine, 'is that a word?'

'No,' she smiled, 'I just made it up.' She started laughing, 'anyway J, the 1960s and 70s American and British Bunnies were as gorgeous as hell.' I knew what was coming, 'I'd loved to have been a Bunny Girl, maybe even a Playmate.' And she winked.

I have a tremendous erection, and I wonder if it's appropriate to ask Lily to service me, even if we are at the dinner table.

'I think Hef would have snapped you up.' I said, 'but I'd have come to the club with you,' I smiled, 'to look after you of course.'

'J? Jealous?' She grinned.

'Hell yeah!' I laughed, 'Jeez Lily, my wife, a Bunny Girl,' I shook my head mockingly, 'just think of all those lecherous men with nothing better to do than squeeze my wife's cotton tail.'

Lily has her foot between my legs; she's laughing; she can feel how hard I am.

'Redheads traditionally wore green satin corsets and bunny ears you know.'

'Lily stop.' I put down my cutlery. I couldn't eat.

'Do you think my ass would look good with a cute fluffy cotton tail J?' She's getting up, sitting on my knees.

'Oh yes Honey.' I ran my hands the length of her sexy thighs.

She hitched up her skirt and I unfastened my trousers, I feared I still had sauce on my chin. I pulled my trousers and jocks to my knees and rucked Lily's panties to one side and she glided smoothly over my dick. I groaned; it felt like ages since I'd fucked her.

J?' she's riding me with wide open legs that I'm holding apart, her girly hands gripping the back of my chair for support, 'would you like to run your hands across green satin?'

'Oh yes...' I panted.

'Would you unpeel my corset, hold my tits in your hands, watching them bounce as you fuck me...'

That was it; game over, I was shooting straight up her, my head thrown back, mumbling obscenities, wishing so badly I could stop coming so quickly, but then with a wife like mine, what the hell did I expect?

Anyway, I have to say, I'm loving her work at the moment, because when Lily's inspired, she enjoys using me as a "sounding board", which means, I'm receiving a hell of a lot of "*classy sexiness*" in the shape of Bunny Lily Ellen, and for that my friend, I have no complaints.

OK, so you must be wondering how these two kids keep up their glamourous and sexual acrobatic lifestyle with a 2 month old baby, well, let me tell you, most of the time, we don't.

See, the days Lily and I do get time together; the times we do feel like having sex, and the times we aren't in bed by 9 because we're so damned knackered, we're the same couple we were when we fell in love; that hasn't changed, in fact, it's deepened, it's now on that "other level" Lily and I often talk about.

I suppose what has changed, is we argue a little more than previous. As you know, my lady is no pushover (in any department) and if she thinks I'm not pulling my weight, she tells me, and this remains her main grudge; she thinks I feel it's OK to carry on writing everyday whilst she looks after Anais,

'I have a life too J!' she shouted at me last night as we were getting ready for bed, 'don't think you can carry on with life as before and leave me to do everything!'

And on times, yes, I admit, I do take her for granted, for a variety of reasons, (1) because she's a fantastic mum, so damned organized and I'm not, and (2) because often she doesn't realise she wants to take charge of Anais; she knows then it's done the way she wants it, but then of course, there are days I can't do right whatever; anyway, despite these small differences with regards to being new parents, we remain solid, for which I'm proud, because outsiders were adamant Lily and I wouldn't make it (except Jeremy – God bless him), and yet I had an e-mail from Joe last week announcing Florence is expecting and already he's been sent to the spare room on a number of occasions for being a "selfish pig" (she's only 3 months gone – oh dear).

Anyway, I am trying to be a more considerate husband as well as an attentive father, honest I am, more than I think Lily gives me credit for on times, but then I can't imagine how it must be for her; after all, she's still just 25 (26 in 2 weeks), and so for her 26th birthday I'm taking her to our Paris apartment for the weekend to completely spoil her. Anais will be staying with my parents (yes – this was a huge decision for Lily, she said she didn't feel "ready" to let her go over night), and I know once we get there, it'll be euphoric.

On a more sober note, Luke is back home, so Lily and I have to meet mum and dad on mutual ground to avert a collision – yes, I do still occasionally receive the odd e-mail from him (the not very pleasant ones). One tends to arrive after something significant has happened in my life, although interestingly, he didn't send anything when Anais was born, but there's usually one if I'm mentioned in the press, and exceptionally nasty ones if I'm pictured with Lily; I can only guess he's not over her, which for me doesn't sit comfortably.

Anyway, that aside, I have a surprise for Lily when we're in Paris, I've arranged for us to meet with a photographer friend of mine, well, actually I know him through Jez, the guy who painted Lily's portrait, his name is Pablo, and he's famous for his nude photography, (in the name of Art, of course), and when I spoke to him a few weeks back about working with Lily, he seemed a little over zealous,

'Your wife; the *red*?' I could hear his smile, 'whoa, of course – no problem.'

'I'm trusting you,' I grinned watching Lily and Anais in the garden, 'I do not want you letching over her.'

'JJ listen,' he said, 'joking aside, because I know from friends how much you love your wife, but I've seen her with you in the papers, she is a beautiful woman and I would love to take her picture but that is where it ends; I am a professional.'

Of course, I don't really have a problem with Pablo taking Lily's picture, I wouldn't have asked if I didn't trust him, besides, I've seen his past work, he is brilliant; he even said he could get hold of a green satin Bunny Girl outfit; after that, the job was his.

I've been in London today to hand over my manuscript to Henry.

'*Red*?' he mused as we sat in Arbutus, 'are you sure about the title?'

'It's become the best way to describe it.'

'It sounds like a book about Socialism.'

I started laughing,

'I don't think anyone who knows my work would associate it with Socialism Henry.'

(Actually, I didn't much like the title either, it didn't do it justice, and after a conversation with Lily a couple of nights ago, she confessed the same,

'I still love *A Genuine Spark of the Divine Fire,'* she said, 'it sums up their desperation and passion.')

'There is another title I've been playing with.' I said coming back to Henry.

Amazingly he didn't turn his nose up when I told him,

'"*A Genuine Spark of the Divine Fire*"?' He repeated.

'And please,' I relaxed back in my chair, 'do not give me a tacky front cover again.'

'See, you bloody writers,' he complained, 'you all get like this in the end.'

'Like what?' I smiled.

'Bloody difficult.'

I poured Henry another glass of red,

'Asking for a decent front cover is not being difficult,' I said. 'But for this novel, it has to be right.'

'Well, I don't know what you've got in mind, but I'm not sure how much Little Brown will throw in for it.'

'Look, I'm not expecting something copyright of Playboy but...' Whoa, a light bulb moment. 'Actually Henry,' I grinned, 'I'll get back to you on that one.'

On the train home, I phoned Lily,

'Hey Honey,' she said rather too sexily since I'm not near her, 'how's it going?'

'Good.' I said sinking into my seat; I'd already taken off my shoes; the luxury of being in First Class, 'missing you.'

'Missin' you too handsome.'

'How's my little Cutie?'

'She's lying on my lap having her milk,' I can tell she's smiling, because nothing makes her happier than looking into our little girl's brown eyes, (although she still maintains her favourite past time is looking into mine), 'when you coming home?'

'On my way,' I said, 'just heading out of Paddington.'

'How's Henry?'

'Miserable.' I laughed, 'nah, he's OK, giving me a hard time because I challenged him over the front cover.'

'Typical,' she said, 'I suppose he wanted something tacky didn't he?'

See, great minds hey?

'I got in there before he suggested anything,' I said stirring a sugar into my tea, 'anyway, I took your advice.'

'Advice?'

'Yeah, "*A Genuine Spark of the Divine Fire*" is officially the new title.'

'Wow J,' her laughter still gets me right in the gut, 'that's fantastic.'

'Only problem now, is the damned cover.' I wanted to see if I could prompt her; tease it out of her. 'See, you know what publishers are like, they don't like splashing out for stuff like that, and well, I did mention Playboy, but I know the copyright would be extortionate.'

Silence.

'Lily?'

'Yes J?' I simply cannot fool this woman; one of the millions of reasons why I love her so much.

'So you know what's on my mind then?'

'I have a fair idea.'

'So what do you think?' I asked cautiously.

OK, if she agreed, it would definitely have to be a more subdued photo of Lily, after all, I do not want my wife's nudity splashed about at every train station and bill board across London; no my friend, that belongs to me.

'Lily, you're so beautiful,' the guy in the next seat down glanced at me over the rim of his specs; I guess he has me down as a fuckwit, 'I'd feel very proud.'

'Jefferson,' she sighed deeply, 'I'd love to do it, but I'm so nervous, you know, with the baby weight and all.'

I try to understand her plight.

'Have a think about it; we can talk about it later.'

'I wish you were home,' she said softly, 'it seems ages since I saw you.'

She's so cute sometimes, although she'd hate me saying it,

'Not long now Honey,' the guy looked over at me again, 'I love you.'

'I love you so much J,' she's pining; I love her like this, 'hurry home.'

After saying goodbye to Lily, I had a warm glow around me; I was fucking buzzing, even the guy opposite nodded to me appreciatively, and I almost said, "if you had a wife like mine, you'd say those things too", instead, I sank back with folded arms and closed my eyes, immersing myself in the woman I now call Bunny Lily Ellen.

May 10

This weight thing is really getting me down. Livvy says I look great and so does mum, J thinks I look even more beautiful with curves, but I'm not finding it a comfort.
OK, so I'm not helping myself by keep trying on all my old clothes; my favourite Diesel jeans, which look like they'll never fit me again, and the gorgeous dresses J bought me when we started dating.
I think my desperate mind has distorted my pre-pregnancy body to the point of despair. I was slim, but I was never skinny, but now nothing seems good enough and I find myself hiding from mirrors and windows; to catch a glimpse of myself makes me want to cry.

Oh, and I promised J I'd do those photos for him, which I really want to do, but I already know I'll hate them.
God, listen to me, some women put stacks of weight on and find it almost impossible to lose it, at least mine is coming off. I should be comforted but I'm not, my body will never be like it was before Anais. I will forever have a paunch and I'm sure my breasts have dropped slightly and I have love handles (J adores these; why are men so like that! It infuriates me!), and no amount of training at the gym seems to shift them.

'J!' Lily came bursting into the study; how I adore that smile, 'I think I have my first *pink cup cakes* discussion topic.'

'Oh?' She's been giving this a lot of thought lately.

'Women and Media.' She announced sitting cross legged on the sofa facing me, 'OK, I know it's huge, so I'm going to focus it a little, I mean, I was reading on the internet how some celebrity women lose their baby fat in just 3 weeks,' she shook her head in disdain, 'and that's after a caesarean, I mean, come on, they slice right through the stomach muscles for Christ sakes.' My stomach churned at the thought of it. 'Anyway, I'd love to start a discussion about it, focusing on post-pregnancy weight and the issues we face as women to continue looking good as well as being a flat out mum and having a successful career.' She finally took a breath, 'I'd like to do a research paper on it, maybe even a PhD?' She beamed. "*Stripping down the Yummy Mummy – choice or societal pressure?*"' and she laughed; but I know she's very capable.

After Lily left the study, I turned back to the PC, but I was still thinking. I'm frustrated for her, because despite views on literature having shifted, I don't know whether it's shifted enough to accept her genre, I mean, if you choose to write a sexually explicit novel, chances are you'll never make it into the general fiction market, (interestingly, my writing has), and yet when I think about Lily, she's incredible at bringing these issues to the forefront; hence her magnetism to Anais Nin (also a contradiction I feel), so this forum could be the making of her. I sincerely hope so.

Anyway, she's already succeeded in something: in me; because my work has changed; my inclusion of women is no longer merely as body parts, in fact, they've become the epitome of *classy sexiness*,

'And that's down to you Lily,' I said, 'my wife the contradiction.'

And she smiles; because she knows just what I mean.

Bunny Lily Ellen

I was beginning to wonder whether the surprise meeting with Pablo in Paris was a good idea. Lily hadn't been in a great space when we started the journey to London; Anais had a cranky night, and we were up and down for most of it, hence why we've been walking about likes zombies. We barely spoke in the car, and when we did, we were snappy. Neither of us is any good with broken sleep, so I'm thankful we've come away for the weekend.

Actually, I'm not in a great space either. I'm a bit pissed off with not being able to visit mum and dads house whenever Luke is around. OK, I respect their wishes, but for God's sake, Lily and I are married now and we have a daughter, how much longer are we going to be isolated?

'What do you think he'd do if we just turned up at the house?' Lily asked.

'I have no idea,' I said truthfully, 'although I suspect I'd cop a load of abuse.'

'J?'

I looked at her briefly as I drove; she wore an unfamiliar frown,

'Yes?'

'You know he blames me for all of this don't you,' she said, 'you'll always be his brother.'

'He doesn't blame you.'

'Yes he does,' she said sounding slightly hurt, 'he said so at your apartment that day.'

I looked back at the road, hands gripping the steering wheel, my knuckles turning white.

'Do you ever hear from him?' I'd wanted to ask this question a few times.

'Not really.'

'Not really?' I shot her a look, 'what does that mean?'

'It means what I said,' she snapped, 'not really; why, do you?'

'Sometimes.'

'You never told me.'

'You never told me either.'

'Stop snapping at me!' she shouted.

Anais started crying; she cries when we shout at each other, and I guess that's because despite us arguing today, we rarely raise our voice in front of her; we don't need to.

'Lily calm down.'

'Fuck you.' She sneered gazing out of the window.

'Look, sometimes he sends me an e-mail.' I stopped at traffic lights and we looked at each other.

'What sort of e-mails?'

'Not very nice ones, so that's why I don't bother telling you.'

'He hasn't sent me one for ages.' She said as we moved on, 'the last one was after Anais was born.'

Hum, interesting; since that was the only time I didn't get one.

'What did he say?'

'Nothing, it was blank.'

'Cunt.' I mumbled under my breath. I felt Lily watching me so I glanced at her, and to my surprise, she winked and we both grinned.

As we approached London, I was thinking about by passing Hampstead Heath (chosen destination to meet the folks), and driving straight to my parent's house. I figured we were going to have to face Luke at some time, so why not now, then maybe he might stop e-mailing his feelings, confront them and get over them; in essence, get over Lily.

In fairness to mum and dad though, they're thrilled to be having Anais for two nights; they've gone all out to get the spare room kitted out as a nursery, to ease Lily's mind. I also figured it was done in the hope Anais would stay with them more often – bless; anyway, this gesture made Lily feel better, and she started to relax.

'I'm sorry I keep talking about her,' she said after dropping off the Cutie, 'it's weird not being with her.'

I squeezed her hand; she's so lovely,

'Talk all you like,' I whispered, 'this is your weekend Lily.'

'Our weekend.' She corrected.

Lily's farewell to Anais was beautiful; infact I still struggle on times to think of Lily as a Mum, because she's the same Lily Ellen that walked into my life almost 2 years ago; the one who loves pink cup cakes and wears pink butterfly sandals; I guess although a lot of things change when you have kids, your personality doesn't (unless you want it to); I know mine hasn't, another popular misconception thankfully.

Stepping off the plane at Charles de Gaulle, I felt a little nostalgic. The last time we were here, it was just the two of us, and although I wouldn't change being the three of us, I intend enjoying every delicious bit of my wife for the next two days.

Lily's reaction as she opened the apartment door filled me with joy. I was pleased I'd decided to hire someone to organise it for us, (it was actually Helena's housekeeper I borrowed), because seeing Lily's face was worth it.

'Oh J.' She turned to me; eyes watering, 'you spoil me.'

I watched as she walked over to the dining table and fingered the bouquet of pink roses. She read the note aloud,

'*My Darling Lillian,*' She whispered, '*just once, everyman...J xxx*'

'This is just the start little lady.' I reached for her hand, 'come,' I said, 'there's more.'

I took her to the lounge, where logs were prepared for a fire this evening.

'Will you join me?' I took chilled Champagne from an ice bucket on the table and showed it to her, she nodded completely beaming.

But this is just the start, because tomorrow its Lily's birthday and I'm taking her to see Madame Butterfly, which is a surprise. However, she does know we'll be eating at *Le Café de la Paix* where I've reserved a table in the private dining area. My other surprise is I've bought her a new dress to wear to the Opera; Valentino, because she wears it so elegantly; she is pure splendor.

I take her hand and she's laughs softly, already giddy on bubbles. *Oh how I love her.* I'm absorbed as she stands beside our bed; a bed we've yet to sleep in, or more importantly, to fuck on.

Desire ripped through me as she ran teasing fingers over the sheets. Like a voyeur standing in the doorway, I watched her discard her drink and lay on the bed, beautiful smouldering auburn shimmering across pink satin. She brought her legs up, her flimsy skirt gliding recklessly to her thighs, *j'adore* polka dot panties. I swallowed, dick straining to find its way home.

'Now you come here,' she has one hell of a kitty cat voice, 'these sheets need ruffling.'

So, after Champagne and a lot of getting sexily restless between extremely ruffled pink satin sheets, I took Lily to the *Quartier Latin* to meet Pablo.

'J, where we going?' Lily took my hand as we left the apartment, both of us shrouded in a post-coital glow. I cupped her cheek with one hand and took her mouth completely; I'm fired about these photographs; about green satin bunny ears; about Lily; about life... 'I know,' she cheered, 'pink cup cakes!'

'Sorry to disappoint you,' I said re-claiming her hand, 'but pink cup cakes are firmly off the agenda this weekend; I think we've had quite enough of those.'

She started laughing; she says I sound "posh" sometimes and I guess that was one of those times.

OK, so let me tell you a bit about Pablo. He's 35, currently single ("too many beautiful women in the world to settle down quite yet" – he should know – he photographs a lot of them). I'd say he's fairly well off, after all, he lives in the Latin Quarter in an apartment spread over two floors, which my friend, does not come cheap, even with its obvious intellectual edge.

Pablo works from home – his studio is the converted apartment upstairs. He's incredibly handsome in a dark chiseled way, and just a little bit egotistical.

'Who's this?' Lily stared at me after reading the name on the intercom, 'Pablo Regatta?'

'All will be revealed Lily Ellen.' I squeezed her hand.

Pablo called us up via the intercom, and we traveled the two flights of stairs to his apartment.

'JJ,' Pablo grinned taking my hand, 'how's married life?'

'Couldn't be better.' I was grateful he hadn't mentioned my slightly expanding waistline. 'Pab, meet my wife, Lily.'

Lily stepped out from behind me, still unaware of what was going on,

'Hi.' She said shaking his hand, 'nice to meet you.'

'Lily,' he still had her hand; he was checking her out; I sensed her uneasiness, but I stayed calm because I know why he's doing it. 'Such a pleasure.' And she pulled her hand away.

'These are great photographs,' she said moving around his hallway, 'is that Kate Moss?'

'Yep.' Pablo's hands were stuffed tightly into the pockets of his Gucci jeans; he looked smug. He was also looking at Lily's ass; I caught his eye, he nodded.

'Did you take these?' Lily turned to him; she is so beautiful.

'I did indeed.' Pablo went over to her, 'this,' he said pointing to Kate Moss, 'was taken about eight years ago, I'd just started out.'

'Wow,' she seemed impressed; damn, 'they're amazing.'

'Well thank you.' Pab looked pleased with himself; sly git. 'So JJ,' he joined me, 'let's talk business buddy.'

Lily looked at me,

'J?' she said cautiously, 'what's going on?'

I took her hands, kissing each one on turn,

'Don't freak out,' I said softly, 'just think "*green satin*".'

She blinked a few times,

'Green satin bunny ears?'

'And corset.' Pablo chipped in, 'oh, and the cute cotton tail.'

Lily gawped at me,

'Oh J, no.' She shook her head,

'Yes.' I smiled.

'I can't.' She backed away; I gripped her hands tightly.

'Yes you can; you said so.'

She took me to one side.

'I thought we'd agreed to do it when I'd lost the last bit of weight.'

'We didn't agree anything.'

Lily pondered,

'True, we didn't.'

'Lily,' Pablo came over, 'JJ's filled me in a bit, and he's given me an idea of the kind of photo's your both after,' he nodded to follow him through to the next room, 'let me put your mind at ease.'

We sat on the sofa, with Pablo on his knees infront of Lily. He was showing her some of his previous work and I've got to say, he was even more brilliant than I remembered.

'You make everyone look so lovely,' Lily said studying the nudes.

'This will be very easy with you Lily, because you are a naturally beautiful woman.'

OK Pablo, enough now.

'And he has all the props.' I added. 'Lily, please?' I squeezed her hand; I've never seen her hesitate before.

She turned to Pablo,

'Please don't make me look fat,' she pleaded, 'if I do, will you cut all the crap off?'

Pablo laughed,

'I can tell you Lily, they'll be no need to "cut the crap off".'

She looked at me, anxiety in her eyes,

'I want to do it,' she said, 'but I'm nervous; it's been so long.'

'You've modeled before?' Pablo's eyes twinkled; honestly, I thought he would be used to this by now.

'Amateur.' I smiled.

'Cool.' And he winked at me, 'so Lily; are we on or off?'

I have to be honest, now that we're in Pablo's studio and his assistant Solenne is helping Lily with her styling (we are currently waiting for the quick dry spray tan to dry, so I'm told), that I understand why Lily's apprehensive about doing this shoot, after all, she is actually going to be posing nude; real life naked photographs.

'Hey JJ,' Pablo threw himself beside me on the floor, 'I've just been to see how things are coming on, and I have to tell you, your wife looks sensational.'

My wife is sensational.

I looked up; eyes stinging as Lily emerged; a goddess in flames. Her hair had been straightened and curled on the ends; her make up, subtle and pretty, she was wearing a white robe.

'OK Lily,' Pablo was straightening out the leopard print throw, 'when you're ready.'

Pablo had stepped into professional mode, for which I was grateful, because Lily, yes, my wife, was just about to slip off her robe and reveal her beautiful nakedness in front of us, and as she did, my eyes focused and my chest tightened.

Pab didn't flinch, but Lily did, worried eyes boring into me. I winked; she is incredible. Solenne assisted Lily into position and when Pab first started snapping, Lily got the giggles, I knew it was nerves, she's cute like that. He called for her to move this way, that way, and to relax, clicking away like a mad man whilst I sat and watched.

By the time she was dressed in the pink corset tying the ribbon (OK so I couldn't take my eyes off her naked ass and yes I did have one hell of an erection), Lily was living the dream. She was my Lily Ellen pre-Anais: sexy, confident and creative, she'd even started improvising, suggesting things to Pablo. Then it happened; the moment I'd been dreaming of, Lily reappeared; my fantasy; my pin up; my Bunny Girl in green satin.

Pab changed his film and Lily came over and sat astride me, holding my shoulders. I immediately gripped her slender waist.

'Hey J,' she has naughty eyes; I am so grateful we're alone tonight; I want to fuck her bad and I am making no secret of it as I slip my hands to her ass, running my eager fingers over the satin. 'Do you think Hugh Hefner would really have chosen me to be Bunny Lily?'

Now let me tell you something, Lily is a bona fide Bunny Girl. She is wearing a green satin corset that makes her waist look so tiny I'm convinced I'd get my hands around it. Her hips are luscious in satin, despite what she says, and right now I'm playing with her fluffy cotton tail (she has just leaned into me to ask if I'll fuck her ass later – I told her I'd do it now if I could). She even has the white cuffs and a collar (complete with black bow tie) and of course, those Bunny ears that make her smouldering auburn hair blaze.

'He wouldn't have hesitated.' I whispered running my nose along her sexy collar bone.

'Do you like my shoes J?' She was wearing green satin heels with a fantastic point.

'Yes Lily.' We kissed, but it didn't seem enough for her, she took my mouth completely. I cupped her face between my hands and we really started going for it, and only as we slowed down could I hear the familiar clicking of Pablo's camera.

'Man,' he grinned, 'you two are smouldering,' he was laughing, still taking photos, 'who says marriage kills passion hey?'

After leaving Pablo's, Lily was feeling more than a little sexy. Standing on the busy Metro, she pushed her ass into my groin so I slipped my hand beneath her skirt; she pushed back harder, and since it was so packed, I wondered if I'd get away with what I was thinking.

Lily sank her body back into mine and I glided my hand down the back of her panties; she gripped my leg and squeezed. I ran an awkward finger down the crevice of her ass and buried my face into her neck; she tilted her head to allow me access, and then I thought we'd better cool it down, people were starting to stare.

With every intention of locking ourselves in the apartment until dinner, I took Lily straight to the bedroom, where I'd asked Angelique to scatter pink rose petals over the sheets, prepare more champagne, a few strawberries with dipping chocolate and then dim the lights.

I opened the door and Lily gasped, blinking at me through wide watery eyes. I gently took her hand and guided her in. She was laughing through her tears.

'Oh my God J,' she whispered, 'it's just like your "unforgettable night"...'

'...with no ordinary redhead...' I fell to my knees, holding her hands, looking up at her, 'Lily, I want to give you all the best things in life.'

'You already do,' I lay her back on the bed, 'you always have.'

I took her mouth and now I didn't feel much like fucking her in the brutal manner I'd been planning, instead, I wanted to lie and gaze at her, so that's exactly what I did.

May 26

It's a year ago yesterday that I met J out in the yard of Livvy and Tom's farm on my 25th birthday. I'm embarrassed to remember I was wearing pink floral wellies! But J didn't say anything, I think he was just being polite. He bought me a diamond necklace that I now know dented his bank account a little, because he loved me that much.

That night I felt his love stronger than I ever had. He didn't hide it from me, so from that moment on it was just a case of WHEN it happened not IF, because I'd already made my mind up in the yard that I was going to give myself to him. I couldn't hold back anymore and after today, I thank God, really I do (I actually prayed to say thank you), that I gave in, that J waited for me, even though we hurt Luke so badly, which I will always regret.

This has been my 2nd best birthday (the first – see above). I didn't hear J get up, but when I woke, there were still pink rose petals everywhere, (although the one's on the bed were slightly

crumpled!), he'd even scattered them on the window ledge. Then he appeared, dressed in jeans and a blue and white gingham shirt, he is so beautiful my husband, I am so lucky to have a man who is out of my league and yet loves me unconditionally.
'Happy Birthday Lily Ellen,' he sat beside me on the bed and handed me a single pink rose, 'I have gifts for you.'
J spoils me. He says he can't help himself. He says for years he spent money on himself, but now he wants to spend it on me.
'This one is for mummy.' And he smiled and I almost started crying. I've been talking about her a lot I know; I wish she was here. 'And this one is for Bunny Lily Ellen.'

I opened the present from Anais, wrapped in pink foil paper and pink ribbon. It was a gorgeous silver and diamond framed photo of me and her the day she was born. I started crying. J gets used to me now, he smiles and cuddles me, I know he thinks I'm cute, but he daren't say it!
'She sends all her love,' J said kissing me softly, 'and a picture to remind you of her.'
He urged me to open the second parcel. It was wrapped in pink paper with a black ribbon tied around it. It was quite a large parcel and I had no idea what it was.
I laughed as torn pink paper revealed green satin.
'It's the real thing,' J said proudly, 'I got it from auction.'
There; I have my very own Bunny Girl outfit – an original; not many people can boast that!
'Here.' J held out my hand and planted a small box in my palm, 'to say I love you.'
I flipped open the box. My chest tightened. I looked up at him.
'I know we've only been married a short time' he said,' but I want you to know that for me, this marriage will be for eternity.'
J took the diamond band from the box and slipped it on my finger with my wedding and engagement rings. The delicate rocks glistened in the sunlight pouring in through the window.

J and I stayed close all day. I had a great need to keep touching him, just to make sure he was real. He didn't seem to mind, in fact, he encouraged it. We ate in Les Deux Magots and walked around the Parc de Bagatelle, where the most amazing pink roses are in bloom. We had a glass of Champagne in the Hemingway Bar and a bottle at Le Dokhan's. We visited Shakespeare & Company and J bought me a book: "Quiet Days in Clichy" by Henry Miller (in French).
'Can we come back again soon?' I said as we headed back to

the apartment after an afternoon of shopping (Printemps and Fifi Chachnil!).
'Of course,' he said pulling me into him as we stood outside our front door, 'besides, you're going to need to spend a bit of time here when you start research for that novel of yours.'
'Oh, I don't know if I'm going to bother, I just never get the time.'
'Well we'll have to make time,' he winked, 'because if you don't write it, how will you ever get published.'

There was a parcel lying on the bed with a note tied to it,

"Lily, you are an addictive allure – don't ever stop. J x"

'Go on then,' he stood beside me, 'open it Honey.'

I knew immediately it was Valentino. J adores me in Valentino. I adore it too. I held up the dress. Red silk and chiffon, all the way to my feet.
'I'll never forget my 'red' in red.' He whispered into my neck, 'because I love her.'

I dressed for dinner. J checked if I was wearing panties (for the record, I wasn't!). After dining at Café de la Paix, our taxi was waiting outside,
'Opéra National sil vous plait.' J said to the driver, then he turned to me and whispered, 'Madame Butterfly.'
Last night I was so happy. Deliriously happy. Always happy with my J and my Anais...

A Light that will never go out

Something happened the following day that Lily didn't write about in her Journal. I guess it was something she didn't want to be reminded of. She has learnt a harsh lesson when it comes to keeping memoirs.

From Heathrow, Lily and I took a chance and headed over to Hampstead. Lily was absolutely gagging to see Anais. In fact, she found one of her fairy bibs in the side compartment of the car and kept smelling it. Her eyes filled with tears, she said it smelt of her, our little girl.

I laughed, but did the same and my God, she was right. My stomach flipped over and I realised how I much I'd missed her; how much I love her.

We pulled up outside mum and dads and as I hadn't seen my daughter for 2 days, I couldn't care less whether Luke was in or not. In fact, if he was, then all the better. Lily though, was not so sure.

'I don't want anything to kick off,' she said as we hovered by the car, 'I've had such a lovely weekend.'

I took Lily's hand. I couldn't guarantee that it wouldn't kick off; Luke is an unquantifiable source when it comes to being unpredictable. I slipped my key in the door and braced myself. Lily squeezed my hand and I smiled at her reassuringly.

'It's only us!' I hollered.

'Through here!' Mum called from the garden.

Lily and I looked at each other and smiled; it was time to put this behind us.

'Hey,' Dad had just finished mowing the lawn, Mum was sitting on the swinging chair with Anais on her lap, 'how was your weekend?' No sign of Luke.

'Fantastic.' I adore Lily's smile. 'I had an amazing birthday thanks to J.' and she winked at me. 'And how's my gorgeous little lady.' She homed in on Anais; it melted me.

Mum got up and handed Anais straight to Lily. I stroked her lush hair.

'Nothing like being back with your mummy hey?' Mum smiled.

There was a sparkle in Lily's eyes as she took our daughter into her arms. I know how much she's missed her, well, we both have; we spent a fair bit of the weekend talking about her.

'Hello my little baby cake,' she whispered stroking her hair, 'mummy did miss you so much.'

'Was she good?' I said to mum, watching my two favourite girls sit on the swinging chair.

'She was brilliant,' Mum beamed, 'she was as good as gold; you have a fine one there JJ.'

'So, umm,' I said looking around, 'is Luke about?'

Mum and Dad glanced at each other; I guessed it was supposed to be discreet, but unfortunately for my parents, they are anything but.

'I'll put the kettle on.' Dad disappeared into the kitchen and I wondered whether I was speaking another language.

'Well JJ,' Mum said as we sat at the patio table, 'he's actually in Australia.'

'Oh right,' I said thinking nothing of it, 'another competition?'

'Umm, no, he's actually moved out for good.'

I looked over at Lily; she was talking sweetly to Anais.

'When did this happen?' I said.

'Yesterday.'

'But why didn't you tell me?'

'He didn't want you to know until after he'd gone.'

'But...'

'Listen JJ, this is strictly between us, but the thing is, he never got over you and Lily, well, not fully anyway, and now with Anais and everything, he just needed to get away.'

'But he didn't have to go for good did he?' I was totally shocked.

'He's got a lot of good friends out there,' Mum put her hand over mine; I honestly didn't know what to say. 'He just needed to, in his words, "sort his head out".'

Dad arrived back with a tray of murky looking tea; how to tell dad never makes tea.

'I'm stunned,' I said, sitting back in the chair, 'I don't know what to say.'

I realise now I'd wanted to see Luke. So much had happened over the last year; so much wasted time, so many things I didn't say, but should have, and now I wondered if I'd ever get the chance to talk to my little brother again.

'Jefferson?' Lily must have seen the expression on my face. 'What's the matter?' She sat down beside me and I grabbed her hand,

'Luke's moved out to Australia,' I said, 'he didn't want me to know until after he'd gone.'

Mum and Lily exchanged glances. They obviously understand these things better than I do.

'As long as he's happy.' Lily squeezed my hand; I was carrying so much guilt, I just never recognized it until now.

'He's got sun, sea, the surf, and well,' Mum said trying to make light of it, 'a lot of other stuff beginning with "S" that I'd rather not go in to.'

'J?' I looked at Lily, 'why don't you write to him?'

'That sounds like a good idea.' Dad said rather jolly; I felt anything but.

'Say the things you've wanted to say but didn't.' Lily knows me; I swear at times she can read my mind. 'Maybe then we can all move on.'

I leaned over and kissed her; I need her so badly.

'Maybe I will.' I smiled, 'right then,' I said trying to cheer myself up, 'where's that tea Dad?'

I've been watching Lily from the study window digging up potatoes; she's so lovely my wife; the glue in this family. Despite talking this thing through with her on the journey back from Mum and Dad's, I still have a pain in my gut, in essence, guilt and a hell of a lot of sadness.

I've been trying to write a letter for the past three hours and I'm still staring at a blank page, for a best selling author, I'm doing a pretty shabby job right?

The thing is, I don't know how to say sorry, I mean, I stole his girlfriend, my brother's girlfriend for Christ's sake, how the hell do I explain that?

'You just have to be honest,' Lily said as we drove home, 'as difficult as that will be.' She put her hand on my knee, 'make that your starting point.'

Dear Luke,

I'm not quite sure how to start this letter, or even if you'll continue reading once you realise who it's from, but I urge you to, please, for all of us.

When Mum and Dad told me you'd moved out to Australia I have to be honest, I was gutted. See, for the past 12 months, I've been carrying around a hell of a lot of guilt, and only recognized it once you'd left.

Listen Luke, I know you must think it's easy for me to do this because you're not around, and yes, I should have done it months ago, but the reason I didn't, is because I'd been hiding my guilt behind my feelings for Lily, but it doesn't mean I don't regret hurting you as much as I did, but I can't ever regret loving her.

See, no one was supposed to get hurt, because as far as I could see, Lily loved you, why would she love me, and believe me when I say this, but I never imagined I was capable of doing what I did to you, but the truth is, I've been in love with Lily from the moment I met her, and no matter how much I tried to avoid and ignore it, it just became more intense for both of us, but please, don't blame Lily for this, she hated betraying you, and the distress it caused her was not a comfort for me, believe me Luke, Lily has given me a conscience, something which enables me to do this now; to be totally honest.

Look, I don't want to rub salt into your wounds by talking about her too much, so I just want to say I am so sorry for what happened between us, and I have so much remorse that you and I never managed to resolve this, or at least try to talk about it; I still think about you a lot.
See, there are things we used to talk about that I miss; things I'd like to share with you, things I know you'd find humorous, such as Anais having your chilled out temperament even though she's still a baby, that there are chickens running around our garden, and yes, I have an expanded waistline (apparently!)

Listen Luke, I know things can never be the way they were, but I would hate to leave this life having never spoken to you again; you are a great person and we were once good as brothers, and before you think it, this is not me off loading, it's simply me trying to tell you I'm sorry we don't talk anymore, and I'm sorry I betrayed you in quite the way I did.

Anyway, I wish you every happiness, and if you ever change your mind, give me a call or drop me an e-mail (but not of the "cunt" variety please!) and let's have a chat; about anything, because whatever's gone on between us, however much you loathe me now, I love and miss you.
Be good,
JJ.

There was a gentle tap on the study door,
'J?' Lily appeared with caution, 'are you alright?'
I held my hands out and she sat on my knees,
'Never been better Honey.' I kissed the side of her head; her fragile arm draped around my neck.

'I was just thinking,' she said, 'about the night you called me up and we drank whiskey in Chabrol.' Lily admired me with dazed eyes, just as she had that night.

'Oh yes,' I grinned, 'heady nights with Lily Ellen.'

'I loved you so much you know,' I adore her smile, 'I looked up to you; you were everything I wished I could be; everything I wanted, even though I shouldn't have...'

It's rare Lily talks quite like this.

'You flatter me Lily,' I kissed her hand and our eyes met; I like this; this reminiscing, 'I needed you so badly that night,' I confessed, 'I wandered aimlessly around London before I called you, knowing once you came to me, it would be the beginning.' I sank my head into her neck and closed my eyes, 'I couldn't stop thinking about you; I was in way too deep to give you up.'

'I wish I hadn't waited so long to tell you I was in love with you,' she was gazing at our joined hands; it feels lovely seeing our wedding bands, knowing just under a year ago she was completely unobtainable, and now, I can't remember her as Luke's girlfriend. 'I wish I'd kissed you at the New Year's Eve party.'

I laughed softly,

'Oh my Lily, you were so sexy that night; so beautiful. I couldn't help myself, I thought maybe just once; one small kiss...'

She started laughing,

'One small kiss would have turned into many kisses and ended up in your bed.' She grinned, 'well, that's how I'd fantasized it anyway.'

'You were all I thought about.'

'Me too.' She said softly, 'I didn't know what the hell was happening to me, this unhealthy obsession I had with my boyfriend's older brother.'

'Lily?' we gazed at each other, 'you have always been a remarkable young woman, I felt it the moment we met.'

She ran a tender finger tip over my two day old stubble,

'A burning connection I'd never felt before.'

'Me neither.' That was the truth.

'For years you'd been the untouchable Mr. Jefferson Howie; my fantasy.' she smiled; *I love her so much*, 'J?'

'Yes Lily?' My nose is pressed against hers; her eyes are closed; I can feel her warm breath on my face.

'Ever like this?' She whispered.

I smiled,

'Never ever like this.'

Last week, Lily and I were in London. For sentimental reasons, we strolled past my old apartment. The lights were on and we both smiled.

Epilogue

THE WRITER AND THE BUNNY GIRL! – Bestselling author in steamy clinch

Words: Melinda Sawyer
Picture: courtesy of Pablo Regatta

Best selling author Jefferson Howie has stunned his readers by being caught provocatively draped in the arms of a Bunny Girl. But rest assured folks, because the sexy Bunny in question is actually Jefferson's beautiful wife, Lily.

The photograph, originally taken by the couple's long time friend Pablo Regatta, will appear on the jacket of Jefferson's new novel "*A Genuine Spark of the Divine Fire*"...

'I love that title.' Lily was jumping up and down on the bed holding a two day old Evening Standard, (we were in a Hotel room in Cardiff Bay – part of my signing schedule), and I have to say, from a sleazy point of view, watching those plentiful breasts bouncing up and down was somewhat of a delight, '*The Writer and the Bunny Girl*,' she threw herself down beside me and we looked at each other; she's cute out of breath, girly and kind of sexy, 'can I borrow it J?' she said.

'It's yours.' I smiled.

'I think I'll use it for a future project.'

"Future Project"; that makes me smile, because Lily has so many projects on the go, I'm amazed she finds time to come to bed.

See, my wife has become somewhat of an enigma. After Melinda Sawyers article and the rocketing sales of my novel, people are starting to ask about Lillian Howie, so I've urged her to come out of my shadow and reveal herself, but at the moment, she's refusing.

'I'm happy as I am,' she said when I asked her, 'I've got Anais, Pink

Cup Cakes, my *Bunny Girl* novel, the Journal, and my MA,' then she winked, 'but most of all, I'm very happy just being your wife J.'

Which was her reason for boxing up her "pre-Jefferson" Journals, which are now stored in our loft.

'I've no use for them now,' she said as she taped the box together, 'I don't care if I never see them again.'

And on a personal level; neither do I.

And further praise for Lily, from a devoted husband, because during this "book tour" (as we've jokingly dubbed it), she's endeared herself to my readers, by getting out and meeting them; chatting to them in the queues, and discreetly hypnotizing them with her *modest charisma* and *innocent creativity*.

As a result, my publisher is currently receiving more e-mails about Lily, than about my book (definitely no hardship there, believe me), anyway, this has led to more interest in her than she can cope with.

'No J,' she shook her head at me last week when I told her the Institute of English Studies at the University of London were on the phone, 'I can't do it, I haven't got time.'

They wanted her to do a talk about writing memoirs, and after a little persuasion (from me), she agreed, and get this, she's called it "*A lot of being Jefferson and Lily*", and here's an extract,

> *"...I know a man. Not a bad man, but a very good man, who I am madly in love with. His name is Jefferson James Howie..."*

And there are rumors of more to come...

OK, so, you might be wondering about the letter I sent to Luke. As expected, I didn't hear back from him, but Jeremy told me something interesting as we chatted on the phone last week, apparently, Luke's met a "lovely" girl called Claire. She's British and lives out there with her folks.

'He sounded smitten,' Jeremy said, 'he sounded happy for the first time in ages.'

I took this as a sign he's moved on. He's finally released himself, and as a result, he's met someone, and I'm truly happy for him, perhaps now I can finally start to let go of that guilt, well, almost.

October 8 – Paris – 1 year wedding Anniversary weekend x x x

Last night as we lay stretched out on our bijou bed, damp bodies resting on pink satin, (actually we didn't leave the bed all day – our way of celebrating one year of marriage!), I asked J a question,
'Yes Honey?'
'Remember that night I stayed over with you; the night we just cuddled on your bed?'
'Yes.' He smiled. 'The night we drank whiskey in Chabrol.'
'Did you wank?'
He started laughing; he said it was such a "Lily Ellen" thing to say.
'Actually I did.'
'I thought so.'
'Did you?' he asked, 'because I've often wondered.'
'Of course I did.' I grinned 'J?'
'Yes Lily?'
'Wanna reminisce?'
'Sure do Red,' he said, rolling me over for the millionth time this weekend, 'I sure do.'
After a year of being married to this most elegant and refined gentleman, my best friend, my husband, I stick by what I said all those months ago,
You are a man that makes life drunk...you are like me.

*